THE EXECUTION, LIFE AND TIMES
OF
PATRICK O'DONNELL

By

GAVIN O'DONNELL

DEDICATION

For Linda,
for everything.

Live a good life. If there is a God and he is just,
then he will not care how devout you have been,
but will welcome you based on the virtues by which
you have lived. If there is a God and he is unjust,
then you should not want to worship him. If there
is no God, then you will be gone, but will have lived
a noble life that will live on in the memories of your
loved ones."

Marcus Aurelius

This work is one of historical fiction. Whilst many
of the characters and events are real and historically
accurate the author has used them in a fictitious
manner in order to tell a fictitious story.

PREFACE

(Dec 17th 1883 - Newgate Prison, London)
Unattributed Account

Patrick O'Donnell walked barefoot along the narrow candle lit passageway; behind him a guard each side held his arms and guided him to the oak door at its end. His hands were bound in front of him with leather and his feet were in chains with sufficient length to allow his short sliding steps over the cold flagstone floor.

As they reached the door the three men stopped; one of the guards placed a white sack hood over his head while the other pushed against the heavy oak; the loud rasping squeal of metal hinge suggested the door was not often used.

He felt a shove and stepped forward, through the opening, as best he could in the heavy chains. The door closed behind him and he heard the bolts slide; top and bottom, inside. The two men had not followed him into the execution room.

Patrick could hear his own heartbeat and was sure anyone nearby would also. He tried to hold it, to slow it and to quieten it; to no avail. He could sense one other person in the room; through the hood he could make out the candles and the shadow of a figure as it crossed between him and them. The figure came around to his back, but said nothing.

He was guided gently forward by the man whom he knew must be the bungling hangman

i

Bartholomew Binns, his executioner. Binns stopped and turned Patrick around and placed the nose over his head, as he did so Patrick shuddered.

'It's cold' he said hastily; hopeful that the hangman had not mistaken the involuntary spasm as fear.

The figure made no reply as he unlocked the shackles and removed them from Patrick's ankles. He rose and stepped backwards, a plank creaked under his boot; Patrick's head turned to the left almost imperceptibly as the shadow pulled the lever to the trapdoor.

As the floor opened a single utterance issued from Patrick O'Donnell's lips;

'Hanora.'

INTRODUCTION

The following are the translated letters of Patrick O'Donnell written in Newgate Prison between December 5th and December 17th 1883 as he awaited his execution for the crime of murdering James Carey, the mastermind behind the Phoenix Park Murders of 1882 and notorious informer who sent five of his compatriots to the gallows at Kilmainham, in exchange for his freedom.

The letters were written in English and in Patrick's native language, Irish; he occasionally reverts back and forth between Irish and English. Translation has been carried out as accurately as possible; certain anomalies in text and words can be expected due to translation not being an exact science and given that these letters were written 137 years ago, when language was somewhat different to that used these days. Where text would have otherwise been meaningless or has been illegible I have added my own interpretation to give it meaning and fluency.

To illustrate some of the translation issues experienced with the letters I draw the readers' attention to how in his first letter Patrick describes himself as being '*staid eagla mór*', which I have taken to mean 'in a great funk' but literally means 'great fear'. I mention this as an example because throughout the letters the aim has been to produce something meaningful as opposed to literal, but without altering the overall message or accuracy. It seems unnecessary to draw the readers' attention to every such detail so I shall not; other than in places where absolutely required. The reader may be assured that where anomalies in transposing from one language and time into another a great deal of time and consideration has been given to every word and nuance.

Fortunately Patrick does seem to have tried to avoid idiom; a translator's worst nightmare... this is probably because when writing in his two languages he himself must have appreciated the difficulties presented by its use. This sometimes gives the letters a slightly more formal characteristic than they otherwise might have had.

As said, the letters were written in both Irish and English, sometimes a combination. It is clear, from his testimony, and indeed from the text itself that Patrick found it more onerous to write in Irish than he did in English. Whilst he was more comfortable speaking in his native tongue he was happier writing in English. This is not an unusual thing for the time for many reasons, not least that Irish was much more a spoken than written language. Patrick's particular circumstance gave him the opportunity to speak, read and write English, an opportunity he took enthusiastically even as a child; but perhaps at some expense to his native tongue.

The purpose of the translations was not to form the basis of a thesis on language, it was to interpret and collate an account of a life which a condemned man wanted to tell and it is my privilege, with the help of translators, to be able to do that.

Locations and some indexing has also been added, some of the letters, particularly the first few, were undated and in these instances dates have been estimated.

Each letter is preceded with a short introduction, or epigraph, intended to provide context to the following letter and to some extent clarification of the previous. Footnotes have been added for obvious reasons. Otherwise the words written are those of the condemned man in the last 12 days of his life.

Herein Patrick will be referred to using the English version of his name though he signs his name variously as 'Patrick' or sometimes 'Pádrai' or 'Pádraig O'Domhnaill'. Occasionally he signs as 'Pádaí Mhícheáil Airt' which is the name by which he was known amongst his compatriots, and indeed to this day is affectionately known in his birthplace. The name is formed from his father and grandfather's names; Michael (1803) and Airt (1770).

Gavin O'Donnell
January 2021

1
THE FOURTH DAY

Cell in Newgate 1883

When I first came across the bundle of papers which I now know to be Patrick O'Donnell's letters I presumed some were missing, but upon having them translated it became clear, and not entirely surprising, that Patrick was in no state to write for the first few days after receiving his death sentence and indeed had not even contemplated doing so until he heard that Victor Hugo and US president Chester Arthur both had made representations to the British Government in order to have the sentence of death commuted.

Hugo in fact also wrote to Queen Victoria on the matter and this is mentioned in her diaries. We see from his first letter that the news of their efforts seems to have given him hope or at least some focus.

The Old Bailey records show that his trial started in 1883 on November 30 and ended on December 1st; with him being sentenced just after 9pm that same day; a Saturday. A mere 2 days to consider the matter and decide the man's fate. The first letter is dated 5th December, several days after the judge had donned the black cap and made the only pronouncement available to him under English law at that time.

The interventions of Hugo and the President are well recorded and are not as surprising as they might at first seem. Victor Hugo was a well-known opponent of the death penalty, and by incredible coincidence author of *The last day of a Condemned Man* published in 1829 and republished in English in 1841. He is reputed to have influenced the abandonment of the death penalty in several countries.

There is no evidence that Patrick and Hugo actually corresponded directly, other than by way of Patrick's letters, which we know never reached their intended recipient. From Patrick's own account however it seems that Hugo sent both French and English versions of his book to Patrick and Patrick did receive them. Inevitably the books would have been accompanied by some note or other but alas, no such communication has ever been found, nor indeed has either copy of the book.

As for the then president of the United States; Chester Arthur; it is very well documented that he sent a delegation to Britain to plead for Patrick's life. After a protracted (and well documented) dispute between the two governments it was agreed by all sides that Patrick was indeed a naturalized American citizen and afforded the rights commensurate with American citizenship, but regrettably for him, not the protection for which he and his legal team had hoped.

To give some context to the futility of both men's efforts it needs to be remembered that Chester Arthur was an ardent abolitionist and Hugo a republican. By contrast Prime Minister Gladstone, whilst not against abolition in 1833 (in British territories) was for much of his life dependent on, and a beneficiary of the slave trade; his father had been one of the largest slave owners in the British West Indies. I shall leave the reader to discover Patrick's observations on the matter.

From the start we see that Patrick is in Newgate jail in his cell; and it is from here that he tells his story. Newgate was a stone built prison and used as such in various forms from the late twelfth century until the early twentieth century; the manifestation in which Patrick was housed being from 1785.

For any prisoner it must have been a most unpleasant place but for those condemned to death it must have been desperately bleak. Newgate had over the centuries accommodated prisoners from the notorious pirate William Kidd (Captain Kidd) to the perhaps not so notorious playwright Oscar Wilde.

It is worth mentioning that although Patrick was supposed to be in the condemned cell, and believed himself to be, he seems not to have been. From his account, the cell he occupied up to the last day had a single window, but some years before he arrived in Newgate the condemned cell had two windows due to the fact that it was constituted of two cells which had been knocked into one. This enabled a guard to be with any prisoner who might cheat the noose by way of suicide. It must be assumed that Patrick was not considered a risk on this front, perhaps due to him ostensibly being a catholic.

In Newgate in 1883 14 people hanged; Patrick was to be the last of them for that year.

One of the things Patrick seems keen to emphasise is that although he did the deed that landed him in the death cell, he did it for no purpose or reason. We will see this theme come up again over the course of his letters; he seems very keen not to be invested with motives he did not have. History shows his concerns were well founded.

The fact remains that he killed the notorious informer and murderer James Carey by shooting him three times on a ship off the coast of South Africa and whilst his motives are disputed to this day, he never denied the killing, and clearly regretted it.

We are also introduced to his wife Margaret in the first letter. She is a steadfast support to him but later we will see that their relationship is unusual, as are all Patrick's relationships with the women in his life, at least 5 of whom are, by coincidence, named Margaret.

(First Letter)
Dec 5th 1883 - Newgate Prison, London.

My Dear Victor,
In my predicament comfort is scant; the inevitability of my fate dulls my spirit. I endeavour as each precious hour approaches and departs to hold onto hope that somehow, someone will see the injustice that I endure.

I have received news of your efforts to have my sentence taken down to servitude and this has raised me from the worst of my depths and given me some small hope and for that I am thankful.

My dear Margaret has visited me each day since Saturday when my fate was pronounced to her and to me and to the world. She was rushed from Pennsylvania by the generosity of the Hibernians[1] and arrived too late for the trial but in time for the verdict. I confess that in the four days since then I have indulged myself in a great funk but have resolved to mend that from this moment.

Margaret puts me to shame with her fortitude. At the sentencing she held herself dignified while several in the court bayed, some with delight and some with disdain. I confess I did not hold so much dignity as my wife and shouted for my country as they took me down. I played the fool I suppose but they cannot hang me twice.

She is permitted only occasional entrance but anyway comes to this damnable place every day in

---

1 The Ancient order of Hibernians. A worldwide non-violent Irish Catholic fraternal organization

hope. She waits from morning and stays until dusk and endures the taunts and abuse of my English bastard jailers in the hope they relent and permit us a precious few moments together.

I know her too well to try to persuade her to do anything other. She has the stubbornness of a mule. I am told what permission she does receive is a great privilege, bought by means I dare not contemplate lest I go to my death out of my mind. Many condemned see no one until the last. I suspect she has passed the jailers coin and more and hides it from me. We are narrow of means but we have the backing of some who are not and the jailers know it and exploit it. I have heard of large sums being gathered in Ireland and in America and I feel ashamed to take it because it is given not for a fool who killed a man but for what they want, for a hero of some cause which is not mine and was not mine when I did the deed.

Newgate is hellish and surely if I am to go downward for whatever transgressions I have made in my life it can be no worse a place than this. Without the food Margaret brings I would starve to death before they have their go at me. She brings bread and cheese and sack and to me it is a feast for a king. My appetite seems undisturbed; no doubt as a consequence of my days as a child in 46 and 47;[2] my body has learned to take feed and drink whenever the opportunity arises. Until a man has in desperation eaten grass from the fields and the flesh of his fellow man he cannot understand hunger, or

2 *The Great Hunger, (the Famine) mass starvation and disease in Ireland from 1845 to 1849*

the fear of it; thus I gorge what I can when I can, and apologise not for it.

Others too have made representations on my behalf to Gladstone and to Coleridge; the president[3] himself has written to the English, though I fear Gladstone is unlikely to have time for the words of an abolitionist. I am a son of Ireland and a citizen of the United States and neither fact will assist when approaching an English noose.

Your gift is welcome. My father gave my brother Michael and me very little but he gave us the gift of reading and of writing. It was good of you to send both *Le Dernier Jour d'un Condamné* and the translation to English. I acquired some small French in Canada as a boy after being wrecked there and later on my travels in the South of the United States and though it is sufficient to read the French book I fear it would take too much time, something which is a scarcity to me.

I received the English edition today and I suppose that the jailers held it for a day or so as the other book arrived before the verdict; though what they would do with it is not known to me because they are unlikely to be able to read; in any language. It seems the only qualifications necessary for their task in this place are cruelty and greed.

One of the keepers is named Mullins and he is from Ireland, he is the cruellest for some reason but also the greediest, so the most useful. They say that if you wish to set a man upon another man, use a

---

3 *Chester Alan Arthur, 21st President to the United States 1881 – 1885.*

man equal in rank or standing for he will be the most brutal to his fellow in order to prove himself to his master. I have seen it enough times from the bog in Gweedore to the mines in Pennsylvania to know it to be true.

It was Mullins who allowed me pen and paper but not before Margaret paid him two shillings; another tanner gets my shackles off by day. He spits in my food but has no idea what I have eaten in my time; as though spit would cleave me from a feed. I behave offended to his satisfaction to slake his thirst for cruelty lest he quench it by some other more troubling means.

I had thought that I was for Long Drop Marwood[4] on the day, which was some small comfort. He did for the boys from the Park[5] and a grand job he did too, barely a twitch from them I was told. Mullins tells me Marwood passed a few months gone and I now have Binns to do the work. It meant nil to me and I supposed he'd be as good as Marwood but only today I got news from Mullins that on Monday just gone Binns hanged some poor young fella named Dutton and he'd got it all wrong on account of being drunk; not just the drop and weight but the rope too and the poor bastard Dutton swung around kicking air for the most part of quarter of one hour. Hanging is not meant to be

---

4 *Hangman at Newgate until Sept 1883. Credited as the first hangman to use the 'humane' Long Drop.*
5 *Joe Brady, Michael Fagan, Thomas Caffrey, Dan Curley and Tim Kelly, executed in Kilmainham jail between May and June 1883 for the Phoenix Park killings.*

fun but at least Marwood seen them off right. I try to put Binns out of my head but it's a worry. Mullins is a bastard to have told me; it was exactly this ill effect on my disposition that he intended.

The Hibernians keep Margaret in London and gave her a small grant for such costs as arise but they are not content to fill a jailer's pockets; Mullins is to be visited by someone. My cousin Edward also sees that Margaret is safe as he is in London but must lay particular low on account of Salford Barracks[6] and his other little pokes at the English. Lucky for Mullins it will not be him knocking on his door, he hates a turncoat more than he hates an Englishman.

If I am not in error the French book is a first and you have kindly signed it so I suppose it is worth something. I assume this was intended and I shall instruct Margaret to realise the best value she can from it for her own benefit. If stupid Mullins realises it has worth he will steal it so I shall conceal it about her when she comes next and she will take it into town or have Edward do it for her.

She is due to visit today or tomorrow and I must break the news to her that the black warrant came down this morning, signed and sealed. The date is to be the 17th of this month. If your efforts and those of others do not prove fruitful then it is done.

Before the trial I was approached and told quietly that regardless of the verdict I would not see

---

6 *Salford Barracks dynamiting in Jan 1881 which killed a boy.*

a rope but now with the date set I find that of no assurance. I am sure my team were of the same opinion and perhaps had they not been they might have pressed more firmly for manslaughter and not self-defence.

I do not wish to be some anonymous soul like your condemned man. I want no guessing about my life and my death. To avoid this I have begun to record, as best my memory and the limited time will serve, all my days on earth but I am not certain that I can purchase sufficient good nature from my jailers to ensure its safe removal from here and eventual delivery to you.

I write in duplicate, and in my tongue, the writing of which I have never properly mastered. It will be slow and wasteful of the precious hours but necessary I fear.

That which may be intercepted one route shall be sent another which I shall not mention now to you and in writing. I humbly beseech that you receive my efforts and you will forgive the roughness of a simple man writing to such as you. If you do not receive these letters then I trust who does will bring them to light to show the good and bad of me and the sum of me, which I hope is more of the one thing than the other. I trust that the twelve days left will be enough for I can only write in the light of day and the days are short.

My small table and stool are furthest from the window and I am not allowed to move them closer for the light. I think they suppose I might climb up and break a way out but it would be impossible. Alas, I am no Jack Sheppard[7].

I shall end this first letter to you and promise to address my task with determination and honesty but alas, not with hope. I am destined to be interred in this place under the slabs with a sack of lime to speed my removal from history and from all existence. Let my writing dissolve this injustice as the lime dissolves my bones.

---

7 *Jack Sheppard 1702 – 1724 notorious for escaping prisons, including Newgate, twice.*

2
BEFORE THE HUNGER

Ploughing to Plant 1844

In his first letter Patrick does not concern himself with his past. He is writing of his predicament, of his wife's visits and his situation generally but he does not address specifics as to why he is condemned, in fact it is not until much later that he addresses that matter properly.

We can already see that he is highly suspicious of his jailers, probably without reason. For example he speaks of his wife bringing him food as a particular privilege; in fact deliveries of food from family and friends and even from local taverns were not unusual at the time, neither were visits for wives and children. There is no doubt that some jailers extracted benefits from the situation and a prisoner with visitors who had money could expect a better level of care than one without, albeit in a dreadful place.

It's unclear to what extent prisoners in the death cells in Newgate were allowed writing materials; certainly there are records of condemned men writing home and to loved ones. It's unlikely however that such privilege was extended to writing an elongated account of one's life. It seems likely that with a bribe here and there various extra privileges might be enjoyed. There are even accounts of prostitutes being allowed access to prisoners, though Patrick certainly would not have sought that particular distraction, as his letters later suggest.

In his second letter he conveys a picture of a happy childhood with the family doing well after his father's return from the British Army in Africa. The family are unusually well set given their position and it is clear that learning, reading and writing play a big part in his life.

Patrick was depicted, at the time of his trial, particularly in the British press, as an illiterate Irishman. He was, as we see from his writing and all other available evidence, very far from it. It is not entirely clear if this impression was one deliberately encouraged by Patrick and his legal team; there is cause to suspect this may have been the case. Several documents exist which purport to have been signed by him with an 'x', some of them naming him as Michael and others as Patrick with a variety of birthdates and birthplaces.

The confusion initially seems to have been an unintended side effect of an attempt at subterfuge by Patrick, pretending to be his long dead brother (Michael) to evade justice while in Port Elizabeth, shortly after he shot James Carey. At least one other time in his life Patrick escapes death with similar subterfuge, simply by claiming to be someone he is not so it is a ploy he has used.

It is here in his second letter that Patrick first mentions his uncle Manus, who immigrated to the United States when Patrick was very young; Patrick does not encounter him again for almost 20 years.

Patrick also describes the turn of bad luck which sees the family travelling from relative comfort and security in County Donegal south to County Clare and to uncertainty. Further bad luck is brought on by what seems to be Patrick's father giving up on life. The loss of the potato crop from potato weevil in 1845, a full year and a half before the Famine seems at first to be a disaster; it is anything but.

(Second Letter)
Dec 6th 1883 - Newgate Prison, London

My dear Victor,

I can report that I am freshly invigorated with the task I have set myself and in the few hours since I last put pen to paper I have had a visit from dearest Margaret, for which I had hoped but only half expected. To crown this she has been permitted to bring me candles and it is by the light of these that I now commit myself again to the page. She has left this place and I still smell the jasmine from her hair and feel her sweet kiss upon my cheek. Even the stench of this place cannot dull what my senses demand. *Why?* I wonder, did I not treasure such small things when I was free? All they are now is memories which fade into distance as the seconds pass.

It seems to me more important now than ever to record what I can of my days on earth; as much as I can recall. My remembrance of dates is not good and indeed until I was long gone from Ireland I had no concept of them other than for the year of 47, no one will ever forget that year.

I have little to say about my earliest time, the time before an Gorta Mór [8], other than to recount the facts as I know them. This is not because I have no wish to impart the information; it is because I have no great memory of my own of that time. Most of what I can account has come from my

---

8 *The Irish Potato Famine.*

mother and from others; only part is from memory and that is not fresh in my mind.

My father was christened Michael in 1803, the year of his birth. I know little of his origin other than he was from Gweedore and his father was named Airt. He had three brothers of whom the youngest was Manus. I remember Manus; he was much younger than my father. I do not recall the others. I know my uncle Manus and my father were very close and he lived with us for a time, after the disagreement.

There had been a dispute in the family; the details of which my mother would never speak but I know my father and Manus took each other's side in the matter against the other brothers and my grandfather, whom I never met.

My father served with the English army in Africa for ten years before returning to Gweedore and the house of his father and his three brothers, where he was not welcome. He had left Ireland ten years before to join the English in Cape Town in Africa. In 1830 he was blinded in his right eye while fighting the Ashanti. His Bess[9] had backfired and ruined his eye and his right ear and taken much of his hair, though that grew back, mostly, his eye did not.

He told my mother that it was the best thing to happen to him in Africa because the Army retired him with a pension of six pennies a day which he cashed-in[10] for £60. He used the money to set

---

9 *Brown Bess was a nickname for the British Land Pattern Musket muzzle load flintlock (1722 – 1838)*
10 *Commutation of war pensions was uncommon but*

himself and Manus right on what was to be our patch of land and to improve it. During this time he met my mother at the Bunbeg fair; he had impressed her with his own horse, which he had named Bess, after his gun. They were married in 1831.

The old cottage, as far as I remember, was small but enough. It was located outside the village of Gweedore, to the east and near the banks of the Clady River just below the lower Lough Nacung. It was built of stone with a roof of reed with a split door to the front on the long wall and a full door to the rear opposite the front. It had two windows to the front and a grand big fireplace on the end wall. To each side of the fireplace was a cot; one for my parents and the other for my sister Nancy who was two years older than me, and Margaret who arrived the last of my father but not of my mother.

I had three brothers; Michael, the eldest was three years older than me; Donald and Daniel came after me, two years between Donald and me and eighteen months between him and Daniel.

In the little house my father constructed a floor to the joists which provided a good space where we boys would sleep - when we were not fighting. It was a happy situation, we had fuel from the bog which only needed cutting and drying and we had crops and livestock along with what fish my father would poach; none of us could realise what was to come.

---

between 1831 and 1832 exceptions were made.

17

I remember sitting at the table and reading by candle light with my brother Michael and my father telling us how important reading and writing would be to us. As I write now I am reminded of those happier and innocent times.

Michael and I in turn would teach our brothers when the time came. Our father told us how he had sat some years before with Uncle Manus in their father's house and taught him to read. My mother always said that Manus was more like a son to him than a brother.

Every day from the age of four I learned my words in English, never in Irish. In the home we spoke only English but outside it was always Irish. My father knew that no one speaking Irish would ever progress in the world and that reading and writing in English was the thing which would elevate us all. No one I knew as a child spoke English, no one apart from Michael and me. Of course many people had the ability but not the inclination.

My mother's name was Margaret. I can remember my father, whenever he had drink taken, declaring to all that would hear it that the most beautiful woman in Donegal and beyond was Maggie McFadden. They never had cross words as far as I can recall and we had a peaceful and happy home.

In 1842 my uncle Manus, unreconciled with his father and other brothers, left for America with his wife, also named Margaret and their son Manus who was a baby. My father paid their passage from his pension and gave them £2 an old trap he had repaired for the purpose and the good horse Bess to take them to Sligo and their ship. The horse they could sell easily before departing across the Atlantic. In all it took one sixth of my father's pension to place Manus and his family in America, it was a considerable sum that required no repayment.

My father missed his brother and had started to make plans for us all to follow him to America. Plans which to me seemed far away and unreal.

Uncle Manus wrote several times and I was allowed to open and read the letters to the family. He told us of America and his adventures and always asked that we join him there. He was well and had found work in the coal mines of Pennsylvania and was living in a place called Tamaqua. They were planning to take a boarding house near to Mahanoy City one day and he said there were more Irish people where he was than there were in Gweedore. My father made promises that we all would go but the day never came; at least it did not come as we expected.

Our holding was 12 acres in all, part bog and rough ground but some good land and my father worked it well and the middleman, who was named Hayes, got paid on time and we ate better than most. Illness visited us rarely and when it did it was thankfully mild.

The place was too much for one man so after Manus left my father took on a cottier[11] to help and I think I can remember him. He took up my uncle

11 A Cottier was a homeless labourer rewarded with accommodation and a patch for growing

and aunt's tiny stone hut which Manus built with my father before they thought to travel away.

My father and Manus had also built a barn to the side of the cottage, about half its size and with a roof of turf. On the wall between the cottage and the barn he also built the stone chimney, which seems now to be something hardly deserving of mention but most of our neighbours had no chimney.

By the time I was born the pigs and chickens were moved into the barn and the floor of the cottage was laid with flat stones. Our neighbours had floors of earth and shared their living space with their chickens and pigs. We were sometimes accused of having grand ideas above our station but I think it did not trouble my parents.

My father had often told us that it is no stain on a man that he progress himself above others provided it is not to the cost of those others. He often said such things which at the time seemed nothing but over my lifetime have carried great meaning for me.

We lived as well as many and better than some but to nobody's detriment. It is a rule I am ashamed, but compelled to confess, that I have not strictly applied the whole of my life.

I clearly remember the poaching. I cannot have been nine years old, going under cover of night, with Michael and our father to fish salmon from the river on his Lordship's ground. I went on only a few trips but always remember the excitement of it; the anticipation and the triumph of the catch, the companionship of my brother and the company of my father who would allow me a sip from his flask, not as a treat but as my right as a man hunting; his companion, not his son. It burned my lips and my throat but lifted my heart and it made me so proud.

I don't remember the particular occasion I now recount but my mother told me of it and I can testify to its accuracy because subsequent events proved it to be true. My father and Michael had gone to the larger lake much further along. They had with them line and a weighted board[12] and they caught a sack of trout; almost too heavy to carry between them.

Normally what my father caught my mother cooked or dried and we ate but on this occasion there was too much. He had been spotted on the night by the gamekeeper but had not been caught. The gamekeeper was by coincidence also named O'Donnell. He might have been a cousin, most O'Donnell's were, but he had no love for us nor we for him. He was fat and lazy and unable to run or even to shout. He needed not to chase as he would note who and what he saw and no constable or magistrate ever doubted his word. Even so, my father might have got away with it but for the fact that the next day he travelled into Bunbeg to sell the surplus fish. He was apprehended by two constables and the gamekeeper was there as proof against him.

It did not go to the magistrate, but it was all the middleman Hayes needed. He knew the fine work my father had done on the place at his own cost and

---

12 *Otter Boards are weighted boards with line and hooks attached. Used by Poachers.*

there were many in the community who disliked us and would happily pay a higher price for the land. When they came and put us out they left us take the pigs, the old nag and the donkey and chickens but would pay nothing for the new room my uncle Manus had built or for the barn or the stone floor. Even the crops were left.

We had three days; my mother told me that Hayes had spoken up for my father to the owner and told him of his good conduct and service so there was no fine to pay or court to face. But his speaking up was not for our benefit, it was for his own. The land was split with Manus' hut in one part and our home in another, the rent was doubled and a new family moved in, taking our crops and our home. The cottier stayed on and took the smaller part. There is something bitterly shameful about my own countrymen which the English have always relied upon, I saw it then and have seen it ever since. One will climb over the dying body of another to profit themselves.

My father had served in the army with a man called Mark Sheedey who had land in Co Clare and had wanted him to return there after Africa and not to Donegal. So with the donkey, three pigs and all our possessions loaded on the cart we started for Clare. I have only some memory of the journey, which I believe took almost two weeks; I was about ten years old and had my first pair of boots for the walk. The boots rubbed my feet something dreadful, not because they were too small but because they were too big. They were bought with growth in mind. They made my feet bleed but it was too cold to walk without them. My mother bandaged them in rags each night.

We slept on the side of the road and though it was cold it was mercifully dry so we managed a good fire each night. My father put his Brown Bess to work once or twice and we ate meat on the journey, though had he been caught we'd have been in trouble. One night we ate a hound which had crossed our path. Cooked well it tasted to me as good as any pig or rabbit but for a slight bitterness and it was exceedingly chewy. I have eaten many things in my life and dog was not the worst of them.

Michael, Nancy, Donald and I walked the whole way, Daniel and the baby Margaret sat upon the heap of possessions that we managed to load onto the trap. It was the tail end of winter and bitterly cold but my father, who was eternally optimistic had told us the timing was good fortune because we could get a crop into the ground for the coming year. I have inherited that optimistic outlook which I wonder sometimes borders on hopeless delusion but I am convinced has kept me going when others may have fallen by the way.

When we arrived it turned out that Sheedey had no land after all, he was a middleman and he rented off the landlord and rented down to us and other families so what land he claimed was his was not his and we paid a premium for it. What was one original tenancy in our case turned out to be one of many; divided so many times that we were lucky to get what we did. Greedy, greedy Irish men who would claim the burden they gave was the design of the landlords who although not blameless, were not the real problem. Irishmen doing over Irish men; there was the problem, but no one says so.

Like most people we had no choice. My father signed for four good acres and 3 of bog just outside Doonbeg and even his optimism was pressed down flat; he was not content and had no spirit to build up a dwelling again, though he made efforts for our benefit.

The new place, which I do remember better than the old, had a single room, a dirt floor, a small fireplace and chimney which leaked smoke into the room when the fire was being lit. For eight of us it was a tight squeeze. My father was reluctant to make any improvements which might go to the benefit of others but immediately set about making a shallow space in the rafters for us boys to sleep. He also sealed up the chimney with mud but it still smoked. Each time the mud dried out the smoke came back and he seemed to be fixing it most days.

He continued to read with us but less and less. His drinking, which before had been mild and jolly took a different turn and he argued with our mother most nights and he had taken to bad company and wild ways. First the money was gone then the horse went then the donkey and then his old Brown Bess. The crops struggled for lack of care. What spare money he could gather he made by making and selling poteen[13] to a nearby shebeen[14], where he

---

13 *An illegally distilled drink made from a mash of potatoes. Illegal since 1661*
14 *Disreputable and unlicensed establishment selling alcohol, often a private house*

spent his time drinking, playing the dice and mostly losing the little he had earned.

It was after such a night that he was found in the ditch on the edge of the bog. He apparently had been blinded by the brew and would take no help walking home. I wondered if having just the one eye might the poteen have afflicted his sight more quickly than had he the two. When he was found his purse was half-filled after what was apparently a rare night of luck with the dice.

I have no recollection of a wake or a funeral or of being sad. It was late summer in 1844, he was 41 years old. In those days in Ireland people died all the time from all sorts of illness and bad luck; he was just another corpse but he was also my father, the son of Airt, the brother of Manus and the father of Patrick and without him I might have been born a pauper, or a king, a priest or a killer of men. I wonder is it all just a throw of the dice who and what we become or is there some destiny or plan?

We stayed on the land and my mother worked hard. She kept the still and made a few pennies that way, but kept them as she neither drank nor rolled dice. Along with my father's full purse it was enough for the rent and Sheedey let it be though easily could have sent us on our way.

Molony, a neighbour who was a widow man came and helped the first harvest after our father died. The crop was terrible, it looked a grand one at first with fine leaves and flowers and we piled the earth up to encourage the spuds. Not a sign of a problem until we came to pull them in the autumn.

Every single spud was eaten through completely; the skin was intact but for the little holes in and out. As we picked them we would tap them and they were all but hollow. Not a single one spared, not one with a bite to be had, not enough even for the pigs. It was a worm[15] and what made it unbearable is that the worm had eaten the previous crop and no one told us the ground was infested. It was not just our crop but two of the neighbouring holdings had it too. No one else seemed to suffer. I was told later that the little worms stay in the ground with their white bellies full of potatoes waiting for the next year and the next crop. The tenants before us had the ground blessed and prayed over but the only way to stop the cycle was to not plant for three years[16]. Starve the little beast to death, if that does not starve us first.

To make things worse my mother had a belly the size of the bellies of the maggots who got our crop, but it was not filled with stolen spuds it was filled with twins. By the following January Molony married her. She was a woman on her own with 6 children to feed and I think love was not a consideration. She was better than Molony and they both knew it. My half-sisters were named Ellen and Mary and they arrived in March of 45.

I remember Molony as a weak and insubstantial man. I had been used to my father and by comparison the man was second rate. To me, all men were less than enough when stood against my

---

15 *Most Likely wireworm*
16 *Larvae can spend three to five years in the soil*

father for comparison. I suppose it is the same with most sons.

It was obvious from the first day that he did not want Michael or me around. I was about 10 or 11 years old and Michael was 13 or so by this time. He did not beat us and he did not work us hard but it was clear we were not needed or wanted. In those times even before the Hunger an extra mouth or two to feed could ruin a family.

Fate is a very strange thing. In a way that year's potato failure probably saved all of us from starvation but we had no idea of the events to come. It was not an easy time but we had enough and we could buy what we did not have. Other than the normal hunger and poverty 44 into 45 was much the same as any other year.

We could not move on but we did have enough money to buy seed. We had no potatoes to split and besides, the ground was no good for them because of the worm. We planted parsnips and turnips and onions in the spring of 1845. It seemed strange that a worm which would eat potatoes and yet not parsnips would be our saving. Perhaps they were Irish and had only a taste for the spud.

It is peculiar remembering these things; one memory seems to awaken another and I wonder how much more I have to say than I had thought to say. I feel urgency now in this task and with each word that urgency increases. I must say it all and there is so little time.

It must be ten now as the guard has changed. He is yet to look in on me but I shall not tempt fate.

It is cold and my fingers cramp around the pen, my breath is a cloud and my nose runs to the page. I shall wait till morning to write my copy. I had resolved to write two copies in Irish but I find the writing in my language is very slow and does not come to me so easy as English. An injury to my hand which I suffered in the mines also grows painful and stiff in the cold and it does not help with my task.

Tomorrow I shall write all day. There are only eleven more days left for me if your efforts do not succeed and I have little hope that they shall.

3
THE HUNGER

*The Village of Moveen, Co Clare – 1847, (Illustrated
London News Dec 22 1849)*

In his next letter, the third, Patrick seems concerned
that he has taken two days to write just two letters.
He is very focused on his task which, one must
suppose, was a distraction to what awaited him. He
makes very little introduction and letter three is a
continuation of letter two, even though written a
day after it.

This letter serves not only to record his life at
the time but also, and probably more importantly it
includes an account of the suffering of the people
of Ireland during the Famine, as Patrick himself
witnessed it.

The exact dates of the Famine are often argued.
It is hard to tell when 'normal' depravation and
starvation for that time became 'exceptional
depravation and starvation' due to potato blight and

the resulting failure of the crop. It is broadly accepted that the Famine was between 1845 and 1852, with increasing suffering from 1845. 1847 saw the worst suffering and is typically referred to as the date of the Famine. The fact is the starvation and depravation was endured long before and long after any crop failure; during 46 and 47 the suffering reached truly biblical proportions.

For perspective; consider that even the most conservative estimates suggest over 1 million people out of a population of 8 million died of starvation and disease during this period. This was over 12 percent of the population. For comparison; 12 percent of the UK population today is over 8 million people.

Potato crops failed all over Europe at that time but it was only the Irish who depended so heavily on them. The Irish did not select potatoes as their staple diet out of choice, but it happened to be a good staple in most ways. Half an acre of potatoes will feed a family of nine for a year; they will grow in poor soil, are easy to store and take no processing; they are highly nutritious in all requirements but for protein, they will even grow in seaweed and are perfectly suited to the damp climate of Ireland.

By contrast it takes over ten times the ground, good ground, to grow sufficient wheat to feed a family the same size and wheat, in common with other cereal crops must be harvested, threshed, processed and requires dry storage. Great for exporting to Britain, as every year the Irish landowners did, but not for sustaining a large population of hungry people, most of whom were without the means to process grain.

Patrick mentions the transit of grain and livestock out of the country in his letter and it was something every person would have seen, and wondered at.

It is also worth considering that a 12 year old in Ireland in 1847 was equivalent to a man in our times. Childhood in Ireland in the mid nineteenth century was a very short event; by 1847 it was non-existent. His observations must be lent the weight they would, had they been those of an adult and not remembrances from childhood.

Whilst much of the suffering during the Famine has been recorded that record is made up mostly from the accounts of travellers, clerics and officials of the time. First-hand accounts from those who suffered most are rare, at least in print. Most ordinary people were illiterate of course so the stories and accounts handed down over the years are often oral, recorded a generation or two or three later as 'hearsay'. Patrick was unusual insofar as he could read and write and he did suffer the terrible challenges of that time. Whilst his account in his letters is not contemporaneous, it is first-hand and all the more valuable for it.

He admits that he had it far from as bad as others but it is clear he endured great depravation, including hunger; though not to the point of starvation. It is also very clear that he realises his own survival was due to a combination of luck and the resourcefulness of his mother. Managing to keep a roof over one's head at the time was crucial to survival, and they did that.

That the family lost their potato crop in 1845 due to potato wireworms 2 years before the worst of the blight; which caused the Famine, must have seemed at the time to be a disaster, as you shall read, it proved indirectly to be their saving.

The letter takes us to the almost inevitable conclusion that he and his brother must leave Ireland to survive. For Patrick perhaps this was an exciting adventure but for so many more the journey to the ports was an attempt to escape from almost certain death from starvation or disease.

It's during this period in his life that Patrick develops a hatred for religion and given his experiences it is hardly surprising.

(Third Letter)
Dec 7th 1883 - Newgate Prison, London

Dear Victor,

Last night I slept like a dog and I dreamed of my childhood and I hasten to write it down lest I forget it. It is not yet light and is bitter cold but I am warmed by my enthusiasm, nay, my excitement to set down for posterity the time of the Hunger and how my brother and I escaped the worst of it.

When it came it came sudden. People who were not there years after spoke of how we should have seen it and how we could have avoided it and how it must have struck in one place and not another but they are wrong.

God help me I was there and I saw it fall upon us like the tar of Satan; there was no escape. What terrible sin could any man, any community or any nation have committed to deserve such punishment from hell's black pantry? They say 47 was the worst of it and maybe that is true but it takes a man and a child and a mother time to die and the dying I tell you began in my tenth year; in the September of 45, but the causes were there before the crop failed. Many more people would have survived the Hunger if they had not also had to fight homelessness and no potato disease caused the evictions; that was our fellow man, the Irish landlord puppets of the English Masters.

One day the crop was stiff, green and tall and had already flowered and the next it was tired and bowed over and the next day after that it was flat and brown. Most neighbours had not even checked in the earth yet, it was devilish fast. By providence we'd planted not a single spud on account of the bastards in the ground waiting for their fill but all our neighbours had planted and when they dug on the third day they dug blackened spuds wet and soft and ruined. Not a single one missed by the disease, not in any field or any patch anywhere. The few stocks left from the year before and stored in mounds were taken too by the blackness. News came that it was everywhere from Wexford to Roscommon. Not a spud to be had in the entire country.

Our own crop of turnips, parsnips and onions thrived as if in spite of the neighbours' failings. The disease ignored everything but the spuds. The vegetables we had planted by what we saw as bad luck would be enough for us to live the winter and spring. Our two sows got by on the peel and scraps and the one of them produced eight piglets, three of which went to Sheehan after weaning as he'd lent us the boar. By that time three pigs were worth ten.

What meagre rations other people had were gone before the winter. Some had grown a few parsnips and onions but nearly everyone depended almost totally on spuds. They soon came knocking, then begging and then thieving. The result was that we had to pull the crops early and before they had made seed. It was that or they were to be stolen. My mother refused calling in the constabulary at first but eventually had no choice. Starving mothers and waifs were beaten off our little patch with clubs and stout sticks. It was unavoidable but I am shamed by it. Few things in my time shame me more than that. It was a terrible time that saw the worst in men and when I look back almost 40 years I remember the hunger but most I remember the inhumanity, the depths we all will plummet when our bellies ache for a scrap of food.

My mother knew too well that lifting the crop early meant buying seed for the next year, so the selling of the onions and the drink was a blessing, one of the very few blessings that year.

Not everyone was starving; the worse off a person was before the crop failure the more they suffered after it. It always has been that way I suppose. The poor suffer first and suffer the most and for the longest.

The grass grew and livestock thrived and other crops grew. Food travelled west and north to the ports and onto England. We all saw it and it angered everyone, carts laden passing the corpses of the starving. The occasional cart was overturned and robbed by hungry people who had been evicted or who were travelling and thought to gather in a mob.

Everyone was on the move looking for a better place. I heard that many headed for the coast and for fish to be had from the sea. Some died on the way and rotted on the lanes where they fell and when others got there they were chased out by their fellow man unhappy to share their spoils and feared of disease, which was all places. The stories of it reminded me of the sharing of fish and bread which my mother had read many times to us from the bible, but not lately.

People took what they could carry and disappeared into the countryside. Families of many generations just disappeared. These were not thieves or robbers; they were hungry people who saw food being driven to the coast to be taken out of Ireland while the Irish starved.

I saw my first dead body on the way to Mass on Christmas morning. It was a mother, or what was left of the wretched creature. Dressed in the flimsiest of rags she lay face down in the ditch with one arm outstretched as though reaching for something unseen by anyone else. Her long hair tangled in the mud as though the ground had started to digest her. Sat beside her were two corpse-like shapes, dressed also in rags, expressionless and motionless but alive, just. I did not know them and we walked past them as if none had seen them. My mother wept silently and I was afraid, not afraid of the death but afraid of us passing by as though it was nothing, as though we were nothing, not they.

Father Sinnott, a fat well fed man with a shiny pig face told us in Mass that morning to pray and to repent our sins as if we had brought the terrible time upon ourselves. I wondered what sins had those two tiny terrible things committed which deserved them to sit alongside their dead mother awaiting the angel of death to take them from their misery. The congregation sat with empty stomachs, bare feet and cold hands and listened and coughed and starved and weakened as we were told it was God's work and beyond inquisition.

Not my mother though, my most excellent mother; as the priest puked his bile to us she stood and pushed back the bench she had sat upon. It overturned and crashed to the floor and everyone looked around. God's servant, in his purple silk robe, raised his head and squinted in the dimness to see her and she looked him in the eye and spat onto the floor in front of her. She shoved her new husband out of the row in front of her and grabbed Michael's hand and he grabbed mine and down the line we all rose and walked out of that church.

So help me I have never stood in a church since and shall go to the noose without regret for that. I shall not be sullied by the blessing of any robed Charlatan as Binns wraps his knot to my lump. I welcome the relief from such liars and a world which allows them to prosper and spread their message. If I am wrong then I am dammed to hell and if I am right they are, either way I shall avoid encountering them in the afterlife and that is good enough for me.

As we walked towards home that cold, damp morning we came upon the sight again. My mother to a mild protest from her husband took one child in her arms and my brother Michael took the other. We left the corpse where it lay. A corpse on the roadside early that year was still an unusual and shocking sight but that was soon to change.

I cannot account for their age, they might have been as old as ten or as young as three, they were emaciated, covered in lice and in a dreadful way. They had no teeth so we each chewed food for them to swallow but they would hold nothing down. My mother went up to Sheehan's for milk from his goat which he gave her but at a thieving price. They held the milk down and we were hopeful for their recovery. Each day my mother would cradle them and hum to them and stroke their little heads. They were comforted and though they never spoke it was clear that they were content; maybe numb. Alas on the third morning we woke to find they had both passed in the night, their tiny hands clasped together as though in the darkness they had reached for each other, for sibling comfort; and found it. God does indeed operate his plan in a mysterious manner and I curse him to the depths for it.

I helped to bury them and remember as I lifted one into a blanket it was like lifting a bag of dry leaves. Such experiences I know can make a man turn to God and to prayer. It made me turn away from the vileness of religious people. I must labour that I did not turn away from religion, which is wholesome and good but for the efforts of the perverters of it and the peddlers of the lies. In this I know you and I Victor be kindred. The only comfort I draw from the experience is the knowledge that the last thing they knew on earth was kindness from strangers; a product not of God but of man in the face of the spite and cruelty of the Almighty.

Even now I think of those two and I am profoundly, profoundly saddened by the pain and the wastefulness of it. I have resolved to make them my last thought as I part this world; to honour them and to celebrate them in some small way. One of the few benefits of being hanged I suppose is that I get to select my last thoughts.

Father Sinnott had come and offered to bury the two children within the church grounds, so their souls could be saved. My mother chased him from our place with a pike and I am sure had she caught him she would have pushed it through his heart, if indeed he was in possession of such a thing.

I never discussed religion with my mother and although she was a devout catholic she let me go my own way with it; a rare thing in an Irish family. She did however pray to the Virgin Mary for the redemption of my soul and informed me of her efforts regularly. My mother was not an educated woman but she was able to read and she could distinguish between a good religion and a bad church; something much finer minds struggle to do.

After chasing the priest off with a pike she still attended church the following Sunday and every Sunday and holyday thereafter. Sinnott wisely kept his distance. Her devotion I suppose was to the Church and not to the man in the purple dress. She was an exceptional woman. She *is* an exceptional woman because she still lives at my brother's tavern in Derrybeg and will outlive me it seems.

It was not as bad for us as it was for many others. As I say we had turf for the fire and were warm, we had parsnips and turnips and onions and we had pork and we had eggs and chicken. We were like a world within a world. Many years later I discovered that there were many like us, people who although not wealthy had the resource and the good fortune to survive relatively well. Yes I was hungry and times were very hard but other families were wiped out in their entirety, in the most cruel and painful way.

The chickens fed from the ground outside and came in at night. My task was to follow them while they were let out, lest they be stolen. I also had the task of forcing one hen to sit on her eggs and those of the others. Through 46 and into 47 we always had eggs and chickens. We never had less than nine or ten laying chickens.

The months dragged from 1845 into 1846 and things got only worse for most people. My mother was careful and she was wise and she spent her money with caution. She bought good seed for turnips, parsnips and onions ready for planting in the second year of the Famine. Her husband, who I never got along with worked hard and by the spring of 46 he had planted about three times what we would need to survive; our family was large and yet we had lost not one of us.

Our piglets had grown and we ate them all and the sow was due again but by the summer time she turned out only two live and four dead. We lost the other sow to a thief in the autumn so we slaughtered the last of them for Christmas of 46 and beyond. Pig is a good beast and it keeps well with little but salt. The meat is good and the fat makes oil for lamps and for preserving other food. They are also fine companions; better than most men I have known.

No one expected the hunger to go into 47, everybody thought there would be help. I am ashamed to say that I grew quite plump towards the end of 46. Pigs grow fast and have many uses but they eat lots so it was I think the best decision to kill the last one; what is the point of having a fine pig if you die of hunger?

So we ate meat and eggs when others starved around us and to the day I die I will not eat eggs and pork on the same plate again; this for my sin of having more than my neighbour and not sharing it. Had we shared we would certainly have starved to death but this does not ease the guilt. Sometimes the hardest facts are the easiest to reconcile but it still leaves a bad feeling. We had food enough but not enough food.

In 46 we even managed oats and wheat enough to sell and pay the rent and to buy seed. We were told that the black blight had not just killed the potatoes but also the worm which needed to feed so it starved like everyone else. My mother said it was nonsense and anyway clean potatoes were not to be found anyplace near or abroad.

With the spring came berries and nettles and fruit which helped. The chickens laid well but by then we had to keep them inside for fear of them being stolen and this meant we had to buy corn for them. Prices went up twice and three times but putting corn into a chicken gets out eggs and when done the chicken is a feed for a day or two for us all and sucking on the bones is good for a child. In turn the bone ground down can be fed back to the birds.

My mother and I forced brood after brood all summer and winter and managed to sell some chicks. The cockerels were eaten or sold as soon as they had some meat on their bones. An egg will keep good for three months in winter and my mother had built a small stock of them. She stored them in hay above the hearth in the loft and we took from one side and placed new eggs on the other. When the stock got low we ate fewer eggs to build it up again. When the stock was too large she would swap the eggs for anything she could get.

Although there was just enough food to get through the coming winter, as we had the one before, we knew that a family of two adults, four nearly full grown children and four nippers was not going to manage another winter after that. The pigs were gone and money was almost gone with no one able to buy an onion or a spare chicken from us things were getting darker and one more turn of luck such as the chickens stopping or the turnips failing and we would be for the ground; all of us.

We continued to get letters from Uncle Manus in Pennsylvania. These depended on the travels of merchants known to the family and often were carried at considerable cost so our replies were less regular than his efforts. In the winter of 1846 we wrote to him telling him of the troubles and to expect Michael and me in the spring. My mother had decided the best for us was to go to America, she had no argument from her husband and he had suggested Nancy go too but our mother would not have it. We were two growing hungry mouths she could not feed and without us the rest of the family stood the best chance.

His reply came in late January and he assured us of a happy welcome in New York from where he had arranged transport to his new home in Pennsylvania. He was arranging passage from Sligo for us all, the whole family. He was acquainted with a person who in turn was acquainted with a captain who regularly sailed from Sligo to New York and the tickets and a sum for the journey would be with the captain. The name of the ship escapes me; it was 'Naga' or 'Nomad' or something similar.

Uncle Manus remembered the favour my father had given him and he wished he could send relief by way of money in his letters but it was not wise to do so. Money sent in such a way was almost never received.

Soon after Michael and I set out on foot to Sligo, we had the ship's name and that it sailed in late March or April. We also had the name and details of the agent in Sligo; all other matters could be discovered later in the port. We did not write to inform Uncle Manus that it would be just us two as we'd be with him before the letter and besides, the courier wanted three shillings for the trouble, my mother gave him a boiled egg and sent him on his way.

4
JOURNEY TO SLIGO

Bridgette O'Donnell and Children, (Illustrated London News, Dec 22, 1849)

We see from his next letter that Patrick's paranoia about his jailers is reinforced due to his brief illness. We however cannot discount entirely the possibility that his discomfort was not accidental.

He also mentions how he is getting the letters out of the prison; it seems he sends them out as they are finished, possibly because the cell would afford very little opportunity to hide anything.

In his previous letter Patrick conveys the horror and reality of how bad things had become by 1847 along with an awareness that the whole family were by now only a stroke of luck from death, by way of disease if not starvation.

His account is of course that of a 48 year old man but the source of the memories is a 12 year old boy. It is almost impossible to imagine the effects such experiences must have had on him; yet, as he faces his journey north to the port of Sligo his tone is optimistic, even jolly.

Patrick by the end of his journey north is accustomed to the sight of the dead and dying and of the terrible situation in which his countrymen find themselves. He is almost hardened and prepared for one terrible sight after another. What he was not prepared for was the sight that meets him on his arrival in Sligo.

(Fourth Letter)
Dec 8th 1883 - Newgate Prison, London

Dear Victor,

Since writing last I was struck with sickness. It was most unpleasant; vomiting and cramps and dizziness. The illness has passed thankfully and I fear it was bad drink that Margaret has brought to me though I do not put it past Mullins to have slipped something poisonous into it, enough to make life unpleasant but not to end me.

I have asked she get the sack another place anyway and to watch it keen when she comes through. Most of a day wasted for my story and I am not yet out of Ireland and I have so much to record.

The letter is gone now in the petticoats so I shall take up below where I left off. They sent a physician whose task I presume was to ensure I do not cheat the hangman from his fun.

If my memory serves I left you with the decision that Michael and I would venture abroad to escape the hunger so reduce the burden on our mother.

It was March of 1847 when we set out on foot to Sligo. I must go back a little because I have forgotten a thing. A week before we left, a neighbour, Ignatius O'Boyle was poaching and got his leg caught in a mantrap. It was severed at the knee, cut off almost completely. What was left was hanging from the blanket in which they carried him home. It took three days for him to die. My mother bought his boots from the widow O'Boyle for four full grown new laying chickens, which had two years of laying in them at least.

O'Boyle was a small plump man but even so his boots were still too large for me and I had to wrap my feet in cloth for them to fit. I'd outgrown the only other boots I ever had and Daniel had them now. He wore them but one time and the local boys had beaten him for having boots so he never wore them again after that.

My mother made me wear the new boots for my journey but as soon as we were out of sight I slung them over my shoulder. Michael, who had boots of his own since our father died did the same. Neither of us gave a thought to the fact that we would probably never see our mother, brothers and sisters again. It was a very strange time and although we knew these things we did not dwell on them.

As we passed through the far side of the village we came across O'Boyle's resting place. No one had the energy to help bury him and Mrs O'Boyle and her children had dug the shallow grave themselves. The priest Sinnott would not have the corpse of a thief in his churchyard.

The rats and dogs had been at it and his injured leg had been detached and pulled clear by some beast and carried off down the lane where it was part eaten. It was full of meat and I picked it up, it looked like a leg of any other beast but was longer and scraggy from the creatures. It smelled rotten but given the time of year had not yet succumbed to maggots.

8 hours later as we settled down for the night I cut the flesh of O'Boyle's leg into cubes and cooked them on a stick over a fire which we had made alongside a stone wall. We ate our fill. What we did not eat we stored cooked in our bags. That is how easy I first ate the flesh of another man. It might seem to you and to others that this was barbaric, particularly as we had 48 boiled eggs and cooked vegetables with us for food. The fact is we had no way of knowing what was next and since coming across O'Boyle's grave we had that day seen three more dead bodies in the verge, and us hardly up the road. These poor people had stopped to rest and simply died of cold and hunger. They were skin and bone and had no chance in a chill or with the least illness that might visit. Eating for us was not just about staving hunger, it was about building up when we could so when times were harder, as they surely would be, we would have the best chance.

I have explained that life for us was better than for most but make no mistake, there was always hunger, always the worry from whence the next mouthful would come. I was not going to waste my precious rations when there was *meat* to be had. It's not something I enjoyed to do. It was something I knew I must do; though I confess that I found the meat to be tastier than the dog I had once ate with my father. Give me a dead rat and a dead man and I would have no trouble deciding from which I might cleave the best cut. Let any man with a belly shrunk for days argue that. Give me a fat man over a thin one too as the meat is superior. I can say this for sure for I have fed on both.

I determined that I would eat the flesh of any beast provided it was dead and from the moment I made that decision all guilt and horror left me. I know it was the same for Michael as we discussed it and we counted our blessings that O'Boyle had been a portly chap and had not died of starvation. There were few pickings on most of the dead we were to pass in the days to come. I am certain this approach is the reason I was to survive the horrors of the next months which would show eating a man's well-cooked leg to be nothing.

The walk took us past dozens of dead and dying, maybe hundreds. Each day more and more, many stripped naked of clothes and many missing limbs and parts of limbs. I had at first thought these wretches were robbed of their clothes but later I saw one or two in the act of undress. It was strange but often when these poor creatures were close to death in the cold they would remove all of their clothes. I saw the identical thing in Tennessee some-time later and wonder about it sometimes[17]. Madness I suppose or the want of a swift end.

For years I have heard that during this time human flesh was eaten by a very few. I can swear on the scant remainder of my life that it was not only commonplace, it was rife. Humans do not lie down and die of starvation when there is a meal to be had, no matter how distasteful.

---

17 People suffering from late stages of hypothermia become confused and are known to disrobe as part of a phenomenon sometimes known as 'terminal burrowing'.

When I speak to people of our eating rats I am believed and understood but when I speak of eating human flesh I am disbelieved. It is not a subject I normally would mention but it is important to me that the facts are recorded herein. Many, many more people would have died in 46 and 47 had it not been for the supply of the meat of their fellow man found on the roadside.

It seemed that our route was one which many others had chosen. The further north we went the more people we saw. Some travelled in our direction and others in the opposite direction, almost all on foot. Our destination was Sligo but many more boats went from Dublin and other places and people were walking there and everywhere. Most had no hope of making the trek as they were but skin and bone at the outset of their journeys.

Had I not seen it with my own eyes I would not believe it so I allow for your own disbelief if you decide that way. I have read records and reports over the years but nothing; simply nothing can convey the desperateness of the situation. At some places there were dead and dying every few hundred yards. As if they had selected one point or another to die in groups. Sometimes a whole family huddled together in fever and soaked from the rain; those of them still alive too fatigued to look up as we passed. Some took to eating grass and their bellies had swollen and they lay dead from the poison of it. Some vomiting the green half chewed mulch back up and still pushing it in again. Perhaps they knew what grass does to a man and that is what they sought. I had not known of this until I saw it in 47.

More than a few times I saw the dying eating the raw body parts of companions and strangers; their fearsome expressions looking up from the ditches as though to challenge anything we might say in objection. Other than recommending cooking the flesh we had nothing to offer. I have a strong constitution as you by now have discovered, but eating such flesh raw would be hard even for me.

One dreadful creature held a new-born child upside down by the leg, biting into its thigh, tearing as best he could into the flesh with the few teeth he had left. I am not saying I would not do such a thing if driven to it, but I would first cut the flesh and form it to look like the meat of a pig or cow and not as man.

We arrived in Sligo sometime in March, I can't be sure of the date; towards the end of the month I would guess. We made our way to the docks and what we saw was incredible. Ship after ship laden with cows, and all manner of crops, onions, turnips, grain and sheep; but these ships were not landing, they were ships leaving the port and bound for England. Of all the horrors I have witnessed to that day and since I have never seen such depraved conduct as that of the English and of their puppets in Ireland. Our people starved and died by the tens of thousands and all the while the English took livestock and food from their very grasp. They might just as well have butchered a nation of its poor and its sick.

5
THE TAVERN AT SLIGO

Typical Town Tavern 1847

Patrick's account of the journey from his last letter is not particularly surprising and for the most part aligns with accounts given by his contemporaries and others. What stands out is his reference to the practise of cannibalism, which according to him was, if not commonplace, certainly practised by some, himself included.

It's well known that cannibalism occurred amongst some during the Famine; interfamily cannibalism in particular. There is little doubt that Patrick witnessed it but we must be a little sceptical about his claims to have indulged, at least how he suggests. This for two reasons; first, whilst Patrick unquestionably suffered extreme hunger, he was never on the point of starvation, not according to his letters at least. In addition, when he claims to have first eaten human flesh he was by his own account rather stout and well fed with plenty of food in his sack.

In the exceptional circumstances when people do turn to cannibalism it tends to be as a last resort, not when they are a little peckish, as Patrick was on the road north. It is my belief that he has exaggerated what he probably witnessed with a view to emphasising the terrible predicament he witnessed and lived through.

The subject of cannibalism was prevalent all during Victorian times; with stories of lost… and found expeditions to Africa and further afield making headlines regularly. In addition in the late nineteenth century many people in city slums were starving and where starvation existed so potentially did cannibalism.

For those readers who doubt man's ability to dine on his fellow man when circumstance demands I mention *The Mignonette*. In the year after Patrick's 'execution' the unsavoury matter was forced into public consciousness with the high profile case of *R v Douglas and Stephens 1884*.

In this case three ship's crew and a cabin boy found themselves in a small lifeboat after their ship, *The Mignonette,* was wrecked. With little hope of swift rescue they decided to draw lots to determine which of the four survivors would be eaten first.

Unsurprisingly the cabin boy lost, and when he became unwell from drinking sea water he was murdered by two of the men, Dudley and Stephens, who then, along with the third man, drank the cabin boy's blood and ate him…. entirely. Miraculously they were then rescued.

The two men admitted that they had murdered the boy rather than waiting for him to die because this provided most blood to drink; a gruesome but relevant fact in terms of what a man will do when faced with starvation.

Dudley and Stephens were of course prosecuted; found guilty and sentenced to death but eventually only served a few months for their crime. The third man, Brooks was acquitted as although he had eaten the boy (apparently enthusiastically) he did not take part in the killing.

Although the main legal issue of the case was whether or not 'necessity' gave a defence to murder it raised to the public consciousness several moral questions. The thing which distinguished Brooks' actions and those of Dudley and Stephens was that he had not killed the boy. Cannibalism incidentally was at the time not prohibited by law.

Whilst few people actually condoned the killing of the cabin boy for the purpose of survival there was a great deal of public sympathy with the survivors and the predicament in which they had found themselves. They were inevitably found guilty and sentenced to death as they had committed murder. Any other outcome would have been impossible to reconcile with English law. The men were however shown leniency, in spite of their guilt and neither served more than 6 months in prison.

Thus not only an understanding and almost an approval of eating human flesh for survival was signalled but even a certain understanding or perhaps a tacit approval of murder for the same purpose was given.

This is not a legal argument; simply an observation which I hope puts cannibalism during the Famine into some sort of moral perspective: It happened and it is understandable that it happened and had it been admitted people would have understood, as they should now..

As an interesting aside to that event; the cabin boy from *The Mignonette* was named Richard Parker. Many years later a book, *The life of Pi*, also concerned with survival after a shipwreck featured a Tiger, whose name was Richard Parker.

Patrick is shocked by the sights he sees in Sligo and on his journey there; by deprivation and death of course but much more by the sight of the fully laden ships heading out of port.

There are numerous theories and excuses and explanations given by history for why ships laden with food left Irish ports throughout the Famine and people who question it or highlight it are often regarded as too ignorant to understand commerce or politics. The fact remains, people starved to death in Ireland as food bound for England and Europe was shipped out from every port in Ireland in order not to upset the British economy.

Some commentators have characterised the behaviour of the English towards the Irish in this period as genocide. Perhaps that is too strong a term for it. ethnic cleansing, in the author's respectful opinion, is not.

It is soon evident from his next letter, his fifth, that Patrick and his brother are either the victims of a scam or victims of the confusion at the time. Regardless of the reasons, there were those in Sligo town who would exploit the brothers. By virtue of their reading abilities Patrick and Michael make the best of the situation until time brings them a chance.

When they do manage to find a means to cross the ocean it is not the manner in which they intended to leave Ireland but it is the only opportunity available and they grasp it in spectacular fashion.

(Fifth Letter)
Dec 8th 1883 Newgate Prison, London

Dear Victor,

I am glad to have got past the matter of
anthropophagy and I hope that you will not judge
me as others might. Though I am not ashamed I
have never told Margaret of it; she is of a mild
disposition and besides she was born after those
days and there seems no reason to burden her with
it. It's not something I normally talk about but it
was an important part of my life. As you will shortly
see, it kept me alive, not in the moment of eating
but later.

Today is colder but the sun is now shining and
it illuminates part of my cell and part of my spirit; I
think the afternoon will be warmer than this
morning. My hand is playing the devil and is stiff as
a board; I manage but am slow with the pen.

Back to my story and the tavern where we met
Flaherty and how we set sail for America. Flaherty
was the agent man who had arranged the trip this
side of the ocean and though we had not met him
we were assured by our uncle that all would be well.
Manus had paid for the passage for the whole family
and we were but two souls so we expected some
compensation for the others who did not sail with
us. In fact we depended upon it. Michael being my
elder would deal with these things I supposed. Even
at the age of twelve I was already weary to the
skulduggery of men but neither of us had

contemplated the twister that this man shortly
would reveal himself to be.

Michael and I had just a few pennies between
us and we asked about the docks, in the taverns and
storehouses as to how we could find Flaherty so we
might discover the location for the arrival of our
ship. The place was chaos, men, women, carts; noise
like I had never known all around us.

We were eventually directed to the man who
did his business in a tavern he and his wife owned
and ran. It was a long and deep brick built place
with slate roof and two chimneys, from which
smoke billowed and the smell of burnt damp turf
wafted down into the street.

The place was located at the edge of a road with
its front to the docks and the side to an alley where
even in daylight a strong man might consider it risky
to traverse. We entered into the dim lit smoky place.
It was a large room with tables and chairs and
benches and a lit fire at each end. The bar was the
whole length of the room and it was my guess that
the ten or twelve men leaning on it and drinking
and talking and spitting into the sawdust were
nothing as to how it would be at night time. A tall,
wiry woman in her forties bled pints into pewter
and clay mugs from barrels resting high behind her
and poured rum into glasses and laughed like a man.

A few tables were occupied by ruffians playing
cards. Here and there a musket leaned next to its
owner, in easy reach for any trouble that might
arrive. At the very end sat a man alone, behind a
large desk, his head down, scribbling and attending
to business of some kind.

The woman looked to Michael and at me, smiled a single toothed smile and nodded in the direction of the man. I supposed that those who had business in that place could have business only with one man; Flaherty.

We found ourselves in front of a stout, well fed man in the back of the tavern. Though there was a window nearby it let in no light for it was thick with the filth of the street and the smoke from peat fires around the place. Two oil lamps hung over the desk from the low beam and a row of thick candles sat on the wooden mantle of the fireplace.

The tavern was filthy and noisy and dark but it was a little warmer than outside where a sharp wind blew off the sea onto the land. We were both thankful to escape that, even for a short time.

Flaherty sat behind his desk which was located immediately adjacent to the fireplace where the peat smoked over the dull red of a fire struggling against the damp. I remembered my father saying;

'You might as well burn mud as burn damp turf'.

It gave off no warmth though I was stood immediately next to it in the hope that it might. On the desk sat numerous bundles and ledgers along with another oil lamp and several more candles, ink well and pens.

Almost hidden amongst the papers and books was a small steel box which we later learned contained coin and notes. Next to the box was a glass bottle, the shape of which I had never seen. A ruby liquid filled it and a half-filled glass alongside it.

The colour of the liquid intrigued me as it changed with every flicker of the candles next to it. One moment blood red and the next crimson like the vests of Father Sinnott. I wanted to taste it.

Flaherty, who was not Irish in spite of his name, smoked a fat cigar, ash from which he occasionally flicked onto the floor. The end of it looked wet and chewed. Each time he placed it back into his jowls he rolled it with his lips and tongue and seemed to chew it but not right through. He wore a thick coat with a large collar and it was opened revealing underneath a dark red waistcoat across which was slung a gold watch chain which disappeared into a pocket in the garment. Perhaps ten years ago this might have been fine attire but now the garb was worn and grubby. The man filled the clothes to bulging; he was small and round and wore spectacles which sat upon the end of his red bulb of a nose; far enough forward so he could squint over the top to see us.

Although I had never attended school I supposed that he resembled a nasty school master; a Master Squeers but with more meat on the bone. My father had read *Nicholas Nickleby* to us many times and he had always laughed at the nasty school master named Squeers and in particular because like my father he had just the one eye. It was one of his most loved books, second only to *Robinson Crusoe*. Sometimes when he was drunk, back in Gweedore, he would flip up his patch and say to our mother:

'I have but one eye, and the popular prejudice runs in favour of two'. They would then fall about in laughter, each time seeming to find the phrase more amusing than last. I missed my father and found myself thinking a good deal about him on our journey north. I knew though that the world as it was could be no place for soft thoughts and I forced remembrances such as this away lest they weigh me down in melancholy.

Flaherty laughed loudly when we named our ship and that we had passage paid for eight, but needed only two and would welcome return of the balance.

He told us that it was not due into port until sometime in June and that we were not the first to have secured passage on her. We had no idea at the time why he found this so amusing. He told us she was an old convict ship and not fit for the crossing but it was our lives and our uncle's money. He was adamant about the dates and when Michael asked to see the ledger in which he had looked before laughing so loud the man removed his spectacles and turned the huge book towards us. As my brother looked down the list Flaherty said;

'So boy, you can read?'

Michael and I answered together 'Yes'

'My word' he exclaimed with feigned surprise… 'and write?'

Again together we responded in the affirmative.

He looked us up and down as he turned the book back in his direction before Michael had a chance to properly check the lists. The fact that we had been allowed sight of the ledger suggested that the fat man had not been misleading us.

'You've some meat on you lads' He smiled, 'There will be none of that left if you wait here for three months without some sort of employment' he paused, 'It's not a trip for the feeble, more likely to make a splash than see the new world'. He chuckled as if pleased with himself. He was of course referring to the many souls who perished on the trip and were buried at sea. 'Thrown overboard' might be a better way to say it.

'I take it you're potless'. He leaned back on the heels of his chair and I was sure it would bust under his weight. We were unsure of what he meant until he made it plain:

'There is a room upstairs, you can share it. In return you can put your writing to work for me'. It did not seem like a request.

'What sort of writing' Michael asked.

'I need these ledgers copying..', he chuckled again and winked as he tapped his glasses on them, '..but with a few details omitted here and there if you catch my meaning young fella. Some promissory notes and other documents from time to time also'.

He made me feel uncomfortable as if by just saying those words he had entrapped us in some scheme of his. We had come to Sligo for passage to America, passage paid two times four. Trouble with the constable or the law of any kind was not our plan.

'Well Lads?' he continued, his mood now darkened.

'I have the bastard in my fingers' he said, suddenly seeming to cheer again. 'and he cracked his knuckles loudly as if to prove the point. 'My eyes too ain't what they were neither'. He rubbed them hard with his thumb and forefinger in a pinching motion.

'Now you pay mind you lads..' he paused, '..the books earns you a bed but if you want to eat you can help the Mrs around here too when need be'. He nodded to the single toothed woman who incredibly seemed to be in some sort of embrace with one of the sailors at the bar.

'Two plates each a day for that'. He banged the table as if it sealed the contract and declared 'Can't say fairer dan dat'.

I took that to mean breakfast and supper, and it did. Michael looked at me and then said;

'OK mister'.

The man returned the spectacles to the bridge of his nose, spat into his palm and offered his stout hand, which we both shook as he added;

'You'll have your bellies filled and a place to put your head and that's a fair bargain'. He was ensuring that the depth of his benevolence had not escaped us. The fact was that as a minimum he had pocketed a good portion of the price of six crossings and probably eight; God alone might guess at his plans for us. It was all I could do not to wipe my hand dry on my trousers.

We both knew it was our best chance at a place to lay and of some food to eat. Regardless of the facts we were lucky and we decided to play the game until better odds struck us. The notion that we would walk into the port and onto our ship had, I can now see, been most naïve.

The bedroom was without question the most comfortable I had ever seen let alone slept in. It was in the loft space and low with four beams crossing which I could not walk under without bending. It was narrow and long and dark and had no window but by candlelight we could make out the brick gable and up it ran the chimney breast, which by touch was warm.

The floor was rough boards and tight and well fitted so no gaps to the rooms below. Four beds sat on the longest wall. They were made of simple iron frames and on them were sacks of straw. Michael pulled one across the floor to the warm wall and I copied. We had slept in our first home next to the chimney and knew the value of it.

We'd had our fill of bread and cheese and a draft of stout from Mrs Flaherty who immediately put us to work in the tavern scraping the floor and clearing up. If Flaherty were fairly likened to Squeers then Mrs Flaherty was more easily Mrs Squeers. Flaherty I did not like and he was a user but she was dangerous and cruel and I could see the venom in her, Michael too could see it.

It was not hard work but after our travels we were dog tired. If there were a God, and he was a creature inclined to bestow a gift or a curse on a man then I can say the best gift he gave to me was the ability to sleep in any circumstance, in any place and at any time. I was asleep the moment I laid down on the first real bed I had ever slept upon.

In spite of the unsure circumstances I was almost content when I awoke in the morning. We rose before light and noticed the two other beds were occupied, one with two people. All three of our room companions were sound asleep and snoring and farting. We learned later that they were deck hands from the ships in port and that other rooms in the tavern were filled with the same, as other taverns with other rooms were also, all through the town. They were sailors but they were also ruffians and by night they spent their money in the tavern on ale and on women and on dice and by day they slept. They never concerned themselves with Michael and me and I guessed that Flaherty had a hand in that, we had after all taken beds and might otherwise have expected trouble.

Over the following days it was mostly Michael who did the writing as our benefactor looked over him. It unfolded well as it happens because Michael was by far the better scribe of the two of us; I, the keener grafter, worked in the tavern. I tidied and cleaned and then served at the bar and dished up vitals, washed the pots, brought in turf, lit the fires and kept them going. Each day I was able to swipe food; one day I was so filled that I did not finish my supper with the speed and greed I normally applied to the task and it aroused suspicion in Mrs Flaherty, and I think I was close to getting on her bad side. It occurred to me to feign sickness but Michael quickly divested me of that plan lest I be altogether thrown out for fear of the Typhus. I forced the last of the food down my throat.

Most of the customers were sailors and crew of the ships and they seemed to be the only ones with money to pay. It seemed strange that in the tavern life went on, people ate, drank, pissed, gambled and outside people died of starvation as cattle and sheep and corn and wheat were loaded onto the boats bound for English ports and English bellies.

The Flahertys were not good to us but they were not too harsh either, as had been my expectation. One time I saw Mrs Flaherty take a shillelagh[18] to a deck hand who could not pay but had drank plenty and she beat him about the shoulders and head with it so severe that he was laid out cold and two more sailors had to drag her clear before she killed him.

She was spitting fury and her eyes bulged and although I had already resolved not to get on her bad side I doubled my resolution in that as I threw fresh sawdust over the poor fellow's blood. I stole no more food for a few days but went back to my thieving because it was so easy.

Before a week was passed in the tavern I was entrusted serving visitors, cleaning rooms and many other tasks and I wonder was the beating more to serve as warning to me than as punishment for the deck hand. I concluded not; because the anger and fury could not have been planned, the woman was out of her mind in the midst of it for sure.

Michael seemed to have the limited trust of Flaherty, even checking and counting cash the man got from his various visitors; of which there were

---

18 *A stout walking stick with a knob at one end; used as a weapon or as a walking aid.*

many; they were in and out all day long passing notes and money and signing things and whispering and shouting. Some well-dressed gentlemen with white hankies pressed to their nose to avoid the air of the tavern and perhaps to maintain distain for the man with whom they must, but did not want to do business.

Flaherty liked Michael; everybody liked Michael. He was smart and quick witted and funny but not with disrespect or too much confidence; but people did not know him. He was a masterful thief and would steal anything and never missed the opportunity. He always had his eye on the next chance and what luck did not come his way he would manufacture for himself. If Michael saw your pocket watch unattended and he left it alone then it was only because he had a larger plan in mind; perhaps a plan for the watch and the chain and the waistcoat to which it might be attached. The more you trusted Michael the more likely he would rob you. I admired him and worked to be like him but I lacked the nature and the cunning and probably the intellect. Stealing food from the kitchen was at the very limit of my cunning, a task even the rats found not to be a particular challenge.

Although we worked long and hard we also had time to ourselves which we employed walking amongst the docks and seeking news of our ship. Much of what I saw those weeks in Sligo is mostly pushed from my mind; not for horror, though that is there, I just have had no use for it. Besides; others better with ink and pen than I have recorded it. I recall it now only in pieces for it serves no end to recount it all and anyway I have an unavoidable appointment soon so am pressed for time.

The sights were not as bad as what we saw on our journey, though they were bad enough. The worst of it is how the hungry were treated by those who had no want for food. I speak of the sailors and the shop owners and the publicans, the constabulary and others. For me the hardest was the sight of plenty next to the sight of need. On more than one occasion Michael and I gave some of our stolen food to beggars. It was a silly risk for one more bite or one more sip never saved anyone. It was hopeless, the local authorities banned giving out to beggars lest they be encouraged more into the port. To do it risked a fine or a night tucked up in jail.

I heard of some who had crept aboard ships and been thrown overboard into the sea to drown. In normal days I would say that was a tale to frighten people but in those times I have little doubt in the truth of it.

It was upon one of our jaunts around the ships that we encountered Captain Thompson for the first time. He was coming down the plank from a brig which had arrived the day before. It was our habit to ask Captains and crew for news of our ship and that is why we approached him. Michael told me that he had seen the man that morning, in the tavern doing business with Flaherty. Flaherty it seemed had a 'cargo' of men, women and children for the captain, and their passage had been bought[19].

It seemed that such cargo was usually paid for on behalf of some Lordship or other through the agent, normally Flaherty, but there were others. The captains however did not want to cross the ocean with a hold less than full so as well as getting their manifest and payment for it, they would come to Flaherty for any other passengers who were not included already in the official cargo.

Those unfortunates looking for passage came to Flaherty with their life's savings, some only affording to put their children on board for an escape from almost certain death. He would put the two parties together for a piece of the fare, which was much higher than that charged to his Lordship for the tenants he was ridding himself of.

All this done under the table; ships unfit for 200 often sailed with many more on board and not registered on any manifest and you could be sure no extra provisions would be bought by the greedy captains. The result was half rations and half water for all on board, except the captain and crew who ate well and drank well for the trip there and back. This required only a few bob to the port authorities who were supposed to check manifests and proper rations. Dozens of deaths on the ships crossing the Atlantic was the inevitable consequence, along with large profits for the captains and the Agents.

Upon seeing us admiring his ship Thompson called us to him and he enquired as to what our business was in Sligo. He remembered Michael

19 Landlords at the time were keen to rid themselves of tenants and many paid passage.

from earlier in the day and greeted him as if he were a partner in some minor ill deed. Michael seemed flattered for the notice. We explained that our ship was late and that we were working for Flaherty while we waited. He asked the name of the ship and we told him and he laughed heartily.

'Boys' you've been taken for fools. Two dozen of you turn up here every month with the same story and the same ship.'

'What do you mean mister?' asked Michael, 'our Uncle paid the passage in America and he wrote a letter and told it was all done for us'. Thompson laughed again.

'Being in America don't make a man any brighter or less able to be skinned'.

He went on to explain that the Naga or more to the point one or two of its crew were almost legendary in how they sold tickets for trips that never happened. They fleeced good meaning Irish families in America and did it with no chance of being caught. He also explained that of all the people in Sligo who knew about the scheme, the one who knew most was Flaherty. He was not involved directly in the trickery but apparently knew of it and definitely profited from it.

The immigrants when they found they had been tricked went to him and they paid their last penny in expanded prices for tickets in the bottom of some rotting hulk making the crossing. No ship took on a passenger without an agent's say so and even if that agent was not Flaherty, he would have a hand in it one way or another and when he did not have the lion's share he still had a cut.

Thompson explained that he was not one to cross Flaherty but that he had a place for a cabin boy.

'The thing is fellas I can help ye out' he said. 'My own lad took ill on the last crossing and he's gone but he was a scrap and so are all the other pups around this place. You boys look fine and strapping and I'd say you have a few crossings in you'.

He was addressing us both but clearly talking more to Michael than to me. Michael was taller and stronger than me and almost three years older. The sailor suggested four return trips for which he would pay Michael fair and on the last trip to let him off in America; if that was what he wanted but he suggested that Michael might prefer to stay aboard and learn the sea. Payment was to be in pennies and not in shillings but food and a bed was enough to anyone in our situation.

He claimed he also had a use for a scribe and did not elaborate but said;

'A man that can read and write and who knows the sea has the world at his feet'…. he winked at Michael,

'The agents might get to decide my cargo but I get to decide my crew'.

Michael seemed genuinely impressed and his mind was set from that moment. Besides, Flaherty was charging as much as £4 a trip, so it seemed to us to be a very good bargain, we had no hope whatsoever of raising £1 let alone £8. Michael agreed but asked that I accompany him and the

Captain countered that he would have £1 10 for my passage, and we must share a bunk.

We had no chance of getting the money but I knew better that to question Michael until later. On the way back to the tavern he told me his plan to find the money and he laughed at the notion that as soon as his foot was in America he would not be getting back onto any ship no matter what the fool captain might suppose.

We saw Thompson again the next day and he told us we were sailing on the first tide on the following Friday, it was to be around one in the morning in four days. We were frustrated with excitement but had to contain ourselves lest Flaherty notice something amiss.

Although we could easily have lived the few days on the dock or nearby it was better to have a bed and food for the time in wait. We also resolved to relieve our hosts of some vitals before departing and we were best placed to do that while in residence at the tavern.

By the third day the brig had been loaded with Lord Palmerstone's tenants and a sorrier bunch I have never seen. We saw them loaded and counted and they might as well have been cows but for the cows were fatter and healthier and of course more valuable.

Not a single one was dressed in anything but rags, only a few had a bundle, most had nothing, many walked with sticks and the children looked as if a slight breeze would lift them off into the sky, *like blackened embers from a chimney.*

I knew nothing of long sea trips but I knew that some of these poor wretches had no chance of surviving. I'd seen worse on the trip up from Clare but not much worse. I took some comfort in the idea that now aboard they would have rations and water. I was very naive. I confess also that although it was a pitiful sight I did not pity them. It is as if they were already dead and they were not humans at all any longer. No person would take these creatures as their fellow man. I suppose that is how the captains and the Flahertys and the Landlords could do as they did.

Michael and I determined to rob the tavern before leaving. In fact Michael had conceived of the notion in order to find the money we needed for my passage. Initially we were set on a loaf or two, some pies or some mutton but as we planned it we both grew in our ambition. We would be crossing an ocean and whatever mischief we were to achieve in Ireland surely could not follow.

We had no particular gripe with old Flaherty or his wife, neither of whose first names we ever learned. We knew she was a cruel bitch and that he made money on the suffering of others but so did everyone who had the chance. If it was not for the misfortune of O'Boyle and a few others along the way I would not at the time have weighed what I did, Michael would not have been as fit either and our passage would not have been found.

It was not a grand plan and neither of us expected much success but we decided to give it the best go we could. If at the last it failed we would forget the ship and find another, but it was worth a go.

Flaherty slept in a ground floor room behind the bar while his wife slept upstairs in her own room; so far as we could tell Flaherty was forbidden entry to that lair. I was in his room only one time and I had seen the large metal safe. Michael had been in there many times. The safe was not something any man or two men could lift, let alone two boys, large as we were; it had only one key and the key, Michael told me, was always in its door.

The prospect was promising and as the time drew near we finalised our plans both waiting and counting the 8 bells, the noise of which overlapped from several of the ships making it hard to be sure. The brig would sail in less than forty minutes, with or without us. The margin of time was narrow but it would serve to cover our retreat. There would be no time to raise the alarm before we were well out to sea, even if we had bad luck and our crime was discovered before morning.

We sneaked past the snoring men in our room and made our way downstairs. First we prised the lock from the pantry and filled our bundles with cheese, meat and pastry and a couple of bottles of rum. If nothing else we would have something to feed on for the first part of the trip. Michael entered Flaherty's room first; it was dark but for the light from the stump of a single candle sitting upon a dresser and our own single candle to show the way.

Flaherty was laid on his back on the bed. We could barely make out his shape at first. He was fully clothed with his right leg hanging over the edge but his boot not touching the floor. Next to him on the floor was an overturned glass and on the bedside table was an almost empty decanter, void but for the dregs. By now we knew it to be port, his favoured drink. He snored as he inhaled and gargled as he exhaled, his big belly moving up and down accordingly.

We quietly crossed the floor toward the safe at the foot of the bed; it was clear that there was no key in its door or about the place. Michael held the candle up and moved it to gradually illuminate each corner of the room. On the top of the dressing cabinet next to a water jug and basin, shining in the light was the tin box from Flaherty's desk. Quietly we crossed over to it, now less than a body length from the sleeping man, behind us. I gently lifted the lid. It squeaked as I opened it; I looked over my shoulder and the sleeping hulk had not moved. Inside the tin an amount of folded notes was held down by a bundle of coins. I was unsure whether or not to take the contents or the tin entire. Michael sensing my hesitation whispered;

'Take the tin'

Neither of us noted the snoring had ceased.

I lifted it gently but as I did I turned and looking past Michael was horrified to see Flaherty, sitting bolt upright in bed, his feet still not touching the ground but Pistol in hand aimed direct for us. A bolt ran through me, as if I had been hit by lightning, he could not miss us both I guessed. I knew the damage a ball from this distance could do as I had seen some of the beasts my father had shot;

occasionally they were split in two, guts and bone splinters and torn flesh.

He said nothing as he pulled the trigger; no warning, no rebuke, nothing; I wonder did he know that it was us. There was a flash of powder, a puff of smoke, yet no explosion as expected. The second needed to be sure of a misfire passed as an hour but the powder in the barrel refused to do the man's bidding and I thanked God for the dampness of Ireland.

Michael, only 15 at the time was not just a large boy but was fast as a whippet; he made his move. In a moment he was upon Flaherty whom he knocked back in the charge smashing his head against the wall. The gun fell to the bed and as it did it spoke with an almighty bang, a flash and a cloud. My father had told me of this. I was once permitted to use his Bess and when the flint had struck and the powder flashed in the pan but not in the barrel I had turned with the gun pointing to him. It was the only time he ever struck me. The gun did not discharge on that occasion but he had explained to me that damp powder can often take a couple of seconds or more to ignite and such delay was not uncommon.

The ball, which would have killed one of us or both hit the safe at the foot of the bed with a crack and rebounded missing Flaherty's head by an inch and embedded itself in the wall next to him. The discharge from the front and rear of the barrel set two small fires on the mattress, where it sat. The noise would have woken up any lodgers and Mrs Flaherty and although by now we observed the safe key around Flaherty's neck we were out of time. Michael grabbed the watch chain from the unconscious man's waistcoat and wrenched it; the watch followed and the waistcoat ripped. I picked up the money box and we swiftly but quietly made our way to the rear door of the tavern, we opened it, dropped the candle and were away. A glance at our new watch while we were still in light showed half an hour after midnight.

By the time we reached the brig they were about to raise the plank and Captain Thomas saw us approaching and ordered it held fast. As we dashed breathless past him he announced that he thought we were already aboard.

Michael had already seen where we were to bunk on the ship; it was in fact my first time aboard the Carricks. I suppose I was the last person ever to board her.

There was a good breeze and as the ropes were untied and pulled in and one sail was dropped; we started to move away from the quay. No light came on shore and no one shouted or rang the bell. Perhaps the shot was not heard or perhaps the open door had given the wrong impression of what had happened. As the one or two dim lights faded into the distance, so my optimism grew, no one would seek us in America for this crime. As I went in search of the bunk I was to share with my brother I noticed on the horizon what looked like a red sky but it could not have been because from where I stood, Sligo was east and it was anyway far too late for a setting sun.

6
ESCAPE OVER THE SEA

The Wrecking of the Carricks – April 1847

Patrick's account of his experience at the Tavern with Flaherty shows a realisation that he and Michael had been victims of trickery at worst and exploitation at best. I think this diminishes their 'crime' during their escape.

It is not clear if Flaherty was the architect of the mistreatment or just an opportunist, nor is it clear which is the worst, but there seems to be a certain natural justice to the events that followed.

The letter ends with some questions as to the fate of Flaherty; I confess I'd rather hoped he had perished but there is no record of it that I can find. If there had been a fire in such circumstances it would likely have been recorded; indeed a tailor's shop set alight the same month in Sligo was the subject of a newspaper report. Perhaps Patrick's account was a little more driven by a desire for 'poetic justice' than by fact, we shall never know.

His sixth letter finds Patrick and his brother Michael on board a brig, heading not for the United States as they presumed but for Canada. It is probably through their father's travels and experience that they would have known of the existence of Canada but they would have had limited understanding of where it was, in particular how far it was from their anticipated destination and planned rendezvous with their uncle Manus in New York. That said, by the time they got aboard they probably cared little for the destination, provided it was away from Ireland, and fast.

Passengers were regularly told they were heading for America when in fact they were not. New York harbour by 1847, would not accept emigrant ships from Ireland into dock, this due to overloading and numerous epidemics of typhoid, a disease the locals named 'The Irish Disease'.

The United States had regulations in terms of numbers of passengers; The Steerage Act 1819, was aimed at the prevention of overloading and mistreatment of passengers. The Act also provided for minimum water and bread provisions for passengers but these related only to ships leaving, not arriving in the USA.

In Britain, much earlier, a small effort had been made to protect emigrating passengers. The Passenger Vessels Act, was enacted in 1803, and updated in 1828. The Act, similar to the American Act, limited the number of passengers, and aimed to ensure sufficient food and water was provided for the voyage. In reality most ship owners, agents and captains ignored the rules and the ships leaving Ireland were invariably overloaded and very rarely had enough provisions. They also were often unseaworthy. Some ships provided no provisions and the emigrants had to carry their own, out of a famine ravaged country.

It cannot be a great surprise therefore that these ships became known as 'coffin ships'. Losses of human life on the 4 to 6 week journey across the Atlantic varied from ship to ship but were commonly between 10 and 30 percent with some ships recording over 50 percent losses.

Given most ships travelled with far more passengers than listed on the manifest and dead bodies were always thrown overboard it is, as incredible as it might seem, most likely that these figures are very much a low estimate. We must bear this in mind if we are inclined to think Patrick exaggerates his account of the trip. These were not well travelled people; they were ignorant, poor, hungry and often diseased; none would have previously travelled beyond their village and here they were entering the unknown, often to oblivion. What hope had they?

The Carricks was chartered by none other than Lord Palmerston, who was Prime Minister to Great Britain, twice. During the Famine he evicted just over 2000 Irish tenants from his lands in Ireland, lands he rarely saw as an absentee landlord. He famously stated that for any improvement in Ireland there must first be *"a long-continued and systematic ejectment of smallholders and of squatting cottagers".*

It was presumably with this in mind that he forced over 173 starving and thinly clothed passengers onto the Carricks, a coffin ship, in the spring of 1847. According to Patrick's letter an additional 50 or 60 passengers who could afford the inflated prices joined the evicted tenants. This is not only easy to believe, it is almost impossible to disbelieve because coffin ships never went to sea without maximum 'cargo' to maximise profits.

Here is not the place to explain the complex evolution of the situation which meant that it was less costly for landlords in Ireland at the time to pay for the passage of their tenants than to allow them to subsist on their land. It is a well recorded fact.

From 1847 over a period of just 3 years many thousands of emigrants boarded such ships in Sligo alone. Many perished en-route and many more died of disease, particularly typhoid, after arrival.

(Sixth Letter)
Dec 8th 1883 Newgate Prison, London

Dear Victor,

I am making good progress with my story but as I
write so much more rushes into my mind and I fear
sometimes that I recount the insignificant and omit
the important. Alas, also, I am no great scribe and I
rely on my memory and no documents. I trust what
does finally get to you will amount to a fair account
of the most important parts which led me to my
final sin.

That sin for which I am to be punished is one I
regret in many ways but not one for which I deserve
punishment, or at least not punishment so severe. I
have given you a truthful account of what I did with
my brother Michael and although I never
discovered if the old tavern burned to the ground or
not I have a strong feeling it may have done and it
may be that old Flaherty did not survive it. I never
did trouble myself to discover the facts, perhaps
because I did not want to for fear of the inevitable.

Flaherty was a blaggard and a user but no more
so than most in those days, he was in a position
where he could do more evil than others who did
not have the opportunity, but would have done as
bad if they had. Those were not ordinary times and
while some people did what they did to thrive most
of us did what we did to survive. Other than the
tickets he never did Michael or me a bad turn, not
that which I know of and if we don't count him
trying to shoot us as we robbed him. I suppose if he

did not burn then he would by now be long gone anyway from the drink or the smoke or the bitch.

So, you have a brief account of my family in Ireland, of my youth and of how I escaped the Hunger with my oldest brother. Here is how we crossed the Atlantic and made it almost to America.

The first thing to note is that on our first day as sea fairing fellows our companions, the crew, who numbered more than twelve, including Michael, informed us that we were in fact bound for Quebec and not for New York. They informed us merrily that New York and indeed no American port would allow such an over laden and filthy vessel to dock, particularly when it came from Ireland. In fact the British in Canada would only allow it because it was a means of offloading the problem tenants.

We were told that the Irish immigrants landing were in such a poor state that a special quarantine station had been set up in Canada to deal with them. They also told us how all previous passengers were similarly misled and most had no idea where Quebec was in relation to New York. Indeed I confess I had only a small idea of it until they told me that New York was about double the length of Ireland south of Quebec; which in turn also meant nothing to me until they explained it was Clare to Sligo about six times, but a good deal colder. That I did understand.

In normal circumstances such confusion as to our destination would have worried me and my Uncle Manus' arrangements for us in New York also would have worried me but I put that aside.

The issue in hand was whether or not we would get to Quebec, let alone America.

I was 12 years old and Michael was approaching 15 and we were thankful to step off the cursed and blackened land of our birth. A land I would see again but Michael would not although that was unknown to us both at the time. We had almost eleven pounds from Flaherty, less the one and a half I had passed onto the captain, and the watch would be worth something though we had no idea what. I had learned to tell time from drawings but had never actually seen a real timepiece nor indeed had any use for one. We kept the valuables hidden for the crossing as we did the money. There was no immediate need for money so I kept it in my boot, which was anyway too big for just my foot.

The crossing was hellish; we were both as sick as dogs and I puked for most of the first three days. The only relief from it was sleep and again I was grateful for my gift.

However bad it was for us it was infinitely worse for the poor beggars in the hold. I call it a hold for that is what it was. To call them passengers would be inaccurate, they were no more than cargo but unlike most cargo the only value they had was in their transportation, not in their delivery or any use thereafter. Payment was made and received and Palmerstone was rid of his liability and by now drinking claret and eating lamb. If every last one of them perished it would amount to nothing but a saving on the meagre provisions they were given.

I grew up detesting the English because like every true Irishman I was taught, and I knew, all the ills that befell our nation or indeed any nation were directly accountable to the English[20]. My detestation for my fellow man, not just the English, grew as I witnessed the great hunger and lived through it. Like many people I hoped even at the age of 12 to one day be in a position to take my revenge on that poisonous nation. I was young and I saw things flat and as I grew I understood more the complexities of life and I no longer harbour any dislike of the ordinary English people but I cannot in good conscience say the same of the English nation, which is another thing altogether to its people.

Unless you have crossed the Atlantic in a brig filled to the gunwales[21] with the filth of the dying and the dead you cannot possibly imagine the horror of it; though investing oneself with the reality is I assure you not worth the experience, so I urge you to settle on my word for it.

As the ship dives down into each wave it feels as if it will never come up, the higher it then rides up on the next wave the greater the drop. Onwards, day and night after day and night the same dreadful ordeal which leaves a man feeling that it would be best and a mercy if we did not rise up at all, instead for the sea to take us in its grasp and smash the sails and mast and planks to nothing and end the misery. I have heard of sailors afflicted so bad with sea

---

20 *Though Patrick is being sarcastic there is some truth in the fact that this view was widely held in Ireland. The author makes no comment as to its accuracy.*
21 *Top of the uppermost of a ship's hull. Modern spelling 'Gunnels'*

sickness that they have thrown themselves into the sea for relief. I did not contemplate that but understand how a man might.

To venture onto the deck was almost impossible; I had to lash myself to the rail or anything else just to get air or to empty my bucket. The one thing which encouraged me and which made me feel this tumbling lump of wood in the middle of the ocean was safe was the crew who shared our billet. They went about their work whistling and singing even in the worst of it and while they aimed not to make us feel better their disposition and apparent lack of concern did cheer me and it cheered Michael because when he saw me worried in the worst of it he would say;

'Pard, we will only need to run for the lifeboat if the deck hands do'.

Most of the trip we were lashed with rain and no passenger could cook or boil water because cooking for them was only allowed on deck. The crew could cook and Michael was a popular cabin boy as he set about his tasks in the galley and elsewhere with vigour. Midway, perhaps on the third week the weather calmed for a few days and I was able to walk about. Curiosity took me to the hold. I wish it had not; it was unbelievable in sight, smell and sound.

There were only cots half way along the place. These were three high to the underside of the deck; hardly enough for sixty people I would say. There was planked flooring and sort of shelves two high opposite the bunks and around the outer edges but not wide enough for a person to lay. I have no clue as to their purpose.

Upon the floors were 200 more 'passengers', those well enough were pushed up to the sides of the hull away from the spine of the ship where most of the foulness sloshed about.. They laid themselves on what blankets or clothes that they owned. Straw and sawdust had been spread thick on the floor but this was long since soaked in sea water, human waste and vomit.

Shit buckets were filled and overflowed and over turned. It seemed these wretches were unaware that they could go to the deck and throw the contents over and swill the buckets. They could have brought down clean sea water and washed the floors and themselves. They seemed to have given up their humanity, or had it taken.

Vomit and waste was everywhere and the air below deck was almost unbearable. In the foremost area, thankfully furthest from where I stood one man stood naked, ankle deep in shit as he emptied himself down his legs into the pile. He made no attempt to wipe himself and he swayed gently in motion with the waste.

Victor I swear to you that this is what I saw with my own eyes and let any man tell you that eating human flesh is the worst that a man can sink to and I shall call him a liar or a fool. This is what our lords and masters had driven us to. The Irish; a nation which could read and write while the English ran around the hills painting their faces blue, subjugated and turned to this, by their betters?

There were dead amongst the bodies, I could see them, pushed to the spine, and they were not few; and there were others near to death who moaned and cried out like Banshees[22]. I know for sure that during the crossing several poor souls perished from black fever and other illness but it would be over ten years before I heard the full story. What was declared by Thompson in the newspapers was not accurate because there were at least 50 more bodies on that ship than had a right to be there or ever appeared on any manifest, perhaps double that. I know because I was one of them, Michael was another.

I was spared the nightmare endured by the other passengers because Michael had been allocated a cot with the crew and none of them objected to us sharing; I helped Michael with his duties and we served the men well so a blind eye was turned to me. I have to say if I had been confined to the bowels of the ship as had others I surely would have jumped overboard and taken my chances.

Of the six pints of water we were supposed to be given each day I never saw more than two and of the pound of bread I rarely got half so I have no doubt that the wretches in the main hold must have been dying from thirst and hunger as well as disease. In spite of my small official ration I ate reasonable well as the crew's food, which my brother and I were allowed to share, was cooked below deck in the galley. The smell of it must have tortured the

---

22 *A banshee is a female spirit in Irish folklore who heralds the death of a family member*

others, though perhaps the scent of stew could not pass the stench in which they sat and lay and perished.

By the time we approached the coast of Canada at least 20[23] bodies had been thrown overboard and the crew had initially refused after that to go below to bring any more up. Never the less excitement filled us all as the crew told us of our location. It was late April as we approached our destination. The captain paid extra to some of the crew to remove the remaining corpses and I was forced to help, I presume it would not look well arriving with fifty or more dead on board. We threw them directly into the sea without even a word over them. The only ritual for each was a sailor searching through the pockets.

Michael and I were asleep in the bunk when the storm struck: It seemed to come from nowhere, one moment we were bouncing along; which was a thing we had got used to, and the next the ship was rising and falling and tumbling something terrible. I'd been unwell for a day or two and had been puking and shitting like never. The crew had threatened that if I continued this way then I would be put with the others in the hold and not allowed to share the bunk. The thought of it terrified me so the nearing coast was more of a relief to me than anyone can imagine.

I was woken with a crack of planks splitting and breaking. I was already dressed but for boots, which

---

23 *Official reports showed 9 of those on the manifest to have died en route.*

I almost never wore anyway and which still housed our loot. I ran to the deck with Michael beside me and already the crew, captain and all were throwing ballast over the side and leaping to it and into the only boat. I could at first see barely twenty feet ahead until with each lightning strike the world was illuminated in sickening cobalt. In those moments I could see the dark frozen figures coming out from the hatch, children wrapped around parents, confused and frightened as they gathered on the deck, no idea which way to turn.

The screams were carried on the howling wind as it tore through the ice laden sails, the largest of which flapped ferociously and cracked like a frozen whip. The ship then began to rotate, as though a giant hand had reached down below its keel and spun it like a top. I slid across the deck unable to catch anything to arrest my fall. To my left dozens of bodies slid across the deck and into the sea, on top and alongside each other. To my right, I saw Michael grab the rail as I hit it with my back and over I went, into the freezing abyss.

I had never felt anything so cold as the water as I hit it. The drop had been only a few feet as the ship had turned and was listing hard; I did not go deep before coming back up. My flesh burned from the icy water but I instinctively kicked and swam away from the turning hulk as best I could. In another flash of light I could see Michael, just a stretch away tangled and stuck to the rail, I could make him out in every detail as it went under and he with it. It was hopeless, my brother was taken by the sea and I never set eyes on him again. My heart was shredded in that moment and I wanted to die.

I don't know how long I was in the water and I had no idea how far I was from land; I could see no lights. The storm died, almost as if having disposed of the ship it had done its work and blew itself away to find another victim. I could hear others in the water crying and shouting but could see nothing. I didn't try to swim and I think I caught hold of a plank or a cot. I remember not really caring about anything.

I was sure this was the end and really was not very concerned about that, I was worried what my mother might say when she learned I had lost my boots. Then I saw the light to my left. It seemed odd that there would be a light in the middle of the sea. I could hear the shouts and I shouted back, the boots left my mind and getting out of the freezing sea seemed again to be important to me. As the light approached I saw the oil lantern on the bow of the approaching boat and above it a heavily bearded face attached to a bear of a man, with a woollen hat. He reached down with one arm and lifted me clear of the water and I gave up to unconsciousness as I heard him say;

"Bienvenue à bord mon petit".

7
THE SHEDS

Farewell - Henry Doyle - 1868

Patrick laments the loss of his brother Michael; he
did not however dwell on the matter because apart
from anything else he had little opportunity to do
so. He recounts the wrecking of the ship vividly,
such a memory surely would be etched into the
mind of anyone who had suffered it; yet his pity is
more for the poor passengers than it is for Michael,
as they go to their fate. Far from feeling sorry for
himself Patrick makes jokes about how the devil has
missed another chance to get him. Humour and
sarcasm are mechanisms he uses throughout his
letters.

The Carricks sank in a storm off the coast of
Canada in late April 1847. Of the 173 passengers
listed on the manifest less than 50 survived the
wreck, many having already succumbed to fever and
starvation did not even make it as far as the coast of

Canada. All the crew made it to safety, apparently leaving the passengers to perish, just as Patrick observed in his previous letter.

On June 29th 1847 *The Liverpool Mercury* published a communication sent by Captain Thompson a month earlier.

CAPE ROSIER 19th MAY, 1847. "I am sorry to inform you that the brig Carricks, was wrecked about four miles to the eastward of this place... out of 167 passengers, only 48 reached the shore. The crew, except one boy, were all saved".

The 'boy' or 'cabin boy' to whom the captain refers was almost certainly Patrick's brother, Michael.

Incredibly between 2011 and 2016 the bones of 21 individuals were found after a storm and beach restorations near Cap-des-Rosiers, north of Quebec. Analysis of the bones proves them to be mainly women and children, most certainly from a coffin ship, almost certainly the Carricks.

It was not just the Irish landing in America and Canada. Of course the Irish were fleeing starvation but many Europeans, were fleeing religious and cultural persecution. Anti-Semitism for example was rife in many countries.

It was the coffin ships which brought the diseases; the passengers were sickly and malnourished before embarkation and the confinement and atrocious conditions on the voyage only served to worsen the situation. Dozens on every ship died of typhoid and those who survived the trip caused outbreaks wherever they landed.

The American rules for loading vessels meant that only the less crowded and therefore less disease ridden boats landed in New York for example; but still, typhoid and other outbreaks were a regular occurrence. British Canada had less strict rules but also had the infamous Quarantine Sheds on Grosse Island in The St Lawrence.

Originally built 20 years earlier for European immigrants believed to have caused a cholera epidemic the place was brought back to use in 1845 for the 'Irish disease'.

Modern estimates suggest that over 3,000 Irish immigrants died in the quarantine sheds between 1845 and 1849. They also suggest that there were 5,000 buried there during this time because some graves contain people who died en-route. It seems unlikely that the coffin ships would have kept dead bodies on board and it is far more likely that these were disposed of at sea, for reasons of hygiene, if not for the shame of the owners. Thus it is reasonable to conclude that many more of the bodies buried on the island actually died there, as opposed to being brought there dead, from the ships.

In 1847 conditions in the sheds were beyond dreadful. Sanitation was rudimentary, in some areas non-existent; provisions very basic and care was crude at best. Immigrants were confined against their will and stayed for a time and if they lived they left, if they died they got buried. Sadly many arrived without illness and contracted it in the sheds and died as a result. Before 1847 those not suffering symptoms were kept separate from those who were. By the time Patrick arrived there was no such separation. Many immigrants for example were housed in basic tents, poorly protected from the elements and the disease.

Quarantine did not always separate the ill from the well, in many cases all mixed together so whilst insulating the local population from typhus it often exposed everyone in quarantine.

There were few doctors and nurses. One doctor at least is recorded as having contracted the disease and died but the fact is doctors in 1847 were anyway in short supply so in the sheds they are likely to have been very few.

Some nurses, immigrants in quarantine, volunteered and were paid extremely well for their work. They often had to sleep near to the sick and share their food. It is unlikely they were actually nurses of course. The authorities also resorted to employing convicts in exchange for reduced sentences. Escape from the Island in the centre of The St Lawrence was absolutely impossible, though that did not stop some from attempting it.

With rare visits from doctors and nurses, none from any guard or other authority and convicts all but unsupervised the sheds must have been a desperate, lawless place to be. Once a convict was recruited the authorities were reluctant to return them to the prison lest an outbreak of disease occurred; thus they were always long term 'volunteers', outstaying all immigrants and most others, and acquiring the power that brought.

It was here in this terrible place with death all around that Patrick found himself and it is here that he encounters a kind woman who would not only save him but would change his life forever. Together by bad fortune and good their future was bound.

(Seventh Letter)
Dec 9th 1883 - Newgate Prison, London

Dear Victor,

It is strange to me; the remembrance of the wrecking of that ship and of Michael's last moment and my salvation from the sea by a French bear. I have thought of it and many times have lived it again in my dreams but never in such a fashion as required to recount it on paper as I now have done. It took an effort for which I was unprepared and if I was not now sitting in a condemned man's cell I would count myself lucky for my escape. I am not full of pity for myself but it is hard to see why I was saved from the sea to now be condemned to hang instead.

Even these many years later I can still feel the bite of that cold in my shoulders making its way down my spine. It chilled me to the very bones and although since I have felt the heat of the Virginia sun on my back and the flash of powder against my skin I have never been able to fully rid my soul of that icy hand which tried to grab me under into the salty green blackness.

It seems that the Devil had me marked and would get me one way or the other even to the extreme of taking into the sea all those souls in search of just one; Patrick O'Donnell.

I can never erase the sight of those poor wretches, unable only hours earlier to step out of their own waste; tumbling down the deck and into the sea, desperately grabbing in vain for children

97

and loved ones on their way to the depths and perhaps the only true respite from suffering they could ever know.

I was one of only a few saved that day. Some floated to shore, some, like me, were fished out of the water by the fishermen. Many perished in the hold and most of those who got out drowned or froze.

I lived because I was near the deck and I had some meat on my bones to hold in the heat long enough for rescue; most were already deadly sick of hunger and fever and could not have survived a lash of rain let alone a dip in the sea.

The crew cut for safety as soon as they knew the ship was lost; all got clean away but for Michael and he would have too but for getting into a tangle at the rails. He and I were asleep while the crew were fighting the storm, so they were already on deck and we were not. They left the passengers, the cargo, to perish. God curse their bones and the bones of their children and their children's children for they could have saved a few if they had but tried.

I have no memory of the days after my rescue; I say 'days' it might have been weeks, I cannot be sure. I assume that the people who pulled me from the sea took me to a place and seeing what afflicted me was more than the cold and the sea they transported me to the fever sheds on Grosse Island. Our ship was bound for the island anyway and although none of the immigrants knew it, we, like all the other coffin ships, would have docked there and not on the mainland, where sickly Irish corpses were unwelcome. That is to say we would have docked there if we had not first fallen upon the rocks in the storm.

It was in the sheds that the Devil missed his next grasp at me. That I lived through it is a puzzle. Perhaps I had some purpose, perhaps if there was a plan for me it did not include me dying just then and of fever. I had seen the Hunger and I had beat it and I had seen the coffin ship the Carricks and lived and then the wreck and lived still. I did not realise it, but this next place was to be the hardest test for me to keep body soul and mind united in one; the death sheds of Grosse Island, took as much of my countrymen as did the coffin ships[24].

I have no idea how long I lay on my cot or how I got there. In my fever I saw things I was sure were true but they could not have been. I saw my dear mother and my father, in the old place. I saw them as sure as I now see the walls of this cell; his black hair over his patched eye; reading with Michael and me. In my vision he let me shoot his Brown Bess, which he rarely did before. I saw Michael and his legs were cut away by tangles of rope from the Carricks and we cooked them over a fire on the roadside by a stone wall and he ate and I ate heartily; we ate our fill on his plump legs and thought nought of it.

---

24 Patrick is incorrect; whilst many thousands of immigrants perished in the Quarantine sheds of Grosse Island in the late 1840s many more died crossing the Atlantic.

It's a dream which visits me even now from time to time. The worms too, coming from the potatoes in County Clare and up my arm to eat me, chattering and laughing on their way to eat my head as hollow as the spuds in 45, before the Hunger and with them an accidental warning of what was to come; which saved us.

By the time I was back in hold of my mind I was half my weight and desperate weak. I have stated it before and I state it again, but for the *meat* I ate in the previous months I would never have had the fortitude to live through the trip or the fever after it. Boiled eggs do not build a lad in the way flesh can build him.

It was a cold morning when I woke fully, early May as best I can recall, but for sure I do not know. I was laid in a bunk under another poor soul. Whatever the fellow or the woman above me (for I could not tell which) leaked, they leaked upon me. Shit and vomit and blood and spit and stuff the nature and origin of which I know not.

I was just twelve years of age but for each of my years since 45 I had lived ten, so I was a man and as a man I knew enough that I would perish if I stayed in that stinking, wretched place. Yet it was here that my new country required me to stay until cured or dead. I knew that I must improve my situation in any way I could if it was cured and not dead that I was to be.

I was too weak to stand so I dragged myself from the pit and managed somehow to raise myself to the bunk above. Pressing my back against the creature in the higher bunk I managed to tip him to the floor, like a cuckoo evicting a smaller weaker chick. It was a hard task for me in my state but not one that would have troubled a boy in good health for the fellow was all bone and skin and nothing more. Some others looked up from their pits, most did not. Those who did gave me no heed and attended to their own miserable survival or demise.

On my journey through Ireland I'd seen mothers bury their children on the side of the road, not a tear or a whimper from them; but this place was not the same. People moaned and screamed as their loved ones passed. All this way, through the terrible hunger, the long walks, the coffin ships, the disease; to reach the Promised Land only for that promise to be broken so bitterly; for them to finally be left to fester and die in this ungodly pit. I concluded that those who slid off the ship into the water were the lucky ones.

I lay on the top bunk and slept again, I felt no guilt and no pity for the thing of which I had disposed. Later, I have no idea how much later; a woman came by and inspected the creature on the ground. I slept again and when I awoke the same woman was returned with a cart and a man. They loaded the body onto the cart as if it were a bundle of straw. One leg dangled free over the edge and the male attendant kicked it up, only for it to fall down again, this time left to dangle as the cart was pushed away, the man not desiring to use his hands on the diseased corpse. A boot was good enough.

As the woman went about her task she looked to me… more than that; she saw me, she saw me in this place where so much went unseen, unseen for the sake of sanity; she saw Patrick O'Donnell; more than that she saw Pádraig O'Domhnaill[25]. Her face was the only human thing in that shed. She paused as I looked back at her. Hope? Was it hope I felt? It was something.

'Water' I said.

The word was a croak which hurt my throat; my first spoken in this land of opportunity, of salvation; this promise land with Irish dead and dying littered about the bunks and on the floor. She did not reply but after removing the cart she returned with a pitcher of liquid which was cold and tasted of tea. She offered to help but I managed to sip the liquid over my cracked lips; it stung. She looked like my mother but younger and when she asked my name, she spoke our language and I replied;

'Pádraig.'

'Pádraig' she replied.

It was the kindest word I had heard in a long time. It was my predicament of course which made it so but over the years that followed I dreamt more often of that voice and the kindness than I did of Michael's legs or the cold sea or the Hunger or other things yet to come.

Later she brought me gruel; later again she dressed me in a clean nightshirt, after washing my body with a rough cloth, soap and water. I am ashamed even now for the state I was in. My boots along with the treasure within had sunk to the depths. When Michael and I had woken neither of

---

25 The Irish for Patrick O'Donnell

us had time to search for boots or anything else and it was a dash for the side before the boat went down. I was by now infested with lice, in my hair, under my arms and in my ears and the crack of my arse which had gone ripe and which this angel now cleaned and dressed in what bandage she could find.

That first day I was awake she returned and scrubbed me again with salt water and she replaced my mattress. She hid a bowl of the food beneath the bedding and warned me to eat only a little each time.

On the second day she told me her name was Hanora and when I smiled in reply she smiled too. It was a thin smile for me and not for her. I could see smiling was not familiar to her but maybe in the past had been.

She scrubbed me again with the water she had brought in a wooden bucket. I saw her attend to a few others in a similar fashion but not with the same amount of care she gave to me. They stayed on the damp filthy bedding and their clothes were not changed as mine were changed.

Many of the other orderlies or nurses or whatever they were called were cruel. I saw them steal from the meagre bundles belonging to the dead and dying. I could only see close by as it was dark, even by day as the windows were so small and I am sure my sight had suffered.

Some of the nurses were convicts, released to work in the sheds for almost no one else would risk it. I later learned that many of them took the work to attempt escape and those who did stay took the opportunity to enrich themselves by stealing from the sick and to do worse things of which I cannot write for the depravity of it.

These poor quarantined beggars often came as whole families, or what was left of them after the crossing. If they were lucky enough to escape infection on the ships they were almost certain to get it on the island. Every day more came and found their bunks and every day carts of bodies were pushed away. I assume they were all buried on the island but am not sure. Some were buried there I know because later I had laboured at that hellish task.

In the evening of the fourth or fifth day Hanora brought more clean clothes. The doctor came later and looked into my eyes and my throat and under my arms. He wore a mask but I could see the tiredness in his eyes. He did not speak to me other than to tell me to open my mouth. Hanora was with him and after examining me he passed her a slip of paper, and was gone.

As I regained some strength I could sit up and then, soon, I could walk around. I discovered that Hanora was living in quarters for the nurses. She had been nursing me for many days while I went through the worst of it. In the moments I was awake she had washed me and fed me but I have poor memory of it, not of anything before we spoke.

My angel, as that is what she was to me, had left Ireland with her husband and her three children; they were infants and had all perished from the fever. Her husband died on the ship and the three children in that place where she now saved those whom she could. The eldest of her children she told me was four and had also been named Pádraig. I suppose that was my saving, a simple thing like that, a shared name and a shared tongue. I think it is why she took such particular care of me and it is why later, I vowed to return the kindness in any way I could, for all her days, or mine, whichever the shorter.

She had nursed her three and as she did she nursed others and stayed after the children were gone and continued to nurse others. She had no hope for herself after her losses but she had hope for others and had determined to spend what days she had left to save those she could. I suppose she had not expected to encounter me any more than I had expected to encounter her and our new found love for one another gave her hope and a reason to live and to me it had given the means to survive which otherwise might have evaded me.

I say 'love' and I mean it. It was not instant but eventually as you shall see my love for Hanora and her's for me was more than a son's love or a mother's or a sister's or brother's or a lover's affection. Only those who have suffered such extremes together can truly share what was given to us in those sheds.

Each day I became stronger because of the food she brought to me and the kindness she showed me. When I could stand and then walk I would follow her like a puppy and I would divide my food and give some to one or two others, just as she did for me. I was not careless, those too far gone, as I had been, I gave nothing, those with more strength I gave some. It seemed to me to be the fair way to use the few rations we had. It is hard but when food and drink is in short supply giving any to a man dying is a waste.

I left my bunk and the stink and would sleep curled up with my back to Hanora who would hold me tight and sing quietly in my ear. It was better with the nurses and they kept their part clean. I was not supposed to be in their billet but no one bothered with us, even the priests stayed clear of the sheds when they could; only now and then coming along to throw their blessed water on the outside of the hut

I learned that the paper the doctor had signed and which Hanora held for me gave me the clear from Typhoid. When anyone did trouble to ask why I was in her place, which they did not often; she claimed me for her young brother.

One of the many bad sides of that place was that some of the convicts working there would steal rations and other things from anyone, including the nurses. There was no authority or law. Many who were robbed cared not because they were either dead or so glad to survive that their small possession mattered nothing.

Though I had nothing I was determined no man would steal it from me. I was cautious of the convicts who worked there and equipped myself with a long thin knife which I tied to my calf. Hanora too carried a similar blade and though she was a gentle and caring creature I could see in her the strength of a mother cow around her calf and I knew her more than able to use it should the need arise.

We had spoken in the night and quietly agreed that as soon as the weather warmed a little we would make our way off the island. It would be a month at most. We did not plan escape, for escape was impossible and anyway unnecessary because we both had our card.

A few convicts had tried to swim for it and quickly discovered the flow and iciness of the water around the island was impossible. Some still tried with no regard for the impossibility; they would try anything.

One convict nurse had killed and stolen the card of another nurse but unable to read was stopped in the harbour and could not tell his name written on the card. He made a dash for the ferry when challenged and been shot in his tracks by the harbour guards.

Nurses who volunteered for one reason or another to do the terrible work were paid a handsome sum and having no place to spend it could amass a large pot. On top of this if a nurse passed due to catching the fever their loot was sometimes divided up. Some of the women had over twenty pounds saved and stashed, normally on their body.

Any person reading my account might wonder at the amount of gold sovereigns and half sovereigns in such a desolate and hopeless place but those who made the trip often had everything they owned stashed one way or another about their person. It was not only the destitute who were quarantined or just the Irish though it was mostly so. Some Germans in particular arrived and Jews from the east carried loot.

I knew of one Jewish man and his wife who had fled from Persia. He and others with him had paid handsomely for a ship to take them from Persia to the New World. They had set off and unbeknown to them they sailed into the Atlantic for a few days and landed in Cork. There the passengers disembarked sure they had reached America but they had been tricked by the ship's captain. Later they booked new passage to New York from Ireland on another ship, only to be landed in Canada and had ended in Grosse Island.

The man was desperate to escape the island for fear of contamination and he foolishly tried to bribe anyone he thought could help. He spoke to every one of his trials and did not seem to realise that no one had any care left to give. It was soon known that he had gold coin and within days he was found with his throat slit and an empty purse, his wife discovering the murder threw herself into the St. Lawrence River.

I had nothing worth stealing but Hanora had warned me of the convicts and of one in particular. He was a Welshman who had come over long before and was planning to work in the coal mines in Pennsylvania but had tangled with the law and ended in prison even before leaving Canada. His name was Littleman; I think his given name was Marcus but can't remember for sure, everyone called him 'Little'. He was a hateful man, as sinful as any on legs and like most creatures which be deprived of good character he pretended an abundance of it with his constant prayers and boasts of good intentions. He made lame attempts to hide his thefts from the immigrants and to conceal the abuse he gave to some in order to satisfy his beastly nature.

I have to tell you Victor that what I now recount is unpleasant but it is the way it was in that place. When bodies were carted away, the attendants, who were usually convicts, would be eager to collect them and cart them out for the pickings to be had. They would not just search their clothing for valuables but would search inside them too. Men and women often would hide what little valuables they had in places[26] not meant for such purpose. If you think that is a desperate depravity then contemplate the nature of Littleman who would not wait until death to make his investigations for loot. He would do his searches and thieving before anyone else got close.

He'd not approach the new arrivals when many were not yet at their worst. He preferred to scour the rooms at night and when unable to find any property worth stealing on or about the dying inmates he often would tear at their privates where many had stored what tiny things of value they had.

To Hanora and to me the worst that Little had done was not that; depraved as it was it was not as

---

26 *Insertion of coins and other valuables into the rectum was a common method of securing valuables*

bad as what he did to Niamh when he found her as sick as a dog. Niamh was a nurse who also had lost children and stayed in spite of it or maybe because of it.

Everyone knew Niamh had a purse of almost 30 pound[27]. Her mistake was to be indiscreet about it. She had spoken of making for Quebec and finding work as a seamstress, which had been her occupation in a grand house in County Kerry. She had been taken sick very sudden and was talking gibberish by the time she put to bed. Sometimes the typhoid did that, it did it to me, it can make the mind mad just as it can destroy the body. She'd been taken to one of the best cots near the door and had died very soon after but not before she had a lucid moment and described how Little had taken her purse when she had asked him to fetch someone to help her.

She confided that he had searched her; she told Hanora and was ashamed of it. I believe that he defiled her and she was too ashamed to speak of it, even to Hanora and I would estimate that it was this and no fever which killed her. There was nothing too low for this man who never missed morning and evening prayer. He was there for opportunity and stupid to the risks, not brave to them.

It was inevitable that the convict and Hanora would cross paths. I had taken the advice to stay clear of him but as large as the sheds were they were not so large as to allow avoidance for ever. There is no doubt that Hanora and I stood out. I was still growing and thanks to Hanora was eating every day

27 *Equivalent to approximately £3300 in 2020*

and I had recovered well. I got extra rations when I was attached to the gang tasked with digging graves, which seemed a never ending job. I had acquired good boots off some poor fellow with no further need of them and some more than adequate clothes. Amongst the others I stood out. It was however not on my account that our paths finally crossed, it was for another reason.

It was late spring and morning; Hanora had gone to the latrine and I saw as Little followed her. I thought nought of it for a few minutes but then it struck me that he might intend her harm. I got up and followed after them, loosing the knife at my calf from its ties. When I arrived he was upon her, her skirts up and he, breeches down forcing himself.

He did not see me and I made no announcement to my presence nor did I issue any warning. I stepped forward and I ran the point of the blade through the centre of his neck below his skull and then thrust upwards into his brain until the blade scraped against the inside of his forehead, whereupon I twisted the handle and the blade snapped inside him. He did not whimper, he dropped as dead as a stone.

Hanora made no particular fuss; she adjusted her skirts and then leaned over the man. She pulled up his tunic and snapped from his neck the pouch which hung on a cord of leather. As she did this she spat into his face. She searched the rest of him; sparing him the indignity he did not spare others and located another purse; one we both recognised as Niamh's. Hanora concluded her search and rose and levelled a kick at his midriff as we were about to leave. The thud that came back was not one of flesh or bone but one of coin, tightly packed.

Between us we loosened his belt which wrapped around his waist twice and we could not believe it as we lifted it clear. It weighed as much as 8 pound I am sure. I lifted my jacket and strung the load around my neck, tucking the tails into my breeches.

Hanora stepped over the dead man and kissed me on my cheek and thanked me for my intervention and suggested that we make our way to her bed, where we could hide our loot and stay low a spell.

Later we sat on her bed in a corner of the nurses' bunk house and counted. We could not count it all for fear of discovery but surely we had more than £400[28] in all. His purse from his neck was filled with gold Sovereigns and halves and other coin; at least some in the belt was Persian gold coin about the size of half sovereigns. The loot he had stolen from the Jew I suspect. Niamh's purse added about £30 to our total.

I was all for a rush to the hills but Hanora, always calm and always right, had the sense to stay until the fuss had died down or we would surely be suspects and hunted down. She immediately set about sewing together a new belt for the coins. It was to have 40 vertical pockets, each to take four coins; in total 160 coins, more if they were smaller than sovereigns. Not so many for me to look uncomfortable or to look out of sorts when carrying

28 Equivalent to £40,000 in 2020.

it around me. She would adjust Littleman's belt to her size and take the rest of the money. We dared not leave the stuff unattended till we were ready to go so by day and night one of us stayed always to guard the bed.

As for fuss, there was none; at least none that came our way. A dead convict who died of a stab or the Irish disease I suppose was of little concern to anyone. The authorities stayed away.

I have not killed many people in my time but I can think of no sweeter moment than the moment I extinguished life from the convict Littleman, Little as we called him, was now less than little, he was nothing; and I number it amongst my killings of coyote, or other vermin, not of a man. That his last place was in human excrement is fitting. I regret only that he did not realise that I was the master of his humiliation.

8
OFF THE ISLAND

Ships waiting to dock at Grosse island - 1847

Patrick begins his next letter, his eighth, on the 9th December, with a firm assertion that his killing of the convict Littleman was justified, which on the evidence given in his previous letter seems to be a fair assessment. However even given the times and the situation it is hard to reconcile such a clinical, merciless and efficient killing as being commensurate with the behaviour of a 12 year old boy.

By any measure, Patrick was by then no ordinary boy. His childhood, the Famine, the wreck, his brother's death and the experience of the sheds all contributed to the person he was becoming; one who could kill without the least compunction if and when he felt justified. In today's world we would call him 'damaged', in 1847 he was probably extremely well equipped to deal with the ordeals to come.

Patrick was a person able and willing to do what was necessary, when required. He was not the first 'boy' of 12 or 13 to kill and whilst in our modern age it seems unlikely one has only to consider the awful predicament of child soldiers, even today.

Circumstance it has to be said will bring out the best and worst in all of us. It was no different in the nineteenth century. Who is to judge that the despatching of Littleman was a product of the best of Patrick or the worst?

As they head towards freedom, almost overladen with gold coins Patrick seems unable to contain his excitement at the prospect of arriving in Canada; wealthy, free and in the company of a woman whom he had come to adore in such a short time. The amount of gold the companions had stolen was truly vast; certainly more than either of them could ever have hoped to acquire by conventional means.

It seems that the short boat trip across The St Lawrence, away from Grosse Island, marks the transition of the first phase of Patrick's life; and the start of the next; Canada, the unknown, wealth and companionship and adulthood.

(Eighth Letter)
Dec 9th 1883 - Newgate Prison, London

Dear Victor,

Before judging me, if that is your inclination or indeed anyone's inclination I would say that the account I have given of how I despatched that convict is not by way of explanation or apology. I make no apology and regret only that his end came swift and he who ended him was unknown to him.

If I were to plead mitigation, and that is not my plan, there would be plenty of it. It was an extraordinary circumstance in extraordinary times and in an extraordinary place with an extraordinary fiend. I saved my friend and untold misery of others who would undoubtedly have suffered at the hands of this man. On the 17th of this month I meet my maker and I shall account to him and only him for that deed. I am confident that it will weigh in my favour and not against when the scales are balanced.

My companion and I resisted running from that place; we concluded that we must not make a move and we did not. Though the place was the very base of hell and one more body should not matter there was always the risk that the authorities might not allow murder and when Littleman did not report back or was found dead there might be questions and maybe an account to pay. We could not chance it.

With the amount we had, if we could get off the island there would be little to stop our progress. Hanora split the money as I have previously described but she kept Niamh's purse as her own, tied safe to the hip. I did not feel rich, though by any standards I was. My share alone would certainly buy a cabin and a patch of land able to grow more than just a spud, and a horse and a rifle and with some to spare.

How swift my predicament had improved. In a month I had gone from the brink of death to being a fellow close to owning land and his own horse. From such a terrible place the flame of life was reignited in me, and in my companion. It was hard to contain my joy and Hanora more than once had to remind me to settle lest we arouse suspicion.

As it happens, with Littleman, fate was once again on our side. Another convict had come upon his body and knowing the man to be what he was and to almost certainly have loot about his body the convict had turned him over and taken a knife to his arse. He'd been seen by a nurse and reported and was arrested the same day and taken off back to the mainland, all the way protesting his innocence of the killing. That they found almost £20 in gold sovereigns which he had taken from Littleman did not help his case. It did make me wonder if we had missed the opportunity but I contented myself that we had got what we did and a scapegoat into the deal for the spare £20.

I think it was a Friday in the first week of June that we gathered our few possessions and made our way to the Harbour. With suspicion removed from us we concluded the best time to move was immediate. My new belt of fortune was tied about me and sewn fast so it could not possibly fall away.

I had in my pocket a few half sovereigns and copper. Hanora had the balance and it too was fixed in a similar fashion and she had Niamh's purse to hand.

Neither of us looked awkward or out of place but it was hard to feel that way with such an amount of gold tied on. I remember that it was a beautiful morning; the sun was shining and the early spring warmth heartened me. It felt like the world was open for me to take.

I could see maybe ten ships, sails down, anchored off the island, all turned to the current, all waiting to offload their terrible human cargo. I did not feel sorry for them, I had been there and earned my life once again and my thoughts were for me and for Hanora and us alone.

Hanora had kept in her hand enough for a bribe or a purchase should that be required; she instructed me only to offer money of my own if the situation got desperate but we did not expect any problems as we both had cards stating we were clear of disease.

Presently we were both stood at the window of the cabin on the dockside. A man whose face was covered in a huge black beard sucked on his pipe as he inspected the cards which gave us free passage across The St Lawrence and away from Grosse. Hanora had told me that we could get a boat all the way to America; from several towns on the coast. It meant little to me but I knew America was months from us, even by boat.

The man tapped his pipe on the counter and declared, in what I took to be a French accent:

'Out of date'

Hanora picked up the card, and looked at it. She seemed as troubled as I had seen her:

'But, but….,'

'Out of date….' repeated the bearded man. 'You can go back and get a new one Madame' he continued.

'But I have been clear these last months Monsieur'

He looked up, he seemed to soften at Hanora's use of French and she noticed, so immediately followed with;

's'il vous plaît', as she slid a half gold sovereign across the counter to him.

He looked over his shoulder into the office and discreetly slid the coin into his pocket. With a flourish he stamped both cards and handing them back to Hanora he cheerfully said;

'Bon Voyage'.

'Merci' she replied with a little smile. I think it was the first time I saw her smile, really smile, not a smile of sympathy for me in the sheds, not for him either but for her; and it struck me that in spite of her being, in my child-man eyes ancient, possibly as old as 25 or 30, she was positively beautiful. She turned to me and said;

'Thank God for that, it's all the French I can speak', and she smiled again, her head high, her back straight as though walking from the theatre to her carriage, not from some stinking death hole dressed in rags with a fortune in gold coin hiding

119

her shapely hips; of course she lied about the language but it was not until later I discovered that.

We made our way along the long causeway and came to the short gangway onto the ship. We were laughing as we handed our cards to the man tasked with checking them; he didn't even look at them as he tipped his hat at what I now understood to be a most handsome woman at my side. Both glad we had no need to dispense any further riches we made our way with the other passengers to seating along the sides of the small ship.

I'd seen steam ships from the hut and Hanora had explained to me about what I had first thought were ships on fire. By the time the huge wheel started to turn the deck was full of people looking only slightly more healthy and wholesome than those arriving. I think that Hanora and I were the only ones smiling. We both left unhappiness and pain in our wake and we looked forward to the future and with a fortune attached to each of us we had every cause for hope and optimism. We did not know at that time that apart from what she carried around her belly a much greater weight was growing inside of it.

9
CANADA

Writing on the same day as his last letter Patrick was busy with his next. Whilst he seems to have given up on the interventions of Hugo and Chester Arthur helping he from time to time does hint at the fact that he does not expect to hang, only to then revert to pessimism. It is strange.

He again mentions Margaret's visits and it seems by now she was visiting him every day. He also mentions his cousin Edward who was a known member of a group called *'The Dynamiters'* but at the time not known by the authorities to be Patrick's cousin.

There was a move by Irish nationalist groups away from gunpowder at the time. Dynamite was very much more powerful than powder, easier to conceal and very stable. In 1880 a man named Richard Rodgers, a Russian Scot of all things, set up a dynamite school in Brooklyn with the aim of training Irish agents in its proper use and safe transportation; Edward O'Donnell attended that school.

One of Edward's efforts; blowing up Salford Barracks; led to the death of a child. Patrick it seems did not approve, not just for the death but he saw such activity on mainland Britain as being counter to Irish interests. It is in his comments in this letter that we first see that he is not a supporter of a violent struggle in Ireland, though he is a patriot.

The letter concentrates mainly on their arrival into Canada. Whilst the experience is somewhat negative for him in some ways it does not douse his enthusiasm. This is not the first time Patrick has encountered overt hostility to the Irish but the situation, here in the land of hope, must have been painful. Let's not forget that he had probably never been inside a store, not seen the goods on display and much of what he was experiencing was not just a new country but a new everything.

Patrick eludes in his previous letter that Hanora was pregnant leaving the sheds. He, or indeed she could not have known this as they set out on their adventure in Canada and the fact that he mentioned it when writing about crossing the river is simply how he has recorded it, he is not suggesting he knew of it at that time.

When Patrick writes about Hanora we can see that there is some extraordinary bond between them. His relationship with her is deeply complex. These are both very troubled people with equally tragic backgrounds and in one another they see a future and reason for hope. After so much grief and pain surely things must now improve.

(Ninth Letter)
Dec 9th 1883 - Newgate Prison, London

Dear Victor,

It's an odd thing that I have always felt the most hope immediately following the worst despair. I wonder is it so for all of us. Not a growing hope or optimism but a wildly optimistic disposition not at all suited to the circumstance at the time. The exception of course being my current predicament here in this cell, for which I anticipate no hope and no reprieve in spite of your efforts, and those pursued by others.

Margaret brought me the *Morning News* this evening and it took a poor view of your approach to Gladstone. Now that he sees I am an American Citizen President Arthur has also made representations on my behalf but his efforts also seem to have fallen on deaf ears, though I understand he and you persist.

There is no appetite in England for any leniency to any Irishman. The boy at Salford was a damn shame and it is but two years since that deed in which I know my cousin Edward had a hand. Edward learned his craft in Brooklyn and has been practicing it since 80, though knowing him I wonder how he has not blown his own head off. If the English knew that he was of my blood they would hang me twice for it; and I would not blame them.

My countrymen with their dynamite have brought the trouble of Ireland to the doorstep of the English. I find it ironic that my own crime, the fact of which I have not denied, was to execute one who took arms against the English and murdered one of their very highest. You might think they would be grateful to me, not vengeful for my neck. But there are things about that deed that I am not sure even now that I can spend on paper and transmit out of this cell.

Enough of my meanderings; I am short of time and must attend to my story. I confess that as I write I am tempted to revisit passages and adjust for names and dates and such things but fear I have no time and anyway, the essence of my story shall not spoil for a day or a month here and there.

It is true that Littleman was upon Hanora, my Hanora; and I spiked the bastard through his brain and stole his loot which he stole from others and I have not a single regret for ridding that place of its most vile inhabitant and the world of a brute.

Hanora and I managed by my luck and her stealth a clean exit and after a short crossing on that beautiful June morning when I was not yet thirteen years old I set my boot upon Canada proper. Alongside me was my companion and protector, the one who had thrust her hands down to the depths and dragged my limp body from hell's grasp; Hanora. I felt fresh and new; as I always felt when a young boy stepping out from the confession box, leaving the burden of my sins with Father Sinnott back in Ireland.

Somehow the short trip on the paddle steamer cleansed us and prepared us for our new birth into the land of our opportunity and our future. The entire world seemed new to me and full of promise and hope. Our ship which took us to freedom was without sail; pushing against tide and wind. It was miraculous and at first I could not believe it. I had not seen a locomotive but I heard of them in Ireland. My father told me of a rail line from Dublin going north; he had not seen it but had heard news of it from a fellow who travelled. I could comprehend it but the idea of a ship with no need of a sail defied my understanding. Yet there I stood on the deck and as another identical ship passed within 20 yards of us in the opposite direction with its whistle screaming and its huge soaked wheel turning and pouring water down leaving a line behind it upon which the gulls danced, I knew for sure that this new world was new in ways I could not have imagined. Things Uncle Manus had never mentioned in his letters and which I would have doubted even if he had.

I am not sure of the place we landed that day but looking back I believe it was a port town named Montmangy or perhaps Montgomery. Our journey there was short; from Grosse to there was less than two hours, including boarding and getting off. I recall the place was busy with life bursting all around. Though it had not rained for many days the street was still mud, and horse and heavy laden carts passed and skidded and churned it up.

There was no sidewalk for parts and for the first time in my life I was thankful for boots. People made lines for provisions and traders in the streets peddled their goods on people, many of whom had not the means to buy. Hanora and I found ourselves in front of a church where I saw a large wooden sign. It stated 'No Irish'. It was not the last time I would see such a sign but the only time I saw it outside a Church. Hanora spat at the sign, an uncharacteristic gesture for her, other than for cursing Littleman. I spat too and I spit now on all the religious and the charlatans who pretend for profit or effect in its truth.

Most shops were closed to us and we approached several who refused us entry. Some would deal with people, even the Irish, who had money but only on the street outside. Hanora had used her French to get past but mostly to no avail. I have no doubt that we looked as what we were. Two survivors from the coffin ships and the quarantine, and few wanted to chance dealing with us.

We managed to buy some basic provisions from one or two street vendors and with enough food and beer, dried meat and a 'new' coat for each of us we made for the south out of town keeping the river to our right.

Buying a horse was out of the question. Not just because no one would deal with us but had we done we'd have been charged a pretty penny and in paying it revealed to every rascal in town that we were heavier with coin than we should be. Hanora, who was wise beyond what her sex would suggest[29], was cautious that we did not attract attention unwanted. Vagabonds were about and we kept low as we could.

---

29 Patrick could not be accused of political correctness.

Hanora tried to buy a handgun from a store; it was in the window and advertised as a Texas Paterson five shot. Alongside it was a row of bullets. It was the first modern handgun I had seen and it amazed me that someone could fire off five shots in as many seconds without reloading. My father took a clear thirty seconds to reload Bess. It would certainly have been a good thing to have on our journey into the unknown.

Oddly enough the shop owner did not refuse to sell it to us because we were Irish or off the island, he simply did not want to sell such a thing to a woman and besides, he told us it was to show for orders, not to take. By our inquisition the man must have determined that we had the means to buy such a pretty weapon and he allowed us into his shop.

Inside the dimly lit room he showed us a variety of blades but most obvious and the one which stood out was the Bowie Knife. It was enormous, sharp to the front edge, to part of the back and with a point which would pierce leather. It needed no selling so far as I could see and it would certainly prove useful for hunting and protection. We took two of them and a stone for the edge and two leather sheaths and belts.

The man in the shop who spoke part in French and part in English took a page of a news sheet and slowly ran the blade over it. The paper split with a slight scratching sound. He assured me that when I reached the age I could comfortably shave with it. He took the time to show us how to keep the blade keen and spat on the edge before stroking the stone up it and down as his gaze on Hanora became more than a little uncomfortable.

She, who I think the shop owner thought should be impressed, was not. She picked up an ivory handled dagger. It was long, maybe a foot long and was almost round but for a groove down its length. The man took it from her and enquired if she knew what it was. She replied that it was for stabbing and that the groove gave easy extraction from the body of the victim. The man was impressed but when he asked double its marked price Hanora pushed the two Bowie knives, the sheaths, the belts and the stone back across the counter and muttering to him in French she turned to walk away. He relented and in a mild panic offered the spike free of charge. Hanora and he knew he was already charging us double what the Bowies were marked at.

As we left the shop it was obvious that Hanora's knowledge of French was greater than she had let on. There can have been almost no Irish Immigrants who spoke French, Irish and English and although I already valued my companion, I was doubly assured of our joint prospects.

Things could have gone better; on our boat trip from Grosse Island Hanora promised me a room in a hostel, a meal at a dining table and a hot bath: All things I had never had so found it difficult to envisage but eagerly awaited. She worked in a great house before being married and had known of such refined things. Her mother before her had worked at the same place and as a child Hanora had shared the classroom and other things with the children of

128

the house. I was not disappointed when no boarding house would allow us in the door but I was sad to see that she had thought she had disappointed me.

She was shocked at the reception we received due to our troubles and our nationality; we resolved to get away from the town. As I say, the place was infested with vagabonds looking to take advantage and an unaccompanied woman with a lad of twelve was likely to be easy pickings. If they only knew what we two would do for one another they would soon find a way around us.

I shall in this letter and in future describe my relationship with Hanora and her's with me but it is difficult and no one can ever truly understand it. I do not make this effort to tell you what that friendship and companionship was, that is impossible; I do it so as to tell you what it was not and to remove the inevitable and incorrect notion anyone might form in this direction.

I can say that I never saw her as a lover and she never became that, even as I grew older and perhaps had thought of it, as perhaps did she, it was never that. I loved her and I loved her more than I loved my mother or my sisters or my brothers or either of my two wives[30] or children. Hers was the only love I have ever enjoyed in the certainty that it would be eternal and unquestioning and always and only mine.

---

30 Patrick was married only once (Margaret) and in 1883 had a companion (Susan) whom he referred to as Mrs O'Donnell but was not his wife.

I know unquestionably that she felt the same for me. It was more than love. It was a bond that only people who have suffered and survived together can ever contemplate. I admired her and I wanted to be like her, in those first years she was mother, father, brother, sister and friend. Every night I slept with her and we held each other. At first, on the island it was to fight the cold but later it was to feel her against me and to have her breath on my neck and to know that with her I was always safe and loved. Hanora was everything to me, as I was to her.

As we walked out of the town that evening I was not low at the treatment we had been given or being unable to find a room; I was happy... more than happy, I was content. We would have preferred a bath and some good food and some new clothes but we were well supplied, and free, most of all we were hand in hand. Hanora's smiles now came often. She carried a burden too heavy for my young mind to fathom but I too carried my own in some measure. My brother Michael and I had been very close and I wished deeply that he could now be with me on this adventure; compared to Hanora losing her entire family it was nothing.

Our provisions packed on our backs and slung at our shoulders included dried meats, beans, tobacco, pots and pans and coffee and all we might need for a month in the woods; along with enough gold to buy anything we might need and much we would not. We were armed and we were rich, I had the love of my life next to me and although a future unknown I knew that we together would make the best of it.

When I look back I wonder how we could have been so naive. No thought of bears little thought of bandits and Indians and only a vague notion of where we were heading. We knew the United States were south so we headed south.

The simplicity of it all was not worrying to me or to Hanora, it was liberating.

10
SOUTHWARD INTO THE UNKNOWN

The Bowie Knife - Early 19th Century

From his words written on the 9th December we can see that this period with Hanora was, in spite of an uncertain future, a very happy and exciting time for them both and he relays it as such, in spite of his unhappy predicament in his cell when recounting the days past.

Patrick continues to exhibit what we must presume is paranoia about his jailers poisoning him to make his life more uncomfortable than it already is. More letters are smuggled out of the prison by Margaret and more urgency can be seen in his efforts to tell his story.

In his next letter he continues with an account of his travels into the wilderness with Hanora, leaving the small town behind. The plan seems to have been a gradual and slow journey towards Quebec and eventually onto New York and then Pennsylvania to his family.

It's easy to see how content they both were as they travelled through the forests, slept under the stars and ate whatever the land had to offer. Food of all kinds would have been abundant and easily caught or found by Patrick given his very rural background and it is likely they could have lived indefinitely in the hills and alongside the river.

Native Indians inhabited the forests and the hills but these were almost always peaceful. Thy had for many decades become used to European travellers, trappers and traders; many were able to converse in French and some in English; they were not troublesome to travellers, they were curious however and sight of them would be alarming to any new arrival to their lands.

Although the two companions seem to have been aware of some of the dangers and equipped themselves as best they could to avoid them they only seemed to consider the most obvious risks they might encounter. To say they were somewhat innocent of their environment is an understatement but they were soon to learn of the dangers of the beasts of the forest, and the worst of all beasts; man.

(Tenth Letter)
Dec 10th 1883 - Newgate Prison, London

Dear Victor,

I had hoped to conclude the journey south in my last letter yesterday but alas I have taken ill again with stomach pains and evacuations and vomit. I am certain that bastard Mullins is slipping some bad thing into my food. It was late last night before I managed to sleep and I have awoken late.

Margaret has been early enough and taken the last packet of letters. I shall start afresh now with the journey in my last letter. I confess my mind is a haze and I shall write quickly and spare some detail and concentrate on the main facts as best I can. I am writing today in English as you see for it is not so much a task as in Irish.

It is more than thirty five years since we embarked on our journey south. It is easy now to see how dangerous that journey was and how foolhardy we were, but we did not see it at the time. Regardless of the dangers seen or unseen, what choice did we have? Waiting in the port for a ship heading south to Quebec and beyond would have been just as risky a project. One or two travellers had already spotted we were not the usual human rejects that came from quarantine. Even in her poor state Hanora was a handsome woman and I looked healthier than any other my age stepping off the boat. We were not leaving the safety of a township to venture into a wilderness, not as we saw it. We were leaving the dangers of the town for the unknown.

The track south was not well used but it was clear and the occasional cart laden with supplies passed us northwards along with people on foot and on horseback, most of whom paid us more attention than was welcome. As darkness began to fall we took off from the main track and travelled south east into the forest until we found a clearing where we made our camp for the first night of our freedom. We made a fire and cooked beans and drank coffee and sat talking of our plans.

Settled down we only then decided to properly count the loot. Hanora knew exactly the contents of my belt for she had constructed it with pockets which held 160 gold sovereigns and there was no need to unstitch it. It was neatly made and I had slept in it since she made it and I was comfortable.

I helped untie her belt and it fell heavily to the ground. We emptied the coins out and counted in the firelight; 240 sovereigns, or other gold coins of that size and weight and 90 gold coins to the size of half sovereigns. In my purse I had £12 in coins and in Hanora's she had the equivalent of £35. In total we had the equivalent of almost £500 pounds, almost all in gold. It was staggering. I had no way to quantify the sum and Hanora tried to illustrate by telling me we could buy 50 horses with this amount[31]. It meant little other than we were rich and could probably live on the fortune for our entire lives.

---

31 A labourer's wages at the time were about $250 a year at best in New York. There were 4.8 US dollars to the pound so this sum represented about 10 years' wages.

As the night drew down it became bitterly cold and we huddled together under the skins we had bought and I cannot remember being so happy. I estimated we were not four miles south of the town and the night was silent but for the beasts, which did not frighten us as we slept with our Bowie knives in hand. Little did we know of bears and wolves and of Indians and bandits?

I awoke with dawn and made my way out of camp to empty myself and shortly came upon a river. It was not the huge river we had walked away from but a sweet smaller river. It was no more than 40 yards wide and looking down into it as I pissed I could see more fish than I could count. I took a limb from a nearby tree and using my knife I sharpened the end. Leaving a barb as my father had taught me. With my very first jab I stuck a big fellow but as I raised it out of the water its thrashing released it from my spear. My second jab, this time harder was just as accurate and I pulled onto the shore a fish which must have weighed seven or eight pound. What breed or make it was I know not but it looked like a salmon; it was fine and shiny and healthy as it thrashed away.

I returned to Hanora who had woken and showed her my prize, she quickly piled dry twigs on our fire as I constructed a crude spit, gutted the great fish and set about cooking it. It had been some time since I had tasted salmon and none had ever been so sweet. We tore the lumps of cooked fish from its body and devoured them to the last morsel. After we ate we picked our teeth clean with the rib bones of the creature.

Of all the things I had experienced since leaving Ireland the woods were the best. The food was better, the air was better and so was the water from the river; most of all the company of my Hanora filled me with hope and excitement and of promise.

Over the next few days we followed the meandering fresh water river, against its direction of flow. It was an elongated route due to the meandering but it was away from the busier path alongside the larger river. The route was not easy as only a few paths were trodden and this I suspect by the Indians we saw from time to time. They seemed interested in us but did not approach.

We had no urgency and each day we ate fresh fish and beans and drank coffee and the sweetest water from our friend the river. We came across a rabbit from time to time so I set a couple of snares each night and most mornings we had one or two. I tell you that in the week we spent travelling south we built ourselves and were fortified in body and in spirit.

On the tenth day we were brought back to our senses and to the dangers which we had put to the back of our minds. We encountered and almost ran directly into a bear. We rounded a bend in the river and come from behind some rocks and there it was; A monstrous beast over ten foot high. It was standing waist deep in water and it looked at us. We froze. I had not the least notion such a beast could exist and here one was not 40 foot from me. The bear looked at us but did not move, it looked back to the river and with a swipe of its incredible paw it

137

scooped a full grown salmon from the river, over its shoulder and onto a pile of fish similarly cast to the land. He was not just fishing; he was keeping his catch on the shore behind him.

There was something also about it which stuck with me and sticks to this day. When he saw us he did not give chase, he looked at us and he noted us but he continued his pursuit of the big fish. They were the better food and the easier catch… for now.

His work was not as some potluck scoop into the water but a calculated swipe of his paw which each and every time struck rich with a fish; no moment of greed to eat the fish while there were more to be caught. This was an intelligent creature; a creature who could balance his need and his ability and opportunity. The only reason he had not given chase was that for the moment the fish were easier for him. Only those who have stood 40 foot from such a monster can comprehend the might and absolute superiority of it.

We were intruders: how many of its forefathers had stood at the same spot over the centuries and taken their food and not been interrupted by man? I knew enough about beasts to not even look at his stock of fish and we both backed away in the direction from which we had come.

Without the utterance of a word between us we turned west and headed back towards the larger river, where we knew there would soon enough come a town or a farm of some life other than bears. The bear had been busy with food and catching while he could but it seemed to me that he would not be so distracted for long.

Though we had put a good distance between us and the bear it was an uncomfortable night. I did not set traps and we did not light a fire and we were both glad to be on the move again the next day.

We were in an elevated position that night and before dawn, to the west, I could see dim light and in that direction we made our way as soon as we had packed our skins. Going was tough as there was no trail in the forest but we knew the direction we travelled would eventually lead to the river and the road alongside it.

After several hours we came to a clearing and found ourselves looking down onto a large lake. It was over a mile long and half a mile wide and surrounded in thick woodland. We made our way towards the south shore. The water was fresh and there were fish and hundreds of ducks, on the water and in nests on what seemed to be an island half way down its length. It seemed a great place to set camp for a few days but we pressed on because there was a clear path going northwest and on it, fresh horse dung. The path had cart tracks too and although we had enjoyed our time of freedom and eating from the land we both knew the time had come to seek out civilisation and some way to make our way in this new place.

We smelled it first, the clear and distinct smell of wood burning…. and bacon. It must have been mid-afternoon. We could not have followed the track more than a mile from the lake when we came upon the place. The clearing was large, some of it natural where no trees had grown I suppose. In the centre was a cabin built with whole logs, tree trunks, and mud between them, much of which had fallen away. It was a large building, at least 30 foot long but not deep, maybe twelve foot or so. There was a stone chimney, from which smoke rose, and the roof, which was double pitched, was made of mud clods, the grass still growing on much of it. There were two windows from which hinged shutters hung open. It could have been a cottage in Ireland but for the size and the wooden walls.

Against the back length of the building was a lean-to and along the southern most wall was a neat stack of logs. There was a crudely fenced paddock within which stood three horses, one of which was drinking from a trough. Numerous racks and frames had animal skins and hides stretched over them. Between them and the cabin was a pig sty with three pigs I could see. Chickens and ducks roamed around free.

The door swung open and a man stepped out. He was tall and lean and rough. He wore boots to his knees and britches held by braces, one strap hanging down over his shoulder. His shirt was a nightshirt with vertical stripes and it was tucked in half way. His hair was to his shoulders and scruffy and unkempt and he had a patchy beard, as though he had never shaved in his life so could not grow a real man's bristles. I guessed he must have been thirty or forty years old and he held a shotgun aloft.

He shouted in French and Hanora answered him in the same language but asked if he could speak English. He confirmed he could;

'Aye' he said as he approached but with the shotgun lowered. 'State your business on my land or be off'. Without waiting for her to speak he snarled; 'Irish off the island?'

'We are off the island but we are clear and I can show you the paper' Hanora replied as she reached into her chest pocket.

He raised the gun as she did so, as though she might be keeping some weapon in there. His foolishness occurred to him and he lowered the weapon again.

'No need for proofs, you look fit enough to me but there's nothing here for you and your boy Madame…' he looked her up and down seeming to balance the risks… 'on your way'

'We have money' I foolishly interjected as Hanora cast me a gaze that cut me to the core.

The man softened more and rather than deny it Hanora said;

'We have small means to get us to Quebec and beyond Monsieur and if you have supplies we will be pleased to buy from you what little we can afford'. She could see that the damage was done and I cursed my stupidity.

Here we were miles off the main track in the woods with a man who knew we had valuables. I was more than twenty feet away and had no hope of getting to him, even if I could free my knife which was buried under layers of clothing.

141

'I have nothing to sell you.'

At that the door behind the man opened again and another man appeared, they might easily have been twins for they looked and spoke identical to one another.

'Now Alain' said the second man, who had an apple in one hand and a small knife in the other, which he used to cut a segment from the fruit. He placed the blade edge into his mouth and slipped the section of apple onto his tongue as he walked towards Hanora.

My heart was beating threefold as he stopped only a foot from her. She stood proud and unafraid and met the man's gaze. This was a woman who had seen death and spat in its eye and no mountain man was going to frighten her.

'What sort of supplies do you have in mind Madame?'

She answered without thought, 'You have apples in June Monsieur, surely they will be at their end and they will not keep much longer, we might take a few,' She nodded to the fruit in his hand, which I noticed did not look its best. 'A horse' she added, 'or a mule; we have walked for days and we can pay a fair price'.

Alain folded the gun into his arms and nursed it as his brother rubbed his chin.

'A horse in these parts is no small thing and what you think is a fair price will be far from what I think is a fair price'.

Hanora continued to scuffle about in her clothing to locate the documents which showed us to be disease free. The brother, observed her efforts and said nothing of them but turned to Alain and said;

'Fetch Pitch over here'

Alain looked surprised and was about to protest and thought better of it. He walked over to the fence of the coral and leaned his shotgun against the post. Hanora turned her gaze to me as he did so and her eyes spoke to me with utter clarity and certainty. We both knew we had stumbled into a desperate predicament and it was getting worse by the second and there was only one way out of it.

The brother dropped the apple core and stepped one pace forward and grasped Hanora's crotch as he said;

'The balance in our fair price and yours can be settled in a commodity other than coin'.

He stepped back again;

Hanora did not flinch but continued to search for the paperwork and muttered her apology but she would find what she sought in due course.

'By commodity he don't mean fur' shouted Alain who by now was slipping a bridle onto one of the horses' heads. He thought better of it and said; 'Or maybe he do' and he squealed with laughter through his rotten teeth whilst involuntarily hissing snot out of his nose, I was reminded of Littleman back in the sheds.

The brother, pleased with his luck so far stepped forward again until he was pressed against Hanora and he grabbed her intimacy again. Hanora looked over her shoulder to me and I knew it was the moment.

'I have found what I was looking for Monsieur' she breathed, almost sexually, and his face contorted while she gently slipped the razor sharp blade of her Bowie into the man's crotch and almost lifted him off his feet as she twisted it and pulled upwards.

Even before she spoke I was leaned into my run and making for the shotgun. Ten foot or so beyond the gun was Alain, already turning but not yet running. The horse he was harnessing rose up on its hind legs and broke free of the man knocking him off balance. I knew that I had him and so did he. I dived and grabbed the gun rolling onto my back in the dirt and aimed at his centre and pulled the trigger, only for it to click. He was all but on me as my finger naturally located the second trigger behind the first and a moment after the cap had blown Alain's head disappeared from his chin up. He flipped onto his back and was gone to hell and *damnation on him* I thought.

The horse Alain had been securing bolted at the sound of the blast. Hanora, as calm as though she might have just gutted a rabbit and not a Frenchman, walked past me and closed the gate to the little paddock, securing the other two beasts, who seemed positively disinterested in the demise of their masters.

She returned to the brother on the floor, dripping blade still in hand she looked at him as he lay on his side moaning and cradling his bleeding crotch. She crouched next to him and said;

'There is no hope for your body but if you wish a little time to save your soul with contrition then do so, otherwise I can spare you the pain and dispatch you swiftly to your destination'.

He responded in French which I took to be curses as his words were ferocious and unrepentant; she leaned over him and replied gently;

'Bon Voyage mon ami' and slit his throat clear from one ear to the other.

I understood her desire to end the man but her approach to it and her mood unsettled me. I have seen her slit the throat of a chicken with more compassion.

I have over the years come to realise that those who love the most can also be the most cruel and ruthless. Her actions did not endear her more to me nor did they do the reverse. She was a creature which could and would always do that which she needed to do. A commodity I think absent in many who have visited the graveyard before their time.

Thus it was that Hanora and I procured our first home together. We had not planned it to be that but events rather than plans have a way of dictating the course of one's fate. It was a good place; some 12 miles south east of the town we had left and where we were unwelcome and only 20 or so miles north of Quebec, where we were unknown. Three miles to our north was a small port settlement, which name I cannot recall , something 'by the sea'. The forest was full of rabbits and other game and the lake abounded with fish and ducks. We could not have picked a place better than that one which fate had chosen for us.

11
CABIN IN THE HILLS

Typical Log Cabin1840s

It's hard not to be somewhat disturbed by Hanora's actions and to a lesser extent Patrick's but it would be a mistake to judge them in our time and with our values and more to the point, other than in the circumstances in which they found themselves. If we get past the shock and the brutality of their disposing of the French brothers it is not difficult to conclude that they had no choice. Perhaps the sin was in putting themselves in such a predicament rather than how they extracted themselves from it.

If there remained any doubt as to Patrick's contentment regards the killing of the men, or indeed of Littleman back in the sheds it is removed by his comments in his next letter.

From Patrick's account we see the companions soon settle into the cabin, meeting other settlers and even locating a trading post nearby. Life on the side of a hill, teaming with wildlife, near to a lake and two rivers full of fish must have seemed to Patrick like being back home in Gweedore, but with no landlords or game keepers to avoid, just the odd bear or wolf. It's hard to imagine a life to which he would be more suited and much later in his letters he laments ever leaving the hillside above Quebec.

They do not just survive, they prosper and this could so easily have been where Patrick's story ended. Trapping on the side of a hill below a lake with plenty of gold coin buried, a trusty gun and a good companion. Many others lived exactly that life, less the coin.

That is not his destiny of course and those things which delivered him to a death cell almost 36 years later had already begun. His life was writ as though the pages in his cell were set down even before he got aboard the Carricks.

Hanora's predicament soon becomes clear and this informs their decision to stay a while in their new home.

Patrick's account of events, particularly Hanora's troubles is exceptionally moving and even many years later he is still deeply troubled by the events he next describes.

(Eleventh Letter)
Dec 10th 1883 - Newgate Prison, London

Dear Victor,

So my dear Victor, you see that before I had attained my thirteenth year I had despatched two men, both in the company of Hanora but both acts I submit were a matter of necessity. Neither has ever weighed too heavy on my mind, it was a wild place in a wild time and survival necessitated behaviour I would not contemplate these days. Both the Frenchmen on the hill above Quebec held ill intent towards us and we got to them before they got to us

I question why a woman such as Hanora must wear her beauty as some kind of burden, like a beast with fine fur, to be filched by any man as and when it suits him. It was clear what they intended and they went to hell without it.

I do not want to be infected with anger and hatred in my last days so I shall leave that there and move on with my account.

We did not expect any other life about the cabin and when we entered we saw just the two births, chairs, a table, oil lamps and such supplies as you would expect. There were heaps of dried skins and furs to one side and store cabinets along with various chests down the other. There was a fire burning in the hearth and a cast iron skillet hung above; inside of which bacon sat spitting. We feasted on the pork as we had that morning not spared the time to cook or eat. Traipsing through the forest with bears in mind was hungry work.

It was not our intention to stay put and our first inclination was to run; but to where? As the afternoon began to turn to evening we decided we would make the best of the shelter, at least for one night. We were, since leaving the boat, aware that rogues abounded and could harm us and we did what we could to avoid them but it was not until our encounter with the bear that we entertained the dangers from the beasts of this place. My recollection of the bear made the safety offered by the sturdy cabin seem to be a gift which outweighed the risks from two legged animals such as man.

We quickly set about removing the bodies of the brothers and although we thought a visit from the local constabulary, if indeed any such thing existed, or indeed from anyone was most unlikely; we preferred caution to carelessness. The nag which had bolted at the shot had by now returned and Hanora set the horse in his gear while all the time showing me how it should be done. She never stopped teaching and I never stopped learning from her.

We used the horse to drag the two corpses a clear half mile into the woods. We avoided the track which from the cabin was clear and ran west. We stripped them of their clothes and boots but we did not bury them. There were enough hungry beasts in the area to dispose of them. I assume they would not have lasted long in the Canadian spring and I care too little to spare it another thought. It was late evening when we returned to the cabin. Hanora took the harness from the horse and returned it to the coral.

Later, with the door barred, the two windows boarded and by the light of candles and oil lamps and the flickering fire we settled down to a warm dry night. A fox had come at dusk and slaughtered three chickens but taken only one so Hanora made a soup with vegetables from a store room on the side of the cabin and the birds. It was enough for a feast; I struggle to remember a better feed.

I inspected the shotgun and at first could not understand where the flint might strike and how it worked at all. Eventually I discovered that the little caps located where the box would be on Bess were in the stead of a striking tray and when struck would fire the gun. I'd loaded my father's gun in Ireland and the loading was the same and easy enough as soon as I had found the powder and shot, which were in a trunk along with about forty American dollars and some shillings.

I was impressed with the simple and much more reliable firing system on the shotgun and I loaded both barrels placing new caps for each. I went to sleep that night feeling safer than I had in many weeks. Even if the bear were to call on us I was confident with such a fine weapon that we could kill him or send him away.

Over the days that passed we felt more secure in the cabin and while we made no real decision about it we just stayed on for a time. We explored the area; as we did we found many traps, some baited and not sprung and some with dead beasts in them. Next to one we found the leg of a fox and no fox.

When I had been poaching with my father I had seen big traps, intended for man, not beasts and I knew how to avoid them which was just as well because some of the traps we encountered around the lake were three times the size of anything I had seen and could only be intended for bears. This told us two things; there were dangerous and big traps about the place which could sever my leg but also there were big bears likely to be around too. Both were worrying prospects.

One or two of the smaller traps had decomposing and half eaten beasts in them and this allowed me to conclude that the Frenchmen would probably not last very long before being eaten up.

In the first few days we made our way down the trail and encountered the occasional cabin. It was well enough worn and we expected it to lead to something. Up to the lake was less worn but we could see light from cabins in the night so we knew we had neighbours of some sort. The nearest cabin westward was a mile or so from us. Most people we encountered showed little interest in us. One or two were friendly. There were no families but one or two of the men had wives, always Indian.

The days went by and we ate well and we were warm and we slept well. Some afternoons we'd swim in the cold lake, and lay next to each other naked, drying and warming in the sunshine.

By the tenth or twelfth day, which seemed to us like only the third or fourth; a heavily bearded giant of a trapper with his mule laden with skins had stopped. He was as it happens an exceptionally convivial and jolly Irishman who had come to Quebec many years before. He told us he had a cabin up past the lake and that there was a welcome for us up there anytime. His wife who was a native was with him, she seemed fascinated by Hanora.

The trapper asked where the brothers were. Hanora told him that they had gone hunting and the man laughed observing;

'Alain has forgot his gun' as he noted the weapon slung over my back.

'Those skins need taking down boy, fore they spoil' he was nodding towards the numerous pelts and hides which were stretched out on various frames. He pointed with his own rifle down the track;

'Three miles yonder is a trading post, take em down there and tell em Murphy sent ye'. He spat a thick black syrup spit into the ground. 'Ye might as well ave em boys' hides as you ave their gun and their place'. He gave a knowing wink to Hanora;

'Never did like em Frenchies myself.'

It was a strange conversation, the like of which could not have occurred anyplace else or at any other time. In those days in that place you assessed a person instantly and made your mind up about them. He had made his mind up about us and we about him. He cared nothing of how we procured our situation, though certainly knew it would have been by violence, and we knew he was not a threat. It was so simple and I loved it.

Hanora asked them if they would like to come in and rest for a time but the man declined without consulting his wife.

'Some coffee would go down fine though' he said in a friendly enough way after it seemed to me he was trying to erase any offence that might have been construed from his refusal of our offer of hospitality.

They sat on the step of the cabin as Hanora poured them a cup each. The Indian woman upon taking hers pointed to Hanora's belly and said something in her own tongue, the Trapper told her in English to:

'Hush woman' and she silently obeyed the command but smiled warmly at me.

Before leaving he told us that the local tribe, of which his wife was one were known as the 'Mountain People' and that as the spring turned into summer they would come down to the river and trade; mostly skins. He explained we could expect to see them and they were friendly people but not to be surprised if they stole anything not nailed down. He told us the Indian name of the tribe but I have forgotten it; Innu[32], something or other. They spoke their own language and good French but little English. As Murphy left he gave me sound directions to his cabin and reinforced that he was a friend if need ever arose.

The next morning on our new friend's advice we loaded up the scabbiest of the three horses with the skins from the frames and some that were in the

---

32 Likely to mean the Innu an Indigenous people

cabin which we presumed were all ready for sale. We decided to walk although there were saddles for the other two horses; we figured not to look too well to do in case it attracted curiosity.

The three or four miles were not so easy and it was mid-day by the time we arrived at the post. There were about fifteen buildings there of various sizes and although not a town it was more than a trading post. The owner of the main store and exchange came out and announced we had missed the boat which carried the skins down to Quebec and he seemed a bit annoyed. He was another Irish. Without being invited he came over to the horse and lifted one skin after another.

'Five dollars' he said. He seemed not in the least interested in who we were or from where we had arrived.

'Murphy said to tell you he sent us' I said instinctively,

'And I'd give you eight in that case but for the fact they are sat upon Adrien Picard's horse'.

I humped the rifle on my shoulder up as though it had dropped down and said;

'Picard and his filthy brother have no use of horses where they have gone'.

The man looked at me and then at Hanora, who smiled back innocently.

'Eight for the skins… and six for the nag'.

'Agreed' said Hanora.

Inside, as the man located the cash, a woman we took to be his wife showed Hanora over some basics, materials and such as she did so she spoke in a soft French accent;

'Those brothers are detested this whole area.' It was an obvious prompt to draw out some news of their predicament.

'I believe they have moved away to Quebec' replied Hanora. 'We paid them for the cabin, the livestock and the stock'.

The woman looked up trying to gauge the mood only for Hanora to continue:

'We have papers to show a fair deal and good title'. She paused as she lifted a bolt of material up to the light. 'This will do' she said referring to the cloth, and continued; 'I agree they were not very nice people but they are gone now and I trust they will find what they deserve in Quebec or on the way there.'

The conversation although already over so far as Hanora was concerned was interrupted by the man who handed Hanora the fourteen dollars. She then ordered and paid for the materials, salt and other supplies and was told to collect in a week.

She also took from the shelves a pair of breeches and two shirts for each of us. She bought other things such as dubbin, polish and needles and thread which were on the shelves. Looking back the store had much of what we needed but was basic. It was the first one I had ever been inside but for the knife shop.

The skins we learned later went down the river all the way to New York State in North America, boats came most weeks and stopped in all the little settlements along the way, picking up skins and furs.

We were not there to trade and had little prospect of ever catching a beast with a skin. We had plenty of money to live indefinitely but that was not the impression we wanted formed of us. For reasons obvious.

It had not occurred to either of us that we had been paid in dollars yet paid them in shillings, some of the currency we had found in the cabin. The large amount of money we had accumulated ourselves, which was by now buried near to the cabin in three separate hides, consisted almost entirely of gold coins. Most were English half and full sovereigns but with some coins from other countries. We needed to be careful how we used the money because though much of the coins were gold their worth as coin in Canada was less than their worth as gold. When dealing in emergencies such as with the half sovereign passed to the guard at the dock we could depend only on the value of the gold, not the coin. We needed to avoid using English gold coins.

Hanora explained these complications to me but I concluded that we had so much money that even getting poor use of it we were richer than anyone I had ever known. We walked home happy with our trade and our supplies and on the way Hanora was sick.

She vomited three or four times more in the three miles. When she got home she took to bed. I rung a chicken and made a stew of it and she ate it but could not hold it down.

The next morning she told me she was sure she was with child. Littleman had managed to seed her;

she had hoped it had not gone that far but feared it might. Hanora was like me when it came to looking to the better side of things and she tried to be keen. We agreed that given the comfort we now enjoyed and the unknown travelling forward that the best thing was to stay put.

We had money, food, water, warmth, shelter and each other. We even had a few neighbours who seemed pleased at the removal of the brothers who by now were consumed by the forest. If all was well the child would arrive February or maybe March. We did not discuss what would happen to it, regardless it was too risky to do anything but stay solid where we were.

Hanora told me of a girl in her village back in Ireland who had been to an old woman named Gillian to get rid of her child and she had bled to death and she had been buried outside the church grounds. I am not sure why she told me and perhaps she had considered that option but it was discussed but one time and not revisited. I was disturbed when I lay in bed that night and contemplated the nature of the deed she had described. How was it that this Gillian witch could take a child and kill it in its mother because it might be inconvenient or a thing of shame for the family?

We spent a happy summer and twice visited Murphy up near the lake where one time he got me so drunk I could not stand. He, Hanora and Maya, for that was his wife's name; laughed at me and I played up the fool for them and when I awoke the

next day I swore a hopeless oath to never drink
again. An oath I have sworn since again and again.

Murphy was a kind man full of laughter and
mischief and he showed me many things, as a father
might show a son. How to trap a beast without it
suffering, how to load a muzzle fast and to shoot
straight and how to skin the hide from an animal
with just one slit. Maya too was kind. She made the
softest bedding and wrappings for the baby from
rabbit and fox and gave Hanora a sling in which the
infant would be secure and we had great laughter as
she demonstrated its use using a pumpkin, which
fell from the sling and smashed upon the earth.

Murphy and Maya visited us also and we shared
food and laughter with them. He was a wise man
and he warned us that people had spoken about us.
At the time it was curiosity but that might turn to
more if they thought about how we were living with
no furs being caught and doing well. If we had
means concealed then someone might wish to find
them and relieve us of them. Twice in the summer
he came down with pelts which I took to the post
to trade for money and supplies, as though I had
them trapped of my accord. I paid him in gold for
his furs and it was as best I could tell a fair trade
and the aim of showing we survived like others, on
trade, seemed to hold; we even stretched out a few
skins outside the cabin to show we were at work
and sure enough, I managed to trap some critters
and to skin them. Most had holes on account of my
poor skill but they sold all the same.

Late September was our last trip to the post
that year. Mainly it was for salt and feed for the

horses. The woman, whose name I learned was Paulette, was very kind, she too by that time was pregnant and it was obvious by her belly. Her husband, whose name I have forgotten, so shall call him 'Jacob' was also kind. Observing that we were buying horse feed he declared that we would never keep the animal alive through a winter and that he would buy it from us. He told us the cost of feed would be more than the value of the horse.

My instinct was caution but Hanora assured me that it was indeed a kindness and so they bought our second horse, this time for the nine dollars, which was probably close to its worth. He told us he could have it on the next boat and maybe make half a dollar on it and that seemed fair. It was a better beast than the nag but he was right, we had no means to keep it over the winter, even if we could feed it we had no stable to house it, and feeding it would be a cost we could now avoid.

Jacob took us back to the cabin on their trap and when there saw the third horse and the saddles and took these for another 35 dollars. I have no idea if that was value or not but without the horses we had no need of the saddles and in the winter they surely would deteriorate.

On the way back to the cabin the storekeeper told us that Murphy's wife had told them in June that Hanora was with child. I had no clue as to how she could know this but I remembered how she had drawn attention to Hanora's belly when she visited.

When the snow came it came heavy and fast. I have never seen such like it. It was a task just to get to the wood pile and I let the chickens in from their shed and the pigs from the sty. Hanora protested that she would not sleep next to a pig and pointed out that we had enough dry salted meat to last a family of four for a year. I returned them to the sty and fed them what I could over the next weeks but they both were stiff one morning. The fresh pork we got off them made a change from the dried and I managed to hump half of one of them up to Murphy, who was grateful as I would not take payment for it.

Although he was grateful he was annoyed I had risked the trip. Sure enough I was froze to the bone. He lent me his mule to return and told me to set it free with a whack on the arse and it would return to him. I had not realised how cold and terrible the winter could be.

All the while as the weeks became months Hanora taught me my lessons. French and English mostly but also how to hold a fork and how to comport myself. She had me pace up and down with my head straight and my back stiff, which often ended in us rolling on the floor in laughter. She taught me how to sew and mend and how to cook. Mathematics was my most hated lesson and Hanora would laugh when I made terrible errors in simple sums. She taught me to waltz with her to the music she would hum and how to bow graciously to a lady and how to give and how to accept a politeness. She told me that accepting a kindness was more important than giving one. She taught me that kindness to others, even those unkind to you, was the essence of a human being and as she insisted this I could not help but recall the image of her gutting the Frenchman, but I supposed as a kindness also slitting his throat.

I can't recall which came the soonest, the start of the thaw or the child. It was a terrible, terrible time and I remember it now only for this journal and I would sooner not recall it at all.

Hanora had been behaving strangely for a few days. She jabbered to herself and made wild gestures as though arguing with some person not manifest to me. I confess I was most unsettled by her behaviour and her muttering. On one occasion she purposefully struck her head against the chimney breast so hard that she split her skin and it bled into her eye and onto her hair. I held her and comforted her as might a man, not a child; and she had slept, whimpering as she drifted off.

I had seen my mother before birthing more than one time and I knew this behaviour was not part of it. I was frightened of what this was, frightened for her and for me.

It was late afternoon and Hanora had been ranting in what was becoming an unwelcome but usual thing. She was going somewhere in her mind, somewhere away from me and I hated it. She stopped that afternoon and calmly asked me to put water on the fire to boil. She told me that the baby was about to arrive. I was thirteen years old and it made me very proud that she trusted me. The child made its way into the world with no fuss and almost immediately took to her mother's breast, feeding greedily from her swollen chest.

'Her name will be Margaret. It was my mother's name' Hanora said. She said nothing else, even as I cleaned her with hot clean rags and I disposed of it all;

'My mother too is Margaret called Maggie' I said, 'along with my sister also'.

She made no reply. I took the child and cleaned her and wrapped her in the soft furs and made a broth for Hanora. Margaret suckled and gargled and made the sounds of contentment only a new born child or a kitten can make. I dared to hope that all was well and assumed that the troubles of mind Hanora had seemed to suffer were evacuated from her along with the other waste of birth.

I have no recollection of going to sleep that evening but I awoke with the sharp needles of icy wind in my face. I knew immediately things were bad and I got out of bed.

Noting that Hanora was not in her bed I made my way for the open door. Beyond, in the moonlight, which reflected off the snow like daylight, I could see her, naked and bent over something. As I drew near I saw the horror of it; a mother, a gentle and beautiful mother holding her own infant's feet with its head submerged in a bucket. I could not comprehend the dreadfulness of it. It was almost too much. For a moment I even thought that perhaps I must allow it, allow her to kill the thing that had, uninvited and unwanted, infected her body.

Instinctively I kicked hard at Hanora and sent her tumbling into the deep snow. She did not try to regain her feet and she lay there as I pulled the child from the bucket of water. The water was warm; the thought of it made the situation even more dreadful, sickening; Hanora had warmed the water for her task lest the child suffer the chill; *what on Christ's earth could have occupied her mind to do such a thing?* I thought.

I took the child to the fireside and placed her on her furs. She was still but she was warm to touch, no breath, no movement but surely some hope for the tiny thing. I didn't pray, I never pray, I never ask that bastard for anything he has already designed to destroy; but I hoped. I did not know what to do so I pushed her little chest with my fingers and upon releasing it she heaved and she coughed and spat out through her nose and mouth at the same time; and then let out a wail to deafen a man, she continued to wail a shaking, quivering screech which announced her survival and birth for the second time.

I felt responsible for the child, I felt a duty to her and she needed my protection but what I felt for my Hanora was love and more and it was to her I now made haste. My duty to the child done, I wanted only to save Hanora from whatever dark thing had taken her.

She lay on her side, naked to the world and as she saw me she turned onto her back and cried out. She wailed so desperate and so deep that it pierced my heart. I knew her pain as if it were my own and I would have killed or died in that instant to take it from her.

'Please God, please Pádraig tell me she is not gone'….

'She is not Hanora, she is not gone and she needs you and she is waiting for you.'

'I made the water warm lest she suffer Pádraig'.

She never called me by the Irish of my name and I knew she was not speaking to me but to her dead son. I answered anyway:

'And the warmth of the water saved her Hanora, it told her that it was not her you were hurting but him, the beast who planted her into you.'

'It was not, it was not, it was not' She cried out.

The tears stung my eyes and froze on my cheeks as she rolled in her agony, her clasped hands between her thighs. I wished I could take her pain. I swear I contemplated for a moment ending us all with the shotgun on that night Margaret, my future wife was born.

It seemed to me that Hanora had been trying to separate and kill the badness of the convict who had raped her and thereby save the innocent child. Extinguishing of the original sin if I must guess; but who will ever know for sure? Of course in her demented and tormented state she could not comprehend that to kill one would be to kill the other.

I have no ideas on how the mind works but it seemed to me that this was the logical basis to her illogical mind and sure enough as she repeated the logic and the reasoning she quietened and calmed. She eventually got to her feet and as she sat on her cot I placed a blanket around her and handed the now quiet child to her. Immediately she suckled and Hanora seemed to be travelling back to me from the dreadful place she had visited.

Just as an injury to a limb or to the body takes time to heal so I suppose does an injury to the mind. Over the weeks Hanora recovered her senses. It was slow and it was troubling and confusing but the one certainty was her affection and love of Margaret and this allowed me eventually to relax. I had for days tried to stay awake longer than Hanora and to keep my eye on any changes which might show a return of her madness.

Late in March with the child not yet a month old, stuck to her favourite left nipple and thriving Hanora said the only words about the matter that she ever would say:

'Relax Patrick, the bad is gone and I am a mother again and I am yours and all is well'

As my eyes closed and I surrendered to slumber, I heard her say;

'Thank you my love'

And I slept.

12
TO NEW YORK

Paddle Steamer 1850s

Patrick's account of the birth and Hanora's extreme mental breakdown is absolutely shocking. It does not need a psychiatrist to work out that she suffered an extreme psychosis of some kind. It must have been an impossibly difficult situation for them both but from what Patrick has written they seem to overcome. It seems that in spite of her stoicism Hanora had finally succumbed, but apparently recovered to her old self.

In his twelfth letter Patrick begins by mentioning a woman named Susan. I have avoided mentioning her other than in a footnote in a previous chapter because I don't want to unnecessarily complicate things. I fear now that if I do not give an explanation; that which I wished to avoid, will become inevitable.

Susan Gallagher was very relevant later in Patrick's life and he does go into some detail about her in later letters but for now it is appropriate to mention that she was a young woman he met in early 1883 and with whom he was to share his journey from England to South Africa and who was with him as a companion when he killed Carey.

They travelled as Mr and Mrs O'Donnell but they certainly were not married. She was from his hometown of Gweedore and she, like Patrick spoke Irish (his wife Margaret did not). Accounts of her age vary and she might have been as young as 17 but was more likely in her mid-twenties, certainly much younger than Patrick who was 48 at the time. She was by all accounts exceptionally beautiful but rather slow of wit.

The relationship seems to have been entirely platonic and partly for the purpose of procuring cheaper passage on the ship together than they might have procured separately. So whilst she provided companionship for him, he would have been a useful chaperone for a young woman travelling abroad. Several accounts exist which suggest strongly that they had no physical relationship, not least his own account and Susan's to Patrick's lawyers before the trial.

Patrick has already informed us that he will one day marry Hanora's daughter Margaret. They married in 1865 when she was 17 and he was 30. He was still married to her when he met Susan. Patrick and Margaret's relationship is explained by him later in a letter so I shall not detail it further at this juncture.

Patrick in his next letter mentions the Confederate Army and his time with the Molly Maguires in Pennsylvania. He writes extensively about these events in later letters so we shall not dwell on them now other than to mention that both are hugely important events in his life.

The letter also concerns itself with the remainder of their time in Canada with and how they managed very well until 1850 when they took a paddle steamer down The St Lawrence and journeyed to New York City.

Although Patrick and Hanora have been together and prospered for a few years; by 1850 their journey to New York must have been extremely daunting for them. Coming from the side of the mountain and their cabin into civilisation would take a few months but it was a journey from one world to an entirely new world. It is clear that Hanora had a degree of sophistication which was to prove invaluable and that she continually tried to impart some of this to Patrick, apparently with some success. Her years in a grand house in Ireland had made her comfortable with things Patrick and others new nothing about, thus providing them both with some advantage over others.

(Twelfth Letter)
Dec 11th 1883 Newgate Prison, London

Dear Victor,

Margaret did not come yesterday and I am concerned as I have no news of her. Susan did arrive and was not permitted entry as she could not show she was my wife, which she is not. She was brought from South Africa by my defence but upon interviewing her they saw she offered more harm than good to my story. I have asked them to pay her fare back to Gweedore and am assured this shall be done. She is innocent in this and had no idea I was married. Margaret is not troubled by the friendship as she knows my use of women is not intimate in the ways a husband and wife normally might be; I would prefer none the less they did not encounter each other in this place.

I shall continue to record my adventures and hope that Margaret will arrive today and remove them safely. I fear that if she has been caught carrying my letters she might be prevented from visiting again. I am confident however that had she been discovered Mullins would spare no effort to inform me. He knows I write but has not the wit to enquire why or what I write. I suspect he would prefer not to boast his illiteracy so leaves the matter to itself. Alas all I can do is continue and hope for the best.

As you see my life was eventful at its start and is, I regret, to be so at its finish but most of it, excepting that time which I spent with the

Confederation[33] and in the mines with the Mollies[34] was not particularly noteworthy so I shall not recount the day to day living of Hanora, myself and Margaret other than in outline. I shall thus spend more effort on the main events before concluding with the true account of the death of James Carey. A truth known only to me and one other, and he is dead. Time now is very precious and I want to conclude before the last day of this condemned man[35].

By June of 48 we had been in our cabin for a year and had not only survived but we had prospered in our health and we were now three. Hanora's malady of mind was behind us and although I kept a casual eye on her it was mostly forgotten.

Margaret grew fast but was slow in some ways. She could not manage a crawl on her hands and knees and instead moved herself around the cabin floor and outside when the warmth permitted, by means of rolling her little body in the direction she desired. It seemed to be a remarkable accurate mode of movement which she perfected.

With the thaw that year came the warmth and it invigorated us both and we did not think of moving on. We had food and shelter, our gold coins remained buried behind the cabin and untouched

---

33 Confederate Army
34 Molly Maguires was the name given to a union of Irish miners in Pennsylvania who used violence to further their aims.
35 Patrick seems here to be making a reference to Victor Hugo's book (The Last Day of a Condemned Man) which the author gifted to him. It seems he was probably making a joke.

and we had used very little of the dollars left to us by the Picard brothers; we were happy and we were safe.

We made our way to the trading post which seemed all a bustle with Indians and trappers coming down to trade and to buy stores depleted over the winter months. Boats were in and out, several steamers but mostly sail.

There were at least another eight buildings being constructed, one was a church I think and huge piles of lumber had built up on the harbour side since last we visited.

Jacob sold one nag back to us for $12, which seemed a bargain to me as they had kept it over winter and surely spent more than a couple of dollars on it. He'd sold the better of the beasts and done well on it no doubt. He and Paulette made a fuss of Margaret and told us two more children had arrived in the little settlement over the winter, including their own boy.

And so we continued our life on the hillside and instead of we two swimming in the lake and resting in the sun it was three. Spring passed and summer came and then went and Margaret grew stronger but even at 6 months she was obviously slow. Hanora spoke to her in French and English and the child understood what was said.

It was before the second winter that we first spoke of moving on. I have noticed over the years that as man acquires the essentials of food and shelter those essentials no longer seem so important and he desires other things and other things again.

171

Man is not a beast; a beast is content with a belly full and to be safe. A man and a woman need more and always will strive for the next thing and the next after that. Safety and warmth we had, it was time to contemplate what else lay ahead for us.

Murphy and Maya visited regularly and sometimes took Margaret away for a day or two. They could see the slow nature of the child but I dared not speak of the events of the night in March the year before. Indeed, as I now write I realise that this is my first utterance of it. I have not hidden the matter; I have had no reason to speak of it. That is all.

The second winter on the hill was better than the first, and although we thought to move on we did not; so a third winter came and it was easier on us because by then we knew the ways of the mountain, the people, the weather and the varmints. That last year we determined that we would in the following May purchase a place on one of the boats heading south.

Murphy told us that a boat could take us all the way to the state of New York in the United States of America. Even the very words excited me. From the great lake Ontario we could take the canal and then the Railroad most of the way to New York City. I had no appreciation at that time of the difference between New York State and New York itself; or of the vast distance and onerous journey between them.

I knew that New York was not too distant from the coalfields of Pennsylvania where I would find my Uncle Manus and my Aunty Margaret along with my cousins. I was also aware that most if not all of that journey could be undertaken by rail. Although I had not seen a railway or a train I knew they existed and could bring us from New York to the coal fields very swiftly.

We purchased a cabin for the journey south for the month of May. It was to be by paddle steamer. The best price, which Jacob had helped us to find, had been for a boat which had a dozen or so rooms and a dining room for passengers but primarily was for cargo collected along the way. It would steam downstream every two months delivering supplies to the various settlements and towns and turn upstream to collect furs and other goods. We were to be on its first spring trip. Passage was a heavy price but the alternative route by land would be impossibly dangerous and arduous even if successful. The river boats could charge much more and would have done had they known of our fortune as we would have been happy to pay many times more.

Jacob and Paulette had been surprised when Hanora paid our passage in gold coin. We were presumed poor and that was by no accident on our part. To have riches in such a place was to attract trouble. We were glad when the day arrived as the knowledge of the possibility of our riches would surely spread amongst everyone; now there was a hint of wealth. We could have used the dollars, we had plenty of them but that might demand using gold later and better we used it where we were familiar and mostly safe than in the unknown ahead of us.

It was a bright June morning when we dug up our gold. Hanora had kept the coin vests which held the coins evenly, each in its own little pocket and in such a way as to not arouse suspicion or discomfort. She also had adapted my sheath so my Bowie now sat neatly on my back between my shoulder blades and I could extract it swiftly and without the suspicion incurred when reaching for a knife in a more conventional location, such as the hip or thigh. Murphy had taken time to teach me how to use it in defence and in anger and at almost 15 years I was not someone with whom to lock horns.

We took what we could carry and I placed the gun under my bed along with the shot, powder and caps. Murphy had often admired it over his own flintlock and I knew if I offered it on the quay he would refuse. I placed five gold Persian coins next to the gun. These roughly the size, so probably of equivalent value to sovereigns, as near to $25 as I could estimate. A handsome enough sum but Murphy had been kind to us and though we would not have perished without him, life would have been much harder for sure.

On the quay, which really was just a wooden structure which felt like it would fall into the river any moment; we said our farewells to people we had come to know over the last three years and whom we knew we would almost certainly never see again.

I explained to Maya where I had located the gun and the coins and bid her make haste to the place lest some scoundrel, knowing we were away, help themselves. I bade her to not inform Murphy until we had set off. She hugged me and kissed me and she placed around my neck a cord of leather with a bear's claw fixed onto it. Murphy hugged me as though a bear might and he bade us good luck and I am sure there was a tear in his eye as he turned away and demanded;

'Home woman, we have traps to clean'.

Hanora boarded carrying Margaret, for the child still could not walk, in spite of being a full 2 years and more. I followed and as the boat slipped away I felt a great loss for the companionship and comfort of our home but also a greater excitement for what lay ahead.

The trip was comfortable and other than in our cabin it was the first time I had laid in a bed with pillows and blankets or eaten in a grand room such as the dining room. Passengers were not this boat's main concern but we were very well treated. Most of the time we stayed in our room and it was there on that adventure that Margaret took her first steps. She still spoke not a single word.

The journey was uneventful but took almost as long as the journey from Ireland. I had no concept of how big America was, even now it is hard to imagine, indeed it is beyond imagining.

We came to what seemed to be the ocean but our fellow travellers explained it to be a lake, named Ontario. We entered a canal after that and travelled onto a place called Syracuse which was like nothing I had ever seen. I had thought Sligo a large town but this place seemed to stretch out forever. I had never seen so many people.

We stayed a few days and nights in a hotel and the beds were even more luxurious than on the boat. We ate in the hotel too and had fine breakfasts and mid-meals and evening meals and we could pull a cord and have more food brought to us late. Hanora practiced me using the cutlery and so on. All our time together Hanora was 'improving' me as she said and I welcomed her lessons and attention as I knew the time would come when such refinement would be needed and if not needed then useful.

We went to the stores and bought fine luggage and good clothes. I visited a barber and had my hair cut by a man with a moustache the likes of which I had never before seen.

We visited a gun shop which boasted some fine instruments and Hanora bought us a .44 Colt Walker which the owner had told us was the latest. It had six shots, each of which contained cap, powder and lead. It was as heavy as the gold strapped to me. The store had a shooting range in the cellar and I almost broke my wrist and my ears firing just one shot. The noise made Margaret cry out in fear. The hole it made in the wooden target was the size of a halfpenny but when the store owner showed me the reverse of the plank it was torn to shreds.

The people in that place were friendly and seemed not to mind us being Irish. Once or twice I was told off for calling it a town. They seemed very proud that it was a city; I had no idea of the difference. But for Uncle Manus and the family I think I would have happily stayed put in Syracuse and I wonder what would have become of me had I done. I suspect very keenly that I would not be locked in a cell in Newgate waiting for my end.

Fully rested and stocked we made our way onward south east towards New York City. We travelled variously on locomotives and carriage. The rail lines were not at that time joined or were under repairs and horse and carriage stations were found along the way taking us and our fellow travellers from one railroad to the next. We stopped in towns along the way and everything was a wonder to me. It seemed that travel in this vast country was fine if you had the means to do it in comfort; and we had the means.

It was September of 1850 when we finally arrived in New York, I have no idea what part but we were delivered to the city on a locomotive. Hanora had no more of an idea where to go than did I but we knew the first thing to do was to find lodgings. We took a cab and asked the driver to find us somewhere not too rich but which was suitable for a respectable woman, her brother and daughter. He showed us one boarding house after another, all unsuitable even from a casual glance from the cab. He seemed to be ensuring his fare was a good one until I permitted him sight of my colt and he eventually reached a hotel which looked clean and was not rough in any way. He suggested it might be beyond our means and Hanora replied;

'You Sir; have no notion of our means, though they are narrowed by some margin on account of the jolly journey you have taken us upon'.

He looked at her, sheepish, but was prevented from speaking as Hanora continued;

'and I am minded not to pay you given we are no more than a mile or two from where we set off four hours ago'.

She had no way of knowing of course if that were true but it seemed she hit the mark. At first he looked like he might reach for a club but upon seeing me step forward, my hand under my coat and on my hip, he thought better of it and mumbled something indistinguishable as he took the payment from Hanora.

'There be no tip Sir.' She said casually as she slapped the arse of the horse and it bolted throwing the driver back in his seat.'

God I loved her. There she stood on the sidewalk of a strange city, in a new world which seemed infested with people going one way and another; a confusing but a promising world. She had never seen the place or the like of it, she had two months of hard travel behind her and yet; with straight back and long neck and grace and pride and a smile she took down a blaggard without even raising her voice. This spectacular woman was mine and I was hers.

The hotel was named *the Atlantic*, and was on a road named Broadway and opposite was a vast green area undeveloped. It was probably basic to people accustomed to such things but to us it was luxury; beds yet again, with clean sheets and pillows and food in a large dining room; good food. Everything smelt pleasant and was clean. The toilets were inside and on each floor. I remembered the sheds and how we had lived in Ireland and could not believe such a difference in fortune could exist. I was a fifteen year old man and yet still an excited boy.

Hanora was charged $1.50 a day with me at half and Margaret at no cost because we shared a room. It was almost nothing to us. I say so not as a boast but as a simple fact. A boarding house would have cost a fraction but we had the money and Hanora had suggested that we must enter the community at the right level; this could not be achieved in a boarding house alongside construction workers.

'Money and wealth is wasted if used just to survive.' She had said. 'Such use will extend a predicament but not improve it. Wealth must be used to improve and to provide opportunity.'

She was correct of course and whilst her theories might allow the reader to believe that she was strongly ambitious; she was not. To her the ultimate progression and her ambition was to open a school house and to teach children. She believed that the advantage of education by far outweighed the benefit of wealth or even food and she often told me that;

'Nourishment of the mind enriches the soul while nourishment of the body makes you fat' or; 'A gift of learning Patrick is a gift for life yet a gift of money is a transient thing, often to be squandered and thrown to the wind by the feckless and

179

ignorant'. Or 'You can spend your wealth, all of it in one bad hand of cards, or on a poor investment but you cannot be divested of an education, indeed the more education is spent the more it profits the spender in the accumulation of knowledge and happiness.'

She would tell me such things every time we paid a bill or made any decision of worth. Over time she seemed to contemplate such matters more and more. I thought nothing of it at first and I confess I could not find fault with her observations. Indeed they have served me well in my life. Alas from her they eventually came so thick and fast that they seemed obsessive.

We could afford to stay at the hotel for as long as we desired but that was not our intention, we had come to America to make a life and the soonest started the best as far as we both were concerned.

Finally we were safe, secure and in America properly. In the days that followed we explored the streets around us and in the nights we sat together in the dining room of that place and ate hearty and Margaret, at 2 years and seven months uttered her first word, it was;

'Pat-tik'.

We would retire to our room and read by lamplight until the small hours. I was fascinated by the instalments of *David Copperfield* and the manager of the hotel told me that Dickens had stayed in the same room as we occupied just eight years before. Of course I did not believe him but it made the reading all the more exciting.

I cannot remember being more optimistic than during these first few weeks in New York. Our exploration was first on foot and later, when the journeys became too arduous for the child we took cabs, each day further afield. We boarded the ferry several times and marvelled at how low the cost was to transport us across the water to Brooklyn and back again. It felt safe in the day time and with my Colt tucked into my belt at the rear of my trousers and my Bowie above it I felt *invincible*.

We had been almost two months in the hotel and come to know some of the guests, many of whom seemed to live permanently there. Autumn would soon be turned to winter and we both knew we must make plans.

Hanora had in the first week taken my vest of gold and hers and made some business at a bank where she converted it mostly to dollars, some $2,400 in all; a vast amount and not safe carried around on the person. I am not sure of the details but she assured me it was safe and that we had dollars, as many as we needed and access to them whenever the need would arise. We visited the place one day to withdraw money and they held the door for her and for me, and they brought her coffee and sweet things and fussed over Margaret and they bowed and complimented us all the way. It seemed I had not underestimated the value of the loot we had acquired. It also seemed to me that in this strange new place that our station was not nearly so important as it was at home, provided we had money.

Day after day we took coaches further and further into the city. Homes it seemed varied from slums with terrible conditions to fine houses on the next street which we could afford but would never pay. It seemed inevitable that we must leave the island and travel to Brooklyn where there were similar slums but there were also good neighbourhoods, where the Jews, Germans and some Italians settled. The journeys grew too arduous for Margaret and many days I would take care of her while Hanora searched.

One day in October Hanora arrived at the hotel in the evening late but in time for dinner. At dinner she announced that she had found us a real home in a good part of Brooklyn. She had suggested that amongst the Irish and Italian Catholics we would be best at home. I cared little for my countrymen at the time and less for Catholics but I had not seen her so happy and I showed her my delight and we explained to Margaret that she would soon have a bedroom of her own. In reality Hanora would no more let the child sleep without her than would I.

Only days later, as November came, we moved into the house which was constructed of neat timbers painted light blue. It had a shingle roof, which was very normal in America and it had a huge garden to the rear where Hanora would eventually grow vegetables and Margaret would play. The rent was high but the building was in a good area and suited Hanora perfectly. The disadvantage was that it was a carriage ride and trip on the ferry into the city and it was there that I would seek employment.

Hanora resolved to buy a trap and a pony as nearby there was a place which would house and keep the creature. Her excitement worried me a little as she seemed to be sometimes a little too much. She would dash and fret and clean and plan and do too much. One day she would be on top of the world and the next down and tired and sad; the difference in mood was noticeable but then it passed, as it had arrived. I assume it was the move and the settling into the house at first but it continued.

To this point we had leaked money and we both knew this could not continue. We had a huge amount still but at some time we needed to have our income match our expenditure or better still to exceed it. We had both been destitute and starving in the past and it had bred in us a desperate desire never to be so again. My recent reading of Mr Micawber's basic rule of personal finance, namely; '*Annual income twenty pounds, annual expenditure nineteen, nineteen and six, result happiness. Annual income twenty pounds, annual expenditure twenty pounds ought and six, result misery.*' had stuck in my mind and we seemed to be breaking it each day:

With this in mind I looked at first on our side of the river for work but found nothing. I returned every few days seeking employment but I was one of many Irishmen and others in the same situation. Employers could take their pick and they did never pick me. I was a good build for a fifteen year old and I looked older but while full grown men with real skills and hair on their face were seeking employment on the buildings I had little chance. I am sure my lack of fancy for rough work must have also been clear to others.

Hanora, who had always been wise instructed me to find work where I have the advantage over others; including having good clothes and a clean and healthy disposition and a gentle manner, a good standard in French and above average English. These were things she had taught me over the years and now they were the things which advantaged me over my compatriots, most of whom could not read or hold a knife or have a conversation, but could swing a hammer and drive a spike[36].

It was with this in mind on a cold November morning in 1850, in a new suit of clothes and with a new hair cut that I ventured across from Brooklyn on the Union Ferry and towards the very fine Astor House Hotel.

---

36 Part of a rail line fastening system which required strength to drive.

13
ASTOR HOUSE

Astor House, Broadway – New York 1860

Patrick now accounts for his time in New York. By that time he was 15 or 16 years old. It's an important time for him and we can see that he matures into a man while at the Astor; though it is fair to say that by age 15 and long before, he already had many of the attributes one might associate with maturity.

It's clear that Hanora is exceptionally important in his life, as is little Margaret, who is 2 when they arrived in new York and 13 when they leave. Hanora we see is continually trying to 'improve' Patrick with her lessons and by example. It is she who pushes him to seek employment in the very prestigious Astor House Hotel. Whilst much more than a parent or a mother figure she at times is exactly that. It is, to say the least, a complicated relationship; but given it was borne from such

185

tragedy and such challenges as they have faced together and alone, is there any wonder? They have found each other and sadly sometimes bonds made in adversity, particularly extreme adversity are unrealistic in terms of expectation and outcome.

This next letter covers an extended period of time; in fact from 1850 for over ten years. We see a 15 year old Patrick mature into a 26 year old man. We see Margaret grow and we see Hanora apparently thrive with her ambitions; at least for a time.

Astor House, as it is correctly named, should not be confused with more recent and indeed existing buildings in New York with similar names. Astor House, which was of course a hotel, though not named as such, was demolished in the early twentieth century after less than 100 years standing on Broadway at the junction with Vesey Street and opposite the splendid St Paul's Chapel, which still stands.

The hotel, which was opened in 1836, was originally named The Park Hotel. It soon gained an outstanding reputation, it was the first truly luxury hotel in New York and its reputation was not just national but international. The hotel boasted bathrooms on each floor, gas lighting (it produced its own gas) and other luxuries unheard of at the time outside of Paris and London.

It attracted the highest in the land and many famous people stayed there, including Charles Dickens, the poet Longfellow and indeed President Abraham Lincoln was a regular; even running his successful re-election campaign in 1864 from rooms in the hotel; he also stayed for a time between his election and inauguration in 1861.

Astor House however started a fierce rivalry for the most luxurious and most modern hotel. When Patrick arrived in New York the hotel was still at its height, with nothing to compare in terms of luxury and prestige; but only a few years' later hotels such as The St Nicholas, also on Broadway but boasting central heating in every room; and The Fifth Avenue Hotel, on Fifth Avenue, naturally enough, with its heating, 400 servants and, incredibly for 1859, private bathrooms.

As a 15 year old Patrick approached the hotel to seek employment he could not have imagined how much of his life it would occupy and how much he would learn there. His quick thinking, his adaptability, his ability with languages and the many refinements taught to him by Hanora made him and the hotel a perfect fit.

His encounters with the high of society, including proponents both of slavery and of abolition are interesting; little does he know how in the years to follow these notions of others will take him places he would have better avoided.

Some of Patrick's revelations about Lincoln are surprising and disturbing but so well documented, impossible to deny… not to ignore however.

(Thirteenth Letter)
Dec 12th 1883 - Newgate Prison, London

Dear Victor,

Margaret, I am pleased to report, arrived today and explained that she had been most unwell and unable even to get from her bed yesterday. Indeed she has the appearance today of a corpse and I insisted that she return to her lodgings. She took with her yesterday's letter. I feel better today also and hope to write a good deal more than I did yesterday.

My time in New York was not exciting but it was important to how I became who I am. I also will tell you what became of us three.

I was almost 16 years old when I went looking for employment in the Astor House and could have had no idea what a huge part it would play in my young life. Hanora and I knew of the Astor, it was on Broadway at Vesey Street and we passed it on several occasions while we stayed on the island[37] in September and October of 50. Hanora would visit the chapel across the road from the hotel with Margaret and I would wait outside and watch the coming and going.

Astor House was a splendid building which looked to be new. It stood five stories high and at least thirteen rooms wide and even though we had seen many large buildings since arriving in the city this one was one of the most splendid.

---

37 *Manhattan is an island surrounded to the west and south by the Hudson and to the east by the East River and to the north by the Harlem River.*

On the top step stood two doormen in splendid long coats and high hats, in rain or shine, one each side of the grand entrance. As I waited outside the church for Hanora I would watch as grand coaches arrived and a line of staff would appear and unload the luggage and then disappear as the occupants were escorted through the doors into what wonders of splendour and luxury I could only imagine.

It was a cold morning when I made my way up to that place in the hope of work. I had taken the ferry and picked up a cab on the island. I could easily have walked the mile or so from the boat but I wanted to be fresh. I dropped the cab a street early as I did not want to give the impression I was careless with money or too well endowed to concern myself seriously with employment.

Hanora had good experience of service and what is and is not expected. She had instructed me that I must be sufficiently well dressed to not be mistaken for a vagrant but not too well dressed to be confused with a client or some upstart with pretentions to that position.

She had also informed me that those most likely to note a person's standing and to use it unfavourably were in fact the staff and servants more than the clients, who due to breeding were well above such trifles. It was how a Lord could be unkempt and it be forgiven.

She told me also that such a man could in fact be unfaithful to his wife and not be measured for it as might an ordinary fellow. I was not entirely sure of what she meant by this until sometime later she

explained to me that she and her husband had lost
their position in the grand house when the Lord had
made an advance on her and his implausible but
believed defence was her condemnation. It was
enough for their ruin. Thus they were on the boat
to the Americas and all her family were lost and the
Lord remained a 'gentleman'.

On the day I approached Astor House I passed
the church on Vesey Street and instead of turning
left to the side doors of the hotel I carelessly
approached the main entrance of the building and in
so doing I made my first error. It had not occurred
to me but later I discovered that Astor House had a
side entrance for the likes of staff and tradespersons
and idiot Irish immigrants looking for work.
Instead, as a fine coach drew up beside me I walked
up the steps to the main entrance whereupon one of
the doormen stopped me and with apparent distain
asked; what was my business at the front door of a
place where I did not belong? He was a tall fellow
of about thirty years and although he sounded
English I detected a slight familiarity to his accent.

I explained that I was seeking employment but
it was clear his attention was by then on the coach
which by now was spilling its contents; one fine
gentleman and one fine lady, onto the footway.
Before he could comment upon my intentions the
large door beside him swung open and a line of
porters all identically dressed, streamed out of the
hotel and began to unload the carriage. Behind the
porters came what I later learned was a day
manager. He greeted Monsieur and Madam Bull,
whom I later learned were the guests, with

appropriate humbleness assuring them that their rooms were prepared. He spoke in English and they appeared to me not to understand. The lady carried a white poodle in her arms and the man carried a violin case and nothing else.

I had begun to return my attention to the doorman when beside me the handle of a large trunk being carried by two of the porters broke free and it crashed to the floor with the distinct sound of breaking glass. The lady scolded the porters for their carelessness and when they seemed not to have understood the message in her native tongue, she resorted to French, which they also did not understand. She looked to the manager who stood shame faced also at a loss to understand what she was saying.

Opportunities, I have found, rarely announce themselves before arrival and though I had not seen the full potential of intervention at the time it seemed to me that it could hardly leave me at a loss. Thus; with no invitation from any of the parties involved I stepped forward and bowing slightly to the lady and in my very best French enquired if I might be of service in translating her concerns to the manager. In that moment, the fuss stopped. The porters looked at me, the doorman looked at me, the manager looked at me and the guests, Monsieur and Madame Bull looked at me.

As she held my gaze I did my best not to look impertinent and it worked. She nodded her head very slightly and welcomed my intervention. I spent the next five minutes distributing the translated chastisements to all involved, including the manager for not having the wit to understand French when working in such a fine establishment as the Astor. The gentleman seemed to want to have an end to the matter and to retire to his rooms;

'Before the children arrive'. He said to her.

Madame Bull was however by now demanding the dismissal of the porter and it was my sad duty to translate to the poor chap that the manager had acquiesced to the demand just to get the fuss from the front of the hotel and settled.

It was at this point that a second coach arrived and from it came what seemed to be a small army of children, their ages between 4 and 13, along with a nanny trying to organise them. Monsieur Bull exclaimed in what seemed to me to be a sarcastic tone;

'Mes enfants' and he disappeared into the hotel.

In the midst of the chaos a man who seemed to be more senior to the manager who so far had dealt badly with the whole situation, appeared. He engaged Madame Bull in French and she offered her gloved hand which he brushed with his lips. She took his arm and they too disappeared into the hotel as she explained in detail just what a dreadful experience she had endured. The nanny rounded up the children, who by now were playing a hopping game on the steps and she ushered them in after their mother. More porters appeared to unload the second coach.

I turned to the doorman who seemed a slice more friendly to me than he had been and he explained that if I was to go down beside the hotel along the road with the church I would find a side entrance and through there I could enquire about work.

'And lose the Irish accent if you want any hope of employment' He said with a wink and a distinctly Donegal accent.

He tilted his top hat to me and as I turned the more senior of the managers re-emerged.

'You', he said

'Me Sir' I replied, feigning a French twang.

'You, yes you with the French, follow me boy'

I did so without question and as I passed the doorman he smiled and winked at me again. *What a fine fellow* I thought and I smiled back. I was at a loss as to why I had been called into the front of the hotel.

Inside, the woman, whom I knew to be Madame Bull stood in what was the grandest room I had ever seen. She had her purse open as the manager brought me to her, obviously at her request. She withdrew some coins and offering it to me in French she said:

'Thank you for your kind assistance young man'.

The manager looked at me and with a nod seemed to be approving that I might take the money. I protested that I could not possibly accept reward for doing a gentleman's duty and that;

'Assistance to such a fine lady was my pleasure and its own reward Madame'

The manager was visibly impressed and when the lady pressed the matter I suggested to her:

'Alongside this great establishment Madame is the finest church in all of New York and it may be that it would be a more worthy recipient of your generosity'. I knew now to strike and as obvious as it might seem I did not care, so I continued.

'Only this morning I have myself lit a candle and offered a prayer within that place in order I might find some gainful employment.'

I have to say Victor I was very pleased with myself. I had no use for the few pennies she was offering but how else could fate have presented me a better opportunity? I had stretched my luck but it paid handsomely. The manager clicked his fingers and summoned the undermanager who approached, enthusiastic to make right anything he could. He was ordered to take me to the porters' station, find me a uniform and put me to work immediately. He looked to Madame Bull and assured her that as a porter's job had only that morning become available I would be able to start immediately. She looked content that the matter had been dealt with appropriately.

I learned later that Monsieur Bull was a very famous musician and he often stayed at the hotel with his wife and five or six children. He was regarded highly and her behaviour was far from the worst I saw in my time there.

That is how I got my first role in Astor House. I felt badly for the porter I replaced until a couple of days later I found him working in the kitchens. It seemed that someone got 'dismissed' most times Madame Bull stayed, only to be relocated until she had left the country.

I had not expected to be given a position so quickly when I travelled into the city and it was ten days before I managed to get back to Hanora in Brooklyn. She had been distracted about my absence and when I arrived at the house she was not in good condition. The place was untidy and Margaret was not clean. It took all of my day off to help organise things and to bring her around to normality. It had occurred to me that she would worry but not to the degree that she did. We had discussed the likelihood of an immediate start and a few days away but I confess not ten days.

Thankfully by the time I went back to the hotel the next day Hanora had recovered most of her dignity and composure. This was becoming a cycle which afflicted her whenever life became too challenging for her. She would descend rapidly into the depths and her behaviour sometimes was extraordinary with flights of fantasy and grandiose ambitions, only to return, sometimes in hours and sometimes in days to her old self[38].

She would make plans which were wildly unrealistic when in her excited state but the difficulty for me was to understand which were achievable and which the result of unreal fancy. So it was when she had spoken of building a school room at the rear of the house. I was at first unsure of its prospects. As it transpired several of the neighbours had petitioned her in that effort due to

---

38 *Patrick's account suggests that Hanora almost certainly suffered from fast cycling Bipolar Effective disorder or similar malady.*

the lack of good catholic education in the area. The landlord, who had two children himself, had suggested he would have no objection provided it cost him nought.

Hanora decided to go ahead and soon busied herself finding builders and such like to elongate the ground floor of the rear of the house. On each of my weekly returns I saw the project develop and her brighten and shine again. Little Margaret now almost three years old followed her mother about, chattering in a language only she and Hanora could understand.

By March of 51 Hanora had not only completed the little schoolroom but had furnished it with two rows of benches and desks and many learning tools including a desk of her own and a chalkboard and slate and chalks enough for 15 children. Outside were a play frame and a sandpit and a sheltered area. She limited the class to 15 from age five to fourteen and was immediately oversubscribed. In spite of the demand she did not charge too heavy a price and for every three paying children she took one for no charge.

Hanora had improved again and while she was occupied building and later teaching she shone and was at her best. It was to be years before I saw the illness descend upon her again, the next time it was to be with a vengeance I had only ever seen once before.

I came home every week for one day and one night and even at sixteen slept with her as I had in the sheds.

I was not paid handsome but at the hotel I got fed every day and I shared a room in the attic, which we called floor six, with the doorman I had met on my first day so I had small need and less use for pay. I gave half of what I had each week to Hanora and when her little school room got going in 51 she was earning too. Between us our income at last was more than our expenditure, a good deal more. Mr Micawber would have been very proud of us I suppose.

My first six months at the Astor were spent carrying bags in and out of the hotel and though the wages were low the gratuities given by the guests were often very generous. I do not recall any one week where these gratuities did not exceed my wage. I also met some very fine people, many of them noted in society. The Manager whom I had met on my first day seemed to find me agreeable and suggested that if I was willing to spend some months in each department that he might be content to train me in management. It was an opportunity I took enthusiastically and so started my journey through the hotel from the scullery to the kitchens, the restaurant and the desk. The most difficult task I found was the pretence with my accent, which dropped only occasionally.

I even learned to be stand-in valet as often gentlemen travellers were not accompanied by their own staff. On one occasion a gentlemen had come and taken part of the third floor for two months and I served as his butler all of that time. When he left he gave me a gold sovereign and suggested that

I travel back to England with him to take up full time employment as his man. I declined because my heart was set on Pennsylvania and my family there. Truthfully the only things that kept me in New York were Hanora and Margaret.

By 1854 I was a junior manager and I knew the workings of the hotel and more importantly the guests, as well as any of my colleagues did. By 58 I was a middle manager and was in sole charge on my shifts.

As my employment continued with success so did Hanora's school. The landlord had for a percentage and his name on the building offered her a new school house. It was two rooms only but large and within a walk of the house. She had employed two assistants and now had almost 30 children. Word had spread and she had a reputation and her pupils shone.

Margaret by then was 9 or so and she did well with her books but by now it was very clear that she could not engage with people of her age or older, other than Hanora and me. She refused to look at people when they spoke to her and she avoided social interactions. She could dress herself and feed herself and play but she was not like other children.

A notable guest I had the honour to deal with in 59 was Abraham Lincoln[39]. Indeed we served more than one future president at Astor House but Lincoln is the one I remember most. At the time I knew not that he would be president within 2 years.

---

39 Abraham Lincoln became the 16th president of the USA in March 1861

198

I remember him so well not because of his part in the war to come or in his death by assassination but because of his person. In particular his face, which when I looked upon felt as though I was looking into a dreadful abyss. I am not one to judge a fellow by the misfortune of his looks but I believe we have instincts and should sometimes pay them more heed than we do.

Aside from the danger I could see in him, which others I believe also could detect; he was it must be said an exceptionally impressive man and for the three days he stayed I did my best to be as near to him as I could manage. As a moth to a flame I was I must admit, drawn to him and his words. I did not speak to him directly nor he to me but I heard what he had to say to others.

It was he who furnished my early views on the Negro; he allowed me to understand that provided the Negro knew himself to be inferior to the white man[40] and did not try to ingrain himself into the life of his betters by way of marriage or other means then he is a useful fellow and to be treated kindly and not held captive against his will.

I confess a bitter shame for ever having harboured such monstrous opinions about my fellow man but it was at the time perfectly proper to think in this way. The leader of our country and future hero of abolition thought this way and so did

---

40 *The abolition of slavery for Abraham Lincoln was a political and not ethical matter. See Appendix 1 for report of his debate with Senator Stephen A. Douglas in 1858*

I. I later changed my views for morality; he claimed to have changed his but I am sure only for political advancement.

I should confess also that in addition to agreeing with Lincoln on Negros at that time I was in some ways harsher in my views, and unlike him, did not want the Negro to be free at all. I later changed my position on the matter and now am firmly of the opinion that all men are born equal regardless of their skin colour but I must be truthful about what I thought in 59 and for a time after.

Until I heard of Lincoln I never contemplated the colour of skin and I had met not a single black man. I knew of them of course; not least because my uncle Manus used to curse them when he wrote to me. He and others in the mines were strongly feared that if the Negro were to be unleashed from slavery in America then they would flood the industry and work for nothing and so destroy his livelihood and that of his countrymen.

I could see the point but had never dwelt on it. I was an Irishman and I was forced out of my country by starvation which many, including me, blamed on the English and their harsh treatment of my country. Many of my country men had died of starvation and disease so I had no particular interest in the suffering of others, it was no better or worse than mine I supposed.

In addition to that or perhaps in spite of it I had no particular dislike for the English, I never have. I detested what they had done to my people and my country but the deed was not of the ordinary Englishman; it was of the landed and wealthy

English and Irishman and that is not the ordinary Englishman. My father along with thousands of other Irishmen served with their army in Africa and he never had issue with them. He taught me that the English were a reliable and decent race of people.

It seems to many English people that all Irish people who have suffered, and that is most, must harbour hatred for them. This is simply not the case; most Irish men I knew were more concerned feeding themselves and their families than correcting the world and its injustices. I was and am no different. I say this to explain that my dislike and distrust of Negros was much as an Englishman's dislike and distrust of the Irish; untrue and a manipulation.

The newspapers now mark me as an English hating Fenian[41] but they have got me wrong I insist. I did not ever kill anyone or do anything for Ireland; all I have ever done is for me and my own. The English papers describe me as illiterate. Do I seem so to you? They say I am a Republican terror man yet what terror or damage have I done but this one thing?

---

41 Fenian is a term used for Irish Republicans. Often used as a pejorative term for Irish Catholics.

14
AWAY FROM NEW YORK

*Lunatic Asylum Blackwell's island – New York – 1853 -
Harper's Weekly 1865*

It's interesting that in his previous letter Patrick
makes real efforts to disclose that he is not
embittered against the English. Many Irish people
disliked the English, often for good reason, but
many did not. Patrick is clearly not an irrational
English hater, as he is portrayed and he wants not
to be remembered as such. Interestingly we shall see
much clearer examples of how he feels about being
characterised as a Fenian and a hero later in his
letters.

He has told us of his time in the Astor and of
his experiences and we can see that he had a bright
future there, possibly one day becoming general
manager. In the following letter that story continues
into 1861. Great turmoil was descending onto the
country, turmoil in which we shall see him

embroiled and which directly and incredibly will see him again in the lobby of his beloved Astor House.

A fact he mentions in his next letter and which I found especially interesting concerned the witnesses to the execution of John Brown, the famous and very ardent abolitionist executed in 1859 for his attack on a government arsenal in Virginia.

A further coincidence being that Victor Hugo made representations to have Brown spared execution... It has to be said his efforts met with a similar level of success as they had in Patrick's case... thus John Brown's body shortly after lay 'a-mouldering in his grave'...

Sadly great personal turmoil is also just around the corner for Patrick, Hanora and Margaret and although the oncoming war would have probably changed the course of Patrick's life anyway, things proved to be very traumatic for the little family.

Patrick is horrified to discover the truth of matters between those closest to him and events demand he acts in a way that would seem cruel to most but was essential in the circumstance.

(Fourteenth Letter)
Dec 12th 1883 - Newgate Prison, London

Dear Victor,

I have just five days to tell the remainder of my tale; more likely four as I know nothing of the last day. I have no doubt they will waste my time and his by sending me a priest into whose eye I shall spit and there will no doubt be other formalities necessary for the legal dispatch of a soul so I shall not depend on that last day. Opportunity may escape me if I press my luck so I shall again endeavour to write at least twice each day, three times if circumstance permits.

For now I return to the events of how Margaret and I left New York and the comfort of my employment in the Astor and alas how my beloved Hanora stayed behind. As with most things it was no single event but a mix of several.

I have told you of my meeting with the long dead President Lincoln, (though he was alive when I last saw him), and I know that many will be in disbelief. I claim no intimate acquaintance but I met him and shook his hand and heard him speak and ensured his comfort at our fine hotel; not many can say as much as that.

I admired his words greatly and at the time saw no contradiction in them. I have known of several presidents, Buchannan, Lincoln, Arthur and others but I hazard it is only one who has known of me. I know this to be true because I have in my cell a letter from the present incumbent of that noble office, Chester Arthur himself. Like you he petitions for a reduction in my sentence; like you he is bound to fail.

Lincoln was a regular enough visitor to the hotel in New York and he was among many prominent politicians and such famous people, many of whom I cannot now recall and it is not important anyway. After I had left Astor House he returned in 64 to run his re-election campaign from the very same place.

In a hotel a person can hear many things and news is often carried more swiftly and accurately than in the press. I witnessed many meetings and campaigns for the abolition of slavery and although not as a guest I was close up to the work of these people. More and more there were speakers calling for the physical overthrow of the slave states and money was collected in hats for the cause of the freedom of Negros. Talk of war with the south was every place.

I have no idea if John Brown had ever visited my hotel but his name most certainly was no stranger to the meetings and the talk in the dining rooms and the halls so when late in 59 we heard of him bearing arms in the antislavery cause it was clear to most people that one way or another this matter would be sorted with cannon and gun.

To me therefore the first real notion of war came in late 1859 and it was northern abolitionists who took up arms against the South and their legal possession of slaves. Brown, with a well-armed gang took control of the US arsenal at Harpers Ferry in Virginia hoping to inspire the local slaves to take up arms and join him. They did not. The task was hopeless and Colonel Robert Lee[42] under the instruction of the US president Buchanan manged to take back the arsenal and capture Brown and kill several of the raiders.

It was clear that Brown was only one man but he held hopes for many and that the guns and financial support had come from the abolitionists in the north. Buchanan did what was the right thing for Virginia and the slave owners and maybe the only thing he could do to stop reprisals. Brown had taken arms against his own country, it was treason but no more treason than that of which Lincoln's people spoke and incited. Brown had to die for it or surely there would be war.

Virginia and other slave states saw it as a northern attack more than just the actions of one extremist and the president was keen to show his disapproval. Everyone knew that Buchanan had also done battle with Brown over Kansas joining the Union as a slave state and he had lost. The president's loyalties lay one way only, which coincided with the direction of his duty. Brown had no chance. I suppose that had he waited 16 months and done the exact same thing he would have been hailed a great hero of the United States, maybe even one day he would have been president, indeed that outcome would have been most likely.

Brown swung[43] in December of 59 for his treason. By coincidence one of the witnesses to the

---

42 General Lee became leader of the Confederate forces during the Civil war which later in March 1861 ensued.
43 Apparently unknown to Patrick, Hugo had appealed to

execution for the State of Virginia was a 21 year old actor named John Wilkes Booth.[44] It is a remarkable thing I think that a skirmish which some say had nothing to do with the war, had included in it; Robert Lee, who later became the head of the Confederate armed forces, John Brown, the hero or the villain, and Booth, the assassin of the president who derided the Negro but freed him anyway because it suited him politically to do so.

I have I hope shown the landscape of early 1859 to 61 and apologise for the detail but it is clear that my world was changing dramatically. Often when one lives through great history one does not realise it. In the United States at that time however, no one could not have seen that history was happening. I was just 26 years old and comfortable, I had a good job and money and a home. Hanora had established her little school house and Margaret had grown into an exceptional beauty, though she was slow of wit and laboured unduly sometimes over simple tasks. She was just 12 years old but for the world a young woman. She assisted her mother in the school house, tidying and clearing away after lessons and preparing for the next.

Most weeks when I would return home, for it was 'home'; she would accompany me into town. On some days she would come over on the ferry and we would walk in the park and I would allow

President Buchannan for leniency on behalf of Brown in 1859 so was well appraised of the history.
44 Booth assassinated President Lincoln on April 15th 1865.

her visit the church next to the hotel while I waited outside. It surprised me greatly that Hanora would allow her to meet me in Manhattan and spend the whole day because usually she was most protective and even jealous of her daughter's time.

Margaret and I had closeness and she was my little charge in many ways; yet I had since Christmas noticed a distance growing between us. She would sometimes shy away when I tried to link her arm on our walks. I pretended not to notice but it hurt me and I could not fathom it as we had always been so close.

It was upon one of my visits that the matter exploded and shattered our three lives. I say three but it is clear that Hanora's life already was destroyed though she was oblivious to it. I have mentioned that in disposition she would go from down to up and sometimes she would stay one way or the other and other times she would fluctuate. More and more as time passed she stayed in her excited or her depressed mood and she was becoming a great worry to me.

It was early January in 61 and I collected Margaret from the house. I noted that Hanora looked tired and more untidy than she normally did but thought nothing much of it. Perhaps I should have noted it more. Margaret and I set out together but after just a short time she complained of the cold and so we returned to the house to find her a thicker coat.

We entered the front of the house and discovered Hanora with bundles and bundles of sheets of paper. When she saw us she tried to conceal what she was about but upon examination the papers revealed themselves to be hundreds of pages of gibberish. Numbers and letters and shapes written in black ink and lines between them and such things that only a mad mind could produce but certainly not comprehend.

In an instant she became like a she-wolf and she grabbed at the papers and screamed that I was not to look at them for if I did then a dark fate would befall all of us. Margaret I noticed did not seem perturbed by her mother's actions and I realised to my deep dismay that this was to her a common enough scene. Hanora threw a cushion in my direction and missed me but struck her daughter. Margaret winced in pain and realising a cushion could not inflict harm worthy of such an exclamation I drew her to me and exposed her arm beneath her dress and under garment to reveal severe bruising to its whole length.

I have accounted previously of this madness which seemed to afflict my Hanora and I concluded that this action now be some manifestation of the same malady. I resolved to co-operate with her and appease her and it was to that end that I agreed not to examine her papers. Margaret, who now disclosed to me that the workings of her mother's mind had for some weeks been deviant, drew me to the back of the house and into the kitchen.

'Do not concern yourself brother with her now; when she writes and draws she is quiet and at her least'

In just those words I could see that not only was Margaret considerably more than I had given her credit for being but that she had been enduring this situation for some time.

'But how long has it been so'? I asked urgently

'For all the time I can remember'.

I was utterly aghast. I had effectively left home when Margaret was just three or four and although I saw her and Hanora most weeks I did not live with them.

I asked her to disrobe so I might examine her damage and she refused, and blushed.

'I am not a child Patrick,' she said 'I am all but a woman, but I shall show you part if you promise not to examine me all'.

With that she turned her back to me and undid her garments. As she lowered her clothing over her back I was nearly sick. There were all manner of bruises of different hue so of different age. Several deep welts which had scarred sat across both shoulders and there were numerous healed and fresh burns, the shape of small circles. I let out a cry and threw my hand to my mouth to stifle it.

'You did not tell me' was all I could muster.

She composed her clothes and turned to me. She was not in the least sorry for herself.

'I thought it was normal… at least at first, I have known for some years it is not'

'But how ….' I attempted

'I have always had beatings, as far as I can remember but this past year or two it has become so much more… almost too much for me to bear Patrick'.

210

I was by now in tears, my mind was on fire with anger and with confusion and with pity.

'What do you mean?'

Only at this point did the pitiful creature burst forth a sob and a tear, she ran to me and I held her, enveloping her like a broken bird, as close as I dare without disturbing her wounds, some of which were fresh. She sobbed her muffled words into my chest as though they were her confession, not another's.

'She has told me of my beginning and of her hatred for me and she has told me of the snow and the bucket and of you stopping her'.

She stifled a sob and sniffed and continued as best she could. I wanted to wrap her up and protect her and make the memory of it disappear.

'She assured you would hate me if I told'. She then uttered the words which shattered what I thought was love and brought me to the realisation of what is love.

'I can bear the pain of the cigars and the whip and the holding down in water but I cannot bear the pain brother of you not loving me'.

In a moment, the girl I had always seen as a slow sister dragged along and amused by trifles and silly games became more to me even than my beloved Hanora had been. Something minutes earlier I would, have said was not possible.

'I will always love you my sister and it is my neglect which has allowed this to afflict you. I swear to you that no one will ever harm you again, lest I shall remove them from this earth'.

In the parlour Hanora was humming to herself and continued to busy herself with her insane scribbles as she rocked back and forth on her seat.

Margaret continued to tell me of her ordeal and as she did it seemed to lift a load from her; so I listened to how Hanora would sometimes bathe the girl and hold her below the water until she passed out. How she sometimes would not feed her for days and not allow her to change clothing and other things I cannot impart to you for they are too painful to recount.

The evening turned to night and I lit the lamps and made food for the three of us. Hanora refused to eat and behaved as though nothing was amiss and it surprised me that Margaret allowed her to brush her hair. I think perhaps that in her insanity she realised that her concealment of it was come to an end.

When both were asleep I made my business in finding all the documents and connections I could to our money and interests in the bank and what capers the demons in Hanora's head had indulged. I did not need to search for long and found a sum of dollars just short of two thousand and some gold coins. I later learned, mostly from her rantings, that she had become paranoid of the bank and removed our money. She had been making substantial donations to two churches in the area, tens of dollars at a time and from the ledgers from the school she was not now giving free places to every third child but to them all. In the 'income' column of the ledger instead for dollars and cents she had inked 'God shall provide'.

I found her Bowie and mine in its leather pouch and I found the stiletto with its groove and I found my old colt. I removed the three knives and the gun out of her reach and into my own bag. She had not apparently been inclined to use these things but who could say what travelled around in the tempest that was now her mind?

I looked in on them before dawn and Margaret was clutched to her mother in the fashion I had held her at night and it broke my heart. The task I had ahead was not going to be a happy one for any of us but it was one which must be done, of this there was no question. I had given Margaret my word and only one course could ensure I did not break it.

I took the horse from the livery nearby and fixed the trap and made my way to the Doctor's, who resided just a few blocks from us but who was old and struggled to walk any distance. He knew the family and had attended to most of Margaret's childhood aliments over the years. His granddaughter had been taught at Hanora's schoolroom for a short time. The Doctor was displeased to be woken at such an hour but the hefty payment I made to him along with explanation solved that. He collected his equipment; on the route back to the house he also brought a large fellow he expected might be needed.

We arrived back at the house before dawn and I made coffee and ham for the Doctor and his assistant. I had insisted that we wait for Hanora to wake of her own accord and that we not intervene in her sleep.

When she entered the parlour she was already dressed and she looked about, guessing what was afoot.

'What is this? She asked me harshly.

'Has Margaret taken ill?' Knowing it was not so.

'Margaret is well my love'. I responded, much to the surprise of the doctor.

I rose and taking her hand I guided her to the chair I had occupied. She did not resist and she adopted her usual graceful and beautiful manner but this lie was betrayed by the bags under her tired eyes, her untidy hair and the rags that passed for clothing.

I had requested the doctor carry out an evaluation and expected him now to ask Hanora some questions but it did not evolve that way. As soon as she had taken her seat Hanora let out a tirade of profanity the like of which I had never heard. It was as though she had a demon contained inside her which now had broken free. She began then to scratch at her own eyes and face and immediately she drew blood. The large fellow took up position behind her chair and grabbing both wrists stopped the harm she was doing.

All the time she kicked and screamed and cursed me for my betrayal and cursed the doctor and his children and the world. The doctor poured a liquid onto a cloth and he pressed it to her face, she continued to kick and writhe for a clear three minutes before the chloroform subdued her and her body relaxed.

As soon as it was done I took to the stairs and found Margaret sitting in bed. She was crying and I approached her and comforted her. I explained that her mother needed to be protected from herself and she seemed to understand and expressed guilt for wanting it so. For one with a slowness of wit she was very insightful. I suppose better than anyone she knew the extent of the illness and the danger it presented, not just to her but to Hanora herself.

She was taken that day to the New York City Lunatic Asylum on Blackwell's island[45], it was January 24th of 1861 and the news that day told of Georgia, one more state declaring its independence from the United States a few days before. Virginia[46] was next and a week later that State joined the others[47]. But I paid little notice on this the hardest day, so far, of my life.

Even in her madness I could see she was there, struggling to get past the demons and she maintained an element of her grace. A moment she would be there only to be pulled down again to the depths by whatever ailed her mind, and to be gone. I could not leave Margaret with her a moment longer and I knew that if taken from her Hanora would do considerable harm to herself. There was

---

45 Now known as Roosevelt Island
46 Virginia did not succeed to the Confederate States until April 17th 1861, five days after the war began.
47 Patrick's memory of events seems to be in error. In fact Louisiana and Texas both succeeded before the outbreak of war and before Virginia.

no option so in a way that helped my conscience but alas not my pain.

I approached my employer and explained the matter to them but lied about the nature of my 'mother's' illness and that I had to deliver my 'sister' to my family in Pennsylvania and they agreed to let me go for three weeks. In fact they were kind enough to pay me for the time. It was a generous amount of time because the journey was no more than a day by railroad.

The day before Margaret and I took the train to Pennsylvania I visited Hanora on Blackwell's Island and was greatly saddened by her predicament. She was no longer confined in the jacket but was subdued by medication. She seemed not to recognise me and her state had deteriorated over just a few days. At the time I assumed we had caught her in time but her disintegration was rapid and complete. Even so, she was Hanora and some part of her resisted the demons for when I leaned over her and kissed her on the cheek she whispered into my ear four words I can never forget;

'End my torment Patrick'.

Her words caused me to contemplate that the one thing worse than descent into madness must be the awareness, of the sufferer, of that journey.

15
TO PENNSYLVANIA

Typical locomotive in service in USA 1861

It's the evening of the 12th December 1883 and Patrick continues to write by candle light, its dark and he is alone. In less than 5 days he is to hang and his writing is becoming furious, and much harder to decipher. He seems to rush from the account of Hanora's confinement as if he finds it hard to recount, which is not surprising; it is however worth a little more consideration.

Diagnosing mental health issues is hard enough without trying to do it almost 150 years after the event, but it's worth trying to understand, if not explain what happened to Hanora. We know that she had endured almost unimaginable trauma before Patrick met her, losing her entire family on the coffin ship and in the quarantine sheds of Grosse Island and even before that. In Ireland she suffered some other difficulties at which Patrick has only

217

hinted. On top of this the assault by the convict and later the pregnancy. It is a wonder she was not totally insane long before she became ill? It is a measure of her exceptional strength of character that she did not succumb sooner.

Her very severe and almost catastrophic break down in 1848 at the birth of Margaret was by any measure a full psychosis, whether that was brought on by pre or post-natal depression is impossible to say but I do venture to suggest, given the recurrence of her very extreme mental health issues it is likely she had some underlying and or perhaps recurring problem.

Bipolar Effective Disorder or Manic Depression as it was historically known certainly was known of at the time, albeit by other names perhaps. Indeed over ten years before Hanora's confinement a French psychiatrist described a malady as "la folie circulaire", which translates to 'circular insanity' and he even characterised it as cycling from mania to depression. Incredibly, as far back as the ancient Greeks lithium salts were used to help treat depression and to calm 'manic' or 'excited' people. Lithium is now the main treatment for Bipolar.

I mention this because it seems that after her confinement Hanora's treatment, if we can call it that, was to sedate her and to leave her to it, in a bath chair by day and a bed by night. From Patrick's letters we see that from the time she was placed into the asylum she remained in an almost vegetative state, for years upon years. Of course Patrick might seem cruel to have left her there but as far as he was aware this was the best place and best treatment for her, what else could he possibly do?

We see also that Patrick was shocked by the conditions in the asylum but it is likely that he, in common with most other visitors, would have assumed the conditions were 'normal' for such a place, necessary perhaps. After all, what comparison did he have to make? Few spoke of the conditions and most who witnessed them were not in a position to do much.

Even now; who of us knows what is, and is not acceptable in the treatment of the confined mentally ill, or, to use the vernacular of the time; lunatics. The fact is that even by Victorian standards the 'Women's Lunatic Asylum on Blackwell's Island' as it was then called, was a horrific, cruel and terrible place.

Patrick would have been unaware while Hanora was confined that the conditions would one day be exposed by the efforts of a most remarkable woman named Nellie Bly (Elizabeth Cochrane Seaman). She came to the world's attention in 1887 some four years after Patrick was writing his letters.

Nellie Bly was a truly exceptional person and whilst the purpose of this book is not to recount her story we can mention some of her work as it relates to conditions Hanora and others would have suffered while in the hospital in New York.

Bly, almost unable to get work as a journalist at the time was offered a virtually impossible assignment; it was to get into the asylum and report on conditions inside. Knowing she would not be given any meaningful access she took lodgings in a boarding house and frightened several other boarders and the owner by feigning madness. As she had expected she was taken off to the asylum where she spent ten days, as a patient, recording the terrible conditions, in particular the brutality to and neglect of the patients.

After ten days she had all she needed and approached the staff to declare that she was not after all insane, she was a journalist compiling a report on them. Of course they returned her to her cell with all the other 'journalists' who also were 'not mad'. It took the intervention of one Joseph Pulitzer (of Pulitzer Prize fame) to have her released.

In October 1887 her exposé was a sensation. She followed it with a book and her efforts are directly credited with helping to reform the institution. As said; this is not intended to be an account of Bly's absolutely incredible life but there is one other thing worth mentioning, a coincidence; in 2019 almost a dozen previously 'lost' novels of Nellie Bly were discovered by David Blixt, and they are now published. Lost writings from the 1880s apparently are not so rare!

Unfortunate as Hanora's confinement was it was a catalyst in Patrick finally making his way to his uncle and aunt in Pennsylvania, which was unquestionably a better place for the child Margaret. A safe place for his ward, who by now was almost 13 years old. Patrick's intention was to return to New York and the Astor and continue his progress up the ranks, but as we see fate had an alternative plan for the 26 year old.

In the coming weeks he will meet his cousins and get to know them and become one of the family. He will use his hitherto untouched wealth to help them and he will find his employer less than happy to accommodate him, thus leaving nothing in New York for him but for his less and less frequent visits to Hanora.

(Fifteenth Letter)
Dec 12th 1883 - Newgate Prison, London

Dear Victor,

I have written a great deal today and it is late but I am in the flow of it so shall move quickly onto the days that followed Hanora's confinement.

We visited her often, both of us at first but later just me alone, and less frequently as the trips were hard and the visits distressing, particularly for Margaret. I continued my employment and disliked leaving Margaret alone in the house and soon determined a solution must be found. I wrote to my Uncle Manus and my Aunty Margaret and they responded swiftly with a telegram to the hotel welcoming and encouraging me to deposit, what was now my ward, with them for their protection and love.

Reassured and confident for her wellbeing Margaret and I filled two large and one small trunk with what we could. We both knew that we would not be returning to the little house that had been home for ten years or more. We sent two trunks of clothes and linen up to the Asylum for Hanora along with her books and a generous sum to ensure the possessions did arrive. Each time I visited I paid staff well to give her what extra they could. The place was hell and any little comfort I could bring her was at a cost. My only consolation was that she was safe. It was not much to ease my guilt and I had vague plans to one day move her to Pennsylvania.

Margaret and I harnessed the horse and loaded the trap and warmly dressed we made our way off.

It was Mid-February. I had no way to raise a child of 13 in the city and I knew that amongst my cousins in Pennsylvania she would be safe and cared for. It was very hard leaving Hanora and though Margaret and I pretended expectations of her recovery we both knew the best we could hope for was comfort and some degree of peace for her. I assured Margaret that once she was settled in Pennsylvania and I returned to New York I would arrange for Hanora to join her, and I meant it at the time. As we approached the railroad terminal we made busy with plans and preparations in an effort to draw our minds to the future and away from the past but with little effect.

We drew up at the train depot and an attendant appeared and took the large trunks from the trap and placed them onto a cart. I noted the beggars asking pennies from travellers. The first of them was a fellow of about Margaret's age dressed in rags and without shoes. I called him to the carriage and asked him to hold the horse for a while and offered him a few cents which he eagerly accepted. The other beggars noticed and moved on to the next traveller and the next after that. When we had taken the last of our luggage I told the boy that he now owed a horse and trap and he should use them to make his living or sell them and prosper from the profit.

He said nothing but as we walked away I looked back at him and he was stroking the beast's nose. I can never know what became of that fellow and I hope he made the best of his chance. I mention it not to enrich your opinion of me, it was not a generous act; the horse and cart were gone to us, I would have no use of them upon my return to the Astor and better some fellow have them than they roam the streets or go to dog meat and glue.

Although my Uncle Manus had by letter over the years petitioned me to come to him in Mahanoy City in the county of Schuylkill, and I certainly had intended that; I am not sure that I would have done but for Hanora's misfortune and my need to find a safe place for Margaret. The ten years in New York had passed as though they had been months, not years, yet in a strange way the sheds and my dispatch of the thug and the early days in the cabin seemed like a different life, not my life but that of another. As I remember these things from long ago and I write them down I wonder *does fate play a hand in all of our journeys? Did my encounter with Hanora and my love for her and all that I learned from her inevitably lead to where I now find myself? Was there really ever any choice?*

I was 26 and a man and I had secure employment in New York from which only disaster could displace me. I had money and I had a place in Pennsylvania for Margaret.

At the time I concerned myself only with these things and not much else; yet war was in the air, there was no mistake of it. No more States had followed the first seven to separate and talk of Texas joining them now seemed to quiet, almost as if to mention it as a possibility might render it a certainty[48]. I had little way to know that this was a

---

48 Patrick confused dates and States. Texas had already succeeded in early February 1861

calm before a storm which would pitch brother against brother and tear my adopted country to parts.

We were collected in Pennsylvania by my cousin John O'Donnell whom I had never met. He was a fine build of a man even at 16 years and he spoke gently and hugged me as though we were brothers and I immediately liked him. The only cousin of this part of the family which I had met previous was Manus, the eldest of Uncle Manus' children who was now 18 years and was not one year old when they left Ireland.

The trip from New Philadelphia station was long; a good ten miles and the road was rough and it was bitterly cold. Margaret slept behind us buried in blankets as my cousin enquired about my adventures and 'Ireland' which curious to me he referred to as 'home'.

It is a strange thing about the Irish that I have noted over the years; no matter how far they are located from the country of their birth or how long they have lived in another place, or what that place has gifted to them; they always call Ireland 'home'. This extends to the offspring too, most of whom have never set sight on Ireland let alone foot. It is a habit of which I heartily disapprove. Most of the immigrants to America at the time were rejected and starved out of their 'home' yet their new country had given them shelter, food, work and a future and a future for their children. It seemed to me to be ungrateful and stupid to not recognise such a place as home.

For my part of course I do not regard Ireland as my home, but I have that right more than most. It is where I was born and grew for my childhood but it never gave anything to me and I dislike my countrymen who suffered as I did and boast affection for the past and for the land that gave us nil. It seems to me like a child seeking succour from a parent who has beaten and abused it. Just as a mother might throw from its womb a sickly or deformed child so did Ireland chuck me; my motherland discarded me and I owe her nothing. America is more of a motherland to me now and it is more by way of regret than pride that my original 'home' is Ireland, as that factor is enough for an English court to decide the balance of my guilt.

As I recounted my adventures to John on that journey and now as I write to you it seems to me that much of my life in the early years is more like decades, not years; yet later the decades are as years, just as now in my cell the days pass too fast, as if they are hours. Time I suppose is relative to a man's place and predicament.

As I have said; I have clear remembrance of some things I have no reason to recall and no image of that which I perhaps should. The things which seemed to matter at the time they occurred do not matter much later and the small things taken for granted are now so important. How many times for example did I not return home from the hotel on my days off when I could; days I could have spent with Hanora at her best, days wasted, never to be regained. What I would not give for one of those days back and put to better use for the things that did not matter to me then but matter above all things now.

I am meandering, forgive me Victor, I have no time to edit this account so do indulge me.

John, who had trouble with the trap due to an injury to his left leg, eventually brought us to a small wooden house in the town of Tamaqua in the county where my Aunt Margaret lived with my cousins.

Uncle Manus, cousin Manus and John worked in the mines and it was normal enough for men to live next to the mine and wives and children further out, though Mahanoy City, where they lodged, was a clear 12 or 13 miles and 4 or 5 hours by trap and it seemed to me to be a very long way. It was faster by horseback but few owned such a thing in the area. My cousin told me that they made good money transporting goods and people on the horse and trap and it had more than several times paid for itself and they were considering purchasing another.

I remembered my Aunty Margaret from Ireland for they had lived on the land my father worked for a time. She had been baking and cooking all day for us. They all waited up for our arrival; and welcomed us warmly asking all about my adventures, some of which I repeated but most already were known to them by way of the postal service. I of course did not reveal the less savoury aspects or news of the vast amount of money strapped to my waist and how Hanora and I had come by it. I conveyed news of the Famine which they knew about; indeed my aunt had much news of the old place, of 'home'.

Manus had already told me by letter that my mother had survived the Famine but my half-sisters had both perished. Nancy, my sister had children now and lived in Ireland but not anymore in Gweedore.

Many people in the coal fields sent funds back to Ireland during that time and brought back relatives as Manus had tried to do for Michael and me and the rest of us. I explained the trickery of the boats which by then Manus had already discovered from his side and for which my aunty expressed her regret. I told her of Michael already by post and of the woman who cared for me and now I told her of Hanora's ills and my aunty regretted them and that they had befallen one who saved me and she assured me she would pray for her.

I dared not to ask that she not do that wasteful thing so I left it be. The multitude of holy statues about the house and the rosary strapped to her hip told me that this was a devout woman. I confess that in spite of wanting to love her I found this characteristic about her to be unsettling and I never did really like the old woman. She was one of those old ones who thought grumpiness and misery to be virtues. If they are then she was most virtuous; though she only ever showed me kindness in her own manner.

She and John complimented me on my fine clothes and my cousins joked that they would not do in the mines. Margaret seemed to enjoy the attention and it was not long before she had opened her trunk and Mary Anne and Ellen were trying on her clothes. Ellen although the younger of the two seemed the older and she was soon walking up and down the kitchen swinging her skirt until my aunt scolded her for her brazen ways.

It was a large family, Manus was the eldest boy at 18 years and I think the only one born in Ireland then followed John 16 years, Mary Anne 13, Margaret 10, Ellen 10, James who was 8, Bridget 5 and the youngest was Charles just 4 years when I first saw him. I learned later that along the way Aunty Margaret had lost two other children but I did not make enquiry to that.

The family did not seem wealthy but with Manus senior, Manus and John all working in the Mines, along with their taxi and delivery enterprise, they had a better income than most. John explained that he had broken his leg some six weeks previous and had no wage for that time but fully expected to return to work soon. He expressed his delight that I soon would join them in the work under the ground.

I was twenty six years old, had spent my last ten years mixing with the best of the land in my service to them and I had absolutely no intention of going into the ground, perhaps if the black stuff were diamonds or gold, but certainly not for coal. It took only a casual glance to see the bent over hard breathing and ancient young men to convince me that underground was not for me; I did not express that to my kin however.

War was on its way and like most fools I was excited at the approach of it but I had no notions which side I favoured and I had no plans to join it. Young men I suppose prove themselves at such times, but not this young man. My contemplations as to the reasons and facts behind the unsettling time came to me later as a realisation as opposed to before, and I recount matters only as I think them to have been at the time. I may be mistaken about much, but I was there and it is what I think of it.

I had no intention of going down a mine and less still of fighting a war. Though I had the vigour of youth I also had spent my life so far dodging death, surviving; putting on a uniform, any uniform... would not align with my like for life.

To the very best of my recollection I had no real preference upon which side had the better of the dispute but it seemed to come down to the Negros; plain and simple. I had heard the notions of Lincoln and they were confusing. If a man was to be free then surely he must also be equal? If not equal why free him? Lincoln's idea that one free man was not equal to the next free man because his skin was a different colour had become disagreeable to me; when I lent it proper consideration.

It was, by now, the end of February, I was due back to the hotel in New York and I longed to see Hanora again. In the last week of my planned visit my Aunt Margaret assured me that Margaret was already part of the family and I could see that it was so. She played with Ellen and Mary Anne and learned with them and she seemed to thrive. I sometimes wonder if her slowness was caused by her isolation and her confinement with Hanora and the troubles she must have endured. I shall never know but her slowness was not so easily detected when she was amongst my family and it is not an overstatement to say that she was reborn.

What mattered was that she was safe and happy and I had never seen her so content. Aunty Margaret had bathed her and seen the marks and she had approached me and I explained without detail that her mother was where she was and Margaret was safe and that was the end of it. She saw my pain and pressed no further. Until I wrote the explanations in my last letter to you I have not mentioned this to a living soul.

Regardless of the promises, sincere as they were, I wanted better for my companion than my family could in their present situation provide. I had sworn to little Madge; as she had become known to distinguish her from my aunt and cousin of the same name, that I would ensure her safety and security but I had in my mind added 'comfort'.

They were good people but my Madge was accustomed to a better life than that which they could provide in the place they had. It was with this contemplation that I determined to discover a better place for her and a better living. I approached the matter initially without regard for their feelings, pride or opinion. It sometimes is the better way.

John returned to work a few days before I was due to leave and I drove him to Mahanoy and was intended to return to Tamaqua with the trap late that day. John agreed not to inform Manus of my arrival in the town and took my word that I had good reason. My Uncle would have demanded to see me had I not asked for John's discretion; I wanted to conduct my business in private.

Mary Anne told me a few days before of a boarding house in Wiggan's Patch which had become available; it was just 2 miles west of Mahanoy. She told me that the family had an ambition to have such a place but would never have the means.

Renting a house in one town and lodging for three men in another meant they never seemed to get much saved. It was hard for any Irish to get property and mostly the better paid skilled Welsh Miners got the best of it. Very few miners were Irish; the Irish were classed as labourers and paid less.

She thought it hopeless but she loved the idea of it and her favourite game was playing hostess. She would listen for hours to my accounts of hotel life in the city of New York. I think she was destined one day to make the trip to that place.

It took only a little time to locate the agent after leaving John at his lodgings. The man took me to the place that same morning. It was a very large house constructed of painted timber with a chimney at each end and with many rooms and situated perfectly for the mines and travellers. There were similar houses in the patch but this was the best looking of them all, the largest and the newest.

By early afternoon back in his office we had signed and sealed the matter. There were some formalities to take care of requiring Manus to sign and some payments to make later but for a modest part of what I had around my waist the house was signed to Manus and Margaret.

The agent warned that the situation would cause some problems as there were others who were chasing the house. Those others did not have my means to tip the balance for their families as I had for the O'Donnell family. It was a place where my Madge would enjoy comfort and could prosper until I could get her with me. I had not pondered how to achieve this at this time and as usual, circumstance determined things for me.

I should mention that although for most of my life I have had more than enough; money has never mattered much to me. I suppose when one has enough then any more is excess and not really needed. This is I am sure a philosophy that only the reasonably well to do can have but whatever the reason, parting with such a huge sum meant absolutely nothing to me. It was not just because I knew Madge would be in a better place, it was just how it was. I have starved in my time and almost drowned and laid amongst the dead and dying on Grosse Island so I suppose having anything at all is a bonus to me.

It was late by the time I concluded my business. The journey back, in the dark, on roads which I did not know would have been too risky so I made my way to Uncle Manus' lodgings where I found him and my cousins Manus and John.

I was hugely relieved when my news was received well. It would be easy for the recipient of charity from a young upstart to take it bad but my

Uncle did not. Indeed he had referred to my father's kindness to him and Aunt Margaret and he thanked me in that spirit. My cousins hit me hard on the back in jolly excitement and we all made our way to a tavern not one street away.

I pressed the point that although the place was theirs that they did not own it and that payments would need to be covered, I also made it known as gently as I could that this thing was done for Madge. This I hoped would defuse the smell of charity and it seemed to do the trick as they loudly calculated incomes and expenditures from letting rooms as I drank beer with them ... and thought of Mr Micawber.

Little could I have known at that time that the O'Donnell's House at Wiggan's Patch would later be recorded as the place of desperate murders; murders sanctioned and paid for by the mine owners of Schuylkill County and caused by the damnable Pinkerton agency. But I shall come to that in due course.

The conversation in the tavern that night took a darker turn, towards the notion off war. It was no surprise because everyone was speaking of the troubles with abolitionists and the possible split with the South. One State[49] had split in December 1860 and in the month before I travelled to my uncle several more had declared themselves away from the United States.

It was my Uncle who seemed to lead the way in the tavern that night, at least initially;

---

49 South Carolina succeeded on December 20th 1860. The first state to do so.

234

'Another couple of weeks and Lincoln will be in the Whitehouse, then there will be trouble'. He started loudly. It was an invitation for other drunken opinion, as it always is in such situations. He struck the table making the tankards jump and spill and looked about for support; he was drunk.

I ventured to ask; 'will there be war Uncle'?

Others in the bar listening and in similar conversations cheer heartily at the word 'war'. It was then that I noticed one man who was silent; he was leaning on the bar and he sipped from his beer quietly... and listened, and watched.

Encouraged by the shouts for war Manus was emboldened;

'There will indeed be war lad, and who knows which side to be on for I know if there is war and Lincoln and his abolitionists win we shall be overrun by free Negros who will work for free or as near to it as they can'.

'So you would be with the slave states in the south'? I asked, less than sober myself.

'I would for the sake of our livelihood, I would'! He took a long swig and wiped the ale from his mouth with his sleeve..

'But....' I tried to interject, but he was on what I later discovered was his favourite topic;

'I hold not with imprisoning a man for his colour but these slaves are fed and housed and treated as good as any horse so why should we upset that matter'?

The others in the tavern roared drunken mob approval.

'A slave has value to his master so it makes no sense to say they are treated ill'.

John was clearly embarrassed, not perhaps at the sentiment of his father's words but more the slurring and drunken way he said them.

'But father if Lincoln does as he promises and sends them back to Africa[50] we would not worry about jobs'. Manus ignored his son and continued;

'The man makes promises he cannot keep and once unleashed the black man will run over us all. A man who will work for food alone will soon replace a man who demands wages and working rights.

The room roared again with drunken approval at my uncle's opinions; that is all but one. The man who had been leaning on the bar and listening now stood straight and stepped forward tankard in hand. He held up his hand and silence swept across the room as might a biblical tide.

He was a man of no particular stature or note, not slight but not large either; sporting a deep and uncontrolled black Goatee beard with anthracite black hair thinning away from his forehead. I knew not then but later discovered this remarkable man to be none other than Jack Kehoe. A man who one day would wed my Uncle Manus's own daughter, my cousin, Mary Anne O'Donnell,

---

50 *Lincoln never actually made such a promise but he did declare it his preference that Negros be returned to Liberia, voluntarily with payments. His extremely offensive and largely ignored views on Negros can be read in Appendix 1 and 2*

He spoke calmly, almost friendly, but make no mistake his words carried warning and not friendship.

'The Negro is a man first, before and above being a slave'.

He approached Manus and the room was silent, I looked at him and he returned my gaze and flashed a wink direct to me and smiled. It was a warm and welcome gesture; yet when he looked back to Manus his stare was brittle; he raised his voice, addressing the room through the one man to whom he spoke.

'Enslavement of any man is sinful and can only result in disaster. Yet here in a room of Irishmen, of all people I must say this'.

He paused and looked around the room but none will hold his stare. It was nothing less than fear. He stepped up to Manus and behind him and placed his Jug on our table and from behind took the larger man's shoulders in his hands and pressed hard. It looked a friendly move but was not.

'It's talk Jack just talk... what harm in talk'? I was sincerely shocked to note that my Uncles was clearly afraid of this man.

'No harm O'Donnell, from Gweedore, from the land of giants and of starvation and of typhoid and of brutality and evictions and enslavement by the English'. His words were caustic and hit hard. One man in the back of the smoke filled tavern shouted.

'Yes Jack, yes! And it was echoed once or twice by others.

'Ahh Jack I meant nothing 'Manus slurred, but Jack was not finished;

'We are a race of enslaved people, enslaved by the English, prevented from practising our religion, from owning land, from any rights….' He then spoke in Irish;

'Even denying us the right to speak our own tongue'; and he reverted to English as the room exploded in rapturous cries of patriotism.

'So we come to this new land where we think we are free, but we are not. We are the black Irish Manus, make no mistake about this'. Cheers and shouts continued and grew louder, and yet he continued;

'While the Black African picks white cotton for his enslavers we; the White Irish, pick black coal for our enslavers the mine owners. It is a matter of colour perhaps to some but to any man ever enslaved it is a matter of freedom'. Jack shouted the word 'freedom' and raised his jug spilling ale over his arm.

The tavern was in uproar.

'God save Ireland'! was shouted by many and 'God save Jack and the Mollies'!

Uncle Manaus shame faced bid Jack a good night and as I stood to leave this remarkable man came to me and thrust his hand into mine.

'One of us lad'?

'O'Donnell from Gweedore and lately of New York'. I proudly replied

'We'll see you again I hope", and he was gone, into the throng forcing new pints of ale in his direction and thumping him on the back.

The next morning I awoke in the lodgings with my first real adult hangover. I had drunk many times but never to such an amount as that night. Rough ale and smoke; I felt sick to my stomach and my head thumped. Uncle Manus assured me the only remedy was to drink a pint of ale with a raw egg and this I tried and vomited again. I have over the years discovered that the very best cure for such a head is the avoidance of drink or alternatively, its moderate use.

Somehow in the previous night's drinking I had undertaken to help move the family and tidy up the house at Wiggan's. I would not have volunteered sober but nor would I break my promise.

I posted a letter to my employer at Astor House explaining that I would need a further 2 weeks to conclude my business and I anticipated that they would receive the letter before I was due back. I let the matter out of my mind and soon put myself to the task of painting and cleaning and preparing the new house. Manus, John and I stayed in it while we improved the place and at night we drank ale and got drunk in front of a fire fuelled with anthracite. How they managed to work each morning is still a mystery to me.

When I look back, those few days were very good days as I got to know my kin. It was a strange time, Abraham Lincoln was effectively the president and alliances were complicated. Manus' boys were not my only cousins in the county and one part of the extended family were keen abolitionists. One of them was also named Patrick O'Donnell and he was roughly my age; his youngest brother Edward is in London now and is involved with the IRB as I mentioned.

A week after I was due back to work at the hotel I received a reply from them which Mary Ann had brought up from Tamaqua; I had not expected a reply and guessed its content before opening it. It was a telegram, the second I ever received. It said simply:

'Services no longer required, employment terminated'

Although I was comfortable in Pennsylvania amongst my cousins, whose new acquaintance I was enjoying, I very much valued my job in New York. I took the first locomotive back up the railroad to the city and petitioned for my employment to be renewed… to no avail.

While in New York I stayed at the same hotel we had stayed in upon our first arrival and in the same room. I journeyed to the asylum to see my beloved Hanora and though I had low expectations I was deeply shocked at her decline in the few weeks since I had left. She did not recognise me and the brief moments of clarity she had seemed to enjoy in the past were now gone entirely. She dribbled constantly and her chin had become sore from it. She was clean and calm and had no restraints. The place was terrible. There was some effort to care for her and they told me she had walks in the grounds but there was no way to tell.

I stayed only a short time because I could not bear the sadness of it. I again left a good sum for her carers to take special care but had no idea if they would or not. I did contemplate bringing her back to Pennsylvania with me but it was not a realistic thing. She could not travel or be amongst others in her state.

I wondered if she might be better dead as I journeyed south again to Margaret and my newfound family, in Pennsylvania.

16
TO PRESERVE SLAVERY

Confederates Open Fire on Union Cavalry - A. R. Waud.

Patrick's next letter takes him from a relatively peaceful life amongst family with a good fortune behind him into the unknown. He is afflicted by that thing which affects so many young men in general, young Irishmen in particular; the need for adventure, far from home.

We see how pretty soon that need to wander leads him into a predicament he had never really properly contemplated; namely into a soldier's uniform and heading on a troop train for action in a war in which he had no place.

Even if he knew which side had the better argument it is unlikely he'd have chosen to join either if he had stayed in Pennsylvania. By March 1863 the Enrolment Act (the draft) would have removed the element of choice and put him into the union army. He'd have been less than two hours' by troop train from Gettysburg, 4 months before that place saw the worst loss of life in any American conflict before or since.

The US civil war was a brutal conflict between the southern (slave states), the Confederates, and the northern (abolitionist) States; the Union. Of course it was about a good deal more, not least the changing economics of the developing country and the perceived decline in prosperity in the South compared to the North. Whatever the reasons for the war the result was catastrophic. Over 600,000 people died; some estimates put the figure nearer to 750,000; even with the lower estimate it remains by far the most costly of all wars for the United States. By comparison approximately 400,000 died in the First World War. In addition and in common with most civil wars, brother truly was fighting brother, father fighting son and so on. Indeed we now see that Patrick could so easily have been on either side.

Pennsylvania for example, as many states, supplied men to both the Confederate army and the Union so when the armies met, in Gettysburg, in south Pennsylvania, it was not just one or two kin who fought and killed each other, it was many.

Patrick's account of the war seems to be accurate and not in the least boastful, so it is probably reliable. He does not claim glorious battle after glorious battle, though he could easily have done that. When it comes to the heat of battle we see a frightened and confused man, not a hero. His account is sometimes moving and often horrific, not in the least self-glorifying.

243

US military archives show that Patrick signed up to the Louisiana 4th battalion on July 1st 1861 and they also show he was captured on Nov 24th 1863; these records exactly coincide with Patrick's own account in his letters.

His war was very far from over when he was captured as we shall see in his following letters but he would not pick up another gun in hostility for over 20 years', not until July 1883 when he shot James Carey dead on board the Melrose, bound for port Elizabeth.

(Sixteenth Letter)
Dec 13th 1883 - Newgate Prison, London

Dear Victor,

Last evening Margaret managed a bottle of brandy past the guard. I have hidden it; which is no easy task as there is little in here but a small table and a stool and my bedframe. Each morning I am required to roll up my bed and it is inside there and safe I hope. I shall take a good swig tonight in my bed after dark and save the remainder for the last day. That bastard Mullins would for sure swipe it for himself if he had the chance, or even pour it away to spite me having any pleasure or relief.

I think three more letters is all I shall manage but the more I write the more I have to say. It's early and still dark outside and I shall make a start.

Herein I propose to account for my part in the war. I am sure without me the outcome would have been the same but I can claim to have perhaps reduced the number of dead. There is much I would say before it and why I chose the side I did but I fear I cannot dwell too long there. Sometimes we make a decision and it is the wrong one and we are too proud or lazy or stupid to amend it. It is enough to say it was the wrong side that I chose, if such a thing can exist in a civil war[51].

Apart from Tennessee I escaped the worst of it; mostly by blind luck. It was not a glorious time for me, nor I suppose for any man caught in it but

---

51 Patrick actually uses the term 'War Between the States', a secessionist term.

245

given the turmoil, it was not as eventful as you might suppose. In fact a bout of dysentery in the spring of 63 in Virginia came closer to ending me than any gunfire or grape[52]. For the entire war I think that I never so much as wounded another fellow, though I cannot be absolutely sure; perhaps I hope it more than believe it.

I am not a historian and my account of the war is that of my experience, some is from memory and some I learned much later. I did not know at the time for example how close I had come to meeting my own kin on the field of battle.

Although I was armed and in uniform I spent much of my time attending to general duties such as building, moving supplies, cooking and so on. Only a few times was I in the dirt; most notably in Tennessee down near the border with Alabama and Georgia. I shall come to that.

It seems to me that when the Confederates fired on Fort Sumter[53] it was more of a trick by Lincoln to get them to attack and then claim his war on the south was just a reaction. It is how I see it now though at the time the details did not trouble me. My sympathies were at the time were confused and partly, not firmly with the Confederates.

Lincoln brayed about slaves and freedom though he hated the Negro and would send him abroad given the chance. He was cosy with the mine

---

52 *Anti-personnel cannon shot, small lead or iron balls.*
53 *Attacked on 12 April 1861 by South Carolina militia and surrendered by the United States on the 13th. Generally considered to be the commencement of the US Civil War*

owners who paid the immigrants, my cousins included, almost nothing and kept them in poverty and the cities were overfilled with slums of poor, diseased and desperate people. That was the North. At least in the South a slave ate every day and had a roof and warmth. To me they seemed better off than many white folk in the north. The notion of freedom is nonsense if your belly is empty. Freedom to me is being able to eat and to sleep in comfort and to live the next day and the next after that.

Before I joined up there was great talk of conscription[54] in New York and in Pennsylvania. Though I had my opinions in favour of the South they were not strong enough for me to take up arms but for sure I would never fight for the North. I had no wish to shoot other men or be shot at, in fact other than heading down a coal mine with a candle on my head I can think of little else I would prefer less to do. The idea of being told what to do by someone of superior rank and inferior sense also did not sit well; on reflection I would have made a very poor slave.

I concluded that with the possibility of conscription Pennsylvania was not the place for me, so I decided to travel west to seek my fortune and for adventure. Many of my compatriots went west at the time to avoid the coming conflict. The only thing keeping me in Pennsylvania was Margaret. I

---

54 *The Enrolment Act did not in fact come into law until March 1863 and had provision for substitution and commutation. Patrick therefore would not have been conscripted even as late as 1863, if at all.*

knew I would return to her and also knew her to be safe and happy. She was content when I entrusted her wellbeing to my cousins, who were I suppose indebted to me. John was especially fond of Margaret and I was happy to see this. He was three years older than her and she looked to him with great affection, as an older brother.

So it was in late May or June 1861 that I set out seeking my fortune. I was too foolish to realise that I already had exactly that around my waist and in Margaret but I was filled with adventure and stupidity.

I travelled into Ohio mostly by train and then to Kentucky, a state which seemed to me not to know which side it was on. As I travelled I saw more and more that preparation for war was not confined to one or two places, it was every place.

I took the Ohio River in Kentucky west until it turns straight south and becomes the Mississippi. I remember little of the journey as each night I played cards and drank and each morning I slept till noon.

I have to say women have never much taken my interest but at each stop some came on and some got off, unaccompanied and painted and smelling fine. I had thought to trying my hand with one or two but for some reason I never did find what they had on offer much more interesting than a good cigar and a brandy and the company of a gay[55] young fellow or two.

I am not a gambler and I am ashamed to record that by the time our steamer arrived in Baton Rouge

---

55 *The Reference here to 'gay' certainly would not have today's meaning.*

I had lost all but $200 of my fortune. It made me sick when I thought of the house I might have got for Margaret and me with that sum, and how we might have managed very well and how we might have brought Hanora down to us and had a good life. I had spent over a month travelling like a lord and eating and drinking like a pig. I often ate until I was sick and I still do overfill but the food was rich and the drink too was heavy so I was bloated out, my belly pushing hard at my trousers.

When I stepped off the boat in Louisiana I had my colt, 21 rounds, my Bowie, $200 dollars and the clothes I wore. I was glad I had at least kept Hanora's ivory handled knife in Wiggan's Patch because surely I would have lost it otherwise.

You may from this account conclude that I was not a great traveller, not at that time; nor was I much with cards. The gentlemen at the tables had bought me liquor and flattered me and taken almost all my money with their skill at the game. The smoky women had leaned over and brushed against me as they did the other players, and we were too stupid or too drunk to see it for what it was. I have since learned of these pairs and how they fleece the young and the ambitious and that is their living and they are very keen to it indeed.

I found lodging in a place off the main street and spent a few days licking my wounds. I was pleased to use my French and though rusty and unpractised I soon collected the local dialect and made an impression on one or two, or so I thought.

249

The saloons were full of rowdy recruits in their new grey uniforms. Several drunken nights ensued, ending in a night of cards and drink and a morning of regret where I found I had lost my last dollar, my colt and the Bowie. Half-drunk, on the first of July 1861 I walked into the recruiting office in Baton Rouge and signed up to the Confederate Army. They promised a few dollars a week and food so I would not starve. I was assigned to the Louisiana 4th Battalion, and by September I was on my way north and east to Virginia with my new comrades.

Being a foot solder carted by train, boat and on foot across the vastness of the country is not exciting and heroic. Most days I remember I was hungry and filthy and my companions were a mix of innocents and ruffians, I am unsure which I preferred, or liked least. I lost almost quarter of my body weight in the first year and whilst I started out overweight and could afford the loss many of my companions were not so well fed and could not. Some, like me, had joined for a meal a day and a pair of boots and they suffered greatly. Many fell ill and died before they saw Billy[56].

Along the way we stopped at one place and another and seemed to be more a building crew than an army. We fixed rail track and in one place, heaven knows where; we helped to build a bridge.

Eventually sometime in 62 we arrived in Virginia, I had not yet seen a Yankee much less fired a shot. I spent a good while building defences along the Occoquan River and helping with never

---

56 Billy Yankee, later shortened to Yankee, Blue Coat etc. were pejorative terms for Union Soldiers.

ending supplies up till early 63. I was told this work was to blockade Washington but it seemed a pointless exercise to me given Washington was connected to Pennsylvania and all the north by train and land.

There were scraps with the Union trying to come down into Virginia; Blackburn's[57] and Bull Run[58] and other attempts by the North to gain more ground in the state but nothing much in late 62[59] and early 63 that I know of. I was never in the thick of it and I spent most of the time transporting supplies up the line. It was like that, some fellows I knew saw the whole war without so much as a shot. It seemed unlikely I would get a chance to meet a Yankee in Virginia and to be honest by then being shot at seemed to me better than doing nothing.

The nearest I saw to action that part of the war was looking for food and rations and horse stealing from anyone we came upon, regardless of side. Every time any real excitement was to be had I seemed to be out of it cooking and cleaning pots and moving things about, which was a never ending cycle of a task. For just over two years I did nothing but travel build, hump, dig holes and cook slop. I

---

57 Battle (Skirmish) Blackburn's Ford July 18th 1861
58 Battle of Bull Run July 21st 1861. Patrick's use of the Union's name for several battles suggests he learned of these from others in the north after the war. Bull Run for example was known by Confederates as Manassas.
59 Patrick seems to have either forgotten or not known about Battle of Fredericksburg or the second Battle of Bull Run, both occurring late in 1862 in Virginia.

was all for a run to the north and the place at Wiggan's Patch by 63.

Strategies and solutions were always the chat over food at the end of each day and it might surprise you to know that the enlisted men knew much better how to prosecute a war than did Lee or Grant, or so we all figured. I had intended that comment to be jest but when I look back on the dead and the sick and the destruction and butchery maybe it is not so funny, maybe it is true.

I was wrong, that opportunity to make acquaintance with the enemy, as the world now knows, did arise and when I eventually heard the account of it from my fellows I am certainly glad that I, by another twist of fate, missed it.

We knew something was brewing when in early June we started to move north, along with other divisions. By mid-June we were in northern Virginia and had swept what little resistance there was aside.

On the morning we were to cross into Pennsylvania, June 27th I think; I awoke with dreadful pains in my guts and I could not stop defecating. I passed pints and pints of what seemed like water and I shortly became delusional; it was dysentery.

It was July 10th when I recovered in a hospital in Charlottesville. The place was filled with ghosts of men and it reminded me strongly of the sheds of 47 back on Grosse Island. I was a bit more than skin and bone, but not much; and the nurse, a beautiful southern belle whose name I cannot recall told me I was lucky to still have body and soul united.

She told me also of our attack on Pennsylvania[60]. Although I knew what we had been doing I was surprised Lee would not be content to hold Virginia and look for some sort of agreement with the north but he did not.

I re-joined the army some two weeks after that; I was reasonably recovered and well fed but underweight; I found myself in another division than my own 4th. Reinforcements, of which I was now one, seemed to go wherever needed. Some regiments 1000 strong were down to 250 men. Gettysburg had been a slaughter and had gained nothing; a massacre on both sides.

All the expectation was that the Union would push down into Virginia and our capitol[61] and we were to be ready but they did not. It surprised most when a month or so later thousands of us from various regiments and divisions under the control of Longstreet[62] were sent west. The war was heating up in Tennessee and Bragg[63] was in need of reinforcements. By this time I had no idea what regiment or army owned me; I knew not one of the men around me and all except me had seen serious work on the battlefield and I wondered did it show on my face.

I confess that I felt a fraud having missed all action on the way to Gettysburg and the battles themselves due to illness. Though, looking back, I

---

60 *Gettysburg battles from July 1st to 3rd 1863.*
61 *Richmond was Confederate Capitol at the time*
62 *Lieutenant General James Longstreet. Confederate.*
63 *General Braxton Bragg. Confederate.*

concluded that because as many in our army died of disease as they did in battle, I had my own fight in a way.

The journey west was a mix of arduous and boring; long periods on the train punctuated by forced marches between stations where the rail gauge did not suit the particular engines. I believe we must have stopped every time the rail gauge changed and one or two stops involved long marches and a river crossing or two. We did not go directly west either, first we went south for a good 200 miles I would say and then west. In total I estimate maybe 800 miles of track.

On the good side we were greeted at every stop by southern women with flowers and food and kisses. Word had gone down the line that this army was on their way to save the day in Tennessee and no end of well-wishers came along at every stop. We ate well and drank well the whole way.

The long periods between stops allowed me to contemplate my situation. It needed not much thought to discover that I had been a fool; not just to travel off in 61 to seek a fortune I could never find, because I already had it, but why had I chosen either side of the war. The generals on both sides were butchers and the soldier's lambs to the slaughter.

During our time in the north of Virginia I saw many Negros, free men and slaves; sent back down to the South to be enslaved. Many of them were not slaves and they protested but their protests were met with abuse and pain from my comrades. None seemed to care for these poor souls and I was most ashamed that I had taken up with such people. What was I to do now? I had been dealt my hand. The little I had learned of cards on the river boat told me I must play the hand dealt, even if I was the dealer.

I also thought of my second cousin who also is named Patrick O'Donnell. He is six months older than me. He had joined the 71st Pennsylvania so fought for the Union. Indeed a good deal of the men in Schuylkill County had sided with the Union and must have seen action at Gettysburg. The idea of he and I facing each other in battle had not occurred to me until I was bound west on a train though it was obvious enough a possibility. He was wounded at Chancellorsville in May 63 as it happens so like me did not get to Gettysburg though I did not learn of it until after the war. Stonewall[64] took a bullet in his arm in the same battle and that had finished him[65]. I like to think they were brothers in arms[66] though in fact it is likely they never met. My cousin Edward O'Donnell, the one skilled in dynamite, had joined my side though I never knew this till much later, long after the war.

Most of us arrived in Georgia on that train from the east on the 19th September; at what became known as the battle at Chickamauga[67]. It

---

64 Thomas Jonathan "Stonewall" Jackson served as a Confederate general
65 Jackson was shot in the arm accidentally by his own side and died of pneumonia several days later.
66 Unlikely as Stonewall fought against the Union
67 An area on the border of Northern Georgia and

had begun the day before. The generals might have known what was going on but no one else seemed to. What I recount about the situation is mostly from what I saw with my own eyes and testimony I have heard since from others on both sides who were there.

All summer the Yankees had pushed Bragg's boys back and back down from Chattanooga, hardly a shot fired. On the 18th September Bragg stopped his retreat and countered; the Yankees had a front 40 miles wide and it was weak and Bragg saw an opportunity, so he took it.

Hundreds were lost, mostly ours. Grape and cannon and musket had reduced some regiments to fewer than 100 with little chance of replacements. That first day, which I did not witness first hand, ended in a standoff, but it stopped the Yankees pushing down.

My own account starts on the 19th September, I think it was the 19th but could have been the next day. We were ordered to take and hold the Lafayette Road to the south of the main battle. We met almost no opposition as we went across no man's land towards the road and the wood beyond. As we reached the road and what I thought was safety suddenly a barrage of shots hit into us, and then another and another and another. Men fell to my left and to my right, in front and behind. My initial belief was that we had run into thousands, but it was not so; there were maybe 200. We had run into the Hatchet Brigade[68]. We were armed with muzzle

---

Southern Tennessee
68 The Lightening Brigade, Founded and led by John

loaded rifles and they had seven shot Spencer repeaters, we had no chance. I dropped to the ground and stayed there until dark and after.

The sweat from my labours trying to kill my fellow man and stay alive myself had left me soaked and now the freezing night air numbed me. All around was the hideous cry of tormented and injured boys who wailed in pain or sobbed for their mothers. No one can understand war until they are in that place where I was; in a field next to a road in Georgia or Tennessee or in a churchyard in Gettysburg or anywhere one man inflicts his opinion on another by way of violence.

One poor fellow lay within a yard or two. He sobbed and groaned and begged to be finished. He was shot all out in the belly and on the shoulder. Two bullets for one fellow and none for me; I supposed perhaps he took mine and his. In such situations the mind plays the fool, mine is no different.

He had no prospect of living past the night but I was bound to help him. He had after all taken my bullet I supposed. I managed to pull myself towards him and though the Yankees must have seen my efforts none fired on me. Perhaps they did not see; I prefer to imagine they did and that even in this desperate place humanity still existed.

I reached the boy and lay next to him and tried to warm him with my body, cold as it was. His head lay on my chest and he calmed, comforted by the

---

Wilder. Also known as Hatchet Brigade. Mounted Infantry armed with 7 shot Spencer repeater rifles.

companionship and warmth I assume. I was
exhausted and I slipped in and out of sleep. I don't
know how long I lay there and I don't know when
he passed away but when I awoke it was still dark
and the boy had breathed his last.

I observed my comrades making their way over
the road. No shots were fired and it seemed the
Hatchets had withdrawn northward in the cover of
night. I had no complaints about that, any man with
a 7 shot repeater against my old front load shooter
was welcome to take his leave as far as I was
concerned.

I have no recollection of proper sleep but
suppose we must have taken some. By morning we
had regrouped with the others of Longstreet's men.
We fed well for breakfast and it was late when we
moved. I know that the Yankees were holding north
of us but they had left a gap to their line and we
headed for it. We breached the line with upwards of
ten thousand men, three full divisions.

Before us was a wide and open space with
thousands of Yankees flooding north. We let them
have it with cannon, shot, and musket and even
chased them back into range and shot at them again.

There were a number of stragglers left below
Horseshoe Ridge to the west of Lafayette Road; we
captured some and others who had run out of
ammunition smashed their repeaters on the rocks
and made off in a scatter north. We captured
thousands and sent them south as prisoners and I
learned later that as much as 4,000 men died in
these few days, the majority were Confederates and
that is to be expected, we were after all attacking

better armed men who ran out of bullets to shoot at us. It's a funny thing but in war the victor often spends more life getting to victory than the defeated do giving it up.

The Yankees made their way back north to Chattanooga in Tennessee and entrenched themselves there. We besieged them and blocked their only supply route[69]. The blockade was effective and the Yankees were reported to be down to quarter rations, hardly enough to keep anyone alive let alone a fighting man. At one point Longstreet with one division managed to destroy 800 wagons of supplies but Sherman[70] soon had the line opened again and the siege was breaking. Both sides needed the town because it was the intersection of so many railroads.

To the South of Chattanooga was Lookout Mountain, which we held. It was a high hill with a flat top from where we could see the entire area and all of Chattanooga itself. To the east was a Missionary Ridge, a long ridge running north to south. We also held this firmly. Along its top we had men, including me, dug in over its entire length overlooking the town. Men were also entrenched along the base of the hill along its length giving us two defence lines if the Yankees tried to break free. Anyone could see we were too thin spread but we had a good advantage in our position, or so we thought.

---

69 The Cracker Line was a supply route into
Chattanooga during the siege in Nov 1863
70 Brig General (later General) William Sherman

We'd expected the Yankees to break west and try to escape over the Tennessee River or past Lookout Mountain to the south but instead they came at us direct up Missionary Ridge. The first attack came in late November and was mainly Yankee reinforcements from the west. They attacked Lookout Mountain and the battle went on into late evening with many shots but very few casualties. It had seemed impossible to take but Bragg withdrew from that position in the night.

The next morning Sherman came from the north and took a small hill[71] on the very northern tip of Missionary Ridge and started up its long narrow spine. In the afternoon of the same day the Yankees in the town attacked the base of the ridge. We were supposed to pick them off from our position on the top of the ridge but as they approached they were too far off and as soon as they got close to the foot of the hill, they were out of sight. The hill had a sort of first ridge and then a second top ridge. We'd made the error of positioning ourselves in such a manner that the Yankees could climb a considerable way up the hill before we had a line of fire on them.

It was chaos, many of our soldiers in the trenches at the foot of the hill turned and retreated upwards and in the confusion were shot by our own boys. Union soldiers flooded up the hill and over onto us while at the same time they attacked the ridge from north and south. I got off one shot and reloaded before two Yankees approached from my

---

71 *Goat Hill*

right, I threw my weapon down and raised my hands and thank God neither shot at me.

One lifted my gun and shot its charge into the ground and threw the gun clear, he had me drop my pack and told me to remove my coat, turn it inside out and put it back on. I did this and he then instructed me to walk north along the ridge. I walked past dozens of Yankees expecting the next one and then the next to shoot me in the face but they almost ignored me.

As I walked along the ridge I was joined by more and more similarly partly disrobed comrades. Some were angry and bitter and cursing their luck for not getting more Yankees; I was just relieved not to be a target any longer and happy I had not killed anyone. The fellows who captured me seemed perfectly agreeable given the situation. Eventually I got to the end of the ridge and off the mountain. We were gathered and marched to Chattanooga where there was already a good thousand others[72] in the same predicament.

---

72 *The number of Confederate prisoners taken at Chattanooga was between 4,000 and 5,000*

17
ESCAPE

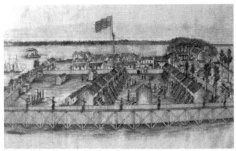

*Prisoner of War Camp, Johnson's Island, Lake Eerie -
1863.*

We can see that Patrick had no particular leaning for
one side or the other before hostilities. He seems to
have had some sympathy with the views of his
Uncle Manus and other miners afraid to lose their
jobs if slavery was abolished but he was also
influenced by Jack Kehoe and his theories of how
all men are equal regardless of colour or creed. It's
easy to see how an Irishman who had escaped the
oppression and servitude of Ireland may have some
empathy for the enslaved Negro. Patrick had to this
point only briefly met Jack but the man had a
profound impression on him.

Lincoln's theories served only to cloud the issue
insofar as he clearly believed and freely espoused
the theory that the black man was an inferior
species to the white man but at the same time he
did not believe they should be enslaved... just
transported to Liberia.

Naturally enough Patrick's feelings about slavery were confused, as were many people's feelings at the time. When it came to joining the war circumstance really made his choice for him; he did not join the confederates for any moral or political reason, it was a simple necessity. He does not say so in his letters but he quite likely had it in mind to run for home (as many did) as soon as the opportunity arrived.

Had there been a Union recruiting station in Baton Rouge (an unlikely thing) at the time he signed onto the Confederate army he would have been as likely to join them as the Confederates. Apart from anything else the pay was better. By 1864 a Confederate enlisted man got 11 dollars a month whilst a Union soldier of the same rank received 13 dollars, unless he was black, in which case the freedom-loving but apparently not equality-loving Union under Lincoln paid just 7 dollars a month; half the salary of the white soldier for the black soldier, who, incidentally, risked almost certain torture and possible execution if captured by the Confederates.

What is becoming clear is Patrick's own realisation that he was fighting for the wrong side but had to make the best of the situation. Thankfully for him he missed Gettysburg, which was the most costly engagement of the entire war with some 40,000 casualties and 7,500 deaths over three days between July 1st and July 3rd 1863. He did as we see however end up in the thick of it at Chickamauga in September 1863 where a total of almost 4000, lost their lives; probably the second bloodiest battle of the war. Just nine or ten weeks later he was captured in the much less bloody but strategically vital battle of Chattanooga.

The battles of Chickamauga and Chattanooga, although about two months apart, were really one extended engagement; the first and most bloody part being Chickamauga, a distinct victory for the Confederates (though they suffered the heavier casualties) who forced the Union back north into the town of Chattanooga. This was followed by the siege of Chattanooga and the eventual breakout by the Union in late November 1863.

Patrick seemed almost relieved to be captured. He had no appetite for war from the outset but after his experiences in Tennessee we see he is determined to avoid further conflict, yet, as we shall see he wastes no opportunity to escape.

As his next letter shows Patrick's arrival on Johnson's Island prisoner of war camp is a mistake, a very fortunate mistake because it was the camp with the lowest mortality rate of the entire war; normally only officers were housed there. That is not to say he or they enjoyed luxury, it was rather better than the sort of camp where enlisted men were housed but still not a picnic, particularly in the winter time, surrounded by a frozen lake Eerie.

Housing of prisoners during the war was a logistical nightmare. Neither side were able or willing to spend resources on welfare; thus conditions were often terrible. Andersonville, a Confederate prison in Georgia housed 45,000 men during the war; an incredible 13,000 of them died there, that is almost 10 a day for the entire war. Almost 11 percent of all prisoners held in the north died and 15 percent in the south perished.

Both sides made efforts to reduce prisoner numbers, and thus losses, and prisoner swaps were made regularly, with combatants undertaking not to re-engage until an opposing prisoner was released in exchange. So; when one prisoner each side was released they both could re-join the war. No one can refute the logic but equally nor can anyone not be disturbed by it. The system was called paroling, a word now used for releasing prisoners early on trust that they do not offend again. The practice, which kept prisoner numbers, so prisoner mortality down was stopped when in 1863 the Confederates refused to treat black prisoners the same as white when it came to parole. That single decision probably cost thousands of lives.

Escapes and attempted escapes were, as a result of the diabolical conditions, an everyday event. Over 100 men escaped from Libby Prison in Virginia in one attempt. Many soldiers died in what were more often than not all but hopeless attempts simply to get away from the atrocious conditions. Better to die running than starving.

Ironically several prisoners were shot at and injured in Johnsons Camp for apparently trying to escape when they were doing no such thing. On September 23rd 1864 Johnsons Island was hit by a tornado which wrecked parts of the camp. Rebel inmates ran in panic in all directions with several going over the broken fences, the guards equally confused shot at them. Patrick makes very brief reference to the event in his next letter.

For prisoners who had wealthy relations willing to send in money, and many did; things were marginally better. The camp had a store and many guards were susceptible to bribery. So when we read Patrick's account of his meeting Robert Cobb Kennedy and the man's keenness to escape we have to wonder why? The chances of survival and of success were minimal at best. There seemed to be more driving Kennedy than just the desire to be free.

(Seventeenth Letter)
Dec 13th 1883 - Newgate Prison, London

Dear Victor,

I fear that I have spent more time on my account of the war than I had intended. I am aware I have but four days left; which is more like three as the last morning I plan to have my brandy drunk down and it will not be a day to me. Sometimes as I write the thought of what is to come goes from me and when it comes back to my mind it does so sudden and as if it had never been as it is. It makes my heart race fast and I sweat even though I am cold.

Though these letters were intended to convey my story, and that alone, they have helped pass the time more easy than otherwise I would have without them.

I had just two sights of battle in that shameful war and came unharmed from both. The first was victorious and a few months later the tables were turned at Chattanooga where I was taken captive by the Union and the next part of my tale begins.

Although the war occupied me for 4 years and more and took me into my thirtieth year I remember it mostly for the young man who died beside me at Chickamauga; a boy who would never see twenty years, let alone my rich thirty.

When I think of it I imagine sometimes a dispatch rider coming down the long approach to a fine house on a plantation someplace in Louisiana or Alabama where the mother of the place stands on the door step waiting for news of her son.

267

She receives the news of the boy's death and she cries out in pain and lost hope and alongside her, the slaves in the field do not rejoice in her grief but they share it and they too wail for the imperfection and cruelty of this world. I wish strongly I could visit that plantation and comfort that mother by telling her he died with a friend and was comforted at his last and maybe give her a cut from his hair or some such thing. Alas there were too many such mothers in the North and the South and it would have taken a great army to do this task; but first the butchering would have needed to end.

After we were taken at Chattanooga we were rounded up and held in the town for a few days, no shelter and only a morsel of food was given to us. We were boarded onto trains; enlisted men and officers together. The badly wounded stayed behind on stretchers in tents but didn't seem to be getting much attention. Some of our boys were allowed to tend them but medical supplies were in short supply. The Yankee wounded were taken away and only the hopeless left as far as I could see.

I can't say I blame our captors and I am not sure I would share my supplies if the tables were turned. We'd been killing each other a day or two before and before that we'd starved many of them for months with our blockade of the town. The town's people were allowed back on the second day and they mustered in to help in what ways they could. They were southern folk thank God and tended to us as kindly as they could before we were loaded onto the trains.

Anyone able to walk got on board regardless of how badly they were hurt. We didn't trust the Yankees to care much for a Reb[73] in a stretcher, so the best chance was on a prison train heading north or so we all figured.

We travelled north through Tennessee, Kentucky and Ohio. The cars had slatted sides with one long sliding door. We were stuffed in like cattle but unlike cattle we were not fed or watered. It was terrible.

When travelling west on the troop train from Virginia in September I had thought the trip was bad enough; that had been in the summer and too warm but we stopped regular and fed and drank our fill just about every few hours. The trip north could not have been more different. It was winter now and colder the further north we travelled.

We begged the Yankees for some sort of thing we could place up against the slats because when we got going the icy wind cut through the cars like a frozen knife. They took no pity on us at all. I don't make that a criticism, they had their pains just like us and no one but the generals, gun makers and undertakers enjoyed the situation.

We were only let out when we had to change trains and sometimes the cars could not come through on account of the track so we'd sit in

---

73 *Confederate soldiers were known by the North as Rebels or Rebs. Confederates disliked the name as they did not consider themselves part of the Union so could not rebel.*

frozen huddles for a while sometimes, just waiting for the previous trains to return and collect us.

Some of my fellows died right where they sat, blood froze wounds, eyes open and faces blue. We took their coats and their britches and vests and their boots and left them, some still sitting upright as we could not stretch them straight on account of them being frozen solid. It was not disrespect and had I died I would have been glad to warm another with my own clothes.

I'd walked past similar human corpses as a child and maybe it came easier to me. I ate nothing of them but was I admit tempted and had any other man proffered the notion I would have been the first to support it.

To my best knowledge no Americans ate each other in that war; though maybe they ought to have and if they had there would be more of them walking about now. Of the two or three hundred prisoners that set out in my group from Tennessee I suppose we lost a good 20 before Ohio.

What do you do with hundreds of, hungry, sick soldiers, when you can't feed and water them; any of whom might set upon you at any time? It was late evening when we arrived at one more stop; we were well into Ohio and it looked like my question would be answered.

We were unloaded and the officers were called out from the ranks. Most stepped out but a few I knew to be captains and such stayed put, they must have been thinking what I was thinking; maybe they were going to be shot, and then it occurred to me, there being so much fewer of them than the enlisted maybe it was the enlisted fellows going to get it. Just as I thought it so it seems had the few officers holding position amongst the ranks. They now stepped forward, along with a few of the enlisted men thinking the same and so pretending about their rank.

It was dusk and in the crowd and confusion I simply ducked down and made off in the half-light behind the station and towards the outside of the little town. In a few hundred yards I was not spotted though I entirely expected to be. My confidence grew as I entered through the rear of a dwelling and lay under a bed. I waited as I heard the train whistle and slowly pull away. I looked about me for a weapon in order to dispatch any occupant who might detect me. I was thankful that no one came; not for my sake but for their's for I would surely have despatched them, man, woman or child.

I have never been grateful to God before or since but assume that the household were at church, the bell from which I could hear in the distance.

I found some clothes which I stole; a good stout coat, a stick and a cake of bread, some salt meat and a flask. It was better food than any I had tasted in months and I ate as I travelled. I made my way from the place and went west first and then south. I had no idea where I would land but I fancied my chances of survival better than back where I had been.

I knew that in Ohio there would be no love for a Reb on the run and I was more likely to be shot than caught but I was following my instinct and that

271

had not let me down before. With every step I took I knew I was further from imprisonment and closer to freedom. It was some hours before I sat under a large oak; exhausted I fell fast to sleep.

I knew if I was stopped or questioned I had a good chance pretending to be a Yankee. My accent was correct and there was no reason to suspect me to be anything other than a poor traveller. As it happens I was not stopped and as I made my way early the next morning I was certain I was free. In the afternoon I tried my hand at stealing again. I broke the latch of a small house, the last in a row in a small town, I entered cautiously. From nowhere without a growl or a bark appeared a hound the size of a small donkey. He pinned me to the floor and I am sure was about to take my neck in his vast jaws when the twin barrel of a gun was pushed into my forehead. I confess I had never before been so pleased to see the end of a gun in my face.

I was not the first to run along the route. Two and three man Yankee units roamed the area with the sole occupation of finding runners. I was soon back at the station accompanied by these fellows. When I arrived it was obvious that the same split of prisoners was happening to another train load. Without being asked I dropped amongst the officers and was reminded by a Yankee guard that I was lucky not to have been shot. He accompanied his comment with a swipe to my head with the butt of his rifle.

I was happy not to be shot of course and just as content that no one had thought to search me as I still had about me my stash of food from the first place I had robbed.

So it was that a day and a half later in early December 1863 I arrived at Johnsons Island[74], along with a hundred or so officers, almost 250 had arrived from Chattanooga over just two days. None gave me away as enlisted and knowing my grub would not last anyway I spread it amongst my fellows and this did not harm their opinion of me. I enjoyed several good slaps on the back for my spunk and getting one over on the Yankees.

So I began almost ten months of confinement, boredom and starvation. For me and for most the boredom was by far the worst of it. I had seen madness come and go and come again in Hanora and I saw the same thing in several of my fellow inmates.

There is little else to say about imprisonment on Johnson's Island. It was harsh and cold and as I say, the worst thing was having nothing to occupy a man. I was fed, though not nearly enough but from accounts I later heard it was considerably better for me than it was for Yankees held in the south. Many perished around me; mostly they were already sickly and some wounded. One man who had a leg removed carried on for three months before he gave way. He stank so bad from gangrene that our whole shed was almost ruined and I have a strong feeling that one of us might have helped him along so as to rid us of the stench. I shall not judge that, I am, I suppose, an eater of men so have no place

---

74 *Military Prison based on a small island on Lake Eyre.*

above any soul who does what must be done; indeed I admit to being glad of the end of Tom. That was the unfortunate fellow's name and while my account might seem to many to be harsh and unfeeling I do know he was someone's son and I remember him from time to time; mostly his smell.

It was not easy but for someone of reasonable health and a strong will a year or even two was manageable. Some had been there since 62. The ones who did best were the ones able to bribe the guards.

Some of the prisoners were well connected, West Point[75] and such, and even though they had nothing to give they had plenty to promise. Letters were carried out and favours returned by well to do relations and contacts. I could not bribe because I had absolutely nothing, the river boats sharps had my loot. However, partly on account of my deed with sharing food one or two real officers included me in their luck, so occasionally I ate as well as some and better than many.

Escape had been on my mind for some time, in fact it was the talk most days amongst the prisoners. The difference with them was they wanted to escape and head south and serve again. I wanted to escape and head north to Canada and away from it all. I wondered if my old cabin was still there and if Murphy would be home to welcome me back. I was a fool to even wander from Canada.

It's a funny thing but of all my time before, during and after the war; the things which most convinced me that the Confederates were wrong

---

75 *Military Academy for Officers*

was my few months in Johnson's island prison. We had lots of time to discuss the war, its reasons, philosophy and attitudes.

I found that the southern gentleman soldier had a peculiar and contradictory personality. They were almost always much more agreeable than their northern counterparts. Yet their obsession about keeping the Negro enslaved seemed to be the only thing more important to them than their hatred for the North. When it came to the issue of slavery all manner of logic evaporated and they became impossible. It is one thing for a society perhaps to agree and enable slavery of Negros but to base an entire economy and philosophy on it must be, to any rational person, utterly insane.

Although I joined the Confederates and I had some sympathy for the white workers who might be affected by freed slaves heading north, it had never really been an issue I had contemplated much. The fact is that I was penniless in Baton Rouge and joining seemed at the time to be the best thing for me if I wanted to eat. I must say that by 1864 I was much ashamed of ever having fought for the South, I still am.

I was where I was however and my plan was first to survive and if the opportunity presented itself to escape, or to wait till the end of the war and to return to Margaret and my cousins whom I had not seen or heard from since 61.

Escape was not impossible, early in 64 five or six men escaped in one go while the lake was frozen. Two came back rather than freeze and one was caught, the others got away.

Getting to the edge of the island was easy and the land to the north was within reach; it was just a mile or so across water and I could swim 3 or 4 times that on a bad day. The problem was that when not frozen the water was near to freezing and the few who had tried had gone under less than half the way across.

It was during one of these discussions about escape that I first encountered Robert[76]. He was a most engaging man and I took to him and believe he took to me immediately upon our acquaintance with each other. Kennedy was a quiet and serious man yet had a good sense of humour. He was popular amongst the others and not just for his charm; he had made a still and managed to cook up moonshine, which he shared with the hut. It seemed to be a skill endowed to most southerners and ours was not the only hut with such a device. The guards turned a blind eye because it kept us busy and quiet but Robert did seem to drink more than was wise. In fact he was drunk most days.

Apart from knowledge of making spirits he had knowledge of a vast variety of things from politics to engineering and to nature. I always enjoy the company of such men but they are few; this fellow was everything I could hope for in a companion and friend. He was two months younger than me and we shared other similarities. Like me he had not taken a wife and saw no reason why he should. Like

---

76 Robert Cobb Kennedy. A Confederate soldier, most
Likely an agent 1835 - 1865

me also he was in the Louisiana's though the 1st I think, not the 4th. He confided he had been kicked out of West Point for being found indiscreet drunk in the company of another cadet.

I never discovered his rank but he was obviously an agent of some sort and later when I witnessed men of high rank follow his instruction I knew he was no ordinary player in this game.

I told him of Margaret and Hanora and of my life and how if I could escape I would make for home and be done with the war. He had responded that it was of no use thinking of the result of an escape without first discovering a means. It was sound advice. He revealed that escape had occupied his contemplations greatly and he had concluded that the coldness of the water was the critical issue in any attempt.

He suggested that if the body could be kept mostly out of the water on a board or some other flotation then the distance could be managed but any man in wet clothes, even if he got to the other side would not last an hour. I suggested that waiting for the lake to freeze would be best and avoid getting wet and most escapes had been done so, walking across; but he was of the opinion that by the time the lake froze the air would be too cold for any success; the key he supposed was to swim fast and to have help from the outside to dry out and warm up upon landing.

Robert waited for my disappointment before revealing that he had managed to get a letter sent and the guard who took it had been paid handsomely by those outside and situated in Canada. It was not possible for a two way correspondence but he had asked that on the night of the 4th October warm clothes and soup and guns and horses for three be waiting at a spot. He was confident in his friends and so was I, though I had no cause to be. When he announced that I was to be one of the three I shook his hand wildly and hugged him. *Here was a tale I could tell my grandchildren* I thought.

After dark that October night he and I made our way to one of the sheds we had discovered to have several loose boards. There had been a terrible tornado just a couple of weeks before and it had taken down almost all the fences, most of which had only been replaced in a rush and not properly. The third man had lost heart and with no time to find a replacement it was just the pair of us.

'All the more food for us on the other side' is all that Robert had remarked, though he was clearly very disappointed.

We removed the planks and made our way under the wires and to the shoreline. Here we broke the planks in two. They were no more than 12 inches wide but a good inch thick and they floated well. Robert started to strip and instructed me to do the same. He suggested that if the dry clothes were not there we would freeze to death but if they were we should not risk being weighted down in the water. It seemed a choice between bad and worse so I did as he said and stripped to my long johns.

I lay atop my two planks which I pressed together and held and the icy water went into my underclothes and the coldness hit me. I pushed off and started to stroke forward with both arms. As I did one of the planks slipped up to my side and I lost it. I was half sunk already but the one remaining board was working to hold me up a little. To my side my companion cut the water gently with his arms so as not to splash loudly and be detected.

As we made distance from the shore we both made more vigorous strokes, partly to move us more swiftly but also partly to shake the terrible, terrible cold from our limbs. As I looked ahead to the blackness I could see a flicker but had by then no honest expectation of the plan working.

'Head for the lamp', he could almost not speak for the chatter of his teeth.

We were barely half way when it became too much for me. I needed to move and to pump my blood so I pushed the board away, and swam like the devil, one arm over the other and as fast as I could, only lifting my head occasionally to spot the light ahead and grasp a breath of air. It worked. I did not warm by any means but I felt my hands and my legs again and I was slipping through the water, leaving my companion in my wake. In a moment he too was swimming for his life in the freezing water.

It was not a long journey and though my hands and feet and legs were like blocks I was not now in fear of failure. I knew I would make it.

We landed, me moments before him and we scrambled up the muddy bank and lay flat, shivering and freezing but daring not to move on until we were sure we were at the right place.

We approached the spot and as Robert passed the oil lamp he picked it up and we were sure we were at the place. The fire in the little clearing was just embers but next to it was cut kindling and in a moment we had a good flame. We stripped naked of our soaked underclothes and rubbed heat into each other. I tried to unwrap one of the three bundles we found next to the fire but my fingers would not oblige so I held them over the fire and the numbness turned to blinding pain as I thawed.

Robert opened the sack, from it I pulled clothing and I dressed as fast as I could. The roughness of the dry clothes was welcome. My friend also now dressing passed to me a hunk of cheese and I devoured several chunks before returning it to him.

Robert's friends had done us well and amongst the goods left for us we found commutation[77] papers for three. These would guarantee free and unhindered passage anywhere in the north. The horses were tied nearby, three of them, saddled and ready to go with full bags. There was even a colt pistol and money left, US and Canadian.

We knew we could not stay to enjoy the fire. We emptied the bags from one horse, removed the saddle and set it off. It was not thirty minutes between us landing and we both mounted, dry but cold and heading for Canada.

The journey was uneventful and we were not stopped or asked our business. In a strange way I

---

77 *The Enrolment Act of 1863 had provisions for commutation at a fee of $300*

had hoped that we would be so to derive the satisfaction of using my new papers of freedom.

It was not until we were in Canada that I discovered why my new friend had taken such an interest in me and determined to have me accompany him on his escape.

18
TO BURN NEW YORK

Robert Cobb Kennedy 1864 (The man who would burn New York)

Patrick now seems less concerned with writing about his situation in the cell or about Margaret and the jailers and concentrates more on getting to the end of his story. It's just 3 days to his execution.

His escape from Johnson's Island with Kennedy seems to have been a mixed blessing. Kennedy was keen to get back to the war but all Patrick wanted was to get back to Pennsylvania, via a stay in Canada to see out the war if necessary. Regardless, their escape was spectacularly risky and had the outside help not been where it was when it was they certainly would have perished in the cold or been captured.

Almost coincident with the escape Jefferson Davis (the Confederate President) was keen to open a 'northern front' against the Union. He believed that there was significant support for the South in some of the northern states. He was probably mistaken and whilst there were many 'Copperheads' (democrats opposed to the civil war who wanted a treaty with the Confederates), they were not likely to take up arms against the Union, though they did oppose the Union draft vigorously and were heavily involved in riots in New York in early 1883 when it was introduced.

The riots only 7 months earlier led to 120 dead; Lincoln ordered in the troops, fresh from Gettysburg and they restored relative quiet to the city but it remained a volatile situation even several months later.

As part of these efforts Davis commissioned Jacob Thompson, (who was before the war the United States Secretary of the Interior) to head up the Confederate Secret Service from Toronto; so the Confederates had a substantial body of spies and activists operating out of Canada, known as the 'Confederate Army of Manhattan', and Patrick joined them, albeit reluctantly.

Thompson developed a plan to attack New York and placed a man named Robert Martin in charge with another Confederate named John Headley as second in command. Martin had been a colonel and Headley was a lieutenant but as spies the ranks were disposed of; this might account for Patrick being unsure as to exactly what the command structure in the group was. Including Kennedy and Patrick there were 8 in the group.

The goal was to disrupt the Union by attacking New York and stimulating riots and panic across the city. The conspirators hoped the panic might re-ignite the anti-drafter riots from the previous year.

Martin and his comrades hoped to achieve the unrest by setting fires in various places around the city, hotels mainly, 11 of them. It seems to have been a strange plan which probably had little hope of being successful. Not least because, unlike Patrick several of the conspirators were very unfamiliar with New York and fine hotel establishments and they stood out rather badly. A Southern drawl in New York in war torn USA was a noticeable thing we should assume.

The initial plan was abandoned when General Butler and 10,000 troops were brought into the city on the 7th November. There was no chance of any rioting. A very amateurish second attempt was made later but like the first it too was thwarted by an informer.

What is obvious as we read Patrick's account of events is that one of the hotels to be burned was Astor House, and thus we perhaps have an explanation for Patrick's hostility to the plan.

(Eighteenth Letter)
Dec 14th 1883 - Newgate Prison, London

Dear Victor,

My new friend Robert Cobb Kennedy was an agent for the Confederate States, as I had suspected and he was not alone. In Canada I met with other such men. Their task was to upset life in the north by damage to rail and other mischief. I would have run but my only escape was south and to go there meant crossing the whole of the Union. I was stuck and I waited for my chance to escape these mad men. That is what they were; they were obsessed with destruction of the North, not with winning the war.

As November approached Robert told me that my use to the cause was my knowledge of New York City and my ability to go about the place unnoticed, in particular some of the hotels. Many of the agents working with him and making mischief from Canada had southern accents and were easy to spot and aroused suspicion amongst New Yorkers. They also had no idea how to comport themselves about the place.

I did not inform him at the time but I had absolutely no intention of working as an agent. Agents when caught were hanged if they were lucky; if unlucky they were tortured and then hanged. I had not survived the war this far to have my neck stretched for some pointless last effort for the slave states.

This was not a feeling I expressed to him but I was already alert to possible escape and now more so; not from the Yankees, but from the blood thirsty and embittered lunatics I now found myself amongst. Those same people with whom I had thrown-in back in Baton Rouge in 1861. I was aware that a dissenting voice in such a nest of madmen might well earn a slit to the throat so I played along in my part as best I could.

The band consisted of about eight to ten men who were sent up to Canada by a general in the Confederacy who must have known the war was lost but who would inflict murder on northern civilians and innocents anyhow as he saw it had been visited upon them in the south. The leader was a bitter man named Bob[78], I was not given his rank or his surname, I assume for reasons to do with security. He spoke constantly of killing northerners and was obsessed with it.

They left it till the last before revealing the plan to me and it was a terrible and wicked thing. Not only was it a plan to set fire to the city of New York but it was to be done not on soldiers or even officials, it was to be done on the people in their hotel beds as they slept.

Here was this convivial and agreeable gentleman with a kindness and warmth I had enjoyed casually speaking to me about the best ways to spark a fire in a hotel bedroom so we could burn Yankees in their beds and hopefully relight the draft riots of 63, which saw almost 200 dead.

---

78 *Colonel Robert Martin.*

Worse than this and the final thing to convince me I must attempt to thwart the plan was that a principle target was the Astor House Hotel. The very place which had taken this boy and grown him into a man and fed him and where I had welcomed good people and their children and put them into their rooms and where now this madman supposed that I would be content to burn them alive or allow it to happen.

The idea was to set fires in the bedrooms of the finest hotels and run. The hope that the fires would spread and start riots seemed to me to be fantasy. It was not glorious and it could not have worked. To cause the deaths was not necessary for the conclusion of the war was near as anyone could see. It was pure revenge by the lowest of creatures.

I was tasked early in November of 64 to travel one day to Broadway with a man named Headley. A detestable man of huge self-opinion, but who was in fact a lowly beast like the rest of them; bent only on revenge for atrocities they had incited in the first place. He had boasted to me once in drunkenness how he had serviced numerous blacks on his uncle's plantation. When sober he attempted to revert to being a gentleman and retract his sickening admissions but he was what he was and he disliked me for I saw it.

My task on the visit to New York was reconnaissance and to plan for our attack which was to take place on November 8th. It was the date of the election for President. Robert and the others knew I had worked in the city in hotels but no one had ever asked which so when I volunteered to enter Astor House and check for routes to the rooms Headley had thought nothing of it and agreed to do the same at another hotel.

It was fortunate that he did not accompany me because immediately upon arriving I was recognised and greeted warmly by my old friend the doorman, the very same with whom I shared a room. I approached the manager and asking him for pen and paper relayed to him the plot as I wrote it down. He assumed me a northern agent and I did not divest him of the notion and knowing my name would be no secret I signed it correctly on the note. I urged him to spare no moment getting the note to the authorities and he, puffed with vigour and importance, assured me he would do his duty.

A brandy was brought to me and good wishes given as I left. I could not get out quickly enough as several of the staff were coming front to wish me luck and to cheer me. My story was overheard and spread within the hotel like the fire itself was intended.

I am certain he did exactly that which I asked of him because a day or so later news arrived that forces had been moved into the city to spoil any possibility of a riot, whatever the cause might be.

The plan as originally set was abandoned by the gang. Even my lunatic companions knew that setting fires without the possibility of wider revolt by then was pointless. It seemed the plans were ditched and we laid low in the houses of sympathisers for a spell.

A week or two later we heard of Sherman's destruction of Atlanta and Bob ordered us to resurrect the plan to burn New York. There is no question this was just plain revenge. On the evening of 25th I found myself back in Astor House, this time with Headley, setting fires in two of the rooms. I was watched closely by him but managed to alert the staff and the fires did no harm. In fact there was not much damage done in spite of us setting fires in several hotels[79]. The authorities were ready for it and so were the staff, thanks to my warning.

Robert did his hotel then as usual got drunk and having some phosphorus left he started another fire in a museum[80] where over two thousand people had been. By luck no one was hurt, by more luck he escaped.

That night we made for Toronto and none of us were caught, which given the fact that Robert was three parts drunk and so were one or two of the others is something of a miracle. The group did not disband and within days they were talking of freeing a train load of Confederate prisoners and other wild schemes which seemed more than pointless to me. It was not hard to escape after this as the situation was chaos. I stole $120 dollars from their funds and made a dash. I regret only that I could not have seen Headley's face when he discovered it.

---

79 St. James on Broadway, United states hotel, St. Nicholas, Lafarge House, Belmont Hotel, Tammany Hall, The Metropolitan, Lovejoy's Hotel, New-England House, The Everett, Hanford Hotel
80 Barnum's Museum

I made my way by train and was stopped on the border, arrested and taken to a police station in the city. I was questioned by a colonel and I made no attempt to conceal anything. I told them that I had been a Confederate and had regretted it and told of my escape with Robert Kennedy from Johnson's Island and my time with the Confederate terrorists in Toronto. I also told that I had been trapped with them. The Colonel listened and wrote and assured me I was going to hang. I requested that I see a more senior officer and he laughed at me;

'You are an enlisted man in the Confederacy and I am a colonel in the Federal Army' He pointed to his shoulder.

'You should be interrogated by a sergeant and no more' he grunted.

'Then why do I have the pleasure of your company colonel?' I asked. He stuttered and thought to say something but did not.

'I am sir the person who brought to you the intelligence which stopped the destruction of New York'. I perhaps exaggerated but everyone knew an informant had prevented disaster.

'How can I know that? Anyone could claim it'

'Take me to the Astor now, it is no more than five miles from here, better still bring the manager and show me to him and ask who wrote the note of warning'.

The man paused, it was clear he was aware of the note and to whom it was given. I took advantage of the pause.

'I have urgent intelligence the delay to which will cost Union lives' I paused and looked directly at him, the guard at the police cell door shuffled uncomfortably.

'Shall you be the cause of delay sir or shall you fetch in front of me a man of general rank capable of understanding the importance of this?'

He looked at me for a moment and I held his gaze.

'Damn you man' he shouted and stormed past the guard out of the room.

I did not wait long before a brigadier-general entered the room. He was smoking a cheroot and offered me one;

'No thank you' I said, 'it's a filthy habit'.

'For a man with a noose near to your neck you seem pretty damn sure of yourself' he said in an unmistakable southern drawl.

'Am I in the right place?' I said and he laughed.

'I'm a busy man, what you got to say for yourself booy?'

I told him how I had warned the hotel and made the note for the authorities and he clearly believed me, I could not have known the detail otherwise. I told him also of the group working from Toronto and their names, as best I knew them. I told him of the plan to take a train load of prisoners and though I did not know the details he acknowledged it was useful stuff. He was keen to know about Headley and Bob, who he told me was Robert Martin but most of all he wanted to know about Robert Kennedy.

I told him all I knew and when we had finished he explained that he had to hold onto me but my actions so far had saved lives and likely to save more and he seemed genuinely grateful. I made no pretence at heroism and explained I was doing what I must to keep body and soul in one. Before he left he stood and shook my hand and ordered the guard to see to it I was fed.

I was transferred the next morning to Fort Lafayette in New York Harbour. Enlisted men were not as a rule held there, it was reserved for officers and spies, they knew I was not the former so I presume they thought me a spy and spies in the war had very short life expectancy. My main fear while there was that word of my treachery, because that is how it would be seen, would escape and the inmates would do me in before I was hanged.

As it was, my fellow prisoners left me be, and I let them be. Most just wanted the war over and to go home. I formed the view that had these senior men any notion of what the war was to be, they would never have prosecuted it in any way whatsoever. They would have found another solution.

Each day came and went and no one came to see me or question me. I made the acquaintance of my fellows but kept my head low and my opinions lower. There were several spies and all seemed to know that some things must not be spoken.

One fellow in particular interested me, his name was Pryor. He was a strange and very handsome fellow who frightened me at first but later we became friendly and though I spent only a few weeks in that place we became close. This man I learned had held the rank of full general in the

Virginia Cavalry. Yet he gave it up and re-enlisted as a private and apparently did so just to spy. It was extraordinary that such a high ranking man should of his own choice drop to enlist. I would have died of concern if I knew then what I know now. He knew me to be the informer on the New York Fiasco and on the failed train job. One word from him and I would have been killed. I know later he renounced the Confederates and became a Union man and even a New York Supreme Court Judge.

You will think it incredible Victor but I saw Pryor not two weeks since. He was advisor to my Legal team here in London. After so many years he saw my plight and remembered our brief friendship in that hellish place and he came across the ocean to help me.

Robert Cob Kennedy was caught trying to get to Virginia in January 1865, just a month or so after my incarceration. They brought him to the same place but I never got to see him. He confessed in bits and pieces to the New York business and they hanged him on March 25[81]. I think that of all the gang involved in that evil work he was the one who deserved least to hang. I would gladly have pulled the lever on Headley who prospered after the war with his lies, or on Bob or the others. Robert was the best of them but I still ask myself what kind of man sets a blaze in a theatre full of people?

I did not have to wait until the end of the war to be let free. The very next day after the hanging the general I had met when I was captured came

---

81 The last Confederate to be hanged during the war
293

and asked me to agree to be paroled. He came in person and he need not have and he again thanked me and shook my hand. I felt a fake as all I had done was for the preservation of my skin and not the benefit of any others. He had asked for my assurance that I would not return to the Confederates to fight and he might as well have asked if I intended jumping into the Hudson with a weight around my foot. I signed a paper to this effect and he gave me two dollars and a coat.

I arrived back in Wiggan's Patch about ten days before Lee surrendered and I slept for three days straight. Each time I woke to turn or to piss Madge was cuddled up to my back, her warmth was indescribable. I swore I would never again venture from that place.

19
MINES, UNIONS, AND MOLLIES 1865

Avondale Mining Disaster September 6, 1869, (Harper's Weekly illustration)

It's obvious that Patrick had a certain fondness for Kennedy, though he could not reconcile the friend with the man who would have burned alive hundreds of people in a theatre. Apart from Patrick, Kennedy was the only conspirator captured, and Patrick, due to his actions was not listed as part of the Toronto group.

Martin and Headley escaped hanging simply because they were not caught. Kennedy had to swing given the crimes he had committed and due to the very ill advised and comprehensive confession he gave. He was after all a spy and it took little to persuade the Union to hang a Rebel spy. He was also the last confederate soldier to hang during the war.

It is well known that the New York fire bomb attack was foiled by an informer and that informer remains unknown. Patrick's claim to have been that informer is not only plausible but most likely to be true. His motivation seems partly to have been his love for the hotel he called home for 10 years; would it possibly have been a different case had Astor House not been a target? Who knows?

A fascinating coincidence also is that whilst in la Fayette prison Patrick met Brigadier General Roger A Pryor. He was not at the time a Brigadier General because he had given up his rank to re-join the Confederates as an enlisted man; a scout and of course a spy. He later became a Judge in the New York Supreme Court and incredibly travelled to England in 1883 to help defend Patrick (unsuccessfully) in his trial for murder.

We see they met, and Patrick mentions this but he does not say anything about their relationship. Why would one of the most senior judges in America, who spent time in prison with Patrick, cross the globe to defend him, an enlisted man, a relative nobody?

Of course by the end of Patrick's trial a vast sum had been donated by the public, over £1 million in today's money so they could afford to pay a good lawyer; but why Pryor? There were plenty of others available.

In his 19th letter we see Patrick at last returning to his cousins in Pennsylvania; he recounts events that occurred from 1865 to 1875 and provides an understanding of the turmoil in the area during that period. We can see that he spent some of that time mining but mining clearly was not for him.

It was an exceptionally eventful time in the coalfields of Pennsylvania; starting with trade union unrest and culminating in murder and mayhem. To understand what was happening while Patrick was away and upon his return we need to understand a little about the background.

For several decades' immigrant workers of many nationalities flocked to the coal fields of Pennsylvania. Life and conditions were hard but work was plentiful. Primarily these immigrants were Irish, Welsh and German, mostly the former two nationalities. Hostility existed between the workers and the mine owners but also between the nationalities; in particular between the Irish and the Welsh workers.

The Welsh, coming from a mining country had mining skills; the Irish, but for a very few who had worked in the mines in England had no such skills. As a result of this almost all the skilled miners were Welsh and the Irish worked as labourers, on lower wages, and often for the Welsh miners. Consequently there were regular fights and disputes between the two groups but these were almost never fatal. Saturday night brawls and such like, often fuelled by alcohol.

For a long time the miners were unrepresented but a trade union; The Workingmen's Benevolent Association, was formed in 1868; inspired and supported by an organisation known as the Ancient Order of Hibernians. The AOH was (and indeed continues to be) an international, peaceful, fraternal Irish organisation; members being Irish or of Irish descent and at the time exclusively Catholic. Its aims were to promote Irish values and culture. During this time relations between the communities were less volatile, probably because the Benevolent Association helped improve pay and conditions for all.

Pay could always rise and fall depending on the fortunes of the industry, the war for example brought high demand for coal and all the workers, miners and labourers benefitted from pay increases and improved conditions on some fronts.

After the war coal prices slumped from 3 dollars to under 2 dollars a ton and as a result various mine owners dropped wages, laid people off and life became very hard. Inevitably this led to disruption and a battle between the Workers Association and the mine owners. One owner in particular was determined to kill the Benevolent Association, his name was Gowen; he managed to buy most of the pits in the area and those he did not buy he could control because he happened also to own the only railway in the region. It was illegal at the time to own a railway and a mine but a blind eye was turned to this powerful man's activities. If any other mine owner disagreed with him he could effectively close them down by refusing to move their coal.

By 1875 and after an elongated and dreadful strike the Benevolent Association was all but destroyed.

Of course all this was a recipe not just for discontent but for some it was a reason for violence. Here enter what became known as the Molly Maguires.

The Molly Maguires or Mollies were a group of mine workers, almost exclusively Irish who took it upon themselves to take action against the mine owners. Ostensibly a labour movement affiliated to the Ancient Order of Hibernians but inclined to use retributive justice outside of the law; a secret Society with roots in rural Ireland during the 18th Century.

For most of this period Patrick worked in taverns and by now had re-made the acquaintance of Jack Kehoe, who was husband to Patrick's first cousin, Mary Ann O'Donnell, so a sort of cousin-in-law if such a thing exists. Kehoe was also known to be the 'king' of the Mollies.

(Nineteenth Letter)
Dec 14th 1883 - Newgate Prison, London

Victor,

I have but three days before they hang me and I am writing now most of the time as I am desperate not to leave my story incomplete. I hasten therefore to the time between the war and my return to Ireland. It was a time of violence in the Pennsylvanian coal mines and of terrible injustice but also, for me, in part, a time of calm where I escaped the mines and kept my cousin's husband's tavern for him.

I left Schuylkill County, Margaret and my cousins early in 1861 and did not return until the closing days of the war in early 1865. When I left I had a healthy bundle of dollars and a need to travel and to see the world. Upon my return I had the clothes on my back and nothing but bitter regret. I scold myself for saying 'nothing' for I had Margaret and my cousins, who were more than nothing. I'd seen more death and destruction than is fit for any man and though many had suffered more than I, it seemed to me that I had borne my fair share. Fair that is for any fool who would seek war.

It was a turbulent time in the country; the president was shot dead a couple of weeks after I arrived back at Wiggans Patch and several Confederate generals had held out for a time but no one really had the stomach for any more fighting. I was glad to see the end and I cared nothing for the rights or wrongs of it and I could not even recall properly why I had taken any side, let alone the wrong side.

While the country endured the turbulence of the time which is well recorded and spoken about we in the coalfields had our own disruption during the war and long after it. In order to inform you of the experiences and the things I saw I must inform you a little of what was happening to my family back in Pennsylvania, while I was off being shot at by my new countrymen.

Whatever the future decides about the past and the story of the Molly Maguires I can tell you that violent reaction is always the result of oppression and injustice. I am making no justification of it; I am saying only how unrest is borne. Without injustice violent objection cannot be conceived because there is no reason or need of it.

The mine owners were fiercely opposed to any sort of labour representation but in spite of this could not prevent the Ancient Order of Hibernians from organising and making attempts to represent the mine labourers and their families. The order mostly consisted of good people opposed to violence but amongst its ranks were a few men of less noble ideals. They were to become known as the Molly Maguires.

When in Ireland, my father had told me of the Mollies, they had first appeared many years before I was born and always lurked in the background of country life in Ireland. These men would dress in women's skirts, and make black their faces, I presume to hide their identity. They would visit any man who took over the house of an evicted family or sold goods at a high price or did something

301

against their fellows. Mostly the Mollies would frighten the new tenant away but sometimes they would beat and even kill him. They were often drunk and the tactics and actions sometimes were at the spur of the moment and not well organised. The attacks were mostly by people aggrieved for one reason or another. There is no doubt they were dangerous people.

'A man with a grudge is worth two soldiers but has half the value of one' my father would say.

Landlord agents in particular were attacked and killed and warnings made before and after so everyone knew who was behind the mischief. The feeling amongst people was that most hated the landlords and the agents but they hated the Mollies more. They brought trouble and violence where enough of that already existed. No one dared to voice against them though lest they incur punishment. It was inevitable I suppose that when such behaviour started in the coal fields in the 1840s in America that the perpetrators would be likened to the Molly Maguires and named after them.

Before going to war I had no knowledge that these people were about the place and little could I know how close I was to come to it all.

While I was in Virginia building defences and carting supplies the Union had decided to draft men from the mines into service. I should perhaps say, 'poor men' because with $300 dollars any man could buy his way off the draft. A few miners might manage that sum and I know of one whose six brothers drew straws and between them collected

302

that payment to free the winner but certainly no labourers would afford it.

Almost all the skilled miners were British; mostly Welsh and almost all the labourers were Irish. More Irish were drafted than others for they were by far the poorest.

When the drafters[82] had come along in 62[83] I was long gone but I was told they had no idea as to who lived in the area or where they were so they went to the mine owners and superintendents for payroll lists of men. Partly due to this cooperation the Audenried mine foreman; Frank Langdon[84] was beaten to death after making a speech. He might have got away with the lists but he spent ten minutes berating the lazy Irish in his speech and berating Irish men is not a good idea.

Events yet to unfold in my tale show he was probably killed by a drunken mob and nothing to do with the Mollies but as you shall see, in the 60s and 70s even the bad weather was attributed to the Mollies.

Another killing which was definitely due to the Mollies was that of the mine owner Smith[85]. That was planned and they went to his house and shot him and it was an exceedingly dirty deed. It was

---

82 Militia Act July 1862 and Conscription Act March 1863 allowed for conscription into Union Army
83 Patrick is clearly mistaken in his account. The Militia Act forcing conscription had not yet been passed.
84 Killed June 14th 1862. The reasons for Langdon's murder are not properly known but probably to do with being a mine foreman and his open criticism of the Irish
85 George Smith: Mine owner

done on the 5th November 1863 and was the filling
in all the papers from the county up to New York. I
think after that there was no doubt the Mollies were
about and they were hungry for revenge by way of
violence against any mine owners or their people. It
was I would say no accident that the killing was on
Guy Fawkes Night. The Mollies always tried to have
some meaning nested into the deeds they did, more
often than not meaningless to anyone but them; for
what could the burning of parliament have to do
with a mine owner and his murder?

Do not confuse the violence of the Mollies with
the Saturday night gang fights on the streets of
Mahanoy city and other places. The Madocs[86] and
the Irish most weekends had their drunken fights
which sometimes included the shooting of guns and
the use of knives. Bitterness was deep between the
Welsh skilled and Irish unskilled mine workers.

Not all was ill on the coal fields during the war,
the hostilities demanded coal and as the price went
up so did wages. By 1863 a labourers wage had
almost doubled to $11 a week. Killings were
occurring but this was seldom and I suspect that
personal grudges were more the reason than
workers' rights or righting of injustices.

Between 65 and 71 there were a few owners[87]
killed but I cannot recall their names, after that no

---

86 Pejorative name for the Welsh immigrants
87 In fact no more owners were killed in that period:
Managers were however. Notably; David Muir,
Superintendent Aug 25th 1865; H Dunne, Superintendent,
Jan 10th 1866; W Littlehales, Foreman. March 15th
1867; Area, Superintendent, Oct 17th 1868; P Burns,
Foreman, Apr 15th 1870; M Powel, Superintendent, Dec

one died until the dreadful year of 1875 when the devil broke loose in Schuylkill County.

By 1868 a new labour union, The Workingmen's Benevolent Association started up in Schuylkill County; it aimed to represent both skilled and unskilled workers but most of the Irish unskilled didn't trust it so much. They managed to negotiate wages fixed to coal prices and that worked for a time and there was peace.

The Mollies were quiet and many of us thought that was because the workers, skilled and unskilled were finally being treated better. Not fair, that was never going to happen but they were paid better and the working day was cut to 8 hours and proper venting in the shafts was done after a bad accident at Avondale[88] and it was a good bit safer. Boys aged less than twelve years could from 1870 no longer be used down the mines, although they still had the terrible task of picking.

So it was very clear to all that things were calm and quiet. That was until Gowen[89] and his Rail Company started to move in taking over most mines. If ever a bastard deserves the fires of hell it be this man. He bought up and illegally[90] mined the

---

2nd 1871.
88 A fire on April 6th 1869 trapped and killed 110.
Pennsylvania passed new safety laws as a result
89 Franklin Gowen; president of the Philadelphia and
Reading Railroad
90 In fact he did not do this illegally. Gowen sought
approval of a subsidiary company (The Laurel Run
Improvement Company) from the senate which rejected
his approach initially, he apparently then bribed 4

fields and even though he did not own them all he owned all the rail transport to move coal, so he controlled them.

The man saw any sort of union or labour representation as a thing to fear and so he desired to kill it off, and that meant killing off the Molly Maguires, which in turn would kill the Benevolent Association union and the Ancient Order of Hibernians. Destroying the independent mines and buying them cheap was just a bonus to him.

To this end he caused all to think that the union and the Mollies were one and the same thing, along with the Hibernians, yet they were very clearly not, both the Hibernians and union had legal charters and most people knew the Mollies were outlaws, disliked as much by the mine owners as they were by the miners they claimed to represent. Of course most of the Mollies belonged to the union and all belonged to the Hibernians but that did not ensure that the good bodies were possessed by the bad.

Gowen and others including the newspaper proprietors and politicians all conspired to make it appear that way. Every time a Molly was caught he would admit his affiliation to the Hibernians or to the union and this was presented as proof that they were the same thing.

In 1868 the Benevolent Association union had made good agreements with the mining companies which guaranteed a level of pay for the workers, not just the miners but the labourers too. No sooner had Gowen set himself against the unions and started his strangle hold on Schuylkill County did

senators and the company was approved.

the coal price drop. He abandoned one agreement and the next and the next and the wages of the workers fell. By 1870 a man previously earning $11 a week was earning just $7.50 a week. Gowen manoeuvred and manipulated the other owners and he tripled the price for transporting their coal and they went bust and he bought more.

By December 1874 the Mollies had started up again with the killing of a watchman[91] just before Christmas. In the following January the union called for a strike[92]. It was an error. Gowen had built up huge coal stocks and he had provoked the strike by breaking agreements with the union. Some owners wanted to end it and let the men go back but he stopped them with threats to ruin them. He was bent on destruction of the union and the Molly Maguires as he thought them the same thing, or pretended to.

The strike lasted until June of 1875 and ended with the starving workers returning on a wage cut by 10 percent for most and up to 33 percent for many. The Workmen's Benevolent Association was all but done. What happened next was inevitable and had been the desire of the demon Gowen.

---

91 F Hesser, Mine Watchman, Dec 18th 1874
92 Known as 'The Long Strike' of 1875

20
MINES, UNIONS, AND MOLLIES 1875

*John (Jack) Kehoe, King of the Mollies 1875,
Husband of Mary Ann O'Donnell*

Patrick has painted a picture of the situation between the workers and the mine owners up to 1875 and it feels as though things are heading to some sort of conclusion or confrontation so the reader might expect in the next letter to read a continuation of Patrick's time in Pennsylvania; but first he seems to step back, he seems to have overlooked his homecoming after the war in 1865 and now addresses this important time in his life.

It has to be said that given he is in a cell awaiting his execution it is remarkable that he does not jump back and forth more often. I confess I was tempted to place the following account into an earlier chapter, where it might have sat more comfortably but for the sake of authenticity here it is, where Patrick himself placed it.

He rewinds to the few days after his return from the war in 1865 and how he encounters Margaret after his years away. It has to be said that Patrick tends to have complicated relationships with women and his relationship with Margaret is every bit as complicated as his relationship with her mother, Hanora. Ever the pragmatist he makes decisions that are logical, if a little puzzling to us in this day and age. That said his account of their re-acquaintance is moving and surprising. We also discover the true nature of their relationship.

Patrick also explains how he worked for Jack Kehoe, his cousin's husband, at The Hibernian Tavern (which is still standing and open for business). He goes on to outline the continuing deterioration in the area leading finally to the deaths of mine superintendents and other officials at the hands of the Maguires.

In 1865 it was the tipping up of coal carts, then the collapsing of mine entrances; the attacks were often random and disorganised, thought up at the last minute, and very often inspired with drink. By 1875 things had taken a much darker turn with more serious disruptions and eventually murder.

(Twentieth Letter)
Dec 15ᵗʰ 1883 - Newgate Prison, London

Dear Victor,

I intended my previous letter to be an account of my return to my family in Pennsylvania but as I wrote it seemed more important to impart to you what one day will be the shameful history of what happened in the county of Schuylkill. The people who manipulated the events must not be permitted to be the people who record them; though I am no fool and am aware that this often is the way of it. I was witness to part of it so let my few words on the matter in some small way balance the account.

Before I move to the destruction of the O'Donnell family by the foul hand of the Pinkertons and Gowen and with the approval of the darkest player in it all, that rat and terrible turncoat James McKenna[93]. I should report to what I found when I came back from Lafayette prison early in 65.

Madge, as I must try to remember to name her in this part of my story; gave me great comfort for the few days I rested immediate to my return from the war. I did not know day from night and I slept entirely in my clothes. It was not a bodily rest like normal sleep but one of my body and my mind. I am sure that the residue of my time in New York and the trials with Hanora and the guilt and the war and jail and all other matters had gathered and weighed me down to the depths of this sleep.

---

93 *James McKenna was the name used by the Pinkerton agent James McParland*

Each awakening I knew she was there and it is impossible to convey the safety and splendid comfort this afforded me. I drifted from dreams of powder and flash and fog and dead men on my lap, hillsides and frozen swims to the gentle hand of my sister and her whispers to my ear. Whispers of things I cannot recall and if I could I would not recount them for they were ours and shall always be.

On the third day I awoke early, just as the sun was rising. I had a hunger I have seldom known. Madge was beside me, sitting on the edge of the bed, fully clothed and watching me. I could not believe that this was the child I had left off in 61. Here was a full grown woman and a handsome one at that. She delighted to fetch me coffee, bacon and bread and without words between us I devoured it all and she fetched me more and after that more again. She knew not to bring me eggs with my pork.

We were in the lowest room next to the kitchen of Manus and Margaret's house, in Wiggans Patch west of Mahanoy City. I knew the house and I knew the room, indeed I had painted it drunk one afternoon with my cousin John O'Donnell, splashes of the blue paint remained on the floor at the edge of the rug.

The bed was large and soft and comfortable, atop it rested a deep patch quilt. At its foot and some few feet from it was a coal fire with embers still glowing pale red; to one side of the bed was a small door leading to a cellar.

311

I knew the fire needed no stoking and would glow its warmth into the room for a long while yet. Anthracite; the black gold that brought my compatriots and others across the ocean and which then subdued them to a life of servitude, to injury, lung disease and eventual death in poverty.

Adjacent to the fireplace on one side stood a wash stand, upon which burned two candles, and on the other side a dresser, the top of which was entirely covered in books, some stacked to eight or nine high. Beside the bed was a smaller child's bed. Above it hung a crucifix.

It did not occur to me for a moment who the occupants of the crib might be; one golden haired girl at the top and a boy of similar size and age at the bottom, both sound asleep. The youngest of the family when I had left was Charles at four years so now he would be eight or nine and much larger than these two. I thought nothing more of it and spoke to Madge;

'Look at you sister' I ventured through my sore throat… 'A beauty you turned into and there be no mistake about that.'

She did not blush, she smiled her mother's pretty smile with the confidence only the truly innocent can possess. She curtsied and almost lost her balance; and giggled.

'I have our dear mother to thank for my looks' she said neatly, 'it is no credit to me.'

That thing which had afflicted her as a child was still there, but it had evolved or changed in some way. No more an obvious slowness or

312

distance, but something I could see and I supposed others close to her would see.

Hanora had told her the truth of the matter of how she came about but Madge had been young and with her difficulties *had she understood?* I wondered.

'*Your* mother my dear' I corrected, 'for we are brother and sister only part way'.

She looked at me quizzically, her head tilted to one side, a little frightened perhaps. I thought myself a clumsy oaf; not two minutes into our reunion and I was divesting her of a brother. I need not have worried and for the first time... no... for the second time I saw her at her most amazing, for the different and deep and complicated creature that she was.

'Brother you are in error'. She spoke so beautifully and I account for it perhaps by the literature she read and which littered the room; 'I shall take thee as mine own blood for in my heart that is what you have always been and shall always be'.

I was dumbfounded that her mind was so deep to contemplate such things let alone articulate them so eloquently. I was also ashamed that I had not afforded her the consideration that she could think so well on the thing between us and that I had not. She was not finished;

'Our union is beyond the measure of simple things such as those that man would apply. We are one and the word 'brother' is convenient but not the thing that we be; alas I have no other word'. She gestured and raised her shoulders in a shrug and another sweet smile. 'Perhaps when I have read all my books and more I shall have that word but until then you are 'brother' to me.'

I had no idea what to say to her. I understood the strength of feeling she had for me because I shared it for her and true enough, it was hard to find a better word than 'brother'.

'Then sister', I replied as I reached for her hand, 'Sister and brother is what we shall be until you read a better book'.

She laughed, leaned down and kissed me. Her attitude was very much as though she had just told me the time of the day and I had confirmed it. She then gestured in a long sweeping arm movement to the cribs and said.

'Would you care to make the acquaintance of your new cousins?' I was not sure at first what she meant. I looked back to her, realising they were her own children and she smiled again.

'I must waken them'.

Inadvertently my eyes were drawn to her very ample bosom which was wetted from her milk. I did not know what to ask first and as I tried to work out what it should be she lifted the first child from her crib sat on the end of the bed and began to feed the infant, in my full view.

'I'll go and we can speak later' I offered and she responded;

'You will go no place brother. When they are fed we shall talk and I can tell you how this came about'.

While I was in the Confederate army several of my comrades had taunted me due to my lack of experience with women. I had seen Hanora naked many times and it was normal to me ever since the age of twelve but this was the first time I had seen any other in any state of undress. I was not aroused in my groin, not by any means, but I was curious and as I watched her feed the little girl I left my shame and embarrassment behind. Madge could detect this change in me and upon changing the child from one side to the other she asked me to fetch the other creature, the little boy, from the crib and attach him to her now protruding breast.

I did not hesitate and have to confess to a great satisfaction when the little fellow attached like a barnacle and began to feed. To explain it as a strange experience would be understating the matter but it made a strong bond even stronger.

In a strange way I am sure that Madge was always endowed with a gift for knowing what was the right thing and how to go about it in the best way. Whatever that thing was robbed from her when she was under water at Hanora's hand, something more special and harder to identify or describe had fallen into her soul. In the minutes together that morning our relationship was not only reaffirmed but the boundary was set for the future. That is to say, between us there never would be a boundary, not in anything. Of course Madge was then and would always be my sister in most conventional senses, a very special sister. She was after all the product of my very own Hanora, the only woman I ever loved as a woman, as a companion and equal and as everything else.

The matter which concerned me and which Madge knew would cause me consternation was how and who? The how of course was obvious but the who was more complicated.

My second or third cousin Patrick and his brother Michael had arrived in Mahanoy city to work in the mines at around 1863, while I was at war. I have always had difficulty estimating the exact nature of relations as I have so many but they were the children of my father's cousin. I shall say just cousin from now. It was not at all uncommon for cousins to have the same names but that these two were Michael and Patrick O'Donnell, just as my brother and me and that they were the same age did cause some issues as I shall mention in due course.

Michael and Patrick took a small house on Wiggans Patch nearby and it was agreed that Madge at the age of fifteen years would tend their house, cook for them and thus she could make a living and the room she left in Aunty Margaret's house could be let to a lodger and all would be well.

My cousin John, who had collected us from the station in 1861, moved into a room with Michael and Patrick in the summer of 1863, he was eighteen or so at the time. Everyone loved Madge but John it seemed took a particular liking to her and they spent much time together. By November Madge had started to swell and John, being given fair warning, disappeared. Some say he joined the Union Army and was lost at the Battle of the Wilderness[94] but,

---

94 May 5th to 7th 1864

no one knows for sure. No one saw him or heard from him again.

It was a pity to me because John was a good man and there seemed to me no reason why he could not be a father and a husband. If a boy of 19 can fight and die for his country why should he not be able to have a wife? He had no relation to Madge either; none at all but I think it must have looked otherwise. Maybe he did not run off and maybe he did not know. No one would speak to me of the details.

For her confinement Madge had moved back to the O'Donnell house and had stayed since the birth, which was a year past.

I was in need of employment and I wanted to support Madge and the children. She needed the shelter and respectability of a husband and I was content to give it. As much as I disliked and cared nought for gossip on May 24th 1865 I married my 'sister' Madge. Of course legally she was not my sister and in fact no relation at all. I was thirty years old and she seventeen, a thirteen year gap between a man and his wife was not at all an unusual thing. The union was entirely for convenience and the good name of Madge and the wider family. I took the children as my own and they were given my name. Edward and Ellen were so far as the world mattered, my children. I still regard them so and I have papers to attest to it.

Madge, the children and I moved into Michael's house on the Patch after getting married and I took a job in the mines as a labourer. Manus who had by now broken all the odds and worked his way to miner took me as one of his and whilst the work was impossibly hard and uncomfortable it was better with him than it would have been under a Madoc.

My first cousin Mary Ann O'Donnell, John's sister, married John Kehoe. He was the man I had seen making a speech against slavery and on other things in the tavern in 1861. Indeed he was still making speeches and had by then become an official of the Ancient Order of Hibernians and later he was elected to the office of High Constable of Girardville. He was also a well-known member of the Molly Maguires then and probably their leader. This explained the reaction to him in the tavern before the war. He was a powerful, respected and feared man. I came to know John (Jack) very well and we were close and he was good to me, Madge and the children; but I never was really involved in the business of the Mollies, not directly or properly.

John always assured me that as his fortune might change so would mine; and his word was true.

I laboured in the mine for almost four years and was all but done with it. In 65 or 66 I hurt my hand bad when I was hanging down to check the fill of a cart and my boot got trapped and dragged me down breaking bones on my hand. I wanted to go back to New York and do what I was best at; hotel work, but on my wage I could barely feed the family so saving for such a venture was impossible. Every night I was spitting black dust from my lungs and I knew I could not continue in the work for ever.

In 1867 Uncle Manus was killed. He'd taken extra work so I was not labouring for him on that day thankfully; he was Robbing the Pillars[95] and was too slow to get away and ended under a few ton of coal. Half the money I had saved till then went for the funeral.

The miner who took his face was a Welshman named Carter and he was a bastard and he paid me lower than Manus had. The Carter brothers were known widely as bullies and inbreeds from a line in family breeding from Swansea in Wales.

Even amongst the Madocs they were hated. Luke was the elder and Martin the younger. They lived 4 miles west of Wiggans and in the manner of beasts in the woods. Sisters and brother made children between them and on that account they were all bereft of normal human attributes.

I complained to my cousin Michael about them and a week or so later their shack was burned to the ground. No one was hurt and Michael never admitted he was behind the deed but everyone knew he was.

Along with the Madocs and after the Avondale fire in 69 I decided that was enough and I took up work in a tavern in Mahanoy City. My hand had got worse and I could not do the labour anyway. The pay was worse and I had to live there and leave Madge home in Wiggans Patch but I got fed and I

---

95 A notoriously dangerous practice of removing coal support pillars when the face was exhausted and the shaft being abandoned, in order to get the last remnants of coal.

got tips, which were often more than the wage; it was a good decision and I was bereft of sense not doing it sooner.

I could breathe again. It was not just the dangers and discomfort of mining, it was all the politics of it; the unions and the mine owners, the gang fights between the Welsh and the Irish, the skilled and unskilled and I was tired of fighting, I had seen enough in the war. When I would take no side I was disliked by both sides; it was hopeless.

Living apart from Madge was not an ordeal. She raised the children and cleaned the house and cooked and she was paid for her trouble and her rent was nil. I delighted in her company as she did in mine and we were very close indeed. We did not sleep in the same bed and she did not look to me for those things a wife might usually look for. I confess I used her firm belief of our kinship, though she knew it did not exist. It was enough for us both and for the family that we appeared to be what they desired us to be.

This brings me Victor to a matter I am compelled to mention. I have considered where and how within my letters to you to best convey this and am at a loss so here it is. I have never been interested in women in the manner which seems to fit with other men. I have been about the place and heard talk and boasting and I have seen love between a man and a wife but I confess it is all a mystery to me. I like women and their company but much prefer that of men. It has always been so with me and I have known others similarly disposed; accounts of which I aim not to make herein.

It is a difficult thing to confess and if it is sinful then I am a sinner but I sincerely believe it not to be a sin. As it happens I believe the idea of sin is a pretence invented by bastard priests and their ilk so as to manage us. Affection in any manifestation or form surely is a good thing and while I know it is not understood by most people I think to lie about it would be worse than to be truthful. I have said it and I trust that in so doing I have addressed questions which may have herein arisen.

I return to my predicament of late 1869. I worked in a tavern in Mahanoy City and John, or Jack as he was better known was a constant visitor, he was by then three years married to my cousin and they had children. He often enthralled the room with his talk of uniting and unions and brotherhood but as he drank more he would always begin on the mine owners and their property and how they might be punished. There was no taste for it I have to report. One or two, equally drunk at the generosity of John would shout support but not many.

It was upon one visit when I was serving and clearing up and chucking out scrappers that John suggested that I should have my own place and make money and not wages. He had been very drunk and I thought little of it and knew I could never afford the rent or the purchase of a tavern. Just a week after that John had brought me out for the day and taken me to Shenandoah where he showed me his tavern which he had purchased and which I was to run for him with my cousin, his wife. I was surprised he remembered a drunken conversation and his promise and I wondered did other things said in drink, things not so good; also remain in his mind when not drunk.

Upon that point Madge and my own fortunes, which coincided, as we were man and wife, changed. She, Edward and Ellen moved in with me and within a year we had saved more than $100 and lived well in spite of it. By 72 John had bought a new place in Girardville which in recognition of the Ancient order of Hibernians he named 'Hibernian House'. I took to running that with John. I stayed in all nearly 8 years, long after he was dead and buried.

By the time the terrible events of 1875 came about Madge and I had worked in taverns in the County for six years or so and we were well known. The children were at school each day and they prospered, Ellen had her mother's fine looks and both had her gentle disposition. Madge continued as always in her own world but also very much in mine, if not others. There was something very special about her. Not a single time did any patron take advantage or attempt to. She had an air of elegance, not superiority, just simple elegance no one dared to breach. She was kind and she was hardworking, she spoke her mind directly and cared nothing for what people thought of her, and partly in consequence of that all thought highly of her.

It was a few years since anyone had heard of the Mollies and the Benevolent Association I suppose was largely responsible for that. But now there were scuffles again and then fights; Irish gangs fought with Welsh gangs and sometimes with German gangs and one or two had been killed. A man[96] was killed on Halloween in 1874 but this was a drunken brawl, Miners fighting Labourers and not organised by anyone, let alone the Mollies.

I do not make a small thing of any death but the few that occurred before 1875 were not significant and had as much to do with drink on a weekend and jealousies over nationality or the best jobs than over Molly Maguires trying to control the mines. I know this because I was at the centre of it; many a crowd left the Hibernian Tavern filled with drink and anger and many a meeting was held there so I got a good feel and no Molly was involved up to 74.

All that changed in the year of 75. The fights in the street between the gangs seemed by then to be happening weekly so I sent Madge and the children back to Wiggans Patch where they lived again with my cousins Michael and Patrick. Aunty Margaret and Cousin Ellen O'Donnell who by now was married to Charles McAllister and had a son John, lived with Aunty Margaret, who by now was known to us all as 'Grannie'. James too still lived at home as did Charles, Charles O'Donnell that is, who was by now 18 years old. Cousin Manus, who must have been in his thirties had long left, married and had children.

I shall not catalogue all the assassinations that occurred because I do not remember them all. I use the word 'assassination' because this is what they were, they were not brawls or fights, these were men targeted and killed directly by the Mollies, because of who they were, what they were and how they had behaved; of this there is in my mind no doubt. As for the right and wrong of it, I am more inclined to say they were right and fair killings; not including Hesser, who was at Christmas 74.

The first was a policeman[97] in July. I forget his name. There followed five[98] more in just two months. I remember the names Uren and Sanger because they along with the long dead Langdon had particular interest to me as you shall see.

When I look back now, or even when I looked back in 79 after the trials of the Mollies it seems so obvious now that the insurrection and violence was deliberately provoked by Gowen and that with the happy cooperation of the church which detested anything that they did not control; and they did not control the Molly Maguires.

It was Archbishop James Wood, a very fine friend of the Reading Railroad president Gowen by the way, who excommunicated all the Mollies. People not Catholic will not understand how significant that would be for the Mollies themselves and for the community which often helped and hid them and their deeds.

From as far back as 73 Gowen had sent in his snake Pinkerton McKenna and with my own eyes I saw this man provoke, instruct and partake in Molly

---

97 Benjamin Yost, July 5th 1875
98 Thomas Gwyther, Justice of the Peace; Aug 14th
1875: Gomer James, Miner; Aug 14th 1875: Thomas
Sanger, Foreman; Sept 1st 1875; William Uren,
Foreman; Sept 1st 1875: John Jones Superintendent;
Sept 3rd 1875

work. He was not just gathering information, he was making it and he was as close to John Kehoe as any of them; even for a time working in the same mine. They drank together and they planned together and many a plot unfolded uninterrupted in spite of his claims later to have tried to stop the bad works.

My explanation of the situation from 65 to 75 is rough I admit Victor and to cover matters full I would need a library and much more time; of course I have neither. For now it serves to disclose the unhappy situation in Schuylkill County at the time. I summarise it thusly: Gowen's Rail Company had a monopoly over coal transport so the few mines he did not by now own in the Schuylkill County he could close at a whim, so the owners did his bidding.

Many owners wanted an end to the Long Strike and peace with the strikers but Gowen stopped that. Coal prices fell to under $2.00 from a high of over $3.00 and Gowen had torn up the agreements made with the union to protect wages. After the unsuccessful strike and by June 1875 the union was utterly destroyed and the Molly Maguires stepped into the void with their retributions and violence, most clearly from July to September that year. Thus they allowed Gowen and his private police force[99], his Pinkertons, the 'Flying Squadron'[100] and his vigilante mine workers to be unleashed.

---

99 Coal and Iron Police of the Reading Railroad.
100 Formed in 1875 between Pinkerton Agents and Coal and iron Police with the aim to break the strike of 1875 and to destroy the Molly Maguires

There is no question in my mind that the situation was entirely orchestrated by Gowen and the violence allowed him to class the union and the Order of Hibernians in the same boat as the Mollies. He would then be able to destroy the two legitimate bodies by destroying the illegitimate, which admittedly they had birthed and to some extent fed.

The Mollies had been busy indeed, and the mine owners were determined by foul mean or fair to put them to an end. Most of the intelligence gathered against them was gathered by McKenna and his ilk. It was faulty, based on gossip and on spite and it was prejudiced and it was reported as fact by the snake and handed to Gowen and his Vigilantes.

Gowen, McKenna, Woods and the rest of them rot in hell for the dreadful deed they next provoked and undertook.

21
MURDER OF THE O'DONNELLS AT WIGGANS PATCH

Ellen O'Donnell Age 20 - 1875

During the Lebanese Civil War it was said in the United Nations that if you were not confused by the situation in the Middle East then you could not understand it. So it is with Patrick and women, particularly with Margaret whom we know became his wife and who had two children whom he took to be his but clearly were not. Not as unusual a situation as one might imagine in a time when 'impressions' were what mattered.

History books will suggest her name and her surname but Margaret had no surname. Given what we know of her entry into the world it's almost certain she was not registered at birth; she is also unlikely to have been baptised. Before her marriage to Patrick she was for all intents and purposes part of the O'Donnell family and would have been known as O'Donnell, as she would have been after. The marriage was a fake and the purpose for it seemed to be to regularise her situation and that of her children. Patrick provided a name and respectability and probably was a good father (or uncle) to the children. He was not, so far as we can tell from his letters, ever a husband in the biblical sense, though given he and Margaret were not related there was no reason why he could not have been.

The last words in Patrick's previous letter are "Gowen, McKenna, Woods and the rest of them rot in hell for the dreadful deed they next provoked and undertook." The following letter deals with that terrible deed. It is well documented and Patrick was there, only barely escaping with his life. Arthur Conan Doyle based his last novel on the Mollies of that time, including this incident and named it The Valley of Fear, it was published in 1914.

Gowen we know was the mine owner and railway giant and main architect of the troubles against the miners. McKenna was a Pinkerton Agent; his real name was James McParland. It is almost inarguable that undercover as a Hibernian and a Molly Maguire, James McParland was an Agent Provocateur acting on behalf of Gowen to cause trouble and attract adverse notoriety to the both groups; the Mollies but also the Hibernians. By 1875 the Workers Association was a spent force.

Gowen was very friendly with Allan Pinkerton, founder of the Pinkerton National Detective Agency. It is impossible to overstate how powerful and all-encompassing the Pinkertons were becoming. They had been bodyguards to Lincoln during the war for example, though stories of their successes in foiling murder plots against him seem to be a fiction devised by Allan Pinkerton to validate the agency and increase its kudos.

By 1910 the agency had more agents than did the US standing army. They were notorious for doing exactly what they wanted, how they wanted; and they exemplified the notion that the means justified the ends. The tactics of infiltration, intimidation and threats were used without compunction. If there were industrial disputes the Pinkertons were always available to bash people and worse.

The intimidation and brutal behaviour of the Pinkertons should not lead one to think they were sloppy or disorganised, they were anything but, they were highly organised and exceptionally disciplined... and they got the job done.

It is interesting to note that immediately after the war's end the Washington Metropolitan Police took over the role of protecting President Lincoln. One of its officers was charged with Lincoln's protection on the night of the assassination. His name was John Frederick Parker. After turning up for his shift at 7pm, four hours late, he sat in an adjacent saloon drinking with none other than John Wilkes Booth. They were not in each other's company but they were feet away from each other.

When Booth enter the president's box Parker was missing. Lady Mary, Lincoln's widow, accused the man of being responsible for her husband's death. Incredibly he was not sacked and later was actually detailed to close protection for the ex-first lady. It is fair to say that Parker would not have been employed by the Pinkertons; it is also almost a certainty that had Lincoln retained the services of that private police force he would have served his second term in full. In summary, the Pinkertons were ruthless and brutal and a law unto themselves, but they were exceptionally good at doing what they did. The ineptitude and disorganisation of police forces at the time led to a vacuum which Allan Pinkerton eagerly and very profitably filled.

The agent McParland embedded himself into the Mollies for two years and seems to have deliberately instigated violence as opposed to stopping it. Thus the Pinkertons could implicate not just the Mollies but also the Hibernians and the Workers Benevolent Association and break them all. He was very close to Jack Kehoe, and that he was testifies to how effective an organisation they were.

There is no doubt that it was McParland who gave Gowen and the so called Vigilance Committee of the Anthracite Coal Region the names and location of the O'Donnells at Wiggans Patch. Yes, you read it correctly; there really was a perfectly legal and openly operating organisation at the time named 'The Vigilance Committee of the Anthracite Coal Region'.

It's worth noting that while Patrick observed all of these events, other than an odd minor caper he was not involved in the work of the Mollies in any meaningful way; most people were not and in fact the Mollies were as hated by the miners and labourers as much as by the mine owners because of the inevitable reprisals and trouble they invited with their actions.

And so equipped with the names of the O'Donnells and the address at Wiggans Patch the inevitable happened in the early hours of December 10th 1875.

(Twenty First Letter)
Dec 15th 1883 - Newgate Prison, London

Victor,

By late 1875 the entire county was in turmoil. The Workmen's Benevolent Association was dead and buried, defeated when they went 'all in' against Gowen and lost. There is no question that the Mollies had been all about the place, killing and attacking and burning mines and turning over coal carts. Maybe that was because of the breakdown of the union, leaving the workers without a voice or part the reason for it, who can know?

That of which I now write was no question procured by the violence against the mine owners by the Mollies. Maybe some people might say this was deserved. Those will be people who have never gone into the black ground with an empty belly.

McKenna had been about his work since 63 collecting what information he could gather and inventing that which he could not divine in the pit and in the taverns but that which his masters Allan Pinkerton and Gowen required. He delivered his report to Gowen and what was to unfold was the result of that.

When it comes to my cousins, the O'Donnells at Wiggans Patch there had always been gossip and spite. I suspect the start of it went back to 61 when they got the house over others who were after it and ahead of them. My family made good use of it as a boarding place and when Michael, my second cousin got the house nearby, where I lived for a time, it made for more bad feeling from others. This had never manifest other than in a fight now and then in the tavern or once or twice coal dust on Grannie Margaret's sheets out drying.

When McKenna started fishing, usually amongst those who hated the family; he hooked gossip, jealousy and spite and reported it as fact. James and Charles O'Donnell and James McAllister, who was married to Cousin Ellen O'Donnell, were, along with several others, listed as the likely killers of Uren and Sanger who had both been done-in in early September of 75.

Them boys would give a beating or they might cave in the mouth of a mine or turn over a coal cart and I know they often did because I accompanied them. It was a lark and nothing more; they were not killers of other men. It was mischief, dangerous mischief but mischief and none more.

I was with the boys most of the time and am sure I would have been given as a killer alongside them but for the fact that when Uren and Sanger were killed I had been in New York City to visit Hanora so could not have been near. They were no more guilty than me but they did not have an alibi. Once again Hanora saved me though she did not know it.

I learned long after the events I am about to describe that a report was made by McKenna and the Pinkertons and it was passed to The Vigilance Committee of the Coal Region[101]. It seems strange

---

101 *In Fact the report was addressed to 'The Vigilance Committee of the Anthracite Coal Region'.*

now to think such a thing might exist but it did and it was paid for by Gowen and the Pinkertons and their Flying Squadron.

A newspaper published the report and it was clearly a murder-note and nothing short of it. It named the killer of Yost as Kerrigan, the terrible bastard who saved his neck by bearing false witness against anyone else he was asked to name. Naming Kerrigan was the only accurate thing in the report. It named James and Charles O'Donnell and three others for killing Uren and Sanger. Bad enough I suppose but it also gave their address at Wiggans Patch and the names of other Mollies who might go there. It named my Cousin Mary Ann O'Donnell as living there but she did not, she lived in Girardville with her husband John Kehoe, the leader of the Mollies in the county.

I cannot recall all that was in the report but it named many men and the homes of a few and its purpose when given to a vigilante group cannot be misunderstood.

I normally worked Fridays at Hibernian House but John and Mary Anne were about so let me off with Madge and the twins to visit Grannie O'Donnell. We did not often visit and it was exciting for the children. We spent much of Thursday at the house and when it came to bed Madge and the children went over to Michael's where we normally stayed when visiting on account of the boarding house being full up most of the time. It was bitterly cold and I walked with Madge and the children and left them at the door. I returned to Grannie's to play cards and drink with

James, Charles and Charles McAllister, Ellen's husband.

They had set up a table as they always did for our cards and drinking. It was in the same room I had occupied on my return from Lafayette Prison and it was not changed. There was the fire, now blazing and not glowing, the bed, next to the tiny door to the cellar and nearby the smaller bed, this time filled not with twins but with Charles and Ellen's boy; John.

At about one a.m. on Friday morning Grannie put her head into the room and gently scolded us for keeping Ellen awake and we assured her we would retire shortly and stoke the fire in the grate and in the kitchen to keep the cold away from her daughter. Ellen had already gone to bed in the room, she was pregnant and due very soon and we men had great amusement at her loud snoring.

Our games sometimes went on until dawn but tired from the journey from the tavern that day and not wanting to offend Grannie I was away to bed back at Michael's around 2 am. I approached the back door to leave and noticed footsteps outside and a lantern. Before I had a moment to think the door burst open and struck me on my face, knocking me over and stunning me for a moment. Men, ten or more stepped over me, their faces were covered and they carried guns, shotguns and hand guns. One leaned over me and swung his pistol into my face, I remember seeing it before the blackness, it was a Colt, the same model Hanora had bought for me in Syracuse. I thought of her as I lost consciousness.

The next I knew I was outside and next to me Charles and James, not McAllister, who had the same name; but my cousins, the O'Donnells, James McAllister was not there that night and Charles McAllister was nowhere I could see on account of him bolting. There was shouting and baying and I heard shots from the house. Even at that moment I took this to be a night of beatings and warnings and no more. I looked at Charles, who was just past 18 years old and no risk to anyone. I noticed around us at least another twenty men on top of those inside the house. All had long coats and were armed, not with clubs but with rifles and pistols. A man kicked Charles to the ground and declared;

'This is Charles O'Donnell'

Another pointed his colt at Charles and asked,

'Be you Charles O'Donnell the murderous scum what did for William Uren?'

Charles tried to right himself and the first man kicked him in his side.

'I'm Charles' he replied, 'but I did for no man on oath I did for no man'.

Without another word the second man discharged his revolver and the bullet struck Charles sure in the forehead. His head threw back, his leg kicked up and he was still. I was utterly dumbfounded as the first man discharged a further five shots into Charles' face. The second man continued shooting also till his gun clicked empty and two more devils stepped forward and emptied their guns into my dead cousin.

I looked to my right and James had broken free and was on his feet and running for the thicket. The three murderers, or maybe there were four, all frantically reloaded their spent weapons and one or two others started firing. I think one shot clipped James and he went down and my heart sank. Then he was up again and running like a hare. James was a fast fellow and not encumbered with a big coat and boots he was long gone in no time.

I knew it was my time and I was ready to go when two men rushed out of the house in turmoil and argument and blame.

'He's shot the woman dead' said the first. 'He shot a bloody woman dead'.

'I mistook her in the light' said the other

'Her fat too with a child,' said the first man, throwing his gun to the ground.

I concluded to my horror that the shot from the house had struck Ellen. And though I am partly ashamed of it I took the chance. It would either speed my end or delay it.

'Brave men have come here tonight to kill women and children is it?' I said to them all.

The man who had decided Charles' fate stepped forward pistol whipped me around the head and called for a rope. The rope already made into a noose was passed to him.

'It's Mollies we seek and if their women get in the way then they can go the same way'. His words clearly were not welcome to some of the gang who made murmurs and shifted about uncomfortable but no one made objection to my fate.

I knew it was the end and any notion of playing their guilt was lost.

'James O'Donnell' said the man, you are a murderer and you are to die, be it by the neck or by the bullet I can leave to you'

'James O'Donnell' I replied, 'is that fellow you just missed and who by now is half way to New York City' I ventured, sounding perhaps more confident than I ought.

The man looked at me. I could not tell what he thought as I could see only his eyes. Another fellow stepped forward and confirmed my comment.

'Your name?' demanded the inquisitor, with his pistol under my chin and a noose around my neck.

I had thought to tell the truth and declare myself as Patrick O'Donnell but I knew that the other Patrick was implicated in the killing of another Welshman[102] and was a known Mollie and arguing the difference between two persons of the same name and same age was not something I thought wise in the situation with a rope around my neck and a Colt under my chin.

'James McAllister' I said, without thinking of the obvious age difference.

The man looked at me and seemed to consider the odds. I think also the killing of a woman and child inside her might have taken some of the fury from them. He removed the rope and holstered the gun. He had me stand next to Charles. He pointed with his gun and said.

'This is what Mollies get in Schuylkill County'. He looked at me again, still seeming undecided and

---

102 Morgan Powell. Dec 2nd 1871

said 'If you had been your brother you'd be hanged by now'.

I was tempted to laugh at the absurdity of what he said but did not. With that they made off to wherever their horses were waiting and I heard the hoofs beating away. I made my way back into the house and on the foot of the stairs I found Ellen; she was dead, shot in the chest. Behind her the fire roared and her son, John stood in the doorway crying. I could not find Charles but later discovered he had hidden in the cellar of the house next to us where he took refuge after seeing Ellen lost.

Grannie came down to her daughter's body, she was badly bruised about the face. She wailed when she discovered Ellen and screamed that she could feel the unborn child moving and trying to break out. The woman, half demented implored me to get a knife from the kitchen and release the unborn child but I had no inclination to do any such thing, but now regret not trying it. Later when she saw her youngest son Charles in the snow full of holes[103] she lost her mind completely; it was only when Madge had come to her and comforted her that she regained her senses.

There have been many accounts of the night at Wiggans Patch and the murder of the O'Donnells but I was there. James McAllister was not there in spite of reports that he was. I took his name to escape hanging and the fact that he is reported as being there shows to me that the reports must have

---

103 It was reported that Charles O'Donnell was shot 18 times, mostly in the head.

come from the actors in this terrible deed. They believed me and went back to their masters, Gowen and the Pinkertons and reported it this way.

I cannot say that this was the end of the Mollies though it seems coincidental that the killings of mine superintendents and foremen and such like ended. Mines were attacked and other mischief was afoot after Dec 1875 but not on anything like the same scale as before Wiggans Patch.

McKenna admitted his part in provoking and instructing the deeds but expressed shame and regret at the killing of a woman and assault of an old lady. He and others expressed delight at the killing of my cousin. I suppose it was a war and in wars lies prevail. I can't say if the Mollies ever hurt a single woman or child, but I think they did not. The Pinkertons and Gowen did both at Wiggans Patch.

In the years that followed many of the suspected Mollies were rounded up and in 1876 the trials began. The Rail Police gathered the suspects, the Railroad prosecuted them and rigged juries[104] found most guilty. Gowen took advantage of the situation and between McKenna's blatant lies in court and his fiction reports they hanged anyone they pleased to hang. The murderer and jailbird Kerrigan was facing a rope and he turned witness against many. On his word alone some men hanged in spite of great evidence to their innocence; at least to the crimes of which they were found guilty.

Several of the men who hanged were Mollies for sure and they did murder but with no proof or a

---

104 Not one jury had any people of Irish descent in it. Most were German, some unable to speak English.

case against any of them McKenna with Kerrigan and other informers made sure they hanged for crimes which they did not commit. The prevailing approach was that they should hang; it mattered not for which crime, provided they hanged.

It was not enough for Gowen to convict and hang the Mollies. He had to do it publicly. By then public hangings were banned but that did not stop the authorities allowing thousands in to inspect the gallows before the executions and immediately after. Four died in one place[105] and six in another[106] that first day of executions.

Doyle, Kelly and Duffy were men I knew well from the tavern, I'd seen a couple of the others too at Hibernian meetings. I can say with certainty that some of the ten men they hanged on June 21st 1876 were innocent of the crimes for which they were hanged. I do not claim they were innocent of all crimes. Ten men strung up in a single day on the word of informers who were paid off with freedom and on the reports of a Pinkerton snake. If you feel I exaggerate when I describe the Pinkerton as the provoker of trouble, consider the fact that until McKenna turned up in 73 there was no trouble and the union prospered. Gowen needed to kill it off. Suddenly all these murders supposedly done by the Mollies, supposedly connected to the union and the Ancient Order of Hibernians took place and needed to be dealt with harshly.

---

105 Maunch Chunk, Carbon County
106 Pottsville

When they caught up with John Kehoe they had no evidence on him other than McKenna's lies and when they were not convincing enough for a conviction they managed to get another defendant[107] to turn informer. John got 7 years for his part in something he had no part in but they had him where they wanted.

When Gowen saw the charges might not stick, in spite of the informer and the Pinkerton liar he pressed for John and others to be prosecuted again. By the time the trial started John was already convicted of the first crime. It was once again McKenna along with Gowen's favourite weapon, a murderer turned informer with the bribe of freedom offered. This time the informer was Kerrigan. It is worth a thought that without the word of murderers turned informers not a single Molly would ever have been convicted. John got another 7 years.

Gowen was nothing if not thorough. If he was to bury the Molly Maguires he needed the leader to hang, not rot in jail. With nothing to call for execution Gowen dragged up a killing of almost 14 years before. A crime John had nothing to do with; the killing of Frank Langdon back in 63. Gowen even acted as prosecutor. The outcome was inevitable and a gross miscarriage and John was sentenced to hang.

Ten more men died by the rope from March 1877 to 1879, most of them in my estimation were most likely innocent. John hanged on December 18th 1878 and he most certainly was innocent. One

---

107 *Frank McHugh*

day short of five years to my own planned exit I note. I knew him to be kind, intelligent, hardworking and trustworthy. He worked hard for the Order of Hibernians and always tried to improve the lot of workers. He was not a killer, at least not of Langdon, of that I am certain.

22
THE ROAD TO MY UNDOING

Phoenix park - The Assassination of Lord Frederick Charles Cavendish and Thomas Henry Burke (May 6th 1882). Le Monde Illustre - pub. 1882.

Patrick's quick thinking by pretending to be James McAllister could easily have backfired, or may have been his saving; there is no way to be sure. In fact Patrick himself was not suspected of being a Molly, ironically James, the person he pretended to be was but with a gun to his head and a noose around his neck he had little time to formulate a better plan. Avoiding the name O'Donnell turned out to be prudent; for whatever reason, it worked.

Patrick, by his twenty second letter, seems content that he has almost completed his task. He explains what happened to the family after the Murders of Wiggan's Patch and Jack Kehoe's execution. His account about the aftermath of the Wiggan's Patch Murders is brief. A good deal happened between the murders in 1875 and the execution of Jack Kehoe in 1878; the event which many people take to be the end of the unrest. In fact Wiggans Patch was the end. After that the murders stopped and the kangaroo courts and hangings began.

The supposed ring leaders were gathered up by the Coal and Iron Police of the Reading Railroad which was the private police force of Gowen and the Pinkertons. Most were put on trial with evidence of informers who were given immunity from prosecution and in front of German speaking juries unable to speak English. They were hanged, several at a time, to best effect. On June 21 1877 six hanged at Postville and four more in Carbon County, ten men executed in a day. Over the following year another ten would hang, some guilty perhaps, most not, and all without a fair trial.

Jack Kehoe hanged for a crime he certainly did not commit. The prosecutor was Gowen, the charge, because they could find nothing else; a 14 year old killing which Kehoe did not do. The evidence was from an informer, promised freedom. In 1979 Kehoe received a posthumous pardon from Pennsylvania Governor Milton J. Shapp.

It's most unlikely that Kehoe was innocent of other crimes but he was certainly hanged for one he did not commit, as were the majority of the 20 men who hanged in the 3 years since the murders at Wiggan's Patch.

From his next letter we see that Patrick could not entirely settle after the murders and so we see he moves on. He makes his way to New York and to the company of his cousin James O'Donnell, who escaped the Patch a few years earlier and had since adopted his mother's maiden name; Devers and married.

He records also of hearing news of the Murder of Lord Frederick Cavendish and Thomas Henry Burke (Under-Secretary for Ireland) in the Phoenix Park in Dublin on May 6 1882. Unbeknown to him at the time that barbaric act is the catalyst which will ultimately lead to his own death sentence.

The Phoenix Park murders have been described as the JFK of the 19th century. It's not easy to overstate their significance at the time. Every paper around the world reported on the event and then for months after as the newly formed 'Special Branch', led by superintendent John Mallon was employed finding the killers. This should not be a surprise because Lord Frederick Cavendish was related, by marriage, to Prime Minister Gladstone, he was his wife's nephew. In addition, his elder brother was Lord Hartington, a prominent British Lord and politician who was to become the 8th Duke of Devonshire and head of one of the most powerful families in Britain. Appendix 3 contains a brief explanation of the significance of the killings in terms of what it meant to the furtherance of Irish Independence.

Other than the same interest any Irish man would have had in the story it is very clear that Patrick was not particularly concerned about the event. He had already resolved to visit Ireland with his cousin en-route to the diamond mines of South Africa.

Patrick seems to know he will not return to the United States but is unclear why. His last visit to Hanora, who is still in the lunatic asylum, is, to say the least, a surprise.

(Twenty Second Letter)
Dec 16th 1883 - Newgate Prison, London

And so Victor I come close to the end of my story, there is but one more tale to tell and I hope you can see that it is not the tale of my life, it is the tale of how it ends and that is all.

Every one of us comes to an end and I have found that the digestion of that reality, although not a comfort, helps me to accept my fate. Today is the last full day of this condemned man, and it has not begun well; Mullins the bastard found my brandy and stole it from me. What sort of a man has such in him that would deprive his fellow of this last pleasure? I think it poetic that the last injury to me apart from hanging is done to me by an Irishman, as were the earliest of my injuries[108].

After Ellen and Charles were murdered Grannie O'Donnell and the rest of the family abandoned Wiggans Patch and for a time lived at the tavern in Girardville along with Madge and me. James was in New York living under his mother's maiden name but we heard nothing from him until 1880 as he was cautious to what extent the Pinkertons would stretch in finding him. They surely would have assassinated him along with Charles if they had been quick enough on that night at Wiggans Patch.

I was free enough. I had associations with some of the wrong people but in a way my closeness to John Kehoe helped. That I worked for him in the

---

108 Presumably Patrick speaks of the Famine and evictions by Irish middlemen.

348

tavern gave reason and innocence to our association, a reason for it other than mischief which although not entirely correct was close enough and useful for me. Although I had set a few fires in my time since the war I had not been too heavily involved in the real trouble such as assassination.

My cousin Patrick who shared my name and my old address at Wiggans Patch was captured and prosecuted and got ten years for conspiracy[109]. He was inside by 1877. I don't know how he got on because I never saw him since and I think he is due to come out soon enough, if not already. I suppose one Patrick O'Donnell might have been enough for them.

On the night of the murders at that place I almost gave my real name and for sure I would have received a bullet for that identity which the killers would have mistaken for my cousin Patrick who was wanted about the killing of the Welshman in 71. Being an O'Donnell was enough in the moment I suppose. As it happens when I gave the name James McAllister I was just as likely to be shot as James was Charles McAllister's brother and himself knee deep in trouble of a serious type.

I think the gang were thrown by the murder of Ellen who was swollen with her child and killing women and children was not meant to be the business of the night. It accounts too for why they gave poor chase to Charles McAllister and James

---

109 In fact it was 5 years for Second Degree Murder of Morgan Powell Dec 2nd 1871 (Convicted Oct 1876)

O'Donnell; I think they were set to end us all but for the way it went. I give them no credit but even they had no want of the blood of women and children. It was what it was and sometimes too much thought is not a good thing. In a war both sides suffer loss and that is where I leave it.

I stayed on at the tavern but my arrangement with Margaret was in danger of being inadvertently disclosed to all. Grannie especially had an eye for things like that. You see we lived as brother and sister though we were married and appeared to be man and wife to the entire outside world. I had never known my wife in any way other than a dear sister and companion. She was the same with me but for reasons different to mine.

We moved back into Cousin Michael's house at Wiggans. The old O'Donnell place was empty and we went nowhere near to it after we fetched out the family's stuff. I worked five days each week at the tavern in Girardville and came back to the Patch, Madge and the children; who were almost fully grown by then.

Michael and Madge formed closeness in that time and when he discovered the nature of our companionship his relationship with her took on the aspects of a real marriage and I was truly then the brother. In honesty he knew the situation from the start but kept his distance for the sake of reputations. By then such things seemed of less importance.

It was a happy situation for me because I had plans to leave and maybe even return to Ireland and knowing Michael would care for Madge, Edward and Ellen was a comfort. Ellen was working as a dress maker by then and Edward was in the tavern, Michael had made it to miner and had his own face and labourers. Edward and Ellen already had the name O'Donnell and true enough they had that look about them, which confirmed to me that John had been about Margaret when she was still a nipper. Michael, Madge and the two offspring looked for the world a family and that was good news to me because I was once again, at the age of 47, ready to seek adventure for perhaps the last time. I wish I had stayed put. At this moment the inside of a coal mine seems a good place to be.

James Devers who was James O'Donnell wrote to me in late 1880 informing me that he had settled in New York, married and started a family. He had good work as a fixer in a large hotel on Broadway and begged me to join him. The last time I was on Broadway I was risking my life informing on Robert Kennedy and the plan to set alight the Astor House and other hotels and to burn down New York City.

It took only a small persuasion from James; I had a belly full of the coal fields of Pennsylvania by then, of the Hibernians and of the now expired Mollies. The drunken talk in the tavern every night was of what they would do with McKenna if they ever caught sight of him; brave drunken heroes who talked the fight. Anyone with a single eye could see who had won the whole game and it was not the 20 Mollies hanging from the gibbet or the miners or labourers. It was Gowen and the Pinkertons, but they one day will have their reward in Hell.

351

What happened to John Kehoe was a terrible thing. I know he had done bad deeds, even killings or the arrangement of killings and maybe he deserved to hang for that but he did not hang for it; he hanged for Langdon and everyone knew he was not guilty of that one. Langdon was beaten by a mob he had provoked and he walked home from the beating[110] and anyway John was not there.

I had liked him and he had been kind to me. Mary Ann kept the tavern in Girardville after they hanged him; John had provided well for her and the children, he was a wealthy man. She need not have kept the business but I suppose it occupied her and she by then had taken in half of the family. Old Grannie looked after John, Ellen's' boy and was useful with John's own five and she cooked and made busy and judged us all for our transgressions which she supposed had attracted all the trouble; and she may have been more right than she was wrong.

With Margaret and the children taken care of and happy with Michael there was nothing to keep me in Pennsylvania so in the spring of 81 I made my way to New York and to James. I stayed with him and easily found work labouring. There was much building at that time and mixing mortar took little skill and paid enough to keep me. Soon enough a fellow showed me the skills for laying bricks and I was about that for the next while. The pay was better and I was able to find my own place

---

110 *Langdon died the day after being attacked by a mob in what was clearly an unplanned attack (so not a capital offence anyway) by thugs.*

352

for a time but the plan always was to collect enough money to head back to Ireland.

In 82 I heard stories of diamonds in South Africa and this took my particular interest, not only because it was an adventure and there was good profit to be made but also I remember how my father had spoken of the place and I longed to go where he had been so many years before.

I had missed the gold rush in California and always regretted that. There is no easy or exact way to explain the matter; wandering the world is in the blood of many Irish men and with me it was no different. James and I had enough money to make the journey and to sustain us for six months, by which time we swore to his wife that we would return. It was on this promise that she gave her leave for us to try it.

Also in that year in the late spring we heard of the terrible deed in Phoenix Park[111] in Dublin. I shall not waste time now recounting that dastardly deed in all its detail for it is well known to the world. It is enough to say that the Invincibles struck down Cavendish[112] and Burke[113] with butchery and without mercy or consideration; as wolves descending upon lambs.

---

111 Please see Appendix 3 for a brief summary of the Phoenix Park Murders.
112 Lord Frederick Charles Cavendish. (30 November 1836 – 6 May 1882). Chief Secretary for Ireland
113 Thomas Henry Burke (29 May 1829 – 6 May 1882). Permanent Under Secretary at the Irish Office

The news was greeted in New York by some in our community as a great victory for the cause of Irish republicanism. Most holding that opinion had never set foot in our country. I and many of my fellow Irishmen and women took it as a great sadness and yet another depravity committed by a few in the name of us all and without our consent. The rational Irish and British Irish and American Irish saw it for the foulness that it was and recognised the untold damage it would make to the cause of Irish Independence.

By this time I was in correspondence with my younger brother Donald in Donegal where he had married a woman named Mary and had a son whom he named after me; Patrick. They had taken a tavern in Derrybeg and encouraged me to come home where they had a room for me. My mother, who by that time must have been past her seventieth year longed also to see me; it was 35 years or more since Michael and I left in the midst of that terrible time in 47.

As we made our final plans to leave New York each week more exciting and worrying news of the murders in Ireland came our way. It was disclosed that the elder brother of the murdered Cavendish was none other than Lord Hartington, who was part of Gladstone's Administration, so no effort would be spared finding the culprits. After no progress in almost eight months a new squad named 'Special Branch' was formed and soon it was in keen pursuit of the killers. Employing the usual English tactics of bribery and torture they eventually rounded up a dozen or so of a group called the 'Irish Invincibles';

a squad of degenerate illiterates who knew as much about Irish freedom as they did morality…. nothing.

By the middle of January the authorities had all of them plus a few others for good measure. By the middle of February the leader of the attack, James Carey and another[114] had turned informer. When I think of it my mind is drawn back to Pennsylvania and Kerrigan the liar and others and it made me sick to think of it. *Was the entire world a cesspool and it filled to overflow with informers?* I wondered. To me there is no more detestable a thing than a turncoat.

During my two years in New York and before I visited Hanora in the asylum most months. I would wheel her in the grounds and talk to her of bears and hunting and trapping and the Innu visiting us in our cabin. I spoke to her of Margaret and how she had grown beautiful and had children and a good man in my cousin Michael. I think or perhaps I hoped I could see something in her face or in a movement or a sigh but I could not. Hanora had left that body many years before.

I wondered then and I wonder now *if Hanora had not been grasped by whatever thing which took her mind where would we have been on our journey?* There would have been no war for me because I would not have gone west without her and if we had gone together she would not have let me fall into the ill ways which saw me gamble and then join a wicked campaign of destruction.

I do not exaggerate when I tell you that as I sat with her and held her bony hand and looked at the

---

114 Myles Kavanagh, the getaway driver

living corpse that she had become that I would gladly have ended my days then and there just for one second of recognition, of a smile or a frown or something that said

'I am here and I see you and I hear you my love'.

Alas it was not to come and upon the visit before my last I had set my mind to the course I was going to take. It was May 14th, 1883 the day they hanged Joseph Brady, the first of the Phoenix Park killers, though I did not know it on the day, I discovered that news later.

I took Hanora as usual out into the grounds in her bath chair and I spoke to her as usual, I held her hand and I stroked her face and I cried as I pulled her close to me. Into her ear I whispered

'I will always love you'

I gently thrust the blade of her ivory handled stiletto up the back of her neck and deep into her skull. As I did she exhaled the softest of breath, and whispered;

'Pádraig'.

and she was gone.

There are those that will judge me and to them I say this;

'Go to Hell.'

My Hanora was gone and my one regret is I did not join her; soul, mind and body sooner. I loved and I do love Margaret like I love no other but even that love is as nothing to the complete and everlasting love I have for my Hanora. I knew I would not be returning with James as my fortunes lay in some other place and I did not want her to suffer any more.

I withdrew the knife and placed it in my belt, I placed her on the floor and called for help for my fallen companion and they came and took her and I left. I made a small effort to conceal the matter but not any great resource was spent in subterfuge and it happens no one noted anything untoward or if they did they could not be bothered to report it.

I cannot ever tell you the gap I have in me, the utter and unbearable emptiness I have felt from then until now. Even when I did not see her, sometimes for years, I knew she was in the world and now she is not. It is not something I felt when away at war or in the mines even though I seldom saw her but knowing now she is gone is almost all I can bear.

As I look to one more day on this earth I confess part of me welcomes the noose and the end of this pain. If I could I would have it done today and be finished with it all but I need to finish my letters.

I shall stop a spell and finish this evening for I will indulge myself and contemplate the times by the lake and the times with old Murphy and I shall think of my darling Hanora at her very best.

23
GULITY OF THE ACT BUT NOT THE DEED

'HE ASSASSINATION OF CAREY—ARREST OF O'DONNELL AT PORT ELIZABETH

The Assassination of Carey – Arrest of O'Donnell at Port Elizabeth.

Of all the adventures and his several acts of violence during his turbulent times none is more troubling than his dispatching Hanora. It's hard to judge Patrick on today's standards and obviously he considered the act to be one of mercy. This is a man who was born into suffering and death and most of his life he has encountered and survived it.

The temptation is to judge the act and the man in the context of his life and of the times in which he lived, but if we do that maybe, ironically, he might be judged more harshly than if he did this deed in our time. Although the manner of it seems brutal was the act itself any different to a man escorting a beloved wife or mother or sister to some Scandinavian country now, to be humanely killed for the avoidance of further pain and suffering?

It's a situation we all might judge but not one which many of us will ever encounter, thankfully. Perhaps what he did was not so bad, not bad at all in fact.

What it does show is that Patrick had a way of determining his own philosophy on killing, one might say, adjusting, or killing his own conscience. Littleman in the sheds and the Frenchmen on the hillside above Quebec seemed to be completely justified to him and frankly it would be hard to argue anything to the contrary. Later it is clear from his letters that he was most unhappy at the concept of killing another human during the war, simply because he was in an army and the army was instructed to kill. He does not say directly but it does seem that he actively avoided shooting the enemy at Chattanooga. He seemed to live by a code, his code, which is not everyone's code but at least he had one.

As we shall see, on the morning before his execution is scheduled to take place Patrick begins what he thinks is his last letter with a somewhat cheerful note. Sometime previous the jailers took his brandy from him but that morning they returned it.

It is in this letter also that he makes his strongest commentary on his motivations for the crime for which he is to hang, insofar as he had any. He was clearly absolutely determined that he would not be remembered for the wrong reasons. It has to be said, that apart from papers at the time and the prosecution no one seriously believed he was ever a member of any republican organisation, far less a violent one such as the Irish Invincibles. So far as anyone can determine he was not even part of the Hibernians. He lived 36 of his 48 years in America and whilst Irish by birth he was hardly a patriot. He, like most people at the time, including many Irish patriots, not least Charles Stewart Parnell, was repulsed by the Phoenix Park Killings for example.

Of course some republicans in Ireland claimed him and attributed to him motives he did not have and this was what he feared. It's ironic that these same organisations or their descendant manifestations now also want the British Government to pardon him due to his mistrial. In July 2021 The Times carried an article suggesting his 'mistrial' might be investigated.

Did he do the deed for Ireland or not? Does it matter? It mattered to Patrick but his opinion and wishes died with him. As he feared his act was hijacked, which is a pity.

His explanation as to what happened on that ship off the coast of Port Elizabeth does seem honest and eminently plausible. More to the point, all alternative explanations seem complexly implausible. Disregarding the detail of which gun was used, what size bullets and so on, what happened was the same thing that happens in bars and taverns every night around the world.

(Twenty Third Letter)
Dec 16th 1883 - Newgate Prison, London

My Dear Victor,
Good news indeed… No, I am not reprieved,
though that would be the best news. Mullins has
renewed some of my belief in man. Late he came
this afternoon and returned to me my brandy. He
shook my hand also and I would never refuse a
hand offered in contrition. I was highly suspicious
that he might have urinated in the bottle. I have
tested it and as far as I can tell it is all brandy, and if
I am mistaken and cannot taste his piss I care not
that it might be contained within the spirit.

I have a swig or two taken and it has cheered
me a little. It is funny how easy it is to come to
peace with your end when there is no question to it.
I derive also great contentment from almost
completing my story. I suppose in a way I have now
lived my life two times; once for real and once in
the telling of it.

I saw Madge in the last hour and I decided not
to inform her of her mother's passing. I wanted to
but did not have the spirit required and I feared if
she was angry or greatly wounded then I would be
in a great funk going to the gibbet. It sounds a
strange thing to say but it is true, I prefer a good
disposition than a bad one in life so why not in
death? As with most of my letters that part is in
Irish and she will not be able to read it until I am
gone. When she then hears the whole story I am

sure she will understand and be gentle in her judgement on me.

She took with her my letters from today and she is allowed one final visit early tomorrow so I will complete my work tonight so she can carry out this last letter.

I am near the end of my story, the end of my life and the end of all things. So now I shall recount to you the thing which it seems is of greatest interest to most people yet to me is a trifle and a mere detail which is notable only because the person I despatched was famous for his badness and I am to die for it.

You will be surprised to learn that the answer to the question why? is not entirely clear to me. It is little wonder that the newspapers have speculated that I am a British Spy hell bent on revenge for the British establishment against the mastermind of Cavendish's murder on the one hand or an Invincible hell bent on revenge for the Irish republican cause against a turncoat, on the other hand. Is it any wonder they have chosen to hang me? The British get their revenge and the Irish get their martyr. My death restores the balance in many ways.

So let us start at the beginning of the event which sees me in this fix. It is after all the only place to start. I can declare without any fear of doubt and with no man on earth capable of contradicting me by word of mouth or by paper proof, other than lies; that I am not an Invincible, that I am not a member of Clan na Gael[115], that I am not a member

---

115 Irish republican organization in the United States

of the Irish Brotherhood[116]. So let it stand that I acted never for one of these organisations and have never had the least affiliation or interest in any of them. I know that even before I am hanged some of them claim me and my deed but they do so without my consent.

I lived in Ireland for my first 12 years and was forced out and away from my roots and from my family by starvation. I landed in a new world and although it was no easy trip and I have fought wars and mine owners and illnesses which would have ended most; America is my home. Not the place of my birth but that of my salvation. I do not hold any loyalty or favour for Ireland and at times have been more inclined to shame than to pride that I originate therefrom.

I say these words harsh I know but I do so lest they be taken and forged by the warped minds of those who advocate slitting innocent men in a park for a cause they steal from democratic and good advocates.[117]

I say this not because I have some dislike of the land or the people but I have a detestation for those that would promote the notion of its independence over the rights and wellbeing of its own inhabitants. They presume to speak for all and in their actions arrive nothing but misery on them. Just as the

---

116 Probably refers to the Fenian Brotherhood, another (earlier) name for Clan na Gael.
117 It is likely Patrick refers here to Charles Stewart Parnell, who was making headway politically in a fight for an Independent Ireland.

Mollies, a handful who, through the extremities of their actions, gave the mine owners the tools to destroy the trade union and the Hibernians because they chose to kill.

So let it be understood by all those who will cry tears and build tombs and monuments and remember the 17th of December, you do it not for me, you do it for you and I will be dead and with my Hanora and I cannot stop you but from my grave I curse you and your good intentions with your bad deeds.

Do not I beg let anyone attribute my contrition for killing poor Carey to some foundation of religion; it is not. Do not pray for me or offer a sacrament and do not build any monument or record of what I have done. Leave me I beg amongst the lime under the slab in this place, it is where I deserve to be, bury my deed with me I beg.

I did not do this thing for Ireland and I did not do it for freedom, I did it because I was drunk, I was stupid and I was vengeful and arrogant and since my loss[118] I care nothing for me. I allowed the situation to run, all the while I could have stopped it but pride and drink were my masters. Nothing noble; nothing noble I tell you and all who will twist my motives one way or the other for their own needs then a curse on you and on yours and theirs after that.

I am not a fool[119], I know that many of those who hate me will remember me for the deed and all

---

118 Presumably Patrick refers to Hanora. He is clearly still grief stricken at her loss, perhaps to the point of 'suicide by court judgement'.

of those who wanted the traitor Carey dead will also remember me for the same deed but for different reasons. I pray I am not remembered or celebrated for taking away a husband and a father and any person who believes me to have done this as some act of heroism or as a blow for the cause, any cause, is woefully mistaken.

So here all of you now read why and how I killed Carey, the killer, the traitor, the man, the husband, the father.

After visiting my family in Donegal in the spring of 83 James decided he missed his wife and son too much to be away a full year or even the planned six months and he took a ship back to New York. I continued alone onto Dublin and then down to London where I befriended a simple girl from my own home town, Gweedore. She reminded me greatly of Margaret, though was no more than twenty years old. She wished to open a new life in South Africa and had some small means but not a vast sum. I do not know for sure but she had some regrettable time in our home town which she was not disposed to discuss. I had the impression it involved unwanted attentions from a man.

---

119 There is no question that although not formally educated Patrick was very learned, able to read at age five, able to speak three languages fluently and an exceptionally good learner and deep thinker. British and American Newspapers at the time reported him as 'an illiterate Irishman', as of course they presumed all Irishmen to be.

We came to an arrangement convenient to us both that she sail as my wife, Mrs O'Donnell and thus we would share the passage in one birth and save. Had we not been man and wife we would not have been allowed to share. I asked a priest in London to marry us proper but he refused.

Susan Gallagher was her name and she was agreeable if simple company and would serve well as a companion and no doubt be of considerable assistance in my venture. I had not planned upon the situation but it seemed to me to be an excellent happenstance.

Susan was not of great wit but she played draughts most skilfully and bested me more often than not. Much of our trip was spent so engaged in the second class saloon of the ship. I cannot recall the name of the ship but it was 'something' Castle[120].

I ask any and all to judge the situation at this point. Does this seem like a man on a mission to murder? I say;

'No it does not'. Nothing was further from my contemplation.

On the trip I met several travellers, some Irish, some British and Dutch and in particular a jolly fellow named James Power along with his wife Maggie (yet another Margaret) and seven children. We found common ground because we both were bricklayers though I confess he was a master of the trade and I was a novice by comparison. In the evenings he would sketch out the complexities of waterproof brick laying, Flemish and English bonds

---

120 *Kinfauns Castle. It sailed for Cape Town July 6th 1882*

and such like. On one occasion he borrowed the children's building blocks to erect an elaborate model of a brick chamber good enough to stop the escape of gas. He was exceedingly knowledgeable.

Most around us, particularly Maggie and Susan found this an exceedingly tedious debate but he and I got along very well. In order to include Susan and Maggie and his eldest two we would always finish up in the saloon playing draughts tournaments which almost without exception Susan would win.

When the women and children were away he and I would play for small wagers and we both won and lost in equal measure. James was always with his cigar and glass of brandy and me with my pipe and whiskey; often too much of it for us both.

As you read this account you will have deduced that this James Power was in fact, unknown to me, none other than James Carey, the leader of the Invincibles, the mastermind of the killing of Cavendish and the turncoat who saw five of our countrymen swing and several of them sent to servitude. You will also deduce that I had absolutely no idea that this warm and friendly family man was one in the same - a jackal. So I ask again that question, how could I possibly be on a plan to kill a man I did not know and I did not know was on that ship? It is a question I will ask again and one that my defence asked two weeks past in court but to not plausible explanation.

The three weeks it took to get as far as Cape Hope passed swiftly. Our new acquaintance with the Powers family, as we knew them to be, made the trip enjoyable. We were to take a coast steamer from the Cape to our final destination because by hugging the coast we apparently would be spared the worst of the weather which that area offered.

We had the chance to go on to land at Cape Hope and Susan and I took the opportunity to look about the town with our new friends, who brought with them the whole family. I was impressed with how the children conducted themselves, they were quiet and respectful. Later of course I realised they were fearful lest their father's identity be revealed. There were many Irish and indeed English on the boat and about the place who would not take kindly to James Carey. There is no question, he had made enemies of all sides and done it particular well.

I have heard since, during my trial and before it that rumours about Power's real name and identity were all about the place on the boat to Cape Town but also and in particular in the town itself. I can tell you that on the 28th of July as we boarded *The Melrose* to continue our journey around the Cape I had absolutely no notion of these things. The Phoenix Park killings could not have been further from my thoughts.

Had the execution of Carey been my mission I could have done it any time over the three week journey and pushed his body over the side into the ocean and been certain to get away completely with the act. So once again I must ask; can any right minded person really believe that was my task?

The new ship set off on the 28th which I recall was a Saturday. The next afternoon, as normal, James, Maggie, Susan and I played draughts. I did detect nervousness or restlessness in Maggie which I had not seen before and she retired to her birth at about two in the afternoon. Susan stayed next to me on the sofa and James sat across, the draughts board between us. He was not his normal jovial self and on reflection I suppose he may have heard the rumours about his identity the previous day and supposed…. incorrectly…. that I too had heard them. I certainly had not and accounts of me being told this by an orderly are entirely fictitious or mistaken. I would not have sat with Carey as he would have been the target of every Irish hero from Cork to Cape Town.

His acquaintance would have been an embarrassment to any man and most likely a danger. In addition although I detest all turncoats and informers I hate more murderers of innocent men and I would have wanted nothing to do with the man.

I was rather more filled with whiskey than normal for the time of day and losing one game after another in bad style. James too was the worse for drink. He leaned back in his chair and for the first time I noted a revolver under his waistcoat. I remarked to him very simply;

'Are you expecting trouble Mr Power?' as I nodded to the handgun. It was a jovial and a thoughtless remark which meant nothing. Though he may have deduced my use of his surname was intended to mean something, it was not, it was natural for me to address close friends by their surname. In addition many travellers carried side arms and in my bag I myself had a loaded colt. I was not in the least concerned with his precaution; he was after all travelling with and the protector of a large family.

At this point James dropped his seat forward and put his hand on the gun while keeping it under his coat. He demanded what I knew. I cannot recall the exact words for I was very shocked but he stated that he was James Carey and declared that I was a Fenian assassin.

Susan who had been half asleep started to rise up at the commotion and I put up my hand and declared I had no idea what he was speaking about. The name Carey at that moment did not mean a thing to me I tell you in all honesty. Although I knew of the matter I had not yet been linked to it as I now am. With this James made a drunken pull for the gun and it flew out of his pocket into my lap. I picked it up instinctively and turned it on him; he was by then on his feet.

Victor; you may say that at this point I had a choice, and I agree I did. I had his gun and I was not in danger and that I freely confess, yet, I have seen men hesitate and whose lives have ended for the want of action so without a single thought and still with no idea who this man was I fired and hit him in the neck. For those who judge my next actions I ask;

Have you disabled a man using a gun and have you been army trained? If 'no' then you cannot judge. The rule is you shoot until the assailant stops moving; an injured man is a dangerous man. He might easily have a knife or a gun about his hip or his ankle. I often had one or the other.

As Carey twisted and fell towards Maggie, who for some reason was coming back into the saloon; I shot him twice more. That the shots hit him in his back was not designed but I am thankful I did not injure Maggie who was so close to him as he fell.

Accounts given to the court claim one thing or another and I cannot confirm or deny these. There are only two certainties in this thing. The first is that I shot dead James Carey on the Melrose on that hot Saturday[121] afternoon and the second is that I had no intention of doing that thing right up to the moment it happened. *I had to do it, it had to be done.*

As you and the world know that is all I have claimed. I am no Fenian rebel or Republican or Invincible. The notion that the Invincibles paid me is beyond unbelievable, they were done for and finished before Brady hanged. I swear I never so much as met a single one of them.

I did this terrible deed because I was drunk and stupid, had I been sober I would not have shot the man because I would have assessed the matter better. It was later that I found out the man was Carey of the Park killings. If I had known his true identity I would have avoided him, not shot him. I have no interest in the business in which he was involved, none other than all the other observers and readers of the news.

By the time I came to my senses I saw poor Maggie and her eldest and I was shamed and

---

[121] *In fact it was a Sunday afternoon.*

shocked. I gave myself to the authorities without struggle and without protest and was more ashamed than proud when some ill guided fools in Port Elizabeth cheered me on and shouted abuse to the dead man as his body accompanied me to the courthouse.

I wanted to protest that I did not do this thing for Ireland or for England but I was instructed to be quiet or my words could hang me. Upon my return to England I was told funds were being raised for my defence in Ireland, in Africa and in America and if I spoke as I do now the funds would not come. I wanted very much to denounce myself as a drunken killer of a father but I was told that would soon stop any collection for my legal case. I am sorry to say that I listened to the lawyers.

Pryor came over from America. I had not seen him since my time in prison on Lafayette Island and it is the measure of how famous my deed and I had become. The killings had been the biggest news since Abe was slain in the Theatre and my deed was taken upon by every side for their own ends. My acquaintance with Pryor in prison had been brief and I doubt he remembered me much but we had both been Confederate spies, or so it appeared, for I certainly was not. It seemed that the Irish Brotherhood and others had collected several thousand dollars and insisted he be on the team to win my freedom.

When it came to the trial, I wanted to plead manslaughter as the act was in the moment and that is how it was. Even when convicted I would have kept my life. The crown would have none of it and

nor would my team, which by now consisted of the
very best and most expensive in the land, including
Pryor, who was not permitted by the judge to speak
for me. The crown was sure of a guilty verdict on
murder, so a hanging; and my team were very sure
of self-defence so sure of freedom.

I believed my team made a fatal error, fatal to
the case and to me. They assumed that the English
would be truthful and honest and would keep in
mind that regardless of Carey's testimony hanging
most of the Phoenix Park killers, he was still one of
the murdering brutes who killed one of their highest
and most powerful people would be glad of what I
had done, regardless of why. It seems to me now
that they were mistaken.

Susan had at first been left in Port Elizabeth
but Pryor with his funds from America paid her
home and put high hopes in her testimony but
when she arrived she was muddled and they felt she
would harm me more than help so she was not put
to use.

Then they brought in two or three witnesses
who swore to me having a photograph or a drawing
of Carey in my case in the birth and that I knew
who he was. I have to tell you Victor that I have
nothing to lose now so you can take my words to be
true. I had no such picture, I had no such
knowledge with which they later endowed me, I
knew not the man's true name or that he was a
turncoat.

They stated I had a gun in my case and this was
true but it was normal enough and it would be no

good in my birth if I was planning to kill the man. They even claimed I had a bomb and threw it over board. It was a box for my hand which I injured in the mines and though they fished it up and saw that is all it was the mention of it to the jury was very harmful to me.

With all the misleading testimony it was turned from a drunken error to a planned murder. This in spite of all the evidence saying if I wanted to do him in I could have done it easy with no detection.

I can conclude that by hanging me it makes a tidy job of the whole business and brings the end to the Phoenix Park killing. The Irish republicans are glad to see the turncoat dead and the English glad to see the Killer of a noble one of theirs dead. I am but the full stop to that unpleasant sentence!

So there we have it Victor. The truth of the matter; I have resigned myself to my fate and as I have hinted, in some ways I welcome it. I hope that my letters get to you and that one day they are shown to the world. Yes I killed Carey but he might as well have been any bricklayer from Dublin. Even now I cannot say if it was or was not self-defence. A drunk man pulled out a gun on another drunk man who got the gun himself and used it to end the attacker. That is how it was.

I have now a few hours and I shall stop writing. Madge is due in the morning to say goodbye and I want to prepare for her. I am glad to say that Michael has arrived today also so she will not be alone. He promised our mother I would allow Fleming, the priest to see me so I shall but I would sooner spit in his eye. I would have liked to see

Ellen and Edward but the fund paid for Madge and later for Michael and would not pay more.

I bid you farewell and whilst, as with Poor old John Brown, your efforts for me have not been fruitful I am deeply indebted to you for making them. Like you I do not believe in the religious but I do believe in religion and I am sure now of one thing and one thing only; that I shall in hours be united forever with my dear Hanora.

Pádraig

24
LOST LETTERS

This next letter is brief and was written on the morning of December 17th 1883; 'Execution Day'. Patrick had not planned to write it. The text is self-explanatory so there is no need to explain further what had happened. Why it happened however; is something that shall forever be open to speculation.

He did not sign the letter but initialled it.

(Twenty Fourth Letter)
Dec 17th 1883 - Newgate Prison, London

Victor,

I am not sure why I write this note as it is most unlikely you will see it, but by some fortune some other might; it must be brief. All my effort is undone. I made a story of my life and intended it for you to do with as you judged best.

I must report that my efforts are stolen from my wife Margaret. She is here with me now and has told me the news that all of my letters are discovered and taken by scoundrels; she knows not who; they pushed her about and bruised her. They went to her rooms and ransacked them and took it all.

All that is left is my last letter from last evening and to it I attach this note. That letter at least tells of the way it was on the boat, the matter for which I am condemned unfairly. If it reaches you then at least some of my task will have been fulfilled.

Thank you for giving me the distraction which you may never know you gave me. Margaret takes this note and the last letter in an empty brandy bottle, they will not search that I hope, or steal it for its contents are in my belly warming me.

P.O'D
Proud to be both an American and an Irishman.

25
THE EXECUTION OF PATRICK O'DONNELL

The Gallows at Newgate 1883

The twenty fifth letter was not actually written by Patrick, or so at first it would seem. From a practical point of view it was written on an altogether different sort of paper, a better quality, and the hand is completely different to Patrick's.

Examples of Patrick's handwriting are rare but in all he uses cursive writing; what in primary school might have been called 'real writing' or 'joined up writing'. This letter was printed and virtually every third word is incorrectly spelt. It is unsigned so from the letter itself it is impossible to ascertain the author; from its content however we can deduce that it was almost certainly or intended to appear to have been written by Bartholomew Binns, the hangman; and likely written many years after the event. Who else could it have been?

378

Upon reading the letter now however there may be one other candidate.

(Dec 17ᵗʰ 1883 - Newgate Prison, London)
Unattributed Account

Patrick O'Donnell walked barefoot along the narrow candle lit passageway; behind him a guard each side held his arms and guided him to the oak door at the passageway's end. His hands were bound in front of him with leather and his feet were in chains with sufficient length to allow his short sliding steps over the cold flagstone floor.

As they reached the door the three men stopped; one of the guards placed a white sack hood over his head while the other pushed against the heavy oak; the loud rasping squeal of metal hinge suggested the door was not often used.

He felt a shove and stepped forward, through the opening, as best he could in the heavy chains. The door closed behind him and he heard the bolts slide; top and bottom, inside. The two men had not followed him into the execution room.

Patrick could hear his own heartbeat and was sure anyone nearby would also. He tried to hold it, to slow it and to quieten it; to no avail. He could sense one other person in the room; through the hood he could make out the candles and the shadow of a figure as it crossed between him and them. The figure came around to his back, but said nothing.

He was guided gently forward by the man whom he knew must be the bungling hangman Bartholomew Binns, his executioner. Binns stopped and turned Patrick around and placed the noose over his head, as he did so Patrick shuddered.

'It's cold' he said hastily; hopeful that the hangman had not mistaken the involuntary spasm as fear.

The figure made no reply as he unlocked the shackles and removed them from Patrick's ankles. He rose and stepped backwards, a plank creaked under his boot; Patrick's head turned to the left almost imperceptibly as the shadow pulled the lever to the trapdoor.

As the floor opened a single utterance issued from Patrick O'Donnell's lips;

'Hanora.'

(Final Letter)
Dec 17th 1883 Tilbury Docks, London

I had not intended to say her name. It just happened that way, she was not even in my mind; my only thought was to hold onto my bowels. I have heard stories of hanged men letting go of it all and I did not want that.

At first I thought the trap had stuck but it could not have done because I heard it open and I heard a man drop and the snatch and the creak of tight rope on timber as its human burden swung back and forth.

Next I heard the steps of a man, the slide of two bolts, the opening of a door and the closing of it and then the turning of a key. I waited, but nothing; my hands were still bound with leather ties and I raised them both to the hood and slowly drew it from my head. Before looking about I loosened the rope under my chin and threw away the noose.

I looked about me and there was no one in the room. The taught rope next to me had almost stopped swaying and I peered into the trap and there on its end was a man, not swinging now but slowly turning as if the rope was unwinding its own coils.

The room was not as small as it had felt, twelve foot by ten perhaps. It was lit with candles on the walls and there was no window but I could feel a strong draft and the candles flickered wildly giving the impression that the walls were on fire. The thought I was in hell crossed my mind.

26
TILBURY DOCKS

Typical Horse and Carriage 1883

The purpose of the epigraphs in this book has been to provide context, sometimes explanation and generally to introduce each letter. It was very hard to do that with the last letter so I have split it in two. Now that the utterly remarkable turn of events is known to the reader we can consider it.

The first thing to note is that the account of Patrick's 'execution' in the unattributed letter may well indeed have been his own account after all and for some reason dressed to look otherwise. The most obvious reason being that he wanted the letter to confirm his execution, but we shall never know for sure. What is absolutely clear is that the last letter, part of which we have already read, is unquestionably Patrick's.

What will have been noted by most, even without further explanation, is the unusual process employed in the 'execution'. People who are executed of course cannot account for the process and what is done and who is there; they will for a short time be invested with the facts but the nature of the enterprise will almost immediately dispose of that knowledge. However, even without expert knowledge it is clear that in the course of an ordinary hanging, if such a thing existed, there would at least be a priest, probably the warden certainly the surgeon and the hangman. In fact there would likely be several other people in attendance also. That Patrick was taken into the execution room alone indicates that things were not in any way usual.

There are those who will suppose such subterfuge in an execution to be impossible, but that is not so. Fake executions though not commonplace certainly did happen. Patrick was after all in a very unusual situation. He was in some parts of English society regarded as something of a hero. He had after all killed Carey, the mastermind of the Phoenix Park Murders, in which Lord Cavendish; part of the highest echelons in English society, had been brutally stabbed to death. There were a great many very influential people who felt that a debt was owed to Patrick O'Donnell.

It's easy to forget that 137 years ago there was considerable speculation that far from being an Irish hero, Patrick was in fact acting on behalf of the crown, having been recruited personally by Inspector Mullins, of the newly formed Special Branch. Apart from reasons due to his occupation,

Mullins detested Carey for the degenerate that he clearly was.

The theory certainly seems to be credible given that Patrick, previous to his involvement with Carey, had nothing to do with republicanism. The assassination, if that is what it was, could not possibly have been more inept and amateurish. This might be why the British would have employed his services, if indeed they did.

On the one hand it needed to not look like a republican coup but also not as though the British had a hand in it. They could not have done a better job; for a bungling happenstance is what it certainly appears to have been.

This is not 'grassy knoll' or 'moon landing' fantasy, it is plausible and indeed highly possible given that the high and powerful of the land would hardly have wanted to honour a deal made by a police man with the killer of Gladstone's nephew.

There is no account in Patrick's letters of any such dealing, one would hardly expect there to be. Though there are hints if one is inclined to look for them.

As a reminder of how deeply the matter reached into British society, in fact to its very heights; Queen Victoria herself mentions the killing in her diaries, where she expressed what might be described as contentment regards the disposal of Carey. In an earlier entry she also expressed the view that Finnian's should be hanged 'on the spot', without trial.

Of course the republicans regarded him as a patriot; they still do; he was Irish and hanged by the British, what else could he possibly be? However, they had no motive or reason to plan an escape; they wanted a martyr, and martyrs are best presented dead, preferably at the end of an English rope.

At the time there was a very real concern, almost paranoia amongst the authorities that there would be an attempt to free O'Donnell and for two days before the date of execution extra police were drafted in to stand guard at the walls.

On the morning of the 16th December 1883, the day before the execution there was considerable consternation about a mysterious ship which appeared off the Tilbury docks. The Boston Pilot, a newspaper, published an account of the event on December 22nd 1883.

The ship, named the Assyrian Monarch, (later the Assyrian) was a steamer which was, according to the London Police, laden with a group of Irishmen intending to free O'Donnell. It had apparently sailed up from Cornwall the previous day with its deadly cargo of ruffians.

When it docked in Tilbury it was boarded by three detectives in possession of warrants. When they discovered that the passenger list was missing this seemed to compound their fears so no passengers, regardless of nationality, were permitted to disembark until after noon the following day.

Restocked, the ship made for New York on the evening of December 18th 1883.

Though unlikely and illogical the authorities entertained as a serious possibility the Irish Republicans breaking Patrick out; in spite of their previous attempts to free their countrymen being spectacularly amateurish.

Twenty years earlier, in 1867 the IRB made an attempt to release a prisoner from Newgate by placing a barrel of gunpowder against its wall. The explosion dented the wall, blew out windows in a tavern and killed 4 passers-by. Had gelignite been available they'd have made the same impact on the wall but probably killed a few more innocents, and themselves. So even if they had the motive they did not have the means. If the Assyrian Monarch was chartered by anyone for nefarious work, it was not the Irish republicans.

For obvious reasons Patrick does not in the course of his first 25 letters say much on this point; not least because he would not have known specifics about any plot to free him, and had he done he would never have mentioned them. He did however make several comments which in hindsight may well have been very revealing. For example in his very first letter he writes *"Before the trial I was approached and told quietly that regardless of the verdict I would not see a rope"*.

He does not say by whom he was approached but in view of his escape, or release, these possibly have a hidden meaning. In addition he does seem a little blasé about his fate at times. And whilst no one in his situation would want to rely on a promise or a hint he does seem confident occasionally.

Although Patrick does not record it in his letters it is known that he was visited by a priest and that they were engaged in deep conversation several times. Something of a surprise given that he was fervently anti priest.

Supposing there was some plan afoot he would not have known the details and certainly by the time he had the noose around his neck he must have lost all hope. Scepticism is to be expected, indeed; by those who conspired to save him it is relied upon.

Perhaps we can leave the last word regards the escape plan and the possible involvement of the Cavendish family and the 8th Duke to the current and 12th Duke of Devonshire; Peregrine Andrew Morny Cavendish. He responded in 2021 to my proposition; not by denying it, but by stating that he was 'agnostic' on the matter. He was also kind enough to congratulate me on my efforts translating and transcribing Patrick's letters.

(Final Letter - Continued)
Dec 17th 1883 Tilbury Docks, London

On the floor in front of me was a set of clothing and on top a leather pouch; next to that was a knife; my Hanora's knife. If not hell then perhaps I had arrived in heaven? I honestly wondered was I dead and this next life was to continue the intrigue and adventure.

I was still soft from the brandy the night before and my head throbbed. My senses and my sense came back to me fast though. I stepped forward, cautious at first and then with pace. I took the knife which served badly to cut the leather bindings and better to untie them. I looked into the pouch and found paper and money. I did not count it but it was a very large amount. I dressed quickly and did not question what luck this was or how it came about.

When fully clothed I took the wooden staircase via a doorway in the floor at the corner of the room; down the two turns and I arrived slightly below the swinging man's shoulder; his face was white and I knew immediately this man had departed long before this morning. Beyond him was an open door, beyond that I could see the wheels and base of a fine carriage.

I shifted back into the shadow to avoid the occupants or the driver seeing me. I waited. The carriage moved inches forward and back as the horse protested at being still. I could hear the voice of the driver calming his beasts.

I leaned forward and saw that the carriage door was open. I leaned a little more and with a growing confidence and the hope that this could be what it might be I stepped forward and I saw into the vehicle. Sitting in a fine dress and a bonnet, illuminated from the morning darkness by lamplight was my wife; not my wife, Margaret but my wife Susan, who was not entirely my wife. My heart leapt and I concluded immediately that this was some plan set afoot by God knows who, to see me free.

I made a dash and as I hit the soft cushioned interior of the vehicle the door slammed behind me and I heard the crack of the whip and away.

Susan engaged me with enthusiastic affection and when I could take breath from her efforts to smother me with kisses I asked what was afoot. She could tell me nothing. I assumed first that some republican group had sprung their hero and then thought better of it as there was no way it could be. She had a bundle on her lap and she passed it to me as I looked through the rear of the carriage, sure that I would see constables on horse come to fetch me back to my fate. I took the bundle from her.

'My letters' I said in complete amazement. 'but how?'

She smiled innocently and shrugged her shoulders. She was a handsome creature but what she had been gifted in good looks had been at the debit of some other part of her; as I so often have found in handsome men and beautiful women.

'This morning a knock came on my door and a splendid tall gentleman with a hat of fine mole hair entered my room. He had this dress for me in a box and it is new'.

She proudly stiffened her back to show the blue and black silk dress to its best effect and I admit she looked in it as beautiful as I have seen her look.

'The letters?' I asked.

'Yes, he had them in a bundle for me and he said that they are for you' She seemed most pleased with herself.

'He waited and I attended to myself and put on the dress and the shoes and this bonnet he had brought'.

She tilted her head so I might appreciate the splendid hat.

I was concluding rapidly that this was not an escape plan; this was a release by people powerful enough to order it and to manage it.

'He took me to this carriage and gave me this'.

She opened her purse and inside was at least £100 and a tiny pistol; a twin shot Derringer[122].

'He told me it was to protect me from Irish assassins' she giggled.

I noted the hammer was cocked and I gently released it and took the gun from her lest she by accident blow her own brains out; though I confess even I, with all my experience in weapons, was

---

[122] *From the description possibly a Remington Model 95 very popular at the time with ladies.*

probably not so proficient a shot so as to achieve that task.

'Where is the man now?' I asked

'Gone' she said; 'he put me in here and told me to go with the driver. He told me no more and I have been here in the carriage waiting for nothing I had supposed'. She giggled beautifully and I caught a glimpse as to how other men might regard her.

I wondered how this wonderful innocent creature had managed to survive so long in the cruel world.

'I expected no trouble from him' she continued 'who would give a lady such an amount of money and a gun if he wished her harm?'

She gave me a quizzical look and her logic was sound enough I must admit.

'Have they let you go my dear?' she asked.

'They have that' I replied and I laughed until I was almost sick.

I looked through my letters and they seemed to all be present, both copies; even the note from that morning and the last letter from the night before; it smelled of brandy.

I knew Madge was not involved in the mystery and had a feeling I would not see her again. Such dealings as this were bound to demand secrecy for all time.

Presently the carriage stopped at Tilbury Docks. I got out and helped Susan out. The driver climbed down and offered me his hand.

'I know who you are' he said 'this is my master's work and he has asked me to shake your hand for him on account of you putting that murdering bastard Carey into the ground'.

His master could have been only one person I suppose, certainly English and very powerful. Only one person involved in the whole matter could arrange such a thing and have the power.

He pulled a large bag from the driver's seat.

'Clothes, tickets, a side arm and a note from my master'. He said proudly. 'The ship is yonder and it will not sail until you are on it. It's a steamer and will see you in New York in just two weeks'

He handed the bag to me and wished us both well. With that he was gone and we stood together at the docks.

By late afternoon we were seated in our splendid cabin with a leg of lamb, boiled spuds and wine and a bath filled. As Susan took the first of the water I opened the note from my saviour. It was simple and it was brief and it confirmed what I suspected, it also assured me that no man died in the plot, confirming what I had suspected about the swinging man in my stead. He will take my place under a slab or two with a bag of lime in Newgate and no record of it will exist.

I cannot recount to you what that entire note conveyed or from whom it was received because he asked that I do not. It was upon this presumption that he allowed me keep my letters which I could one day send to you Victor, though the urgency of the task is not what it used to be.

Binns knew of it and the warden and surgeon; they have been handsomely rewarded. If any ever spoke of it then such testimony would be worthless for who would believe such a plot? No other knew of the plan but the driver, who was not a driver at all but a man in the service of my benefactor in other ways. Madge knows nothing of it and never shall and that is fine.

For this reason I ask that if you ever reveal my letters that you end the story with my execution. It serves no one to know more.

I also cannot tell you of my final destination, I am sure I could go no place in the world and not have the risk of being recognised so I suppose that going to the place where I might most be recognised might be as good as any. I have thought of Wales and shall say no more as to what part. It is a place which produces coal and I have some knowledge in the matter of the excavation and transport of that thing. Ireland is a possibility or perhaps back to America or Canada, near a lake or between two rivers. One day perhaps.

So here ends my tale. I have a good companion who knows my limits in companionship and who demands nothing of me. I have money and the wit and means to make more of it. I have shaved off my whiskers and I shall grow my hair and if people think they know me I can say that man is under a slab and who can argue that?

For now I will set about the roast lamb and the potatoes and wine and enjoy what is left of my time. The steward is a handsome young man and I fancy I may engage him later in a game of cards.

Your servant
Pádraig O'Domhnaill - December 18th 1883

Appendix 1

Abraham Lincoln (1809–1865).
Political Debates Between Lincoln and Stephen A Douglas.
Fourth Joint Debate at Charleston

Extract from Mr. Lincoln's Speech
(September 18, 1858)

"I will say then, that I am not nor ever have been in favor of making voters of the negroes, or jurors, or qualifying them to hold office, of having them to marry with white people. I will say in addition, that there is a physical difference between the white and black races, which I suppose, will forever forbid the two races living together upon terms of social and political equality, and inasmuch, as they cannot so live, that while they do remain together, there must be the position of superior and inferior, that I as much as any other man am in favor of the superior position being assigned to the white man".

Chicago Press and Tribune on 21 September 1858

Appendix 2

Abraham Lincoln (1809–1865).
Extract from Mr. Lincoln's Speech in Peoria
(October 16 1854)

"If all earthly power were given me, I should not know what to do, as to the existing institution. My first impulse would be to free all the slaves, and send them to Liberia,—to their own native land. But a moment's reflection would convince me that whatever of high hope (as I think there is) there may be in this, in the long run, its sudden execution is impossible."

Appendix 3
The Phoenix Park Murders
and
Their Significance in Irish History

Much has been written about the Phoenix Park murders and the following is a brief account of the act itself and its relevance to subsequent events in Irish History.

On the evening of May 6th 1882 a group of men set upon two gentlemen walkers in Phoenix Park, Dublin. They brutally stabbed the men, both of whom died from their wounds. One of the victims was Thomas Henry Burke, the Permanent Under-Secretary, he was an intended target of the killers; the second victim who was not an intended target was Lord Fredrick Cavendish, the Chief Secretary to Ireland.

The event was cataclysmic in terms of how it impacted on Britain's attitude to Ireland's future thereafter. At the time it was seen around the world as a brutal and unnecessary murder which even Parnell, an ardent Irish republican condemned unequivocally. With the benefit of hindsight we can see it was even more catastrophic to the Irish cause than realised at the time.

The killers were part of an extreme Irish republican organisation borne of the Irish Republican Brotherhood and funded largely from the United States. They were known as the 'Irish National Invincibles' a group which concerned themselves primarily with assassination and existed for a short time between 1881 to 1883.

After what was initially a very slow start to investigations a new team in London's Metropolitan Police was formed. It was known as the 'Special Irish Branch' or as we now know it; the 'Special Branch'. The unit 'lifted' and interrogated known republicans and by the 13th of January 1883 had arrested over a dozen suspects, including one James Carey, a local Councillor and master builder living in Dublin and the mastermind behind the killings.

By February 13th Carey had admitted his part in the deed. He became a witness for the prosecution, or as the republicans would say, an informer. As a direct result of his testimony five of the gang hanged in May and June of 1883 and seven were given penal servitude. This was effectively the end of the Invincibles. It was however not the end of the matter and the ripples into Irish history continue even today.

It is not an exaggeration to state that had the killings not taken place then there may well have been an Ireland independent from Britain before the turn of the twentieth century, probably by 1886. There might have been no Irish war of independence against the British; there might have been no devastating Irish civil war, no IRA and so on.

It is almost impossible to think of a single deed, done, as it happens by mistake, that has had such a terrible and long lasting effect on any two nations over such a vast period of time.

How can this be? You might ask. Make no mistake, these were not assassinations they were heinous murders carried out by thugs. Murders which were unnecessary and almost as fatal to the Irish cause as they were to the unfortunate pair that May evening in 1882. But the assailants were too ignorant to comprehend.

To understand this bold assertion you first need to understand that Charles Parnell (Irish Parliamentary Party) had been petitioning since 1870 for Home Rule for the Irish. By 1882 he had made such headway that the weight of opinion in Britain was to approve this in parliament. Not devolution, but near enough Independence. Whilst it was by no means a certainty there was considerable momentum in the desired direction. The British were sick of Ireland and even the objections from unionists seemed unlikely to stop any Home Rule Bill.

What changed everything was one coincidence; that coincidence was manifest in the person of Lord Harington, a senior member of Gladstone's government at the time of the killings. Lord Harington, who also happened to become the 8th Duke of Devonshire, was an exceptionally powerful man who wielded huge influence, particularly amongst sycophantic parliamentary colleges, on all sides. He also happened to be the butchered Lord Cavendish's elder brother.

Harington was not a supporter of Irish Home Rule, indeed he opposed most things that favoured the Irish but he was not obsessed with the matter. Not until the murder of his brother. Naturally enough he swore vengeance on the Irish and true to his word he had that.

He petitioned and pressured every person he could and effectively blocked the Government of Ireland Bill 1886, known later as the First Home Rule Bill. The rest as they say is history.

The second and third Home Rule bills were watered down to a weak devolution and both failed anyway. The British since 'Phoenix Park' had lost any sort of willingness to co-operate with the Irish in self-determination.

The fourth Bill in 1920 (Government of Ireland Act 1920) might have been enacted but for the fact that the Irish got tired of waiting so had a revolutionary war, between 1918 and 1921; which they partly won. The fourth Home Rule bill though never enacted was likely to succeed and in a way it did. The main aspect of it was the splitting of Ireland into the 26 county Free State and the 6 northern counties (Northern Ireland) which stayed part of Britain. This typically British tactic of partitioning, which was ostensibly to placate unionists in the north, was actually to preserve Lloyd George's and several of his colleague's massive personal investments in the shipyards there; of course it led to the Irish Civil War and more unnecessary and pointless death and turmoil.

This is a brief summary and it will no doubt be disputed but in essence, the killing of Cavendish in Phoenix Park unquestionably had monumental repercussions. What chance the Home Rule Bill

had, even if that was a small chance, was destroyed.
A bunch of illiterate ruffians took it upon
themselves to act violently on behalf of their nation.

Appendix 4
The Author's Relationship to Patrick O'Donnell

My relationship to Patrick, as it happens is irrelevant to his story and when we discovered the letters I did not know exactly who Patrick O'Donnell was. Of course I knew I had an ancestor with that name and that the British had hanged him in the eighteen hundreds and I knew that the shame and reluctance to speak of him was not to do with whatever he had done, it was to do with the lineage and relationships. I suspect the following will not be an entirely unfamiliar story to many families from Ireland at the time.

I studied the Phoenix Park Murders in school in Terenure College in Dublin but even so I did not make the connection between my ancestor and the famous murders. There was no reason why I would. It was not until I read the letters that I realised that this Patrick O'Donnell, was the very same Patrick O'Donnell my father often mentioned when he'd had a bit too much to drink and became ultra-patriotic.

My grandfather was named Edward O'Donnell, his wife was Catherine Foley; they married in 1926 and the family disowned them amid scandal. The reason they were disowned, or the reason given to us, was that they were first cousins and had grown up together as brother and sister. In fact they were not really related, though they did grow up together.

Edward was born in Brooklyn in 1901. His father was William O'Donnell, the 17 year old son of Manus O'Donnell, who was first cousin to Patrick O'Donnell (Manus' father, Manus and Patrick's father, Michael, were brothers).

William impregnated a very young woman in Schuylkill County Pennsylvania; no one knows her name and I have not been able to discover it but she was apparently of Welsh descent and worse, she was not a catholic. She was taken to the home of John O'Donnell and his sister Catherine O'Donnell for her confinement. John and Catherine were cousins of the family; they lived at Clymer Street in Ward 19 (Kings) in Brooklyn.

There in 1901 the young woman died in childbirth; the child was Edward O'Donnell my grandfather. Census records in 1911 show he was still living there with his relations and he is shown on the record as 'nephew - Edward ODonnell aged 9', yet no birth certificate is registered for him.

At the age of 11 Edward was sent to live with his distant cousins; the Foleys in Co Kerry in Ireland. He and Catherine Foley grew up together but were not related, other than by great distance. William O'Donnell, Edward's father, who by then had married and had his own family, aware of no relationship between the two agreed to be witness for them at their wedding in 1926; upon that certificate he openly declares himself father to Edward and witness to the marriage.

Thus Patrick O'Donnell was the first cousin to my great, great grandfather Manus, albeit via an illegitimate grandfather.

Printed in Great Britain
by Amazon